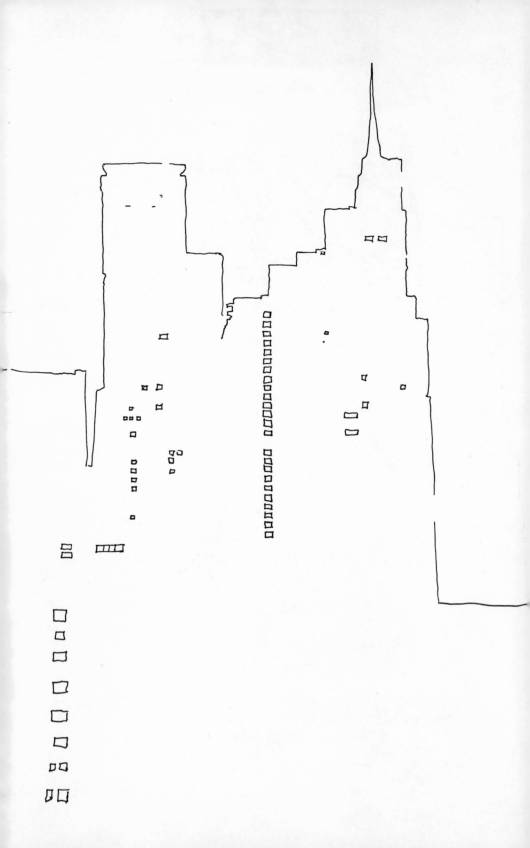

# Dear John

## SUSAN LEE
## SONDRA TILL ROBINSON

RICHARD MAREK PUBLISHERS
NEW YORK

**Library of Congress Cataloging in Publication Data**

Lee, Susan.
   Dear John.

   I.   Robinson, Sondra Till, joint author.
II.   Title.
PZ4.L48163De   [PS3562.E365]   813'.54   80-15417
ISBN 0-399-90091-8

Printed in the United States of America

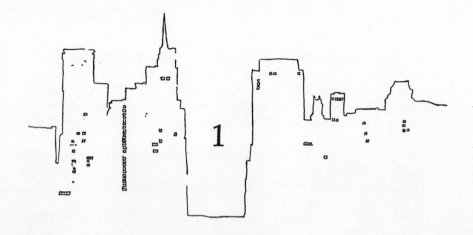

1

Kate raised the window and grasped the black iron bars, testing them. They were heavy and firmly set in their stone frame.

The man with the keys watched. He was bored and impatient. "You're letting in the rain," he said finally.

Kate said, "I assume there are also bars on the other side of the air conditioner sleeve?"

"That's right. Also a grid in the chimney." Smug and off-hand.

She carefully closed the dripping window, then scanned the large, almost square white room. She went to the small raised fireplace made of recently laid old bricks. "I sure don't need this."

The man played with his huge ring of keys.

Kate's heels clicked on the bare, pseudopegged floor as she walked back into the bedroom and the tiny bathroom with its already chipped sink and tub that were supposed to look like heavy porcelain. "But this is better than any of the others I've seen."

"You don't have much in the way of choices." He shot his cuff, pushed his digital watch button and flicked his eyes at the red numerals.

7

She slowly reexamined the rooms and came to a stop before the fireplace again. She stared at it. "In a place like this," she opened her hands from her wrists as if to include not only the apartment but all of Manhattan, "you only need a fireplace to keep from freezing if the furnace goes on the blink, or to create an artificial atmosphere."

"Lady like you doesn't need candlelight. You can do okay in a hundred and fifty watts."

"Thanks. I assume that when this brownstone was renovated a new furnace was installed?"

"Oh, yeah. Brand-new furnace and new electrical wiring. Plumbing. Miss Delling, I'm meeting people at the office to look at this apartment in twenty minutes. I'm going to be late for them."

Kate frowned at a thin crack in the plaster angling down from a corner of the window. "Okay. I'll take it. But, come on. What did the former tenant pay?"

The man rose from his slump, all perky and businesslike, adjusting the clothes he chose to wear to meet whatever types he had to escort in the Seventies and Eighties and Nineties on the West Side. "I can't tell you that, Miss Delling." He hustled her through the door and locked all the locks. "My assistant will help you with the lease and I'll cancel the other people. Look," he said after he popped open his big black umbrella and they were headed for Broadway, "that apartment only came in today. I'm exclusive agent. You're the first person I've shown. That's a very well-run building."

"It seems safe." Her Ferragamos were probably being ruined by the puddles. She ordinarily carried plastic shoe covers and an umbrella when the weather was threatening. But today had begun so bright and clear. "I mean the window bars and the three locks. Plus the security intercom and buzzer."

"You're as safe as a bug in that brownstone. All you have to do is stay away from the park side of Central Park West after dark and also from Amsterdam Avenue, and you're fine." He steered them around a drunk or a junkie or a Vietnam veteran or a corpse whose khaki-clad legs drooped onto the sidewalk from a brownstone's stoop. "You aren't from New York, originally, I mean. I can tell from the way you talk," he said smoothly, confidently. "Originally, you're from . . . Portland, Oregon! Am I right?" He beamed at her under the enforced intimacy of his huge black umbrella.

"Los Angeles, California."

"Really? I can usually tell Los Angeles." He gave his head a little shake. "Wherever. Anyway, Miss Delling, I can tell you've been here long enough to know how a woman has to act to take care of herself. I can tell you're a very savvy lady."

Kate didn't know which was more annoying, the man's previous bored impatience or this present chatty coziness. Unless one had many friends who had many friends who had contacts, one was at the mercy of rental agencies. The man holding the umbrella had, during the past month, shown her six apartments. He no doubt assumed he had well earned the check for fifteen percent of her first year's rent she would soon be writing in his office. "I know how to take care of myself."

He ignored her. "Women who drink too much or smoke dope usually have troubles. Women should always take taxis if they've been drinking. Otherwise they are just asking for it."

"I think I know how to manage myself on the street," she said crisply, then followed with, "Besides, I never have more than two glasses of white wine over an hour or two. I seldom drink hard liquor. I don't like the taste of it. Especially whiskey."

Damn it! She felt the little giveaway tic begin, and she knew it was visible to others. A muscle above her jaw, about an inch in front of her right ear, an autonomous throbbing having nothing whatsoever to do with her pulse or breathing. Whenever it happened she was in confined circumstances in which she was simultaneously tense and felt she was required to explain herself or her family or her circumstances.

Kate moved as far away from the rental agent as she could without becoming soaked. She no longer heard his explanations and admonitions for women alone on the streets of New York.

Superimposed upon the intersection of Broadway and Seventy-ninth Street with its shops and people, the printing of the newspapers and magazines on the stands was the image of successions of grayish-green waves folding over themselves. The waves came endlessly, never the same: governed by gravity, the configuration of the shore and whatever mystery the moon exercised.

Kate tensed her jaw without clenching her teeth and willed away the waves.

"One thing you have to give New York City, it's certainly more dynamic than L.A."

The man turned to her. "Said like a true Californian. You've never had any problems on the street or in the subway? Don't mind the claustrophobia and the weather here? Don't miss all that space? Jesus, I hated all that space out there, and the light was unreal."

They were waiting for the signal to change. The agent's office was across the street and three floors up. The elevator was out of order. But he could see the grimy windows of his office. Another small conclusion for him, signatures on leases and checks. And no doubt the last he would ever see of Kate Delling.

She said, "No, I don't miss the West."

They hurried across the street.

"You aren't a woman who goes around asking for it, Miss Delling. Know what I mean? A provocative type."

Kate knew how the rental agent saw her. She was a category to him. Men like the rental agent, most men, were not very observant. If they were, they would not so readily respond to the subtle and not-so-subtle signals by which women are taught to define or protect themselves. Kate did not want to give the rental agent or anyone else a provocative-type signal.

She was a physically healthy woman of twenty-seven who was a moderately successful professional working for a large New York-based company. God, she thought as she tramped up the dusty stairs, there must be seventy-five thousand of us on this island. We run the spectrum, from ugly-mousy to gorgeous-flamingo.

As she was in most areas, Kate was objective about her appearance. She possessed thick, reddish-brown hair, the sort that usually goes with freckles. But she had fair, freckleless skin that took an even tan. Her eyes were light brown, almost round and deep-set, giving the upper part of her face an awed, innocent aspect. This, though, was contradicted by her broad mouth, strong jaw and cleft chin. If the proportions of her torso and legs had been differently distributed, she could have worn a size nine. Her long waist required an eleven. Still okay for five foot six. Her short, casual hairstyle, softly tailored clothes and her subdued makeup were chosen to give the impression of brisk neutrality.

And that was how the rental agent responded to her—as a moderately attractive, self-confident and disinterested woman who happened to have grown up on the West Coast.

He turned Kate over to a brusque woman in her middle sixties whose tightly corseted torso resembled a barrel. Her hair was dyed a pale pink and her hands and fingernails were dirty. The cheap nameplate on her desk said Mrs. Belle Wyler.

"You already filled out the credit forms?" Mrs. Wyler said, shuffling through a stack of papers.

"Yes. My name is Kate Delling."

"Delling, okay. Here you are." She shoved three long forms across the desk. "Sign here and here and here. Where the red Xs are."

Kate lifted the top form and began to read.

"You're not going to read all this, are you, honey?"

Kate smiled politely. "Sure, I am. Don't you think I should know what I'm agreeing to?"

"Are you a lawyer? This is just a rental agency. All you're signing is the lease for an apartment and our commission form. No. I see you work for Federated Computer Systems. A computer programmer, is that what you are?"

"Yes." Kate rapidly, carefully read the small print.

"Pays good money. I didn't know computer programmers did so well. This is almost as much money as my grandson makes. And he's an engineer."

"I have specialized training in computer systems and programming."

"So why did you decide to move? That's nice, the park block on Eighty-sixth Street."

Patiently, Kate said, "The building is going co-op. I considered the advantages and disadvantages of buying my apartment and decided against it." She resumed reading.

"Most girls your age aren't as particular as you. The young men either. They hurry in, sign and hurry out."

The woman named Mrs. Belle Wyler talked on while Kate read every word.

Kate moved into her new apartment on a warm day in June. Using graph paper, she had drawn to exact scale the floor plan of the apartment. She had made scale-sized pieces of paper representing her furniture. She was able to tell the movers exactly where to place every piece of furniture and every labeled box.

She had previously lived on the seventh floor of a fifteen-story building faced with pale, taupe-colored brick. The building contained one hundred and twenty apartments. During the five years Kate had resided in the building, she had learned the names of the super, the elevator men and the tenants on her floor. Now she was on the parlor floor of a renovated, six-story brownstone on West Seventy-fourth Street, a narrow street that she hoped would be quiet. Two apartments to a floor.

By six o'clock all of the kitchen boxes were unpacked.

A knock sounded on her door. With hands black from newspaper wrappings, Kate fumbled open the three locks and opened her door as wide as the heavy chain permitted.

A beautiful woman stood in the hall. She was wearing faded jeans, a loose terry-cloth top and sandals. Her long hair was pulled back in a rubber band at the nape of her neck.

"Sorry to bother you. I live in three rear. My name is Margaret Elias. I seem to have lost my cat."

Kate pushed her door closed in order to free the chain. She opened the door. "Hello. I'm Kate Delling. I just moved in today. I haven't seen a cat."

"His name is Roberto."

"Oh."

"My God, you must think I'm crazy," Margaret said. "You see, two of us in the building ended up with kittens from the same litter a year and a half ago. Art, who lives just above you, and me. The cats are almost identically colored. My cat's name is Roberto and Art's is named Phyllis."

"The outside doors were propped open while the movers were bringing in my things. I hope Roberto didn't escape."

"He doesn't like to go outside in the street. He does like to visit in the building. He climbs out my window and wanders ledges until he finds an open window. He climbs up and down the ivy."

Kate opened her door all the way. "Come in, won't you? Maybe he's here and I haven't noticed him."

Margaret looked around the living room. "You are certainly organized for moving day. My place didn't look this good for a month."

Kate went into her bedroom. A large gray-and-white cat was comfortably lounging in the depression between the pillows on her neatly made double bed.

"Roberto?" she asked.

The cat yawned.

"He's in here, Margaret. He must have slipped through the bars over my window."

Roberto's mistress walked into the bedroom, swept up the purring cat. "Boy, are you pushy, fella. You haven't even been introduced. Kate, this is Roberto, the wanderer."

"I've never been introduced to a cat before," she laughed.

"I'm afraid you haven't seen the last of him, or of Phyllis, not with hot weather and open windows coming up. Say, you can't have begun dinner yet. Or do you have a date?"

"I brought food from my old apartment."

"I made a vat of cassoulet yesterday. It's better the second time around. Will you join me? You must be pooped."

"I'm also covered with newsprint."

"Pop in the shower, then. I'm 3-R." With Roberto in her arms Margaret walked into the hall. "See you in about forty-five minutes."

Kate stood in her doorway. She should, she was certain, have declined an invitation from another tenant, especially on her first day in a new building. But she was quite hungry. She loved cassoulet and she liked Margaret. Roberto was another matter.

Her father had considered dogs, cats, fish and birds to be dirty and inconvenient. Her inherently impetuous mother had never been impelled to possess a kitten or a puppy, although she and Kate's aunts had grown up with cats and dogs and even rabbits and desert tortoises. Kate was not afraid of cats, especially not an amiable creature like Roberto. But she found the idea of being intruded upon by a cat or a person unsettling. She would need to see about window screens.

As she showered and dressed in linen slacks and a flowered silk blouse, Kate considered how she could, on the one hand, accept Margaret's hospitality, and on the other, politely and firmly make clear her need for privacy.

She shouldn't have accepted the invitation to dinner.

Kate sat down on the edge of her bed and frowned at the window—open only three inches now. She could see nothing but a blank brick wall beyond the black bars. She had not eaten a meal with anyone else in almost two weeks. Warren, from Documentation, wouldn't be asking her out again; she had, the day before, turned him down for the fifth time.

Her stomach rumbled. Cassoulet of all things! She loved cassoulet. It was such a chore to make that few restaurants served it, and the one time she had prepared it she had sworn never again.

Additionally, if she had not immediately sensed an easy civility about Margaret she would not have accepted. Kate was not an impulsive woman.

Margaret greeted Kate with, "Welcome. And I hope you realize I don't make a practice of asking strangers to dinner."

"I've been trying to figure out why I accepted."

"Probably because you were tired and hungry. Come in." Margaret still wore the jeans and casual terry-cloth top. "We probably won't see each other again for a month. I come and go at irregular hours, and I cherish my privacy."

Kate was immediately reassured by the other woman's calm directness. "So do I. I mean, I really do."

"Then you won't have any difficulty in this building. A drink?"

"White wine?"

While Margaret was in the kitchen, Kate settled in a wing-back chair and felt herself relax.

Kate's mother had come from a wealthy family; her father had been an art curator. Margaret's apartment, she could see, contained beautiful and valuable furniture and decorations. The mixture of styles and periods was eccentric, yet perfect. The apartment was not the product of a decorator's efforts. The place was too comfortable: a Shaker table set for two with Finnish stainless and Dansk stoneware. Then there were the Eskimo carvings on a low, golden oak table on an afghan carpet. The sofa was of no discernible period, yet the lines were serene and classic, the cushions covered with deep rust velvet.

The framed prints on the walls ranged from Da Vinci studies to Polish circus prints to two Picasso line drawings.

The person who lived in the spotless, uncluttered rooms was responsible for every inch of them.

"I like your apartment," Kate said. "Especially the mix of Picasso, Polish, Da Vinci and Eskimo."

Margaret handed her a glass of Chenin Blanc. "Did you study art?"

"No, no, I didn't. My mother painted, though, and my father was with a museum. And my aunts and uncles collected." She could hear her words speeding up. "My parents didn't collect.

They couldn't afford what they liked. But the rest of the family was quite rich. My father advised them."

The phone rang.

Kate sat back and released the arm of the chair. Thank God; she had begun to babble.

Margaret made no move to answer the phone. After the second ring Kate heard a soft click and then a low, whirring sound. She peered around the side of the chair.

Margaret's phone rested beside an expensive telephone answering machine. Kate had not previously noticed it.

"What sort of music do you like? While you were searching for Roberto I saw your stereo." Margaret sipped her wine. "That's an excellent one."

"Classical, mostly. And Joni Mitchell and Bob Dylan." This was safe and comfortable territory. "I've never been able to stand rock. And now disco!"

"Disco won't last. Have you listened to much Cole Porter?"

During the next hour Kate and Margaret discussed music and musicals. Wonderful smells from the kitchen perfumed the room. No harm in a second glass of wine, she was safe within her own building, her triple-locked door was only two flights down.

Dressed as she was and without makeup or jewelry, Margaret was a flawlessly lovely woman. Her pleasantly modulated voice, her diction, were Eastern private school and one of the Seven Sister colleges. Kate wondered which one. Margaret sounded like and possessed the manner of the Wellesley roommate one of her cousins had brought to California for a Christmas vacation when Kate was eleven. Her cousin Beth, by her junior year, had picked up some of the style, some of the idiom. But she would never, ever sound or move like her friend from college. Kate had thought then, if Beth said, "indeed," or "boring," or "disgusting," one more time she would scream. Beth would never get it right, not the way Margaret did it.

Kate, recalling the recorded phone call as they ate the superb cassoulet and French bread and salad, wondered whether Margaret was a lawyer or in publishing or an executive with one of the multinationals on Park Avenue.

She had not asked Margaret about her work because she did not want to discuss her own. Three weeks earlier she had learned that her suave immediate supervisor had claimed full credit for a job she had labored over for eleven months. Scotty Rogers had done nothing, he had proven to be a complete blank on the system she had developed for a nationwide chain of wholesale auto parts distributors. When she had had a problem he had fiddled with his vest buttons and assured her she could solve the problems. She had. She had worked fourteen-hour days, six days a week, and she had developed a system that was clear and accessible to the high-school graduates who would be feeding day-to-day data into the kitty as well as the highly technical data for the accountants and M.B.A.s who would later need to interpret it.

And there was Scotty Rogers of the three-hour lunches, Scotty Rogers of the weekends at his rustic place in one of the Hamptons, Scotty Rogers who could always find instant tickets for the Yankees or the Rangers or the Knicks, Scotty Rogers who had not only taken fourth in the AAU javelin, but who had also been the drummer in a popular Grosse Pointe, Michigan, band. The walls of Scotty Rogers' office were plastered with photographs and hand-lettered documentation of his interests and achievements. Something for everyone, with the exception of assistance for the group head who was preparing a difficult manual for a computer system for a chain of wholesale auto parts distributors.

Eleven months! It was finished, and now he was saying, "Thanks. Monumental effort. Now it's on to the Welles-Keeler project. Kate who? Oh, you mean Kate Delling. One of my assistants. Sharp girl. Needs constant reassurance. You know the type."

She wanted to be directly assigned to the Welles-Keeler project. So did Scotty, so he could hand it to her. She did not want to think about either Scotty or the projects. She was not worried about Roberto who was draped over Margaret's window ledge. She no longer paid attention to the phone, which had rung seven or eight times, to be answered by the efficient machine attached to it.

She was tired and she was at ease. She and Margaret had shared many of the same responses to plays, books, concerts and films. And, to Kate's delight, Margaret's succinct observations were more amusing and cogent than any of the newspaper reviewers or the rehashings by her dates.

"Your phone. You've been letting it answer itself for hours. You'll be up all night returning your calls. I'm afraid I've taken advantage of your hospitality."

"My callers either can or cannot wait."

"What do you do?"

Margaret smiled gently at Kate. "I have never found a way to be tactful about my work. Not even by the use of euphemisms. I am a very expensive whore."

Kate was not aware of her jaw dropping or of her eyes widening. All she could feel was heat rising from her breast, up her neck and into her face. Was this a terribly sophisticated joke? Should she laugh or respond with a witty quip? "I don't understand," she said.

"I am a very expensive whore because I neither look nor act like an inexpensive whore. My clients are men who can afford to indulge their fantasies and illusions. Prostitution is an illusion."

"But I thought you'd gone to maybe Wellesley and were a lawyer . . . or something."

"My formal education ended after six months at Hunter College. As James Thurber said, I became disenchanted. Or to use Salinger, I saw it all as phony." She gracefully lit a Carlton.

"I don't know what to say." Kate slowly shook her head.

"You don't have to say anything. I'm not embarrassed by my work. Come on now, Kate. We're only twenty years from the twenty-first century. You can't be as shocked as you look, for God's sake."

"Do I look shocked?" She stared down into the coffee cup in her hand. "That's probably because I'm . . . surprised. I've never know a prostitute before." She looked up quickly to see if the word had offended Margaret.

"I'll bet you've known many, many women who have been paid for sex, one way or another. The only person in this building who is unaware of my work—and believe me, I work very hard—is Mario. Our super has convinced himself I am hot shit with an advertising agency. Why he picked advertising, I have no idea."

Kate carefully placed her cup in its saucer and set them on the polished oak table.

She was too embarrassed to look at Margaret. She had trusted her instinct about a cultivated, scrubbed stranger searching for her cat. This did not have the feel of another New York test-the-hick "in" joke.

"Those phone calls your machine answered?" God, why did

she sound so childish? She had not known of this woman's existence until a few hours before.

"Clients, Kate," Margaret said softly. "I'm sorry you're as shocked as you are by the way I earn money. I think you're possibly overreacting. I am twenty-six years old. I have another six, maybe seven years. I'm like a professional football player. No matter how well I care for myself, gravity's big tug will begin to tell. Even very old men prefer firm flesh. Thank you for coming up." She stood.

Kate hurriedly rose. "Thank you for asking me." She tried to smile.

In her apartment with all the locks set, Kate did not prepare for bed.

She sat on her sofa staring at the fireplace. She sought reassurance from the symmetrical pattern of the cemented bricks and found none.

Moving into a brownstone had been a mistake. Large apartment buildings afforded more anonymity. Margaret spoke as if all the tenants in this brownstone knew each other and their work.

All right, now. Be rational! You met someone for the first time late this afternoon. You liked the person. You accepted the person's invitation to dinner. You enjoyed a pleasant evening. The woman volunteered the information that she is a high-priced prostitute. You are acting like a silly, naive child. You were rude and insulting. What that woman does has nothing to do with you.

She did not understand why she was so upset because a virtual stranger expressed no shame about being a whore. Good God, there must be hundreds and hundreds of high-priced prostitutes in Manhattan on the East Side alone, and they certainly wouldn't wear badges or armbands. Not like the women and girls who walked Eighth Avenue advertising themselves by their appearance and actions.

Think of work!

Think of a way to be assigned the Welles-Keeler project directly, not as Scotty Rogers' peon. Plan a strategy. Arrange a way to bring up the subject with Mr. Hamilton.

Her anger focused now, Kate went into the bathroom and splashed her face with cold water.

That goddamned, sonofabitch, hypocritical thief Scotty Rogers!

Before she left for her office the next morning, Kate leaned a book Margaret had said she wanted to borrow against the door of 3-R. Inside was a note: "Sorry I made such a fool of myself. I make genuine California enchiladas (L.A.-Mexican version). Please let me know when you can have dinner, and give me a day's notice. Kate Delling."

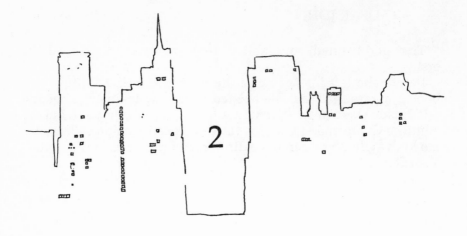

# 2

As Kate rounded the corner onto Central Park West, a dusty blue M10 pulled away from the bus stop. Sometimes the damn things came in caravans of three or four. That, or the wait could be twenty-five minutes. None was in sight.

A man had hurried from an apartment building as Kate was turning the corner, glanced uptown, then muttered, "Damn it," and strode down the sidewalk to the Seventy-second Street subway entrance.

Kate waited for the next bus beside a canopy support, fully aware that buses were slow and less regular than the subway.

When she had first come to New York she had used subways—for almost seven months—until one morning when the rush-hour local, so jammed with passengers her arms were painfully pressed against her sides, suddenly darkened and coasted to a stop.

The men and women on the train were held immobile by the raincoat-padded torsos of strangers. No one spoke. She could not take a full breath. She turned her head two inches, encountering a shoulder. Her mobility was reduced to the approximately four-inch arc in which she could rotate her head.

Just one full breath. Impossible.

With all her strength she tried to thrust her elbows away from her body. She could not move. She was sweating heavily now. As her panic built she felt herself shrinking, growing weak, becoming a terrified small person in a stuffy darkened room. The salty smell of sweat became the seaweed smell of the ocean.

"Please," Kate panted, "let me out. Please."

"You'll be okay, lady," a deep voice to the right said. "Try counting slowly."

"Please. I can't breathe," she whispered.

"Shit," said a disgusted male voice directly in front of her. "Fucking hysterical women. Next time why don't you walk, honey?"

Several people snickered.

She squeezed her eyes shut so tightly red and yellow sparks appeared. She was certain she detected the scent of tanning lotion mingled with the salt and seaweed odors. Kate found a tiny dot of focus. A fantasy. If she had in her hand the gun she had been given in Arizona, she would find the will and the strength to raise it, press it into the body of the foul-mouthed man and pull the trigger. When he slumped down there would be more room. She would be able to breathe more easily, move her arms away from her sides. In her mind she carefully repeated the act over and over until she heard the train's engines hum to life. She opened her eyes. The lights flickered on.

At the next station, even though it wasn't her stop, Kate pushed her way out of the train. She ran up the steps to air and space, where she stood in light rain taking huge breaths.

That had happened five years ago. Kate had never again entered a subway station.

The only times she thought about the gun Alex had given her were when she wondered, occasionally, if she was breaking New York laws by keeping an unregistered firearm in a shoebox at the back of a top shelf. She kept the thing for the same reason thousands of other people had guns stuck in bottom drawers or on top shelves: she didn't know what else to do with it.

Buses were sometimes as crowded as that subway train had been. But on a bus one could always see freedom beyond the windows. The possibility existed of making such a disturbance that the driver would let off a passenger in the middle of a block. Because the immediate possibility of escape was always present, Kate had never lost control on a bus.

The next M10 followed the one she had missed by almost twenty minutes. Kate and three men pushed their way aboard.

"Move to the rear. Room in the rear." The bus driver did not raise his voice.

Kate doubted he could be heard five feet behind his plastic shield. Surprisingly, though, people inched and shuffled toward the back of the swaying bus, providing a bit of space on the park side.

Muscles stiff from packing and unpacking boxes, eyes a bit sore from too little sleep, Kate stood erect, gazing at Central Park's greens and smooth dark stone. She hung onto an overhead handle and wondered why she felt so alert and energetic. She had been filled by an unusual vitality since she had written the note to Margaret and placed it and the book against the door.

Why?

Why were colors more intense, lines more crisp, the faces and movements of other people more immediate? She found herself smiling as the bus made its right-hand turn at Sixty-third. She automatically found her balance and felt almost a joy from defying centrifugal force, a joy and a sense of her own strength and coordination, a pleasant rhythm.

But why?

The day before she had met, enjoyed dinner and conversation with a woman who admitted—no, she had not admitted, confessed or apologized—who, without apology, stated that she was a prostitute. Margaret was evidently earning a great deal of money from men willing to pay for sex the way they pay for a beautifully prepared and delicious seven-course meal.

Now the bus was negotiating the left turn past Lincoln Center. Like a dancer, she confidently leaned into the pull and gracefully lowered herself onto a vacated seat.

Margaret said prostitution was an illusion. Just like a seven-course meal prepared in the stainless-steel kitchen of a fine restaurant is an illusion. That thought elated Kate.

Between the Lincoln Center and Columbus Circle turns, she made an attempt to catch the blowing feather of the emotion she was experiencing.

Why was the thought of a man paying a large amount of money for sex suddenly a pleasant thought? Why was she equating that with an expensive dinner?

She could not imagine how Margaret earned her large fees. No doubt she had become the mistress of some mysterious knowledge of appetite and ritual. For a man who occasionally found himself in need of more than leftover pot roast on the familiar dishes. For a man who occasionally liked to think himself a grand duke whose grateful chefs and servants designed new and lovely ways to please him. Candles, perfect flowers and table service; a first course calculated to be savored for itself yet set the palate for the next. Wine poured. Dishes unobtrusively placed and removed. Tender meats under subtle sauces. Piquant fish molded into astonishing forms. Exotic vegetables and fruits. Precious cheeses from the caves of devoted monks.

Solicitous waiters, a murmuring sommelier, chefs sweating behind the swinging door to the kitchen. All for him.

Sated, he signs his name on the line the deferential attendant indicates.

Kate smiled at an orange-and-brown Bun & Burger signboard.

What a marvelous joke!

The duke-for-a-moment enjoyed the illusion that all those people had undergone their apprenticeships and mastery with his pleasure, alone, in mind.

The truth was they had not even known his name.

No. Kate stared at the marquee of a cinema without reading the words. No. They know the man's name and it meant nothing. Nothing. All that mattered was that he be able to pay.

Good for Margaret. She was an entire expensive restaurant. Of a sort.

Between Forty-sixth and Forty-fifth Kate saw six jacketless policemen and about thirty civilians in a loose cluster on the sidewalk. They were all gazing at someone on the ground. Probably a knifing. Drugs.

She looked away, upward to a shiny bus ad for menthol cigarettes. A man and a woman on a granite boulder beside a waterfall. Ferns and pines.

A traffic jam forced the bus to a stop in the middle of the block. Horns were honking. Her own phlegmatic bus driver leaned on his horn.

Kate folded her hands on her lap and gazed at the lovely pool beneath the waterfall.

Whatever it was that Margaret was doing to or for her clients did not debase her. The men who needed to pay her were debased.

Margaret was the person in control. She decided whether or

not she would answer her phone. Last night or this morning, presumably, she played back the machine's tape. Margaret had said the men either could or could not wait. That meant some of those men were angry and frustrated because Margaret had not been available. Margaret had chosen not to be available.

The corners of Kate's wide mouth turned up.

What did men who were accustomed to their prerogatives do when they were forced to state their needs to an answering machine, then wait for a response—one that didn't come? Men of wealth and power?

She wanted to shout, "Ha!" as she stepped from the M10 at Thirty-fourth Street.

A crosstown bus arrived in less than a minute.

She put away thoughts of Margaret, yet retained the faint buzz of excitement. Because, thanks to Margaret, she had gained a secret knowledge, possessed a new poise.

Kate was going to speak directly to Mr. Peter Hamilton about her contribution to the Foster Automotive project and about the Welles-Keeler project. Screw protocol. She was going over Scotty Rogers' head.

Federated Computer Systems occupied the fifteenth, sixteenth and seventeenth floors of the Bellcroft Building on Madison Avenue. Kate's small, windowless office was on the sixteenth floor, Mr. Hamilton's on the seventeenth. His view was to the east and his potted plants looked as if they were on loan from the New York Botanical Garden.

Kate asked for Peter Hamilton's extension before she looked at the memos in her tray.

His secretary, the woman responsible for the plants' condition, told Kate Mr. Hamilton was in a meeting.

"I would like to see him today."

"Mr. Hamilton's tied up most of the day. But I'll see if he can fit you in. What shall I tell him you want to see him about?"

"Just tell him it is important and private."

"Your extension?"

"Three five six one. Kate Delling."

"We'll get back to you."

When Kate replaced the receiver she discovered her hand was slippery with sweat and her ear hurt from the pressure.

Each time her phone rang that morning she gave a little jump and settled herself before answering.

By three thirty her resolve was lapsing into momentary tugs of anger and frustration. His secretary, at the least, should have reported back. She had been told it was important.

At four fifty Scotty called to ask her to come to his office.

"Have a seat, Kate." He waved to the chair at the corner of his desk.

He looked especially natty in his light gray three-piece suit and his aviator glasses. His thick dark hair was not cut, it was styled. He laced his fingers behind his head as he tilted back in his junior executive leather chair.

"So?" he asked as he studied her.

"What do you want, Scotty?" She wanted to be in her office to answer the phone.

He sat there, tilted back, with a pleasant smile on his tanned face.

"I'm in the middle of a revision that has to be finished today," Kate said.

He brought himself forward, folded his hands on his desk and said, "What is this important matter you want to see Pete Hamilton about?"

The self-assurance she had been filled with when she had ridden the elevator to the sixteenth floor at eight fifty that morning dissolved. Kate cleared her throat.

"I want to speak to Mr. Hamilton."

"So he told me."

"When did you talk with him?"

"Oh, sometime this morning. Around ten. He called to ask me what was going on."

"I told his secretary it was private."

"That's what he said. Important and private. He wanted to know what was going on in my department. This is the first chance I've had. What's on your mind, Kate?"

She rose. "If I wanted to discuss this with you, I would have."

He tilted back again. "Right. Let me tell you something, dear. Peter Hamilton is fifty-four. He is only a division head. There is a reason for that. He is a very nice, very bright man. But he has no balls. He will go no higher than division head. I'm surprised he's managed that. Now then, what is it you feel is so important and private? Let me guess. You want to talk with him about Foster and Welles-Keeler, right?"

"Tell Mr. Hamilton I won't discuss the subject with you, Scot-ty."

He lifted his right shoulder and lowered it. "Okay. Today's Wednesday. He's flying to Atlanta tomorrow. He'll be there until Friday. I hope whatever you have to tell him can wait until next week."

"It will have to, won't it?" She left his office.

Kate walked back to her own office. On the way she greeted or spoke briefly with three women and four men. Her voice and body were under control. She spoke and moved the way she ordinarily did.

At her desk she stared down at black marks on white paper. She was unable to discern meaning in them. None.

Now then, she said to herself. Now then.

That almost always worked.

Now then.

She became absolutely still and imagined herself, her rational and composed self, to be approximately two feet above her disor-dered and crumbled self.

At approximately 10:00 A.M., almost seven hours ago, Peter Hamilton, disregarding the "important" and the "private," had contacted Scotty. Scotty would have immediately known what Kate wanted to tell the man directly over him. He would also have understood that Kate was anxious, on tenterhooks, waiting for Peter Hamilton's call. He had waited until ten minutes before he left for the day to call her to his office. Then he had happily, smugly dumped his bucket of shit on her head.

What are your options, Kate?

Not many. Not considering the two men involved.

Hamilton, who had found his way to Federated Computer Systems by way of a bachelor's degree in math from Bowdoin, wore wrinkled seersucker in the summer and baggy tweeds in the winter. His large apartment on East Eighty-eighth Street (site of the division's annual Christmas-Hanukkah party) was crowded with heavy, dark furniture. The bathroom was deco-rated with dried, pressed flowers in frames. His wife was as pale and faded as the flowers. Mr. Hamilton was a gentleman and he was New England–collapsed.

Scotty Rogers was not nearly as intelligent as Peter Hamilton, but he was very ambitious and possessed an amazingly accurate instinct for the precise persuasive words and inflections, the forceful, yet graceful gesture, the perfect timing that would carry him to a certain level of success. Not many people at F.C.S. would be able to stop him. Not Peter Hamilton.

No options, Kate?

One. On Monday she would not call Mr. Hamilton for an appointment. She would go up to his office and demand to be heard, then and there. She could present her case in less than ten minutes.

Then that's settled. See how pointless it is to become angry?

The black marks on the white paper became numerals and letters. In a few minutes the numerals and letters possessed meaning.

Kate was able to complete the revisions and deliver them to Documentation by five after six.

The Thirty-fourth Street M16 crosstown bus was crowded with tired office workers and women carrying bulky shopping bags from Altman's and Ohrbach's. The M10 uptown was worse than the M16.

A traffic jam forced the bus to stop in the middle of an intersection. Taxi drivers, truck drivers, civilian drivers, her bus driver, leaned on their horns.

Kate could clearly see the cause of the tie-up. Just west of Eighth Avenue, on Forty-fifth Street, six police cars and a police bus with heavy mesh over its windows blocked the street.

Police were milling on the sidewalk under a canopy that announced, Pink Sultan Massage Palace. There were at least fifteen uniformed policemen. They were amiably talking with each other, smoking cigarettes.

Kate hung onto her overhead handle and watched, as did everyone else on her side of the bus.

Slowly, clumsily, out they came.

First the women, about ten of them. They were hastily dressed in wrappers or street clothes; some clutched clothing against their breasts. They appeared to range in age from late teens to late thirties. Not one of the women looked dramatically attractive even from a distance. Some were homely.

Then the patrons. Kate counted nine men. They were fully dressed. A few held their hands over their faces. Some wore suits, some work clothes. None was younger than twenty.

The women looked weary and resigned, the men, embarrassed and annoyed. The police herded them all into the bus.

The M10 crept forward.

A middle-aged man, who had been twisting in his seat to view the activity, said, "Those hookers'll be right back there doing business tomorrow," to the plump young woman beside him.

She glared at him. "And what about the men?"

The man shrugged. "They pay for those lazy sluts, don't they? Nothing will happen to them."

The young woman sneered at the man, "Phallocrat!"

He drew back. "What's that mean?"

"It's French for sexist pig." She pulled a copy of *Rolling Stone* from her bag and began to flip through it.

Red-faced, the man muttered, "I still say they're lazy sluts."

The young woman glared at her *Rolling Stone*.

A gang of twelve- or thirteen-year-old boys wearing T-shirts with the emblem of their prep school over their hearts got on at Fifty-seventh Street and managed to appropriate every seat as it became empty. They evidently considered it to be a triumph of sorts to beat out a man with a briefcase between his feet who was reading the *Post*—given the glances they directed toward schoolmates.

Street smart.

That was how many upper-middle-class parents proudly described their preadolescent sons—on the West Side, anyway. Scotty Rogers had been born street smart in Michigan. Peter Hamilton probably found the phrase offensive and would one day be mugged on East Eighty-eighth Street.

The bus was now in the Sixties. The boys who had taken seats from people too tired to make an issue were getting off. They would all be off by Ninety-sixth, leaving the stained plastic to people who had more to worry about than a bus seat.

The boys would be admitted by uniformed doormen, borne to their floors by elevator men who knew less English than the boys did Latin. The boys would courteously greet the black women born in Jamaica or Guyana or Flushing, Queens, who had made their beds that morning.

Street smart, as Kate understood the words, meant more than survival. They meant confidence with a swagger, an offensive, rather than a defensive or neutral stance.

In California, boys had been more furtive in their early adolescent assertions. They had been more fascinated by the manipulation or destruction of objects. Very few boys took on people their parents' age or older—whatever the person's color or language.

The M10 jerked forward and stopped, jerked and stopped, creaking and groaning through a single lane of Central Park West, past a crew of workmen tending a breakdown under the street.

Kate looked down at a boy seated to her left. His T-shirt with the school emblem was spotted with mustard and dribbles of dark pink. He was reading a *Times* he had retrieved from the floor. Reading the first section with absorption. Not the sports section. That boy had aced out a distinguished-looking white-haired woman, and now he was avidly reading an article on Indochina.

Kate was no doubt being unfair in her negative thoughts about the kid, because she saw him as a budding Scotty Rogers, only smarter. Therefore worse.

Two boys sitting on either side of a middle-aged woman with blue-black skin began to reach across her to poke each other.

Looking straight ahead, the woman said in a loud, hard voice, "You lean against me once more, I'll whip your skinny asses. Hear? I been on my feet ten hours. Now I'm resting."

Immediately the boys stopped, their faces instantly expressionless.

The black woman's inflectionless authority was conclusive. She was no more than five feet tall, and wiry. Kate did not dwell on the question of how the woman came by her certainty.

Kate turned away from the woman who would be stepping from the Eighth Avenue bus into a neighborhood beyond her imagining.

Her own streets were a virtual sanctuary compared to those above 125th Street. That was how the black woman would consider them, Kate was sure.

So what if four or five men standing in doorways on Columbus or Amsterdam drinking from half-pints muttered obscenities in Spanish and English? So what if troops of teenaged athletes in tight pants and forty-dollar running shoes moved in behind a woman on a side street in the Seventies and Eighties? There were always people out walking their Dobermans or German shepherds. The police patrolled the streets and responded to calls. So what if the trim, young white woman was afraid to walk at night on streets with trees protected by foot-high metal fences, functioning streetlights and supers who made tidy mounds of bagged trash and lidded cans and swept up after garbage trucks?

The rental agent had sized her up and she had resented his instant, offhand assessment.

She was afraid of the drunk men in doorways and on stoops. She felt completely defenseless against the gangs of tall, strong boys. Women had been pulled into passageways and down stairs to service entrances on brilliantly lit Eighty-sixth Street and on Central Park West. With knives or guns pressed against them, they had not made one sound while a man or several men raped them amidst the garbage cans. Only the worst cases made the papers.

And what was the rental agent's advice? Women must be very careful. Not show weakness or vulnerability. Not invite attack. Take cabs after dark. Walk on the curbside of the sidewalk. Walk fast and purposefully.

Kate glanced at the tired black woman before she got off the bus at Seventy-fourth Street. The boys had either exited or moved elsewhere. The woman was still staring straight ahead, clutching her cracked patent leather purse.

The day had not gone as Kate had planned. As she unlocked her apartment she willed away the image of the woman on the bus.

"Now then," she murmured and placed a record on the turntable.

Jean-Paul Gallardon playing Chopin mazurkas.

By nine she had eaten, washed and put away her dishes and made considerable progress with the remaining cartons. She took a shower and put on a nightgown.

The apartment would be the way she wanted it by about noon on Saturday if she kept to her schedule.

She poured a tot of the Calvados a man whom she had met at the Frick had given her after their third date. She placed the Beethoven Fourth Piano Concerto on the machine and lay back on the sofa.

Midway through the final movement someone knocked on her door.

Margaret! Oh, God, she wasn't prepared to see Margaret tonight. The Margaret-generated confidence she had felt in the morning was gone. It hadn't worked with Mr. Hamilton or Scotty or the woman on the bus.

A second knock sounded.

Kate grabbed her robe from the hook on the bathroom door. "Who is it?"

"Ms. Delling, my name is Art Gilman. I live directly above you. I have a problem." The man sounded worn out.

A pipe had broken and water was about to begin dripping through her ceiling, Kate thought.

"What's wrong?"

"Green beans."

"Did you say green beans?"

"Could you open your door to the chain? I'm too pooped to shout."

Kate snapped open locks and looked through the opening. A very sunburned man wearing a denim shirt and brown corduroy trousers was looking back at her.

"Isn't it a little late for green beans?"

"It's not even ten thirty, and I could hear you playing Beethoven."

"Oh, I'm sorry. I'll turn it down."

"That," he said patiently, "isn't the point. The point is about thirty-five pounds of green beans. I just got in from the country. My hosts seem to have had an extraordinarily bountiful early crop of green beans. I don't know what in hell to do with them, and I wondered, since you are awake . . . Look, this isn't the best way to introduce myself. Look, will you please take a few pounds of these green beans?"

"I suppose so. I'm very fond of green beans. Thank you." She undid the chain. Maybe she had moved into a madhouse occupied by curiously generous lunatics.

The sunburned man stood between two large wooden crates in which green beans were mounded. A trail of green beans was strewn along the waxed hall. "You see my problem."

"Good God. I won't make a dent in that. I mean, there are only so many green beans one person . . ."

"Just take what you can use. While you're looking for a large Baggie, may I have a glass of water? I've been driving for three hours."

Within a little more than twenty-four hours, Kate waved a

second stranger into her new apartment. The man went directly to the kitchen, opened the upper-right-hand cupboard door, found a glass and filled it.

He drank two glasses of tap water. She stood in the doorway holding open the door. His denim shirt was stuck to his back with sweat.

"Thanks for the water." He turned to her. "Jesus, you look nervous." He pushed his glasses up his shiny red nose, frowning. "Of course you are. You shouldn't have let me in. Except I'm past the lobby door. Still, you've never seen me before."

"Margaret said someone named Art lived above me."

"Ah, Margaret. You've met Margaret? I hope she'll also relieve me of some green beans. I don't know how long they'll keep." He opened the door under the sink, stopped and peered into the space. "Aha. Very organized." He pulled forth a large, folded grocery bag. "Honest intentions, truly." He went past Kate into the hall and began to stuff green beans into the bag. "I don't blame you. Maniac knocks at your door offering veggies."

"Stop! I can't use half of that if I ate green beans for a week. Three meals a day."

"You're sure you don't want more?"

"Positive."

He carried the bag to the kitchen and set it on the drainboard. "By the way, have you seen Martin Fried's new play?"

She shook her head. "The reviews were good."

"Thing's sold out for months. I have a single ticket for Friday night, if you'd like to use it. I was planning to go with the woman I love, but she's frantic about her dissertation so we'll go another time. I gave one of the tickets to my aunt, which leaves me with the single. And don't offer to pay me. I'm a free-lance journalist and I always get freebies."

"Thank you. But I was planning to use Friday night to finish unpacking."

Art came into the hall where he slowly shook his head at the two crates of green beans. "Finish on Saturday or Sunday. My Aunt Lenore doesn't snore, cough or engage in conversation with people she doesn't know. The seats are sixth row center."

"I have been wanting to see *Pardons*," she said reluctantly.

"Okay, I'll shove the ticket under your door tomorrow. Thanks for helping me out with the green beans. I wonder who's in the building and still awake?" He shoved one crate against the wall, lifted the second and walked to the door of the rear apartment.

Kate closed and locked the door.

She liked the way he matter-of-factly had said, "the woman I love." She had never before heard a man say that.

She made room for the bag of green beans in her refrigerator and went to bed. She fell asleep while she was wondering what to do with so many green beans. She did not dream that night.

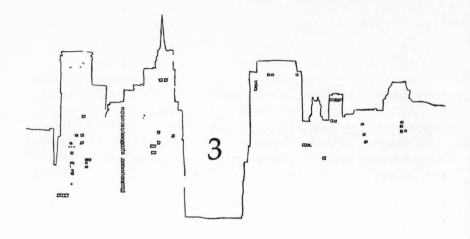

3

Thursday morning at eleven thirty Scotty Rogers' secretary brought Kate a scribbled note on his memo paper:

Kate,

I can't make Harvey's meeting. It begins at one and should be over by five. Give me a rundown tomorrow.

S.R.

"Oh, that bastard," she said.

"Harvey's meeting," as she well knew, was to be a presentation by one of their hardware suppliers. Federated Computer Systems was considering a contract to develop a program for a modification of CARNOR. The technical reps were to explain the difference in the computer language, its advantages and applications.

Every department head whose people and products were affected was expected to attend the presentation.

When the meeting had been announced several weeks before, Miriam Graun, who was also a group head in Scotty's department, told Kate over a quick lunch, "Rogers won't be going to Harvey's meeting. What do you want to bet?"

"Not a penny. He'll send you or Ralph or me."

"And at the last minute. That sonofabitch is so obvious I am in constant awe of his ability to bullshit Hamilton and almost everyone in the company over him."

The two women angrily ate frozen yogurt.

"He'll send one of us," Kate said, "because he won't know what the tech reps are talking about. Any question he asks would give him away."

"But he'll do it an hour before the meeting. He's such a fathead he'll assume if he tells anyone he can't attend they'll reschedule it."

Early Thursday morning Kate had assumed she was exempt. She had a pile of programs to debug by Friday afternoon and Scotty knew it.

She called him immediately after receiving his note.

Neither Scotty nor his secretary answered his phone.

The meeting was over at five forty-five.

Kate worked at her desk until after seven.

At least at that hour the buses were less crowded.

Kate was washing the dishes and the pan she had used for making a scrambled eggs and bacon dinner and listening to Verdi's Requiem when a knock sounded on her door.

"Oh, hell. The green beans," she whispered.

They were still in the big bag stuffed in the refrigerator.

"Who is it?" she called.

"Margaret. Have you a minute?"

Kate stared at the chain. She had not thought about Margaret since the night before when Art had said he'd give her some of his green beans.

"Kate? Can you hear me?" The knock sounded again.

"Yes. Just a moment."

She unbolted the locks and slid off the chain.

"Hello." Kate opened her door.

Margaret swept into the apartment. "I hope all I'm interrupting is the opera you're playing."

"That isn't an opera. It's a requiem. I was just finishing my dishes."

Margaret looked around the living room. "You're amazing. Only four boxes to go and the pictures to be hung. Kate, I feel terrible about unnerving you the other night and I want to apologize."

"No. Please don't apologize." She vigorously shook her head. "I was startled, that's all. But I see everything quite differently now. Honestly."

"May I sit down?"

"Of course. Would you like a drink?"

"I brought my own." Margaret extracted a can of Miller's Lite from her large Vuitton shoulder bag. "I'll accept a glass, though."

Startled, Kate went to the kitchen, poured herself a glass of wine and brought Margaret a glass.

"Actually," Margaret said, carefully pouring, "I don't like beer. I've found, though, that beer works best."

"Works best?" Kate sat down opposite Margaret, who was gracefully arranged on the love seat.

She was dressed in a full skirt and loose matching blouse. She wore a pearl necklace and earrings. Her hair was softly pulled up and back; her makeup was subtle. The effect was tastefully subdued elegance.

"My first trick tonight gets it off when he's peed on. Fortunately, my next date has different requirements. Thus the beer."

"You . . . urinate for men?"

"Not for, on. Right in this one's face." Margaret sipped, watching Kate over her glass. "And you thought I was a lawyer. Last night my services were required by a Methodist minister, among others. Every three months or so he leaves a coded message on my machine. Takes him that long to come up with the scratch. That's part of his turn-on, paying what I charge." Margaret rolled her eyes. "My experience has been that some men of the cloth are living at least two separate lives. I mean, some of those men are not after a pleasant, furtive bang. They're crazy men. I suppose they can't let themselves go with their wives. After all, I don't have to listen to those turkeys preach on Sundays or counsel the young marrieds." She sat back against the cushions. "I came here to apologize to you."

"I've already asked you not to apologize." Kate was rigid. She was quite tired and she was now disoriented. "What you do . . . the way you earn money, is alien. To me. There's no need to discuss it."

"Yes, there is a need to discuss it. You're rather straight, you know. Vulnerable. I set you up the other night. I enjoy shocking people. Ordinarily I enjoy being outrageous, watching people's reactions. The other night after you left, I was sorry. Kate, I'm used to my games and illusions. My apartment is my own fraud. For myself. I rarely ask anyone in. I'm an actress." She poured the rest of her beer into the glass. "What are you doing in New York? Why do I feel you don't like it here?"

"Probably because in many ways I don't like New York."

"Then why are you here?"

Margaret's question was spoken in a different tonality and accent than she had used before. Was it Queens or The Bronx or Jersey? Kate was never able to sort them out. Margaret's was a grandmother's voice. Accepting, without reservations. Wise and patient.

"I didn't come to New York to conquer," Kate found herself saying slowly. "I came here to hide. I came here to hide in the crowds and I find I'm claustrophobic."

"If you can't tell me, you can't tell anyone. Whores don't gossip. Or did you know that?" She pulled another can of beer from her bag, popped open the top and poured. "So why are you here?"

Kate switched to a different chair. She got up and refilled her glass, seating herself in yet another chair.

"Okay. I'll tell you about my family." She let her eyes slide over the leaning, unhung pictures, the unpacked liquor store boxes. "I don't like to talk about my family."

"Then let's talk about the Yankees. How about solar power or the gasoline . . ."

"My family, my mother's family, is a prominent California family. My grandfather and great-grandfather were important men in California and Arizona and Nevada." She spoke slowly, carefully, enunciating each word, as if she were an advanced audiocomputer programmed to the definitive *Who's Who in the West*.

"I'm a fifth-generation Californian on my mother's side. My father was born in Maryland. If I ever met anyone from my father's family I've forgotten. Although he sometimes mentioned a great-uncle who had served in the U.S. Senate. I don't know when. I do know about my mother's family." She looked from the unhung pictures to Margaret. "My mother was a Meade. That means nothing to anyone here in the East. In the San Joaquin

Valley there is a town called Meade. South of the Tehachapi
Mountains there are Karl W. Meade branch libraries, Meade
boulevards, and Karl W. Meade parks. Karl W. Meade the Second
was my grandfather. He died before I was born."

"I've never thought of California as having a fifth-generation
anything."

Kate nodded. "You don't know Arroyo Avenue in Pasadena.
My mother and her two sisters grew up in what is called 'Meade
House.' They loved it. Now it's preserved as a historic site and
used for wedding receptions and sedate parties and meetings.
I've been there a few times. It's hard to imagine anyone actually
going to sleep and waking up in that house. It was built in 1905,
my aunt Catherine liked to say. The people who put on the
receptions own it now, and they're required to maintain the
house and grounds."

"What happened? Why did your people sell it?" Margaret
appeared sincerely interested in the chronicle of an authentic old
California family.

"My great-grandfather was the Karl W. Meade the libraries
and streets are named after. My mother's father, his son, was a
speculator. Boiled down, he finally lost everything in the late
forties. My grandfather, as my aunt Sarah said, often, believed in
applied science. More specifically, he had absolute faith in an
assistant professor at Cal Tech who was developing an inexpensive method for converting ocean water into pure water. Needless to say, Dr. Hazeltine's venture failed. I don't know what
happened to him. I'm told my grandfather went into a severe
depression and died in his sleep."

Kate paused to sip her wine. She looked at a corner of the love
seat when she resumed talking.

"My mother's older sisters were safely married to successful
men from prominent families before my grandfather lost everything. My mother, whose name is Anne, was determined to
become a painter. She studied in San Francisco and with several
painters in Europe. She met my father, whose name is Lloyd, at
an opening at the county museum where he was an assistant
curator of art. They fell in love. My mother became pregnant.
They were married."

Margaret belched softly and excused herself.

"My father was very handsome. He was socially ambitious. In
his work he was able to meet the sort of people he enjoyed—rich,

important and cultivated. He was one of those not-quite-Southern men who enjoy being gallant and amusing. My mother was intense and often distracted. Her sisters liked to think of her as an eccentric artist.

"Aunt Sarah and Uncle Hugh Willoughby live in Pacific Palisades and they have a huge, two-story house on Lake Arrowhead. Aunt Catherine and Uncle Gordon Van der Kemp lived in Hancock Park and owned a great stucco and tile-roofed pile at Laguna. We seldom visited their city homes. Arrowhead and Laguna, though. Most weekends and during vacations we were at either Laguna or Arrowhead. We never vacationed anywhere else. My father never earned much. My mother sold few of her paintings. My mother didn't care whether or not we were invited to her sisters'. My father, though. My father's life was focused on being a houseguest at one place or the other. People in the neighborhood where we lived thought we were terribly lucky to have rich, generous relatives."

"Then what went wrong? Something went wrong, right?"

"Yes."

"You rattle off your past and your family as if you're quoting from some sort of résumé. Why did you come to New York?"

"After I finished college I had an affair with a married man. In Arizona. His name was Alex. I didn't want to go back to L.A. I applied for jobs in New York. I received a good offer from F.C.S."

"Why do I feel you've left out the important parts?"

"I don't think of parts of my past. Ever. The past is past."

"Don't bet on that, Kate." She glanced at her watch. "Are you curious about why I'm a hooker?"

Kate realized, after she began to relax and consider Margaret's question, how rigid she'd been. "Yes, I suppose I am. But from what I've heard, women in your work don't like to talk about it. Is that right? They hate their clients to ask, and they invent conversation that isn't true."

Margaret laughed. "You've been listening to pop psychology. The truth is, I really don't know why I do what I do. Sometimes I look in the mirror and I'm astonished. Is that you, Maggie? Have you ever noticed that most of the time when you look in the mirror you don't see yourself? You see your hair or your makeup. As if you're looking at a manikin. Then every once in a while you see yourself. And it's frightening. That face looking back is all you are. Whenever that happens I become aware I'm alive, in a different way. I stare at myself. I think, Maggie, this is you. And I become so aware I'm alive, I'm terrified."

"But of what?"

"I consider my death—it follows." Margaret shrugged away Kate's hesitant, raised hand. "In answer to your unasked question, I am turned on by the unexpected, by weirdos." She examined the two inches of beer left in her glass. "I don't mean sexually. I am basically unsexual. So? The men who can pop for the money I charge don't want, as they say, normal screwing around. That they could get from their wives or the women who are usually available to them. These guys need a kind of anonymous female they'll never see in any other context. They may have a wife and four girlfriends. They don't want to reveal some private sicky aspect of themselves to those women. I can do, or fake, anything their regular women can. They don't want that. My johns are usually hiding some kink they think would cause them to lose face with their regular women. Can you imagine the wife's reaction if Joe Bluster-Cool or Frank Wall Street came dancing into the bedroom done up in Frederick's of Hollywood? Hairy legs under the garter belt and midthigh nylons?"

"Then is that what you do? Help men save face sexually? Secretly submissive men? Transvestites?"

"Hardly. I've told you a part of my first client's requirements. The one I'm drinking this beer for. No, my johns' requirements run the spectrum. The rainbow. Shit, the entire rainbow. Kinks Krafft-Ebing never encountered. I don't do heavy S and M. Oh, if some guy wants me to trail a piece of leather over his rear, I've done that. But I've never been bruised. Not once."

"How can you tell beforehand whether or not a client is crazy?"

"I'm an expert with voices. People can fake everything about themselves except their voices. I don't mean regional accents; they're a snap. I mean a person's state of mind. I can pick up a loony in ten words or less, from a message on my machine or directly. The words aren't important; the way they're spoken is everything. And this works both ways. Many, many ads and phone numbers are available to interested men. What do they have to lose in a phone booth with a pile of dimes? They listen to a voice over the phone—recorded or live. They want quality for their money. It's easy to hang up and call another number. Selective shopping."

"I can't understand how you can talk about what you do so objectively." Kate was trying to imagine a sane, successful man married to a sane, enlightened woman, with several children, unbuttoning his vest, preparing himself to be urinated upon by a very attractive woman who dressed well and spoke properly. "What do you feel?"

"Feel? If I let myself feel I'd be in trouble. I'm an actress. I've told you I deal in illusions. I can't be bothered with a shrink's interpretation of why men need to pay me to play games. I'm an actress who's never seen a script. I have to improvise. And fast. Timing is important. The johns provide the cues; my job is to pick them up." Margaret drained her glass. "I may have the most obliging bladder in the tri-state area. By the way, if you were a whore, you'd have a very salable voice."

"What!" Kate laughed.

Margaret shrugged away Kate's surprise. "Nicely modulated, middle register. Confident and educated, but not too confident. Then, beneath that is a great combination of innocence and anger." She collected her purse and carried the empty beer cans to the kitchen. "You don't look innocent or angry, though."

"That's because I am neither angry nor innocent." Kate stood in the center of the living room.

"Hmm." Margaret tilted her head, calmly studying Kate for a moment. "Maybe I'm too full of beer. Does the offer for enchiladas still stand?"

"Sure. But after I finish unpacking."

"Great. Off I go." She unlocked the locks and let the chain drop.

Kate closed the door and locked it.

The power for the record player was still on. She turned it off and put the Verdi records in their slips, then into the album.

If anyone else knocked on her door she would not respond. Too much had happened during the past three days to be assimilated and ordered, both at work and in this new apartment.

She no longer enjoyed the idea of spending an entire evening with Margaret. She would put off the dinner invitation as long as possible.

Margaret saw nothing disgusting about what she was blithely going off to do.

"That's sick," Kate said and slumped into a chair.

She was so tired she ached and her eyes burned. She should have been in bed an hour ago, but she felt agitated and unfocused. If she went to bed now she would be unable to direct her thoughts.

Now then, she said to herself. Now then.

What did you think expensive whores did?

I didn't think it out.

You're confused by Margaret's openness and nonchalance. She doesn't even consider what she does as being sexual. She's an actress.

The men, though! They all look and act completely normal. Just like Uncle Gordon.

Now then. Now then. That is past. You can do absolutely nothing about that. Nothing.

Correct. Nothing. That's past. Margaret's a grown woman who chooses to do what she does. She chooses and so she's safe.

Outside, from the street, nearby, a man yelled. Not in rage, not in fear. He bellowed forth one word. Kate listened for the next yell. It was the same word, probably someone's name, but the intonation was different.

She had heard men yelling on the streets at night many times since she had come to New York. They were men alone and drunk. The ones she had seen were poorly dressed, in their thirties or forties. They stood, weaving, trying to interpret the sidewalk at their feet. After a while the men straightened, lurched, wound up and sent forth their one-word shout.

Kate concentrated on the man outside.

His word sounded like "Segundo," and from the placement, he was several doors west, on her side of the street.

She did not count the number of times the man found the strength to call out his word. She did not time his progress along her street to the corner. He shouted and pleaded and moaned "Segundo" in a hundred different ways before he turned the corner and could no longer be heard. He was safe. The police had more urgent business. He wasn't worth a mugger's trouble.

The man's past, present and future were reduced to whatever the word "Segundo" meant to him. In his drunkenness and despair he still knew and felt something. He, none of them, to her knowledge, just lay down and gave up; not the men who yelled in the middle of the night. The act of yelling saved them.

Kate envied the man who had found the word "Segundo" upon which he could simultaneously lean and rant, oblivious to anyone or anything else. An absolute focus. All of his experience reduced to a single word.

She held his many voices in her mind when she fell onto her bed. They were not hers.

Everyone was safe.

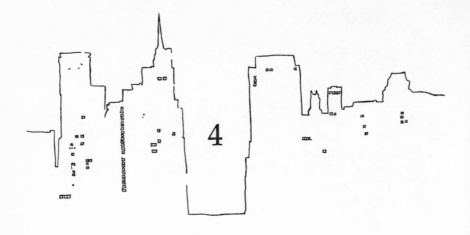

4

Sometime during the night Art slid an envelope containing the ticket for *Pardons* under her door.

Friday morning, Kate selected clothes that were a compromise between work and the theater. While she drank her instant coffee she examined the unpacked cartons and the unhung pictures.

"The hell with it."

She wanted to see the play and it was Friday. She would make a reservation at the Russian Tea Room for six thirty.

While Kate explained to Scotty the content of the presentation at Harvey's meeting, he doodled. He asked no questions.

"Arrange to fill in Miriam and Ralph. They need to know this." He fiddled with his Dunhill pipe. "Pete Hamilton will be back Monday."

"I intend to speak with him then."

He yawned, rudely, vastly. "Nice man. He's a great listener. He listens and becomes immobilized. You've heard that. He can't make decisions. He calls in the department heads when one of his plants droops. He doesn't feel comfortable with dissension."

Kate gathered up her papers. "Does anyone?"

44

"I love dissension, sweetie. Keeps me awake. Speaking of which, did you know you have circles under your eyes? Boyfriend keeping you up?"

She worked until five forty-five.

The captain at the Russian Tea Room seated Kate midway back against the wall. A perfect place for observing the other diners—the concertgoers, the musicians, old Russian women who smoked cigarettes like male detectives in French movies from the fifties, men and women with familiar faces, most of whom she could not place. Her waiter was attentive and efficient. The salmon with capers and raw onions was delicious. She drank one glass of wine and three cups of coffee, two more than she ordinarily did after dinner.

She walked to the theater, hoping the exercise would serve to stimulate her. She was tired. And she must appear exhausted if Scotty noticed.

A portly, graying man who wore a clerical collar occupied the seat on her right. The seat on her left remained empty. Evidently Art's aunt was unable to attend.

Kate found the play disappointing, although the minister or priest beside her laughed loudly and even slapped his thigh at lines she thought were corny or tasteless or both. He wasn't alone. She wondered if she was the only person in the audience who was not amused. Perhaps it was fatigue.

There was something more. While her body felt weary, her mind was acutely, almost painfully alert. She was aware of minute details in the set, that the actors were acting, of the people around her, their rustlings and laughs, of their participation in the elaborate deception.

Midway through the final act she decided she would take a taxi home, rather than the bus.

Kate headed west on Forty-seventh Street. She did not hurry. Eighth Avenue would be lined with theatergoers trying to flag taxis.

A great heap of bagged trash lay on the curbside of the sidewalk. Someone had slashed open most of the heavy plastic bags, causing garbage to spill over the width of the sidewalk. It smelled foul. Kate crossed the street where there were fewer people and where fewer taxis were stopping.

Well-dressed men and women stood on both sides of the street facing downtown, an arm raised. Kate remained on the sidewalk. Ten or fifteen minutes didn't matter. She would not set her alarm.

The garbage stench wafted across Eighth Avenue. Kate walked uptown to escape it. At Forty-eighth she glanced to her left. She had heard a moaning, a woman's voice. The street was not as brightly lit as the avenue. She stopped, squinting. About nine car-lengths from the corner she saw a girl with long, straight, light brown hair writhing facedown over the front of a dirty VW bug. Three men drinking from bottles in paper bags leaned against a building watching the girl. Farther down the street Kate saw another cluster of lounging men looking at the girl. There wasn't a woman to be seen.

Kate considered the possibility that the girl was a decoy of some sort.

But what if she wasn't?

Too tired to be logical, she straightened and hurried toward the figure laid over the VW.

There was, after a few steps, enough light so that Kate could see the blood running down the girl's legs.

The girl's short shorts had absorbed all the moisture they could hold; the dark red was spread up to the waistband and in streaks over her hips. Now it flowed over the backs and insides of her thighs.

"What happened?" Kate bent over the girl.

She lifted her head and looked at Kate. Her eyes were not in focus.

"I'll find the police. An ambulance." Kate searched the street.

The men with the paper bags poked each other.

The girl wailed. She looked thirteen. What was she doing here made up like a clown, dressed in short shorts and a tank top? Kidnapped?

"That sonofabitch. Oh, shit," the girl muttered.

"What happened?" Kate tried to ease the girl off the car.

"Leave me be." She fell back on the grimy hood.

"I'm trying to help you. Don't be frightened. People will help you. It's all right now." She was amazed by the blood. It ran down the girl's ankles onto the cement. "You may be in shock."

Kate slid her arm under the girl's chest.

"Shock, shit. Are you a dyke? Where's André? It hurts!" The child's head bounced off the windshield wiper. "André said it's okay."

"Look," Kate growled the words, "I think you've been sodomized! You are hemorrhaging. Do you know who did this?"

"André told me, okay. But, a big, big man."

"André told you okay? Okay, what?" Kate heard the men with the paper bags chuckling and making comments. "You need attention. I'm going to try to help you to Eighth Avenue. We aren't far from Roosevelt Hospital."

The girl was thirteen or fourteen, no older, filthy, and ghastly from loss of blood.

The men crinkled their paper bags and moved in closer.

Kate tried to pry the girl off the car while she searched for a police car. Long-drunk, sagging men formed a half-circle.

"André," the girl moaned.

"You need a doctor!" Kate screamed.

The men's heads wobbled.

"Where are the police?" Kate desperately asked the girl, the men with their half-pints, the dark windows. "Where are the police! This is a child!"

Kate could see men and women walking along brightly-lit Eighth Avenue, ignoring the neighborhood, the side streets. She screamed "Help! Rape!" toward the people whose arms were raised for taxis.

The paper-bag men shuffled, mumbled, backing off.

"André said go with the john," the girl was saying. She had a country voice. Now she spoke in a monotone. A string of drool slipped from the corner of her mouth onto the car. "Grabbed me from behind once we got in the room. Never said one word. Threw me on that bed and it broke under us. Crashed to the floor. And he was at me. From behind. André never told me about that."

"What is your name?" Kate asked as gently as she could.

"Fuck my name. Where's André?"

The blood was congealing. The girl continued to lie on the car, arms draped over it.

"Where are the police?" Kate looked to Eighth Avenue, then west to Ninth Avenue.

"Where's André?" The girl slammed her cheek on the car. "He's my main man."

Kate kicked a man who had lurched over to the VW for a better look. He hobbled off laughing and saying, "Hoo-hoo. Hoo-hoo."

"How old are you?"

"Twenty-two," the girl said flatly. "Twenty-two. Where's André?"

Three women clattered around the corner on wooden platform shoes.

"There's a girl here," Kate called to them. "She's hurt." She recognized the women as prostitutes. "She needs an ambulance."

They sauntered over to the car. The oldest one, a black-haired woman who looked to be in her mid-twenties, glanced at the girl, then slowly, contemptuously ran her eyes over Kate.

"Yeah?"

"Will one of you find a policeman and call an ambulance? I was afraid to leave her alone." She gestured to the lounging men.

"She's André's. He'll take care of her."

"He already has! He sent her to a man who tore her to pieces! She's a child, goddamn it!"

"Yeah?" a woman with Dolly Parton hair said. "She's old enough. Lou Ann," she said to the girl, "you wanted to come here to the city, didn't you?"

The girl closed her eyes and nodded.

"André was asking about you awhile ago," the third woman said. "He'll be along."

"Just exactly what is André going to do when he gets here?" Kate was shouting.

"Listen, lady," the first woman said, "why don't you go back over to the East Side or uptown where you came from? Who do you think you are? You want to take Lou Ann home with you? Feed her banana instant breakfast? She'll be back on the street the minute her tushy heals. Lou Ann likes the life, don't you, honey?"

Kate tried to control her voice. "Will a doctor see Lou Ann?"

The three women laughed softly.

"No one ever died from what happened to Lou Ann," the blonde said. "Next time you won't feel a thing, honey."

Lou Ann began to moan again.

"I'm going to find the police!"

"Sure," the third woman spat, "you do that."

"Here comes André."

Kate saw a tomato-red Oldsmobile, not a new car, slowly cruising along the street.

The black-haired woman gave a small jerk with her head.

The car stopped beside the Volkswagen.

A very tall, very thin black man gracefully emerged.

"André," Lou Ann cried. "André."

"Baby, you're messed up." He brushed her hair back. "André's here. Shit," he said to the three women, "that dude did look funny." Then to the girl: "Lou Ann, you come with your main man. You come along. You want to get cleaned up. I'll fix you up. You know André will take good care of his girl. You know."

He opened the rear door. Lou Ann permitted two of the women to lift her from the VW and ease her onto the white leather upholstery. When she sat she screamed.

"Who's that?" André eyed Kate.

"She found Lou Ann. She wants the police."

"You won't take her to a doctor, will you?" Kate said to the tall, smiling man.

"Sure I will. That's just where I'm taking her." He ran around the front of his car, climbed in, slammed the door and drove off.

The three women, the drunk men, were all looking at Kate. She had not thought to look at the pimp's license number.

What would have been accomplished if she had? How many tomato-red Oldsmobiles were there in Manhattan? Not many. If the police wanted André they could find him.

The prostitutes, all of whom smelled of sweat and strong perfume, watched her with expressionless eyes.

With effort, she said quietly, "What about the man who did that to a child?"

The first woman, the one with shiny black hair, said, "What about him?" She laid her hands on her hips and leaned forward from the waist. "He didn't kill her, did he? He didn't bite off her nipples, did he? Shit."

She clattered and swayed back to Eighth Avenue, followed by the other women.

One drunk began to vomit, another to cough.

Kate slowly walked toward the lights.

She could not remember why she was walking uptown on Eighth Avenue. Yes, a taxi. There had been a play. Her calves ached. She had lost her day.

Skinny, freckled Lou Ann had run away from somewhere. André had exerted his pimp magic on her. Kate couldn't imagine what it was. Lou Ann worshiped the man. Whatever empathy the street whores had begun with, whenever they had begun, had evaporated.

Not one of those women indicated concern for the bloody girl. "She's André's girl. André will take care of her." A terrified fourteen-year-old; at most fourteen.

Kate bumped into a tall, thin black man done up in skintight, mouse-gray suede pants and a puffy-sleeved satin shirt. A wide-brimmed hat topped with a peacock feather was tilted jauntily on his short Afro. He looked like André. Kate bared her teeth. The man said, "Hey, whoa, lady, you on a bad trip?" in a deep, amused voice.

He wasn't André.

But he was probably a pimp.

Where had André taken Lou Ann?

To some filthy room. Somewhere in Manhattan where his red car would be safe on the street.

And somewhere within a subway ride of Eighth Avenue and Forty-eighth Street was the man who had hired Lou Ann's body.

The three whores had shrugged off Lou Ann's blood and pain. The girl belonged to André. The man who sodomized Lou Ann gave André the money.

Kate stolidly continued up the avenue, concentrating now on discovering a manageable explanation. How did Lou Ann's bloody legs connect with salmon and capers at the Russian Tea Room and Scotty Rogers' pipe and a paper bag full of wilting green beans and a banal play and Margaret's two cans of beer?

The connection was between Lou Ann and Margaret.

Beautiful, poised Margaret with her comfortable apartment in which she served cassoulet while a machine collected requests from men. Grimy, ignorant Lou Ann whose existence was reduced to the demands and whims of one man.

Kate was dimly aware of people she passed. It was well after midnight. The theatergoers were now home or elsewhere.

She tried to focus on the connection.

Lou Ann was raped. Margaret urinated on rich men.

The ocean waves began to rise and break, obscuring the people and cars, the garish stores. The distant sound of children laughing and shouting in the surf overlaid voices, motors and horns. The smell of salt water and suntan lotion almost gagged her. On came the breakers, pounding the beach, retreating, forming again to rise and curl and fall under their own weight. The waves were endless and provided no resolution. Never a resolution.

She clenched her teeth, made her hands into fists, stopped and squeezed shut her eyes.

There is nothing you can do, she said to herself. Nothing.

Lou Ann didn't need your help. You didn't help her. If a police car had shown up Lou Ann might have been helped.

When she opened her eyes the waves were gone.

Two teenaged Hispanic boys were standing a few feet from her, grinning.

"Fuck off," she spat and walked around them.

She saw she was in the mid-Fifties. She should stop and wait for a taxi. Her legs and back ached from fatigue and tension.

Kate continued to the next corner and walked around a parked van into the street. Taxis approached, but all were occupied. She saw a light on a taxi a block away, on the east side of the street. She hurried to the other side, dodging traffic. Two men caught the taxi halfway up the block. No others were in sight.

When a taxi finally stopped for her, she gave her address. She was not aware of being driven home, of unlocking and locking her door, of undressing and getting into bed.

She lay on her side, knees drawn up, wrists crossed over her breasts. She could not close her eyes.

Now then. Now then.

They pay for it, the man on the M10 had said about the patrons of the massage parlor.

He didn't kill her or bite off her nipples, the street hooker said.

A rich man gave Margaret money to pee in his face.

A large, silent man paid André for the use of Lou Ann.

Policemen lounged under a canopy, smoking and blocking traffic. Everlastingly drunk men sucked their half-pints in little paper bags. And they watched.

The drunks looked at Lou Ann and went, "Hoo-hoo." The red-faced man called the massage parlor women lazy sluts.

Kate, curled on her bed, could see Margaret's lovely face, Lou Ann's stained and contorted face, the glum faces of the massage parlor women, the impassive faces of the street whores.

It was now after three in the morning and Kate lay awake and sweating.

The men's faces, finally, had become very important.

What did Lou Ann see before the big man threw her on the bed? How did Margaret read her clients' needs? What did the street whores and the massage parlor women find on the men's faces when they hurriedly described what they wanted?

She knew, Kate did.

She stared at the bedroom window and she remembered the men's faces. Each of them.

Now then. Now then.

And they had not paid for what they did. In no way had they paid.

Not her father. Not Uncle Gordon. Not Alex.

Hoo-hoo. Hoo-hoo.

Now then. Now then.

Her shoulder and hip pressed heavily on the mattress. She could see the bars silhouetted behind the curtains.

The words now then, now then weren't working.

The faces of those men weren't dissolving.

Not one of those three men had cared or was sorry for what he had done. It hadn't mattered to them.

And there was nothing she could do.

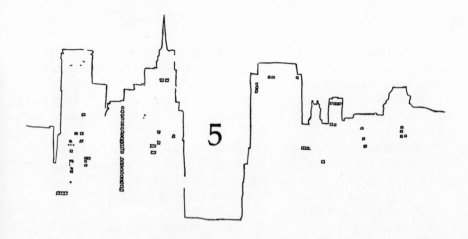

5

It was early September and Kate was almost twelve years old. They were at Aunt Catherine and Uncle Gordon's Laguna Beach house again, for a five-day Labor Day weekend. The number, relationships and ages of the houseguests made it necessary for Kate to be put up in a small, ill-ventilated room that usually served as an auxiliary dressing room. One door opened onto the beach, and another onto the hallway that ran from the kitchen to the storage rooms where great quantities of wine and liquor, food, beach equipment and tools were kept.

Although Aunt Catherine was apologetic, Kate didn't mind the folding cot and the stuffiness. This was better than sharing one of the guest rooms with friends of her cousins, who were much older and were either patronizing or contemptuous.

The summer was not going well. This had nothing to do with the heat and smog, which people said were the worst they could remember.

Following Easter vacation, when the summer half of the year began, Kate had begun to see and hear her parents in a different way. Before, she had paid little attention to Lloyd's words, his observations and judgments. They all seemed to be about art and artists, or art patrons and their collections, or evaluations of guests he had spent time with or wanted to spend time with at

53

either Lake Arrowhead or Laguna Beach. Before, she had been able to ignore the amount of vodka Anne drank and its effect on her, both when she was drinking it and the following day.

What she had begun to notice, but not understand, was that there was a correlation between the quantity of vodka and her father's words.

The second-to-last day of Easter vacation, which had been spent at Lake Arrowhead, Kate overheard Aunt Sarah and her oldest friend, Cynthia Rodriguez, talking about her mother.

"What in God's name has happened to Anne, Sarah?"

"You knew she drank."

"You drink, I drink, we all drink. Your baby sister has been falling down drunk for six straight days."

Kate had been sitting on a rounded white boulder halfway under the Willoughbys' private dock on the north shore when Aunt Sarah and Cynthia Rodriguez had strolled out onto it. She was supposed to be on a nature walk Uncle Hugh had signed her up for.

"I am very concerned. She's never been this bad before," Aunt Sarah said.

"You have, I assume, discussed Anne with her husband?"

"He phoned me about three weeks ago. Lloyd said he was worried about her. Something to do with a new painting technique she was trying that wasn't going well. He thought she needed a vacation very badly. He was able to juggle his work at the museum in order to be with her here."

"I wonder how Kate's affected by Anne's drinking? Doesn't she seem unusually shy for her age?"

"Not especially. I think she's quite bright. The truth is, Kate's always been so self-contained, I've never paid much attention to her."

"Sarah! Your own niece!"

"Don't look at me that way! Whenever Anne and Lloyd and Kate come up here the house is always bulging with other guests. I cannot remember a time when my sister and her family were our only guests. Thank God Lloyd can always be counted upon to be helpful."

"Well, I'm still concerned about Anne, no matter how solicitous her husband is. How in hell can she write her name, to say nothing of painting, if she drinks this much?"

"Lloyd says she goes for ages without touching a drop."

"If he says so. Shall we get back? I'm due for mixed doubles in a few minutes."

Kate listened to her Aunt Sarah and Cynthia Rodriguez walk back over the wooden planks, and she watched sailboats and powerboats towing water-skiers wearing wet suits. The water in the lake was still very cold; it gently lapped against the white boulder.

Aunt Sarah had not told her best friend the truth.

Anne was frustrated by the series of canvases she had been working on since Christmas. That was true. But she had wanted to stay home and try to figure out what she had been doing wrong. Lloyd had a week's vacation from the museum and he was bored because he had finished the catalog for the next exhibit and there wasn't anything interesting that had to be done for a while.

Besides, Kate was positive Lloyd had told Anne that Aunt Sarah had called and begged them to come. Something about her needing them to help entertain a crabby director on one of Uncle Hugh's boards.

Now Kate sat cross-legged on her cot in a room that smelled of the ocean and tanning lotion. The ceiling of her room was a portion of the wide deck that hung over the beach. Five months after she had eavesdropped on Aunt Sarah and Cynthia Rodriguez, Kate listened to her father and Aunt Catherine.

They were up there alone and they were talking about her mother.

She rubbed sand from the sides and bottoms of her feet, from between her toes, then brushed it off the cotton spread onto the rattan rug.

The words Lloyd was saying to Aunt Catherine weren't lies, but they weren't the truth either.

Many things had become confused and unsettling since Easter vacation at Lake Arrowhead, since she had begun to look and listen carefully.

For instance, at that moment he was telling Aunt Catherine that Anne was having difficulty with her work and he was certain that this time spent with the Van der Kemps and their stimulating houseguests was exactly what she needed.

But that wasn't really true.

Kate had been paying attention. Everything was so complicated.

Aunt Catherine was saying she hoped Anne would behave herself with vodka that night.

"When you phoned to ask if the three of you could come down this weekend, I had serious reservations."

"And I understand. Catherine, please, I trust you not to let Anne know I made that phone call."

"Sarah and I love her so much and we both feel so helpless. It must be a thousand times worse for you, Lloyd."

Her father murmured something Kate couldn't hear.

"The reason I told you I'd have to talk it over with Gordon first was because the other guests are out-of-town clients of his firm. Also, he's treating this little musicale tonight as if it were a full-fledged concert."

Kate's father murmured again.

"I can't understand why she's become so self-destructive. I'm baffled. She wants so much to come down here, then acts as if she can't bear being here."

"Anne's pride, Catherine. But that's my problem, not yours."

A group of people clattered out onto the deck. A man said something and everyone laughed.

Kate screwed up her face, lay down on her back and tried to make sense of what she had just heard. She couldn't, so after a while she opened the door onto the beach, being careful to lock it and drop the lanyard to which the keys were attached over her head.

Anne wasn't proud! She didn't want to come! She had said, "Why don't you take Kate, Lloyd? I'd truly enjoy spending five days by myself. Truly!"

Lloyd had become almost angry. "I have already told you, darling. Without you the situation would be awkward. How in hell will Catherine manage the seating with an extra man? She can't ask another woman. Where would she put her up?"

Anne had poured vodka into her glass. She hadn't bothered with ice cubes or tonic. "You know Sarah's and Catherine's floor plans better than you do the one of this house."

"Go to your room now, Kate," Lloyd had said.

Kate couldn't hear his words from her room, although she had been able to hear his voice. He had still been talking when she had gone to sleep, and the next day Anne had stayed in bed with the shades pulled down.

He had told Anne how happy he was the Van der Kemps had

invited them. There would be interesting people from New York and Boston.

Kate stood on the hard, wet sand. Foamy water from spent breakers washed over her feet, a few rose to her knees. Her feet began to sink into the fine, dark sand.

So the Van der Kemps hadn't invited them. Lloyd had more or less begged to come for the holiday. And Aunt Catherine had left it up to Uncle Gordon.

The problem was that Anne did get drunk and knock over lamps and fall over furniture. She said strange, slurred things no one could understand.

So maybe all those lies Lloyd told Aunt Sarah and Aunt Catherine were his way of trying to save them from worrying about their sister. Except, that didn't make sense either, not if Anne didn't want to come in the first place, and told Lloyd that very clearly.

Kate waded along in the water until she was across the beach from the Van der Kemps' big white stucco house that was out-lined against the chaparral-covered hills. Their wide deck was filled with people; no one would notice her. She could hear them talking and laughing across the flat expanse of footprint-dimpled sand.

This was the four o'clock cocktails crowd. They would be gone by six thirty. Then the adult guests would begin to shower and dress for the formal dinner which would begin at nine. At least that was what Guadalupe, Aunt Catherine's cook, had informed Kate. "The kids get tacos and burritos from the takeout. You be in the family room for that at seven. I'm making guacamole and nachos for you kids and that's all. I got two helpers in my kitchen for tonight. Jesus, Maria Almighty!"

The offspring of the guests from Boston and New York were tanner than Kate. The youngest was four years older than she was. Her name was Elizabeth and she thought everything about Southern California was "awesomely boring." They all seemed to have come by their tans on "The Cape" or at "The Hamptons."

Back in her room, Kate pulled off her bathing suit, rinsed it and hung it over a towel rack. She showered and put on a pair of cutoff jeans and a loose, faded, navy blue T-shirt.

She settled on her cot with a book of acrostics. The people on the deck above were scraping furniture, talking and clinking ice cubes and glasses.

Kate glanced over when the door to the service hall opened. She wasn't frightened. She had double-locked the door to the beach, as Aunt Catherine had told her.

"Here you are," Uncle Gordon said.

"Yes."

"Why aren't you out on the beach with the other kids? You enjoy volleyball and swimming, don't you?"

"Swimming. I'm not a good volleyball player."

"Then why aren't you out there in the sun?"

"I just came in from the beach, Uncle Gordon."

Gordon Van der Kemp stood in the open doorway looking at her with his head tilted a bit to the left. He was a tall man, much taller than Lloyd who was exactly six feet tall. Uncle Gordon had been on the tennis team at Stanford and he still played every day. His shoulders were broad and muscular, he didn't have the belly bulge most men his age did, and his legs were as sinewy as his sons'. His thick, graying hair was trimmed short. His heavy eyebrows were sunbleached over his pale blue eyes.

"Are you comfortable down here?"

"Yes." She wondered when he would get whatever he had come into the dressing room to get.

"Not too warm?"

"No."

He shook his head. "Christ, those people up there are noisy as hell. Doesn't that bother you?"

"Not really."

"Well, it bothers me." He stepped into the room and shut the door. "That is, being up there among them sometimes gets me down. Mind if I hide out here with you for a while?" He unfolded a canvas-and-wood director's chair and sat in it with his long legs stretched out. He wore chinos, a pale green shirt open at the neck and leather sandals.

Kate did not know what to do or say to this man who, before he had opened her door, had never spoken more than a hundred words directly to her. She knew he was a partner in one of the most important law firms in Los Angeles. He was a trustee for banks and corporations and even the museum her father worked for. He had been to Washington to advise a president. And he still found time to practice the cello. Kate had heard him; he was a very good cellist. He was big and powerful and authoritative.

"Would you like me to get you a drink?" she asked. "Scotch?"

He shook his head without looking away from her. "Not this afternoon. I'm playing chamber music tonight. I've found that even one drink affects my coordination." He spoke seriously, pensively, as if she were an adult.

"Maybe a glass of plain soda water?" She felt she was the hostess and she should see to the comfort of her guest.

"No thank you, my dear." He said "my dear" in the same way he said it to gorgeous, distinguished women. "How did you know I'm a Scotch drinker?"

"I guess I just noticed."

"And I guess I've just begun to notice what a very lovely young woman you've become."

Kate blushed. Uncle Gordon was looking at the front of her T-shirt. It was loose, but maybe he could see the two small mounds that had begun to grow beneath her nipples sometime last winter.

"You're almost twelve?"

Kate nodded.

"I suppose your mother has spoken with you about the changes that occur to girls your age? To your body?"

She gave one tiny nod. The body he spoke of had become rigid.

He frowned the way she had seen him frown when he was engaged in a very serious discussion.

"Has your mother taken you to a grown-up person's doctor yet? Well?" He sounded as if were talking business over the phone—brisk and impatient.

"Not yet."

"Not yet! My God!" He stood and walked to the cot. He was so tall that when Kate looked up to see his face the back of her neck cracked.

"I want you to stand up, Kate. Here, right next to your bed. I can't believe your mother hasn't had you checked yet." He put his large tanned hands on her shoulders. They were hard and heavy. He lifted her by clasping her shoulders.

"Uncle Gordon, I have to go help Guadalupe."

He looked crazy. The corners of his mouth were curled up at the same time that his eyebrows were lowered.

She could clearly hear the voices of people above them, distinct snatches of conversations. She was afraid for herself, and for Uncle Gordon.

"Guadalupe will have to wait. You must say nothing or your mother will be in serious trouble. She drinks too much. Child neglect."

He popped open the copper fastener on her jeans, unzipped them and pulled them to her knees along with her cotton underpants. With one painfully strong hand he held her shoulder, the other made proddings and stabs at everything the crotch of her panties had covered.

"No! Please! Don't!" She whispered because she was dazed by humiliation and confusion.

"Do not say one word!"

She could not see his face any longer, but she could hear the change in his voice, even above the noise from the deck.

"I am doing this for you. Oh, yes!"

The hand that had been digging at her body went to his fly. He jerked down his zipper, yanked out his shirt. A great, hideous, veined flower was freed. Now he pressed that against her chest. He pressed and pressed. She could not find air. Both hands were on her shoulders. Her head was flopping back and forth. She bit down hard on her lower lip.

Her eyes were frozen open in terror.

That was why, in the dressing room's wall-to-wall mirror, she saw the door open. In the mirror she saw her father. She even saw he was holding a fresh bottle of Beefeater's. She saw his mouth open and then close. She saw his eyes seeing what Uncle Gordon was doing. All this she saw, even though her head was being jerked back and forth. Lloyd would know a way to make all of this stop. He would know the right words.

Lloyd did not speak or come into the room. She saw him carefully close the door.

She felt, as the door was closing, a crushing pressure and a spurt of moisture drenching her T-shirt.

"Ah," Uncle Gordon said. "Ah, God!"

He pulled her with him when he crumpled onto the cot.

Kate's T-shirt stuck to her chest. Her left arm was under her body and Uncle Gordon held her right arm.

"Nothing has actually happened to you," he said. He sounded

very tired. "No one will believe you, Kate. I know. You could prove nothing. You aren't damaged."

Kate rolled off the cot. She tugged up her panties and shorts, ran to the beach door and frantically fumbled with the locks.

"The top one," he said, "turns clockwise. The lower one, counterclockwise."

"I hate you!" She could not manage the locks.

From the corner of her eye, from the mirror, she saw him rise, deftly tuck in his shirt and pull up his zipper.

"One moment; you forgot the keys." He scooped up the lanyard and settled it over her head.

Kate ran across the sand to the ocean.

She splashed through shallow water to the point where the waves were breaking. Not the gentle sets of small waves, beyond them, to the big ones that came separately and towering.

Instead of diving under the breakers for protection, she stood straight up facing the walls of green water and took the force. She was knocked down and tumbled about underwater. Again and again she exposed herself to the might of the water. She would either be cleansed or crushed. One or the other.

Neither happened.

A short, stout woman whose curly brown hair was streaked with gray, a woman Kate had often seen walking a black Labrador retriever along the beach, determinedly pushed her way out to Kate.

"Enough!" the woman shouted.

Kate turned away from her.

The next wave battered Kate. The woman dove under it.

"I said, enough!" the woman yelled when Kate's head emerged from the foamy water. She grabbed Kate's hair and towed her into shallow water where she let go.

Kate was on her hands and knees. She panted and sobbed.

The black dog pranced and splashed around her, wagging and barking.

The woman stood above her. "Whatever is wrong, think it over."

"You don't know," Kate gasped.

"I'm sure I don't."

"Leave me alone."

"Not until you're back up at the Van der Kemps."

"I don't belong to them!"

"Nevertheless, I'll wait until you're up there. Try time, my dear."

Kate did not thank the woman; she was not grateful. But there was nothing she could do except cross the sand to the door to her room.

She tore off her clothes and stood under the shower that she had turned on full force.

That didn't help, just as the ocean had not helped.

She still felt the weight of hands on her shoulders, the pressure against her chest, the hot liquid that soaked her T-shirt, the smell of tanning lotion and after-shave.

More than anything she wanted to erase the image of Lloyd's face as she had seen it in the mirror.

Kate threw the sodden T-shirt into a wastebasket and dressed.

She sat on the cot staring at the woven squares of rattan that covered the floor.

What should she do? Tell her mother? Anne loved her. Kate was certain of that.

She rushed along halls and up stairs.

Anne sat in a chintz-covered chair gazing out at the ocean. Lloyd was on the double bed leaning back against a mound of pillows reading a *Saturday Review*.

He continued to look at the magazine when Kate said, "Mother, I need you to help me!"

Anne continued to gaze at the ocean. "Sweetheart, I was watching you play in the water. Why weren't you wearing your bathing suit?" Her speech was very slow and inexorable; she was therefore on her fifth or sixth drink. "I said, 'Lloyd, Kate is certainly being tossed around by the waves. I would feel better if this beach was protected by lifeguards.' Then the woman with the black dog dragged you in by your hair. Were you frightened? I wonder why she pulled you in. I was sitting right up here watching. Why did that woman interfere with you? Silliest damn thing I ever saw. That is what I said. I said, 'Lloyd, Kate ran out into the water with her clothes on. Come here and look. What in the world is Kate doing?' And your father looked at you in your wet T-shirt and he said, 'Oh, for God's sake! You know she likes to attract attention.' Isn't that what you said, Lloyd? Kate likes attention?"

Kate's mother set down her glass and opened her arms. "Come give me a great big hug and kiss," Anne said. "Aren't we having a wonderful time? Your Uncle Gordon is going to play the cello for us with some professional musicians after dinner. You may tiptoe up and listen after dinner if you are very quiet."

From behind his magazine, Lloyd said nothing.

Stiffly, Kate went to her mother to receive a sloppy smack on her cheek.

Anne began to cry. Kate brought her a handful of tissues. She wouldn't be making it to her sister's formal dinner party.

"I wish," Anne said, "I could paint you the way I saw you in the ocean. Why can't I remember what I saw?"

Junior high and high school passed.

Lloyd grew increasingly bored and talked even more. Anne painted and drank vodka.

Once or twice a year the three of them were asked to Lake Arrowhead, always in the off-season, when, if there were other guests, the people were unimportant "duty," or distant relatives from Uncle Hugh's family who could not be gracefully entertained in the city.

The Van der Kemps never again invited them to Laguna Beach. About once a year Anne said, "I used to love the ocean at Catherine's. I wonder what happened to it?"

Anne painted on smaller and smaller canvases. When she painted. Several people from La Cienega galleries whom Lloyd brought to see the paintings acted quite enthusiastic. But Anne laughed at the gallery scouts. She said if they liked her paintings they were incompetent. She laughed at everyone and Lloyd become morose.

None of that mattered because Kate could do nothing about it.

Kate attended UCLA on four academic and financial need scholarships. She lived in a dorm on campus and studied hard to maintain the grade point average required by her scholarships. She seldom saw her parents.

She accepted dates and almost never enjoyed herself. She looked in her mirror and saw that she possessed a pleasant face, an excellent complexion, thick and glossy hair and a well-proportioned body. None of that mattered because she was not comfortable within her own skin. She felt herself to be awkward and without some essential rhythm. And the young men who asked her out acted distracted and mechanical during the first part of the evening, and then became single-minded and mechanical during the latter part.

Kate was convinced, by the beginning of her senior year, that sex was propaganda that not even men believed; or if they did, they had no idea how to go about it comfortably.

By age twenty, Kate was no longer interested in intricate contests between men and women. She found pleasure in the certainty of her studies—computer sciences and technical writing. Computers did not deal with ambiguities. The answers were built into the questions: yes/no, either/or, right/wrong. A computer program did not contain answers for Anne or Lloyd or Uncle Gordon. Therefore the questions were not possible.

The recruiters began to descend in the early spring of Kate's senior year. Her adviser assured Kate that as a woman with 3.8 grade average in her field she could call the shots: anywhere in the country; anywhere in the world, with one of the multinationals.

Her adviser was correct. But Kate was not elated by the quantity and quality of the offers neatly stacked on her dorm desk—she was overwhelmed. Everyone wanted her. She began to receive follow-up letters and brochures celebrating the advantages of working and living in San Francisco, Houston, Atlanta, Boston, New York, Denver, Minneapolis-St. Paul and New Orleans. Also, London, Paris, Milan, Cologne and the large cities of Africa, the Middle East and Asia. She could not make a decision.

Alexander Harding, president of Arizona Computer Services, arrived in Los Angeles in June. By then Kate was receiving second follow-ups from Atlanta and Milan and Boston and Seattle and Minneapolis-St. Paul.

Alexander Harding did not go about recruiting the way anyone else had. He was neither businesslike nor serious. He told anecdotes about life in Tucson that made the place sound utterly dull. He talked about his two sons, about camping in the desert and mountains, about problems with his swimming pool. Kate laughed a great deal and was sorry when he said, "Okay, now to business."

He scanned her résumé.

"Miss Delling," he said after less than two minutes, "I'm not going to make you an offer. I can't afford you, and you'd hate Tucson. Now that that's settled, I am consumed by a desire for abalone. Do you know Russell's in Hermosa Beach?"

"No."

"Good. Then Russell's hasn't been discovered yet. You'll be impressed by their abalone."

"I don't like abalone."

"Then you can have red snapper or scallops. If the IRS ever audits me, tell the fellow I was trying to hire you." He buttoned the top button on his shirt and pulled his tie tight. "You're free, I hope?"

"Yes, but . . ."

"Have no fear, Kate. The words Arizona Computer Services will not pass my lips. I don't want to think about computer services."

The waitress at Russell's greeted Alex by name and immediately informed him the abalone was fresh that day.

Kate's red snapper was the best she'd ever eaten.

Following dinner, Alex said he wanted to see who was playing at the Lighthouse. Two excellent jazz groups.

When Alex returned Kate to her dorm at two thirty in the morning, he said, "You know what I'd like to do tomorrow if I can finish the interviews I've scheduled?"

"What?"

"There is a great Basque restaurant up near Santa Paula. Have you ever eaten in an authentic Basque restaurant?"

"No."

"At the conclusion of a Basque dinner you will be unable to stand up. So I'll call you by three if I can manage."

Kate was in the lounge of her wing at the dorm at noon. She looked at a textbook and at women talking on the pay phones. She thought about Alex Harding.

He was in his late thirties and he was not a handsome man. He talked about himself and Tucson and people he knew. He was relaxed and amusing. He was interested in her. He caused her to feel like a different person, like a soprano in an Italian opera. She did not understand why she woke up that morning thinking of herself as Musetta, for God's sake. But she had, and she liked it.

Alex called at three thirty.

He was quite serious. "You'd better be hungry."

The Basque restaurant was an old wooden building in the hills above lemon and avocado groves. The customers sat at long wooden tables and were served family style.

Alex explained each of the dishes and conversed with Kate and the other people at their table. Toward the end of the huge meal, she was laughing and talking with the sheepherders across the table and with a distinguished couple who had flown their private plane to Santa Paula from San Luis Obispo just for the dinner.

Alex made no effort to ingratiate himself with people. But people were drawn to him. Kate watched it happen. He possessed an appealing combination of enthusiasm, confidence and kindness. He was not in any way self-conscious. He was the center of attention at their table ten minutes after he sat down and he neither noticed nor cared. He was enjoying himself and others enjoyed him.

Her uncles and her father and the male guests at Lake Arrowhead or Laguna Beach spoke of skiing (both snow and water) and yachting and tennis and golf.

In the course of the conversation at the long wooden table Kate learned that Alex had fished for black marlin off the coast of Peru and yellowtail east of New Zealand. He had hunted grizzly bears in northeastern Alaska and had bagged a rhinoceros in Nepal.

He talked about deep-sea fishing and big-game hunting in faraway places the same way she had grown up hearing men discuss the way a golf course played or a mountain skied.

During the drive back to Westwood, Alex did not talk much, yet the periods of silence were comfortable.

"Why is it," Kate asked, "you never mention your wife?"

"Because whenever possible I do my best not to think about Sharon."

"Oh, I'm sorry."

"Why should you be sorry? Sharon is a very unpleasant woman. The regrets are all mine. Tell me, did you get enough to eat?" He turned to her and smiled.

"I must have consumed five thousand calories!"

"Closer to seven thousand, I'd say. But you don't need to worry. I'm the one who's thirty-nine and growing a pot. Tell me which of your offers you'll be accepting."

"God, I can't decide."

Alex listed the advantages and disadvantages of the companies and the cities.

He stopped in front of the dorm and went around to open her door. "My suggestion is, take the Boston job. That's a very good operation. Kate, thank you." He gently held her face between his hands and kissed her forehead.

"Alex?" she said.

"Yes?"

"Good night." Kate hurried across the courtyard and into the building.

She wanted to ask him when he was going back to Tucson. She wanted to look at him, listen to him, touch him. She was in love with him. She had never been in love before.

The next day at five thirty in the afternoon, Kate was called to one of the phones.

"Kate, this is Alex. Tomorrow I'm due in San Diego. Do you like cannelloni?"

"How did you know?"

"You are very definitely a cannelloni person. Is seven convenient?"

Kate hummed Puccini as she showered. She didn't know what cannelloni was, but she was certain it was a form of ambrosia.

Alex reached for her hand as soon as she was seated in his car. He did not look at her. "Best we don't talk about it, okay?"

"Yes. Okay."

Kate ate less than half her dinner.

Alex did not take Kate back to her dorm. They went to his hotel on Wilshire.

That night Kate experienced her first orgasm, as well as her second and third orgasms. She slept with her arms around a man she loved.

He phoned her six times a day from San Diego. He was back in Los Angeles four days later for two days. They did not leave his hotel. Next he was in San Francisco and Oakland for a week. He called whenever he could, eleven times on a Tuesday. He returned to Los Angeles for a week. They flew to Catalina Island for two days. They went to a concert at Hollywood Bowl. They ate chili at Chasen's. They spent a day and a night at Alisol Ranch. Alex went to Texas. He called from Texas. He flew from Dallas to Tucson.

He called from Tucson.

Kate's existence was centered on the lounge and the pay phones. She left it only to attend an essential seminar. She slept and ate in the lounge. She was aware of the comments and gestures directed toward her. She didn't give a damn.

Letters from companies in Houston, New York, Cologne, Boston and Indonesia lay unopened on her desk.

Alex came to Los Angeles for three days in late July. Kate was now graduated and was still living in the dorm. She had signed up for summer session because she could not imagine being in Germany or Minnesota or New York or Japan. The house where her parents lived, where she had grown up, was occupied by a woman with wild gray hair and a grotesquely fat man who sat in front of a large color television set watching Mexican soap operas. The only place in the world she thought about was Tucson, Arizona. She dreamed about Tucson, Arizona.

"Alex," Kate said while they were eating a room service breakfast, "give me a job with your company."

"You won't like Tucson. The air is very dry."

"I will love Tucson. I've been reading about Tucson. It is historical."

"Boston is far more historical."

"I don't want to be in Boston or Paris. I want to be in Tucson. We could be together. No more phone calls."

"A.C.S. cannot pay you what you are worth."

"We could see each other every day."

Alex fed her a bite of honeydew melon. "We will have problems being together in Tucson. Tucson is Sharon's territory. She is, as I've told you, a nasty, vindictive woman who is crazy in the head. I'm not kidding when I say she has her spies. I come home at night and she says, 'I was planning fish tonight. But since you had crab salad for lunch, I've switched to veal.'"

"I will be the essence of discretion. I will call you Mr. Harding."

"Kate, put down your spoon. I love you."

Kate knew, that day in late July, that Alex loved her.

She moved to Tucson in August. She did not notice the weather.

Her duplex was small. Her salary at Arizona Computer Services was just over half of the highest offer she had received from other companies. Other companies did not include Alex Harding.

They could not appear publicly together. He was known by everyone in Tucson. The same people he knew, knew Sharon. So they often drove separately to a place near Rosemont, or to a café above Oracle. She could not phone him at home. At the office they needed to be carefully businesslike.

Sharon was mean. Sharon was crazy. Sharon's brothers and uncles and cousins were judges and lawyers and employers of many workers. Alex loved his sons. Sharon was determined to keep both her sons and Alex, by any means.

Kate was afraid to become friendly with people at A.C.S. She was concerned she might say or do something that could jeopardize Alex, that would get back to Sharon.

After Halloween, three weeks passed with only two calls from Alex. He was having trouble with Sharon. His boys needed him. Sharon was a dangerous woman.

Kate stayed in her little duplex watching television and did her best to be patient.

When they met at the Red Dot Café for a Sunday lunch in late November, Alex told Kate he was worried about her safety.

"My safety?" She held his right hand while he lifted his coffee cup with his left hand.

He looked out through the steamed window at what could be seen of the highway and gas station beside the café. "Your safety, honey. And I'm not kidding."

"Has Sharon found out about me—what?" She did not realize she was digging her fingernails into his hand until Alex pried loose her fingers. "How could she? Other than at work, I haven't seen you for a month!"

He set down his cup and wrapped his hand over hers. "It's my fault you've been spending so much time alone. Goddamn Sharon! But you could and should be doing more, with or without me."

"Yes, I suppose I should. I'm not following you, though. What's this about my safety? Am I really in danger? Is Sharon going to hire a hit man because I love you? Is she that crazy?"

"We're talking apples and oranges. No, I don't think Sharon knows about you. Yes, you are in potential danger. You could be followed home. Someone could break into your duplex. Honey, I worry about you."

"Well, stop then. I can always scream." Kate relaxed.

"I'm not getting through to you. Honey, you need a gun."

"Why? I don't want a gun. I don't like guns. Other than you, I don't think I've ever known anyone who's owned a gun."

"Kate, do you fully understand where we are?" He waved to the waitress for more coffee.

"In the Red Dot Café."

"Be serious. We are just a little more than sixty-five miles from Nogales—in the state of Sonora, Mexico."

"So?"

"South and west of where we are now seated are the San Xavier and Papago reservations. At this moment we're in the foothills of the Santa Catalinas. A virtual wilderness."

"Yes?"

"Many, many Mexicans and Indians are freely coming and going."

"Alex! You're sounding like a fanatic!"

He raised his eyebrows and shook his head. "In addition, there are men at the Air Force base and on the campus, plus doped-up, long-haired hicks in four-wheel drives passing through on Ten. I don't care what color those men are or what language they speak, this little corner of the U.S.A. is still the Wild West in some ways!"

She had never before seen him so solemn and adamant. "All of which means you think I need a gun?"

"Yes."

"Alex, I've been in Tucson for almost four months. Why am I suddenly in danger?"

He held his forehead in his hands. "I never should have let you come here."

"But I wanted to come here, remember? We love each other."

He straightened. "Exactly! But I can't look out for you the way I'd like to, damn it! So, I'm always worrying about you, and I can't call every ten minutes after you leave the office. This is driving me batty, Kate."

She sighed. "I've never held a gun in my entire life, let alone shot one. I have no idea how to even begin to buy a gun."

"You don't have to buy a gun. I have one for you in my station wagon and I'll teach you how to use it."

Kate shook her head. "When you learned all about guns it was so you'd be able to shoot gophers and jackrabbits. I'll be learning how to shoot people."

"No, honey. Not people. Don't look at it that way. The Bill of Rights very clearly states that citizens have the right to keep and bear arms. That's the Second Amendment, directly after free speech. You'll only aim and shoot your gun at a man who is trying to harm you or someone else. Or, you won't shoot anyone."

"Alex, I don't . . ."

"Okay. Hell, don't, then. You've sure as shit made my day! All I'm asking you to do is shoot at some tin cans today. But, okay. You don't want me to sleep . . ."

"All right. Darling, don't be so angry."

Alex paid their gum-popping waitress.

"I'm heading up the canyon. Follow me in your car."

He drove to a side road and continued along it for five or six miles. Kate parked her Ford beside his Chrysler station wagon in a small box canyon.

He helped her from her car, then held her chin in his hand. "I know you don't like the idea of owning a gun." He kissed her mouth. "Do you trust me?"

"Alex! Of course!"

"You'd better, honey. Because I know more about some things than you do."

He opened his glove compartment and removed a gray-flannel bundle. Inside the cloth was a blue-black gun with a short muzzle.

"This is a Smith and Wesson thirty-two-caliber revolver, Kate. I am going to teach you everything there is to know about this gun."

Patiently, Alex explained how guns worked, showed her how that particular gun worked and had her shoot it at rusty beer cans set on a fallen tree.

Two hours later Kate was able to hit a beer can from fifteen feet four times out of five and Alex was beaming. He said she was much better than average.

Afterward they made love on a quilted mover's pad in the back of his station wagon. She drove back to Tucson in her own car.

By the first of the year Kate was working long hours. Alex had accepted the contract for a job A.C.S. did not possess the capacity to execute.

"Alex," Kate told him, "you don't have enough qualified people for this!"

"I'll find them. Help me out, honey. It's go-for-broke time."

He did not find the people he needed. His response to the

pressure was to disappear for long weekends in his four-wheel-drive camper.

Kate worked, ate and slept. She came to hate Tucson. Alex called once or twice a week for ten or fifteen minutes. He said he was depressed. They met infrequently at the Red Dot Café, drove into a secluded ravine and climbed into the back of the station wagon.

She felt helpless to deal with his apathy and depression.

On a morning in late May, Wilma, Alex's secretary, came into Kate's office, dropped a pile of papers on her desk and plopped onto a chair.

"Her majesty is coming to call at eleven thirty," Wilma said.

Kate rubbed her eyes. "Who is her majesty?"

"A.C.S.'s bankroll. She comes once a year to look us over."

"What do you mean, bankroll?"

"I mean, A.C.S.'s grubstaker. The bottomless-pit bank account that keeps his majesty in three-hundred-dollar boots and me on a regular salary. Kate, honey, if you were a little more friendly with the rest of us peons, your mouth wouldn't be hanging open the way it is."

"Do you mean Sharon Harding?"

"I mean, Sharon Bagley Harding. It's the Bagley that counts. As in Congressman Bagley, Bagley Timber, Bagley Copper. This annual walk-through is required by some clause in some trust in someone's will. Don't look so peaked, honey. She's never been known to snap or bite. I've been here for twelve years."

Kate drank cold coffee from a Styrofoam cup. "Isn't she crazy?"

"Who isn't crazy these days?" Wilma lit a second cigarette from the one she was smoking when she came into the office. "Hell, the woman is only in the state six months out of a year. She just came back from two months in Greece, for example."

"Mrs. Harding has been in Greece for two months?"

"Ain't that the life? On a chartered yacht, yet. I'm glad I don't have to pay that phone bill. An hour every day to Greece!"

"To Greece?" Kate was looking at the stack of printouts on her desk.

"To Greece, and I have to place the damn calls. This spring I've been learning Greek. Last fall I learned French."

Wilma sauntered out.

Two months?

"Kate, darling, please be patient with me. I have that mess at the office and a maniac at home."

"But when can we be together?"

"This is a very rough time. I'll call you when the witch is in her cave."

I'll call you.

For God's sake, don't call me. For your sake.

Darling, you're the only person I trust in this town.

In June we'll go to Cabo San Lucas in Mexico for two weeks.

For two months Alex's wife had been in Greece?

Wilma was lying. Crazy Sharon had hired her.

Kate watched the clock. At twenty-five past eleven she slipped to the women's rest room where she entered a stall and fastened the latch. She sat on the edge of the toilet and waited. At one she emerged.

A small, deeply tanned woman wearing a simple linen dress was seated in one of the plastic chairs in the small lounge. Kate had seen the woman before, walking along the sidewalk, in the drugstore, at the good deli. The woman's naturally blond hair was cut in a short, casual style. She was neither beautiful nor homely.

"Kate, I'm Sharon Harding." She spoke in a soft, careful voice.

Kate stood unmoving, waiting for the signs of excitability.

"Alex has probably told you," she breathed deeply, "that I am a violent lunatic. I have never known how to act in these situations." She rested her hands on the arms of the chair. "One of your predecessors who found out about Alex on her own took an overdose of drugs and has still not recovered. I am paying her hospital bills."

"Predecessor?"

"A very bright young woman he found at Pitzer College. She too turned down far better offers in order to work for and be with Alex. You are the fifth—that I've been unable to avoid knowing about, that is."

"What is it you know about me, Mrs. Harding?"

She sighed. "Your qualifications. You came here last August. You've lived a miserable life waiting to hear from Alex. You've worked hard and well. Sometime, oh, last December, Alex's calls and visits with you began to decrease. He probably told you he needed to watch our sons because I might beat them, something

along those lines. The truth is, our sons are in a private school in
Santa Barbara."

"Why are you telling me this?"

"I hoped you would figure Alex out on your own. In a nut-
shell, then, Alex has been exploiting you. That is A. B is, he is no
longer enamored of you." She peered questioningly at Kate.
"Can't you tell, for heaven's sake!"

This woman was worse than Kate had expected. A crazy person
who was able to seem so completely sane.

"Thank you, Mrs. Harding. I have to get back to work now."

"Kate"—her knuckles on the arms of the chair were white—
"I'm going home now. Go to Alex's office. Close the door. Ask
him." She rose and left the lounge.

Kate went back to her office.

Wilma had lied about Greece, about Sharon paying A.C.S.'s
bills. Alex wasn't exploiting her, she had asked to come to Tucson—because they loved each other. Each other! Alex was unable
to see her as often, much less often because . . . Because he was
depressed? No. Because his wife . . .

Kate strode to Alex's office. She passed Wilma. Alex was at his
desk talking on the phone. Kate closed the door. He frowned
when he saw her close the door. She stood before his desk.

"I'll have to call you back," he said. "A minor emergency." He
replaced the receiver. "Yes, Kate?"

"Your wife knows an awful lot about me, Alex."

"You ran into her today?"

"I've run into her before, but I wasn't aware she was your wife.
Just how crazy is Sharon?"

"Ah, shit, honey." He opened his palms to her. "What can I
say?"

"How about the truth?"

"The truth. Okay, the truth. The truth is, Sharon is a rich and
boring woman." He cleared his throat. "I fell in love with you
last year. That is the truth."

"When"—she tried to swallow and could not—"when did you
fall out of love?"

He pursed his lips and pondered the question. "I would say
October. Late October."

"That was over seven months ago, Alex."

"I guess it was. Kate, honey, what can I say? I'm sorry, but
that's the way I am."

"Is that what you told the woman from Pitzer?"

"Sharon told you about her?"

"On November twenty-ninth you gave me a gun and taught me how to use it."

"That's right. So?"

"Because, you said, you were worried about my safety and couldn't sleep. Because we loved each other so much. The last of November is a month after late October, Alex."

"Ah, come on. You're not thinking what I think you're thinking. Christ!"

She could only stand in front of his desk staring down into his face. She felt a numbness assault her lips and cheeks and fingertips, and the rapid thumping of her heart.

"Over seven months," she whispered.

He gave his head an apologetic shake.

Her humiliation was stupefying.

"You must want to take a swing at me, Kate."

As she looked at him his features shifted, stiffened and froze. His face became abstract, without intent or information. A mask.

Alexander Harding, Kate later read in a paragraph in *The New York Times*, was killed in an avalanche while skiing near Aspen, Colorado, with a Miss Beverly Danforth who was also killed. His death was noted by *The Times* because he was the husband of Sharon Bagley Harding, of the Arizona Bagleys.

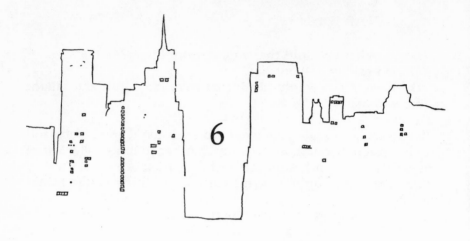

# 6

Kate fell into heavy sleep just before five o'clock Saturday morning. She lay on her back tangled in the sheet.

She was awakened at ten thirty by the straining roar of a diesel truck engine and the grinding of metal against metal.

She mumbled, "Damn," and turned over, pulling a pillow onto her head. The pillow did little to muffle the noise.

A filled dumpster across the street was being connected to the truck that would haul it away. That was an unpleasantly familiar sound. A succession of large dumpsters had been placed on the street and removed at all hours when a town house on Eighty-sixth Street had been renovated. The operation could take a half hour or more.

So tired. For a while she could not remember why. She was not fully awake.

Ordinarily upon awakening in the morning Kate immediately pulled herself to a sitting position and dropped her legs over the side of the bed. She then switched on an all-news radio station. Never music. She had learned that during the period when her mind was floating from deep sleep to full consciousness she was most vulnerable to images and memories she was unable to manage. Fragments from the past flowed through her, unchecked, as if greatly magnified pictures of tiny parts from an enormous tapestry were rapidly being clicked through a slide projector: Anne's hand bringing a sweating glass to her mouth; the receiver of the telephone in her Tucson duplex resting on its cradle; Lloyd's face disappearing behind a closing door; Uncle Gordon's heavy, lowered eyebrows. She could not expand the images, nor could she resolve them. Whenever she had experienced those disturbing, half-awake images, Kate had been agitated and distracted for the remainder of the day.

Saturday morning, though, after only five and a half hours' sleep, while metal screeched and clanged, and the diesel engine whined, Kate clearly recalled Lou Ann.

Kate hurled away the pillow. She pressed her forearms hard over her eyes and rocked from side to side. She was too tired to annihilate André's tomato-red Olds or find the strength to sit up.

And so she saw the car containing Lou Ann speed off toward Eighth Avenue. The men with their paper-bag whiskey, the three street whores in their wooden platforms, stood and watched. Kate lifted her arm, pointed her right index finger at the car and zapped the rear tires. The red pimpmobile swerved into a parked car. Good, a soft impact. Instantly, uniformed policemen surrounded the car. They had been waiting in the dim light. Lou Ann was saved.

Kate kicked the sheet off her feet.

Policemen flung themselves over the top and hood of the car. They yanked open the doors. Two of them pulled Lou Ann from the backseat. Kate hurried up to help and explain.

The driver's seat was empty. There was no André.

The policemen twisted Lou Ann's arms behind her and snapped handcuffs over her wrists.

Street barricades, row after row of them, were thrown between Kate and the red car and the policemen and Lou Ann. Kate shouted as loudly as she could. No one heard her. The policemen pushed Lou Ann into a patrol car. They turned on their lights and sirens and drove off with Lou Ann.

The drunks smashed their empty bottles on the sidewalk while the street whores stood in place clattering their wooden platform shoes.

"No!"

Her own voice startled her. It was louder than the diesel on the street.

She raised herself on her elbows. Her nightgown was soaked with sweat. Heat was not the problem, the diesel and the dumpster were not the problem, the thudding disco music coming from an apartment nearby was not the problem.

She was too exhausted to arrange and control her thoughts in order to slip into deep, dreamless sleep. The most dreadful memories caught her with undiminished immediacy: the days after she had walked out of Alex's office, when she had sat in her duplex without eating because her rage was so great she could not swallow—generalized, impotent rage without the possibility of relief.

"Get up!" she growled, pushing herself off the bed.

A cool shower and breakfast followed by two cups of strong coffee began to dissipate the events of Friday night. Kate concentrated her mind and energies on unpacking the four remaining cartons and the placement of the pictures. By three thirty, she was able to turn off the all-news station and play records.

She was on her fourth cup of coffee as she experimented with the best height for a watercolor when a cat padded into the living room from the bedroom. The creature was half the size of Margaret's cat, but the coloring was almost identical.

Kate sat down.

"You must belong to Art," she sighed.

The cat daintily sniffed the toe of her old sneaker.

"What am I supposed to do with you?"

The cat rubbed her whiskers against the shoelaces and purred very loudly.

"You don't live here, cat. You live upstairs."

Kate grabbed her keys and picked up the cat, which went limp in her arms.

Art's response to Kate at his door was, "Hi. I'll take Phyllis off your hands if you'll come in for a few minutes and let me fill another bag with green beans."

Kate remained in the hall. "I haven't eaten one green bean from the first batch."

"Not one? Christ, then yours must be going bad the way mine are. What should we do?"

"Before you decide maybe you can take your cat." Phyllis was pressing her head up against Kate's chin.

"Look at that! She likes you!" Art stroked the cat's back without removing her. "Females are generally less friendly than males."

"She likes the smell of my sneakers." Kate held out the cat.

He accepted Phyllis. "Damn kitty. She isn't usually the wanderer her brother is. Come in and have a drink with me. I finished a project this afternoon."

"What kind of project?"

"A two-part series on Hollywood's discovery of New York's scenic street wonders for *The Times Magazine*. Haven't you noticed the way film crews have taken over the city? No? Half the police force has been assigned to direct traffic, both foot and vehicular, around a location that will appear for twelve seconds in a movie. And be polite about it."

"Last night," Kate said, "I saw a young teenaged girl, a prostitute, bleeding on the street. There were no police. Only drunks and other prostitutes."

"Where was this?"

"Just off Eighth Avenue in the upper Forties."

"Oh, well." He tossed Phyllis onto a chair where she immediately stretched out her rear left leg and addressed herself to the vigorous licking of her fur.

"She was very young. Do you know what the police were doing?"

"Directing pedestrians around a film crew in a penny arcade?"

"Probably raiding a massage parlor." Her throat was raw and scratchy from tension and lack of sleep. "No. That was earlier this week. I watched them from the bus."

"Was the kid seriously injured?" Art thoughtfully ran the back of his hand over a three-day stubble. "Christ, don't stand there looking so fucking formal." He walked away from his open door to sprawl in a chair that looked like a dumpling with armrests. "I assume she wasn't white." He looked over his glasses at a tenspeed bike leaning against the wall.

"As a matter of fact, the girl was white." Kate perched on a chair just inside the door. "Her color was beside the point, though."

"Not in that neighborhood it isn't. Little pink girls and little pink boys. It has been so for a long time and not just on Eighth Avenue. Fortunes were made from commerce in fair-haired kid-

dies during the nineteenth century in this country. Northern
Europe immigrant families fresh off the boats. Best-sellers were
certified virgin blondes who looked like illustrations from children's storybooks."

"Who bought them?"

"Some were shipped off to Brazil or darkest Central America.
Most of them went to your pillar-of-the-community captains of
industry by way of the better bordellos."

"Then what happened to them?" Kate closed the hall door
when Phyllis sauntered toward it.

"No one was keeping careful records. Not of the kiddies. Some
of the madams were careful bookkeepers, though. A rosy blond
virgin could bring as much as a thousand dollars. That, of course,
was the price of the defloration. From then on the kid's value
plummeted." Art wiped his glasses on his Mostly Mozart T-shirt.
"Most of those girls didn't know ten words of English."

"What happened to them?" She sat forward.

"The girls?" He ran his fingers through his already tousled
hair. "Awhile back I was thinking of doing a long piece on white
slavery, as it used to be called. What happened to the girls? Some
died their first time around. The guys who placed the orders
wanted their money's worth. Some stayed in the whorehouses
and became prostitutes. Some went West. Often the girl's parents
believed their kid really was being taken away to learn a voca-
tion. Wasn't this the land of opportunity?"

"The girl I saw last night was an ignorant, scrawny child from
the Midwest. Her pimp handed her over to a man who sodomized her." She looked to him for an explanation.

"The pimp got ten or fifteen dollars, of which the girl may see
a dollar, plus food, plus whatever drugs the pimp can
scrounge."

Art squinted at Kate. Her hands were tightly folded on her lap.
He went to his kitchen and came back with two glasses of
wine.

"Try this Soave."

Kate's hand was trembling so hard the wine spilled over the
rim of her glass. "Thank you. This has been a difficult week."

"Moving is always a bummer. How was the play?"

"God, I'd forgotten I'd been to a play. I saw the girl right after,
on my way home." She downed half the wine, then looked into
the glass.

"Hey, Kate, you couldn't do anything for that kid."

"But if the police had been there?"

"She'd be back on the street in a few days, with or without the police. So will the john."

"To sodomize another little girl?" She spoke in a loud, tight voice.

"Kate, I'm with you. The bastard should be castrated. The pimp should be hanged by his thumbs." He refilled the glasses. "Maybe the reason I chucked that series on white slavery—I don't know. I became very depressed. In a hundred years the only change is in appearance. And rape is increasing. Fourteen-year-old boys are raping nine-year-old girls. One psychologist I interviewed told me the boys are bored, another blamed it on TV."

"What becomes of fourteen-year-old rapists, Art?"

"They grow up and become twenty-four-year-old rapists."

She set down her glass and stood. "What should I do if Phyllis comes through my window and you aren't home?"

"Just dump her in the hall; that's what everyone else does. Nice to have another tenant in the building who enjoys classical music, by the way. I go a little crazy trying to concentrate over disco thumping." He walked her to the stairs. "I'm glad you told me about your experience last night, although I'm sorry it happened. Now may be the time for me to finish that piece on the nineteenth century."

"What about Lou Ann in the twentieth century?"

"Yeah. That's where I bogged down last time around. There was a distant antiseptic quality to those old, yellowed ledgers the madams kept, with the girls' first names. Whoever they were, they're all dead now."

"Lou Ann may also be dead now."

"Why do you think I dropped the project?"

Kate hung her pictures and stacked the empty cartons filled with crumpled newspapers outside with the garbage cans. She vacuumed and dusted, scoured the bathtub and the sinks, wiped the refrigerator and stove. The apartment did not need the cleaning she gave it.

She needed to keep moving in a composed, deliberate way until her rooms had become familiar and ordered. Until she was certain she could fall immediately asleep.

That time came a little after ten.

Still damp from her shower, she lay on her taut, cool sheet, selected for her mind a Monet she had memorized, a garden path at Giverny. She entered the familiar, safe colors and was asleep.

A long, harsh, brassy sound followed by a continuous series of shorter blares, not quite even. Nearby, but not outside. From inside the apartment. Maybe the bedroom radio had short-circuited.

Kate flipped on her bedside lamp. A quarter to three. Dark outside and raining. The radio was not turned on. She stood before it baffled, more asleep than awake. The loud electrical noises continued. Something wrong with the record player. She shuffled into the living room and stopped by the wall. The sound was in the hall.

Her bedroom lamp provided enough light for her to see the place where the noise originated: the intercom connected to the outer vestibule, beneath which were two buttons.

She pressed the one over the word Speak.

"Stop this!" she said.

The buzzing did not stop.

As she depressed the intercom and shouted, "I am calling the police," into the little speaker, she heard a faint, distorted voice. All she caught was the word "Margaret."

"This is not Margaret's apartment!"

Through her own words she heard, "This is Margaret, Kate."

The noise stopped. Kate rubbed her eyes. How would one of Margaret's clients know her name?

Whoever was out there was now steadily pressing the buzzer.

"Go away or I'll call the police."

From the speaker came, "California enchiladas."

The noise stopped.

How stupid. Margaret had lost her lobby key. Kate pushed the button that opened the lobby door and headed back to her bedroom. As she fell onto her bed she heard faint knocking on the hall door. She forced herself up.

"Margaret, please!" she called through the door. "I'm asleep."

"Kate, help me." The voice was a monotone.

Kate opened her door to the length of the chain. "What's the matter?" All she could see was the other woman's hair; her face was turned away.

"I need help." Margaret faced the opening.

Kate staggered and hissed.

The flesh around Margaret's eyes was grotesquely puffed and purple, as were her lips. A huge welt stood out on her cheek.

Kate jerked off the chain and helped Margaret inside. Margaret whimpered when Kate took her arm, supporting her to the couch.

"You were mugged?"

"Sorry. Couldn't find keys. Can't see."

"Where?" Kate began to shake. "I'll call the police."

"No. No police." Margaret sat sprawled, her head lolling to one side.

Kate hurried to her bedroom for a bathrobe, slipping into it as she returned.

"You don't want the police?" she asked incredulously.

"No." Margaret's lightweight raincoat was open, bunched under her; her dress was pulled midway up her thighs. Her legs were also covered by ugly discolorations. "No police."

Kate felt for a chair. She sat. "An ambulance? A doctor?"

"No. In a minute," she said slowly and with effort, "Help me upstairs."

Kate turned on lights. "Oh, my God!"

Margaret's face was so swollen Kate hadn't seen the split in her upper lip. It was caked with blood.

"I'm calling an ambulance."

Margaret lurched to her feet. "No. Please. Trouble for me." She fell back onto the couch.

Kate knelt beside her. "You weren't mugged?"

"A john. Important man."

Kate looked at Margaret's limp hands. They were streaked with dried blood, her fingernails were torn.

While she helped Margaret drink a little Calvados, Kate discovered one of her front teeth had been broken off just above the gum line.

"Upstairs now," Margaret said.

Kate concentrated only on getting Margaret to the elevator and then into her apartment. She eased the injured woman onto her bed.

"Codeine in bathroom. Two."

After Margaret swallowed the tablets, Kate carefully removed the raincoat, then the rest of her clothes. The woman on the bed, every inch of her, was shades of purple and blue and deep red. Even her feet. Kate did not believe such a thing was possible. How could an entire body be so terribly mauled? When she turned Margaret slightly to get her into a nightgown, Kate saw that her back was no different from her front.

She pulled up a chair so she could sit beside the bed. She tried to think logically.

Margaret needs medical attention. She may have broken bones and internal injuries. She may be dying. She should be X-rayed. She hasn't moved for ten minutes.

Suddenly Margaret gave a loud moan.

"Have to pee," she said thickly.

Kate rose, looking frantically around the bedroom. "Do you have a bedpan?"

"No. Get up." Margaret brought herself to a half-sitting position.

"You shouldn't be moving. "I'll find something." Kate ran to the kitchen. She hurried back with a copper pot.

Margaret was hobbling into the bathroom.

Kate checked the toilet after Margaret was finished. At least there was no evidence of blood. She flushed the toilet.

"Codeine's helped," Margaret said when she was back in bed.

"You must be seen by a doctor."

"Tomorrow."

"It's already tomorrow. It's six A.M. Sunday."

"Mean . . . Monday."

"You may not be alive Monday."

"Okay. My doctor. Crawford."

Kate found a W. Crawford in the address book by the phone and called the number.

A raspy voice answered on the seventh ring.

"Dr. Crawford?"

"What!"

"I'm calling for Margaret Elias. She's been badly beaten. She won't go to a hospital."

"Stupid whore. Is she conscious?"

"Barely. She's taken two codeines."

"Okay. All right." Dr. Crawford hung up.

Margaret was moaning softly.

Kate made two ice packs from smashed ice cubes wrapped in towels and laid them on Margaret's face. She was unable to determine from Dr. Crawford's voice whether the doctor was a man or woman. She was now operating on reflexes. She sat by Margaret's bed taking her pulse. She felt the little throb beneath the flesh. She looked at the second hand on the bedside clock. Thud, thud. Tick, tick. So? What was fast, what was slow? She couldn't count. All she could determine was that the thuds were regular.

Margaret said words Kate could not understand.

Kate held her wrist. She could not look at the exposed parts of her battered face, the hideously distended lips and chin.

Dr. Crawford arrived at eight thirty.

"Who are you?" he asked.

"I live downstairs."

"Are you on drugs?"

"No."

"Then why do you look so strung out?"

"Why don't you look at Margaret?"

"You aren't a hooker?"

"No. I'm the first doorbell she leaned on."

Dr. Crawford was not a happy, graceful fat man. He was a rude, clumsy fat man.

Kate followed him into Margaret's bedroom.

"Well, Maggie"—he lowered himself onto the chair by the bed—"this is clearly terminal clap."

"Need shot, Waldo."

"In due time." He shoved aside the ice packs, pried open her right eye and rose over her to peer into it with an instrument he had pulled from his jacket pocket. Margaret whimpered softly. "You should," he breathed into her face, "try to stay away from the Port Authority Terminal."

"I hurt." She grabbed his fat hand; he shook it off.

"You will hurt even more when you receive my bill for a Sunday-morning house call."

Dr. Crawford touched Margaret's flesh with seeming disregard for her shrieks and groans. He sat her up and shoved her down, bent her arms and legs, her fingers and toes. He pressed her gut, felt and thumped her back and chest.

"Were you raped?" he grunted.

"No."

He lit a cigar, puffing vigorously. "New trick?"

"No. Longtime john. Shot, Waldo."

"In a moment." He leaned back in a chair beside the window. He was savoring his cigar. Margaret lay naked on her bed. "Nothing broken but a central incisor and that will cost you a lot."

"He'll pay. Shot, Waldo."

"Rich and famous? With an image?"

Margaret nodded. "Said he'd pay."

"He couldn't get it up this time?" Dr. Crawford rolled his cigar from one side of his mouth to the other and back. "Not even a little? That causes rage in the rich and famous, Maggie." He heaved himself up and extracted a syringe from his case and filled it from a small bottle. He shoved Margaret onto her side, swabbed her hip and gave her an injection. "If he had no difficulties, he'd have no need for you, would he? You must think of it that way."

Margaret fell back and went limp.

Kate covered Margaret with the top sheet and a light blanket.

"You two lovers?" Dr. Crawford asked as he packed his instruments.

"No. I just live downstairs."

"Tell me, now that she's out cold, what are you on? One of my hobbies is drug guessing."

"I have had very little sleep in the past five days, Doctor." She spat the word "Doctor."

"Don't tell me then." He tossed a small bottle on the bed. "Demerol. Give her one in six hours. She'll want one long before that." He looked down at Margaret. "Try to make her hold out for as long as you can. That lady was a true beauty. A natural beauty." He clucked.

"Do you know what you're doing?"

"She told you to phone me, didn't she?" He drew his raincoat over his shoulders. "Don't call me unless she goes into convulsions. I'm giving a brunch for eight."

"Convulsions?"

"Unlikely. Very. But she should be watched during the next twenty-four hours."

Kate sat beside the bed and watched.

Sometime during the early afternoon she made herself a boiled ham sandwich and drank a can of V-8. It was then she became aware that she was wearing a nightgown and robe and was barefooted.

Margaret didn't ask for Dr. Crawford's medication until two thirty. Kate gave her the pill with a glass of milk.

"Do you think you can eat some soup?"

"Try."

Kate heated a canned beef-noodle soup.

Margaret was able to manage half a cup of the broth. As she was spooning the soup through Margaret's swollen lips, Kate studied the flesh on her face. Her mother, if she was alive, would not have recognized her daughter. Only Margaret's hair looked familiar, and it was matted.

Later, Margaret asked the time.

"Quarter after seven."

"You here since last night?" She spoke very slowly and with effort.

"Yes."

"Must be tired."

"I am tired. Don't worry."

"Call Angie. Good friend."

"Can she stay with you? Dr. Crawford doesn't want you left alone."

"Call Angie. In my book."

Angie said she could come, but not until around ten thirty.

"Never had a bruise before," Margaret said after Kate had given her a second pill. "Looked at myself in bathroom mirror." Tears slid down the sides of her face.

"Why didn't you fight back?"

"Tried. He was crazy. Strong man. Very strong."

"What did he hit you with?"

"Hand. Once. First. Then wood. Driftwood."

For a moment Kate saw a man pounding a slender, naked woman with a chunk of gray driftwood. A large, muscular man with sunbleached hair on his forearms and the backs of his hands.

"Why?" Kate said, more to herself than to Margaret.

"Usual didn't work. Worked two hours. Nothing." A half-grunt, half-chuckle came from her throat. "Got it up from beating me. Came, too. Or I'd be dead."

"He came because he beat you?"

She made another throat sound. "Yeah. Said that was best yet. He'll pay Waldo."

"But what about you?"

"Sending money. Messenger. Monday. He will."

"Who is he?"

"John."

"His name is John?"

"Just a john." Her lips pulled to the side in what might have been a grimace. "Fucking bastard."

"Margaret, that man is crazy!"

"Maybe. Called in spurts. No call six, eight months. Then calls all time for two, three weeks." She was slipping into a doze.

"Before Saturday night you didn't realize he was violent, not at all?"

"No. Just called me. Afternoon. Evening. Not middle-of-night john. Maybe planets. Sunspots."

Whenever Margaret's phone rang the machine answered it.

Margaret would need a new message for a few months.

Angie arrived at a quarter to eleven. She turned greenish-white when she saw Margaret.

"Holy shit! Maggie, baby!"

"Yeah. Shit."

"Waldo been here?" Angie asked Kate. "Dr. Crawford?"

Kate told her what he had done and when Margaret could have her next pill. "She should try to eat, I think, even though she doesn't want to."

Angie tugged Kate into the living room. She looked frightened. "Do you know what happened? Maggie's always super careful. She can smell muscle over the phone. Long-distance."

"All I can tell you is that I gather he'd been a client before and that whatever she had done on other occasions wasn't sufficient. In the process of beating her up he had his orgasm."

"Oh, oh!" Angie lit a cigarette with matches from The Four Seasons. She was a slender redhead with a sweet, pert face. "Then she'd better pass the word on that fucker in a hurry. He'll be wanting more of that now."

"She didn't mention his name."

"Not to you she wouldn't. You aren't a pross." She chewed the inside of her cheek for a moment. "Maggie will give me that bastard's name. I'll make some calls. By tomorrow night he'll be lucky if he can get a fifty-year-old junkie who'd fuck King Kong for a fix."

"He did that"—Kate waved toward the bedroom—"with a piece of driftwood. He hit her with his hand first."

"No shit? I hope he broke all five fingers."

She poured a glass of sherry and sat staring at the dark fireplace while she sipped it. She was not sleepy.

Margaret was, at this moment, the colors of the Monet garden path she had gone to sleep visualizing the night before. No. There was no green on Margaret's body. The purples, blues and reds, though, were close to Monet's palette.

Kate thought about Margaret's feet. She had never before seen deep purple feet. The soles of her feet were purple. How could the soles of feet be made purple?

She drank two more glasses of sherry. Feet were what she thought about. Purple feet. The feet were not swollen and blotchy. They were solid purple, as if they had been dipped in ink.

It was not possible to think about Margaret's face. What lay on those pillows was no longer a face. And if she thought about Margaret's face as it looked three days before, she would have to think about a piece of driftwood in the fist of a very strong man smashing into the carefully tended and made-up flesh. That was not possible. So she thought about feet.

Kate did not wash her face or brush her teeth. She set her alarm and lay on her unmade bed in the same nightgown she had worn all day. She fell asleep wondering about toenails.

The alarm went off before she could decide what color Margaret's toenails were.

Automatically, Kate sat up and turned on her radio. She could not remember the day of the week. The announcer was talking about heavy Monday-morning traffic on the bridges and in the tunnels. Who in the hell was Major Deegan, anyway? And what were Throgs Neck and Gowanus?

This Monday was something more than two buses, an elevator ride and a stack of crap Scotty Rogers had dumped onto her desk. Today Peter Hamilton would be back from Atlanta.

Kate spooned instant coffee into a mug, turned on the gas under the teakettle and went into the bathroom. The face in her mirror was very pale, the dark circles under her eyes had become bags.

She quickly showered, drank black coffee as she dressed and made her bed. She was not hungry. She would go out for a Danish and juice after she talked with Peter Hamilton.

The day was warm and muggy. On the M10 she tried to formulate her opening words to Peter Hamilton. She could not organize her thoughts. She could make no sense of a public-service bus ad, in both English and Spanish, that instructed women how to care for their hair. Always rinse thoroughly. She saw Lou Ann's scraggly, thin hair dragging in the VW's grime. She saw Margaret's matted golden hair on her exquisite pillow-cases.

Kate bought a *Times* on Thirty-fourth Street. The crosstown was so crowded she read only the headlines on the front page. The price of gold was soaring. Five adjacent buildings in the South Bronx were destroyed by fire. The PLO had bombed a bus near Haifa. Always rinse thoroughly.

She glanced at the messages on her desk. Only two. None from Scotty. Of course not. He wasn't in yet. He probably hadn't gotten back from whichever Hampton his summer cottage was located in.

She rubbed her eyes. Think!

Peter Hamilton should know the truth. He should know that she was doing most of the work that Scotty was claiming and receiving credit for. Just be calm and relate the facts.

Peter Hamilton's secretary looked up. "Mr. Hamilton is expecting you. Go right in."

"He is?" How could he have known she intended to march into his office?

Peter Hamilton was seated at his desk surrounded by luxurious foliage. He appeared ill at ease. "Ah, Kate. Here you are. Take that chair."

Kate sat in the chair beside his desk. She did not take her eyes from his face. She felt completely disoriented. "I don't have an appointment with you."

"No, you don't. But Scotty here"—he gestured toward a couch against the wall upon which Scotty sat, ankles crossed, hands clasped behind his head—"told me you would be up first thing this morning."

"Hello, Kate." Scotty gave her a grave, solicitous smile.

She faced Peter Hamilton. "I want to speak with you alone.

Scotty knows that. As a matter of fact, I want to speak with you about Scotty."

"That is what I have been led to understand. You are, ah, certainly one of our up-and-coming people in the division. Scotty has nothing but praise for you. Indeed he tells me that without your hard work the Foster Automotive project could not have been completed on schedule. He gives you all the credit."

Baffled, Kate turned to Scotty. He was still giving her the serious, concerned smile. "Mr. Hamilton, I'm glad Scotty acknowledges my work on Foster. The reason I'm here is to discuss the Welles-Keeler project. Did Scotty mention that? I want to be directly assigned to it. I do not intend to be Scotty's flunky any longer. We're to begin sometime this week, as you know, and I do not intend to do Scotty's . . ."

"Kate, my dear, there is no reason to shout."

"I am not shouting!"

"You have raised your voice, my dear." He glanced at Scotty.

"This is a business office and we are discussing business. Please don't patronize me by calling me 'my dear!' "

"Kate"—Peter Hamilton assumed an unfamiliar soft and syrupy voice—"do you know how long it has been since you've taken a vacation?"

"No! What does that have to do with what we're talking about?"

"You have not taken a vacation in"—he looked at the papers on his desk—"seventeen months. Scotty and I think you should. At least two weeks, and beginning today."

"Oh, I see! I should take my vacation now, when the Welles-Keeler assignments are being made. No way! No way, Mr. Hamilton. Can't you figure out what Scotty's trying to pull, for God's sake! If you give me the Welles-Keeler assignment I will demonstrate my capabilities—on my own. On my own, not as Scotty's peon. Jesus Christ, I can't believe this! Take a vacation! No, I will not take a vacation!"

"Kate"—firmly now—"Scotty has been extremely generous in his remarks to me about your work. He has expressed concern about your, ah, well-being. I see before me a young woman even more troubled and tired than I had expected. I'm afraid I must insist you take a vacation or a medical leave, whichever you . . ."

Kate jumped up and planted her hands on Peter Hamilton's desk. "Okay, I've had a rough week. Today I am tired."

"Yes, ah, of course you are." He gave Scotty an alarmed look.

"So, you see, the very last thing I need is a vacation. I must be absorbed by my work!"

"Kate, you are in no condition to work. Not at all. Your color is not good, and"—he stared at her hands—"you are quite visibly trembling."

"Mr. Hamilton, I am just tired! Today! I will get a good, long sleep tonight and I'll be . . ."

"You will take a taxi home. Now. You will consult with your doctor. You will not return to this office for two weeks. Longer, if necessary."

Kate turned to Scotty. He was sitting up straight and he looked genuinely apprehensive.

"What am I supposed to do for two weeks, Mr. Hamilton?"

He adjusted his tie. "Rest, relax, see your physician. You do have a physician?"

"All I need," she found herself pleading, "is one good long sleep. Truly."

"No. Now I have a great deal to do, Kate. I can't spare any more time for this. I am not suggesting. I am ordering." He walked back to his chair, sat down, picked up his phone and punched buttons. "Get me Dale Marquart." He swiveled around forty-five degrees. "Dale. Peter here. Do you want a rundown on the Atlanta meeting now? Fine. I'll be over in five minutes."

Kate returned to her apartment by bus.

Scotty had set her up. He had even come to work early on a Monday morning to set her up. She must look terrible. No sleep. Shaking hands. But Hamilton already had the information about her vacation on his desk. One way or another, Scotty was determined to have her out of the office during the first days of Welles-Keeler.

"Now then, now then," she said as she unlocked her door.

She wandered through her rooms.

There is nothing you can do.

She lay on her bed.

There is nothing you can do.

She got up and paced.

Kate, there is nothing you can do.

Two weeks!

She ate a piece of toast and drank a glass of orange juice.

I will sit down and read the paper.

Her eyes moved over the words. The president. Congress. Energy. Inflation. Recession. Africa. China. Arson and bank robberies. Obituaries. A tennis tournament. Ads for clothes, furniture, vodka, movies, plays, concerts.

Then, a small boxed article titled simply, "Notice."

Jean-Paul Gallardon's sold-out recital at Carnegie Hall on Tuesday night was canceled and would be rescheduled. The pianist was indisposed.

"Oh, no!"

Kate had a ticket for that recital. She stood in line in the rain for hours for that ticket.

Someone like Gallardon wasn't supposed to become indisposed.

Such a word—indisposed. A cold? A slipped disk? Severe migraine? One of his four children was seriously ill?

Kate collected the scattered *Times* and put it back in order.

Maybe Scotty would tell Miriam and Ralph she was indisposed for two weeks. Because her eyes were bloodshot and her hands shook.

Kate went up to Margaret's apartment. Angie was not there. A woman named Doris had taken her place.

"I brought Margaret a *Times*," Kate said.

"Are you kidding!" Doris snorted.

Margaret looked worse. She was in more pain.

"Waldo," Doris said, "told her this was to be expected. He just left."

"Can I go to the market? Do something?"

"Ah, fuck, shit," Margaret muttered. "You know what hurts worst?"

"I can't imagine."

"Tooth. Not vanity. Hurts terrible."

Kate sat on a chair at the foot of the bed.

"Why," Kate said, "did the man do this to you?"

"Don't know. Most weird." Margaret's eyes were closed because she could not open them. "Passive before. His kick. Always takes time. Concentration. Pays well. Two hundred."

"An hour?"

"Two, three hundred. Hard trick. He knew it. Weird. Rainbow. Said he wanted rainbow."

"He said he wanted the rainbow?"

Margaret gave a slight affirmative nod. "His word. Liked to hear it. Could pay for rainbow. What he wanted done. To him."

Kate leaned back in her chair and looked at Margaret's face and shoulders and arms. "That man is evil."

Margaret made a tiny shrug. "Just weird. Had to be. I gambled 'cause he's well known."

"Maybe you better shut up, Maggie," Doris said from the doorway.

Margaret ground the back of her head into her pillow. "Don't know who john was."

"And maybe you better go home," Doris said to Kate. "I'll take care of Maggie. She doesn't know what she's saying today. Do you, Maggie?"

"No. Don't know. Fucky, shitty. That's all."

Kate slowly walked to her apartment.

Fucky. Shitty. That's all. Everyone will take care of everyone.

Angie and Doris and Waldo Crawford will take care of Margaret. André will take care of Lou Ann. Scotty will remove Kate for Peter Hamilton, or vice versa. Sharon will remove and take care of Kate for Alex Harding. Lloyd will take care of matters for Uncle Gordon.

No one ever wanted to upset anyone.

For the first time since she and Anne and Lloyd drove north from Laguna for the last time, Kate realized with a heavy certainty that she was not the first child whom her big, strong, successful uncle had used in that stuffy dressing room.

What had he said that afternoon?

No one will believe you, Kate. I know. You could prove nothing.

He had been wearily certain that afternoon.

Then he had gone on to entertain his friends and admirers that evening. They had laughed and talked and clapped and clapped and clapped. She had heard them from the hot, humid dressing room. Talking and laughing and clinking glasses and applauding.

There was nothing, nothing, ever, she could do about any of it.

Two weeks of being able to do nothing but try not to think about doing nothing.

She should go back to bed. She was tired, but not sleepy, and she did not want to stay in her apartment. Kate wanted to be outside, she realized. Central Park was early-June green and shady, and full of violent and nonviolent crazies, hyped-up sinewy boys and men on ten-speed bikes.

She considered Riverside Park. Space there, grass and the broad Hudson. Fewer people than in Central Park; that was a plus and a minus. Then there was the gauntlet of clusters of idle, salacious men to be run.

Certain women carried themselves in a manner that forestalled the obscene mutters and gestures, with a demeanor the men recognized and respected. Kate had observed those women; she had tried to walk and bear herself as they did. It never worked. The men sensed her uncertainty. And this was because she was afraid and unsure of herself.

The idea of a few hours on the sloping grass of Riverside Park, watching boats and barges on the river, appealed to her. If there was a cool breeze, it would blow over the Hudson.

Her apartment was becoming a brick and plasterboard cage. And she was her own captive.

Riverside Park: escape.

The four-block route to the park: torture.

She let her eyes run over the irregular bricks above and around the fireplace. The mason, Kate realized, created order from those old, irregular bricks, a symmetry. Working from the floor up, the bricklayer had caused the wall to be almost perfect, working with imperfect materials. A long labor.

So why couldn't she walk a few blocks and forget Scotty and Peter Hamilton and Lou Ann and the purple-and-blue woman upstairs?

Words and truth did not work with any of them, and she had nothing else.

The brick wall began to undulate.

She needed the safety of space and air. Soon.

Pensively, Kate went to her bedroom closet, climbed on a chair and reached for the shoebox at the back of the top shelf.

She carried the old Hush Puppies box tied with heavy string to a table where she applied a paring knife to the brown twine. The box had not been untied and opened since she had left Tucson.

First she removed wadded, yellowed Tucson newspapers and dropped them on the floor. Then she lifted out the gun neatly wrapped in a piece of gray flannel. Nestled in a corner of the shoebox was an almost full box of cartridges.

The Smith and Wesson .32-caliber revolver with its two-inch barrel appeared to be in perfect condition.

Kate opened the chamber, checked the six cylinders and looked through the short barrel. Empty and clean and gleaming. She snapped the chamber back into place, aimed the revolver at the wall and pulled the trigger. She had almost forgotten how much strength that required. "Fifteen pounds of pressure for double action," Alex said. "If you cock the hammer first, then you have only three pounds of pull."

She began to remember Alex's explanation and instructions, along with the timbre of his voice and the way she felt about his voice and his hands and his eyes and his mouth.

That first time he had taken her out to the box canyon to learn how to use the revolver and shoot at old beer cans, he was so earnest about the damn blue-black hunk of metal, and she wanted to touch the wiry hairs on the nape of his neck.

She remembered the essentials because he had made her repeat them.

A small revolver like the Smith and Wesson is usually inaccurate even at close range. The slightest movement of the wrist causes the muzzle to shift in a much wider arc than one would expect. Additionally, the pressure on the trigger pulls the muzzle up or to the side. Practice is vital and the hand and fingers must be strong. Concentrate, and if you are in danger, wait until you're less than a yard from the man before shooting. That takes self-control, but it is imperative. You may not kill him, but you'll stop him. Most people are misinformed about handguns. You might be able to scare an attacker just by pointing the weapon at him.

Kate walked to the brick wall and stood two feet from it.

There was Alex in his office in Tucson. He was smiling his crooked smile and saying, "Kate, honey, what can I say? I'm sorry, but that's the way I am."

Kate held her hand steady, concentrated and aimed at the center of his chest and pulled the trigger six times.

But Alex had no regrets because he was already dead. Killed by a wall of snow with Miss Beverly Danforth.

Kate placed the contents of her purse in a large canvas shoulder bag with a side pocket held closed by a snap clasp. The revolver easily fit in the side pocket. She hung the bag on her shoulder with the pocket on the outside. Pop. The flap of the pocket opened and the revolver was in her hand aimed straight ahead. Maybe four seconds. She replaced the pistol and jiggled her shoulder. The gun wasn't heavy, about thirty ounces. The weight was reassuring.

She imagined herself walking past a man on a dimly lit street, her hand on the snap clasp. She pulls out the pistol and the man looks at it and then at her. He can see from her eyes the gun is empty, and so he laughs.

Kate slipped six cartridges in the chamber.

Maybe all that those men on stoops and in doorways ever did was act and speak filthy to amuse each other. Macho showing off. Maybe the men alone who looked and acted threatening were bluffing. Maybe. But maybe one of them was the man who had gone after Lou Ann. Men who raped did not wear labels. According to the clipping from the *Los Angeles Times*, Gordon Van der Kemp's funeral was attended by the mayor, three ex-governors, as well as senators, congressmen, business leaders and conservative members of the film industry. None of them knew he used little girls sexually. God knew how many little girls.

Kate changed into jeans and a cotton blouse.

She did feel more confident as she walked toward the river. None of the men she passed said anything abusive. None of them appeared to notice her.

Small children played on the grass and paths near their mothers or the Hispanic or black women who cared for them. Teenaged boys and some girls threw Frisbees. Old people sat on benches. Shirtless men, and women in halters and shorts, lay on the grass taking the sun. Two men wearing stingy-brim straw hats played cribbage in the shade of a plane tree.

Kate settled on the grass and watched the river, her bag leaning against her hip. After a while she pulled out a book of Double-Crostics. She completed two.

Now she was beginning to relax.

She acknowledged her aching fatigue. On her way home she would stop by the Italian café and pick up a slice of pizza and an antipasto. Her saliva began to flow. God, she was hungry.

Perhaps it was the heat; few people remained on the grass in the sun now.

Kate walked up the slope to the path that ran parallel to and below Riverside Drive.

"Hey," a male voice said from close behind her, "you got a match?"

She turned and saw a slightly overweight man wearing a wrinkled gray work shirt and greasy gray trousers. He was balding, in his mid-thirties.

"No."

The man's face showed no expression. None. "How about a lighter?"

"No." She shook her head, laid her hand on the side pocket flap and hurried along the path. She could hear his footsteps behind her. The man was not holding a cigarette. His right hand was shoved into his trouser pocket, clenched, as if he were holding something in his fist. Like a knife.

"Stop following me," she said loudly, without turning around.

"It's a free country. The park belongs to the people." He made a laughing sound.

The laugh was ominous in a way she did not understand. She began to run. She heard him running, gaining on her.

As she was about to pass a culvert that ran under the street, the man caught up with her and shoved her toward the arched stone mouth. She staggered backward into the shadows, struggling to retain her balance.

"Get in there." He jerked his head toward the stonework, keeping his right hand in his pocket.

Kate fumbled with the snap catch. She was almost gagging from rage and terror. Her hand slipped into the pocket, her fingers found the stock, the trigger guard, the trigger. The gun came free. She aimed it at him, holding her right wrist with her left hand.

"Oh, shit." He glanced at the wavering revolver and snickered. "You can hurt a guy with one of them."

He was five feet away, his back to New Jersey. Kate willed him to come closer.

"I'm not going to hurt you. I'm only playing. This is just a nice day, you know?"

"You stupid, evil bastard." Her teeth were clenched; only her lips moved.

"Hey, I won't hurt you. I'm not a bad guy. I swear." His hand came out of his pocket and he lunged toward her.

Kate squeezed off two blasts. One struck him on the right side of his chest, the other on the left. His knees gave way and he crumpled forward, landing half-curled on his side with his mouth hanging open.

She had forgotten the sharp, loud, cracking sound, the jerking recoil and the smell she associated with little red firecrackers. The noise had been amplified as it echoed off the gray stones.

The man at her feet was moaning.

"Oh, shit," she heard him say, "I'm gonna die."

"I hope so," she said.

"Mistake . . ." He coughed violently. "Oh, God . . ." His eyes remained open and unblinking.

Kate pushed his hand with her shoe. It was empty and flopped loosely.

Oh, God? Mistake?

They all made mistakes. Sure they did. Every one of them. For a half hour, a day, a few months.

She was not in the least regretful. The man had intended to rape her in the culvert. Because he couldn't help himself? Because he didn't have fifteen dollars to give André?

Kate looked away from the man's pale, still face.

She had seen the movies and television programs. A policeman and a group of silent, horrified onlookers would be staring at the woman with the pistol dangling in her hand.

She saw worked stone and shrubs and trees and grass and an overflowing rubbish can and a sliver of the river and the Jersey cliffs and the sky. No people. Not one. Nothing moved but the leaves.

Are they hiding out there, the Frisbee throwers and chess players and joggers?

Kate stepped over the man's body to peer past the entrance to the culvert. A black woman was changing a white baby's diaper on a bench about fifteen yards down. An elderly man and woman were reading the *Post* about ten yards up. Three women jogged toward her from uptown. She watched them jog right past the culvert entrance. They were facing straight ahead.

Two shots and nobody noticed?

Above and behind, on Riverside Drive, Kate heard tires screech, motors race and either a car's backfire or a cherry bomb.

The woman mopped the baby's bottom and the man and woman continued to read the *Post*.

What would have happened if she had screamed for help and not had a gun in her bag? After the man had raped her she would have crawled onto the path, and some caved-in drunk with a half-pint would be weaving and looking down at her and saying, "Hoo-hoo. Hoo-hoo."

But she did have a gun and she had killed the man with it.

The dead man's face possessed no particularity. He was a nameless, unsuccessful rapist. Most rapists remained nameless, both the successful and the unsuccessful.

Kate pulled a plastic wallet from the man's hip pocket. She dropped it into her bag, fastened the .32 in its pocket and walked past the man and woman hidden behind their *Posts*.

She heard the wailing of a siren when she was between Broadway and Amsterdam on Seventy-ninth. The car was speeding downtown on Broadway toward Lincoln Center or a massage parlor farther on.

The man's name was Joseph Warburton. That was the name on his Social Security card and on two laundry receipts. According to the receipts he lived on either West 126th Street or on Amsterdam Avenue in the mid-Nineties. Two tens, a five and four ones occupied the bill compartment.

Joseph Warburton could have afforded Lou Ann after all.

Kate set aside the money. She burned Joseph Warburton's Social Security card and his laundry receipts in her fireplace. She ejected the two spent cartridges from the .32, wrapped the gun in its gray flannel, placed it in its Hush Puppies box and put it back on the closet shelf. She wiped the wallet with a damp paper towel, then completely covered it with tissues. The spent cartridges she wadded in toilet paper.

Now it was seven o'clock, but still fully light.

She dropped the wallet in a trash container by the Museum of Natural History and the cartridges in a trash basket on Columbus Avenue and Seventy-sixth Street.

How much did the trial of an indigent rapist cost? A rich rapist? A poor one, like Joseph Warburton? The salary of a public defender alone? The judge and the per diem of all the jurors?

Then, there was the cost of food and lodging in prison. Then there was the next victim and another public defender.

She had saved the State of New York many thousands of dollars.

She reached the Italian restaurant well before darkness settled and ordered antipasto and two slices of pizza to go; she was very hungry. When she got back home, she ate every bite and licked her fingers. She showered thoroughly and slowly and placed a recording of Rachmaninoff's Symphonic Dances on her record player.

She choose that record because of all those she owned, it contained the spectrum of tonal colors. And she wanted to evoke a man who wanted and could pay for the rainbow.

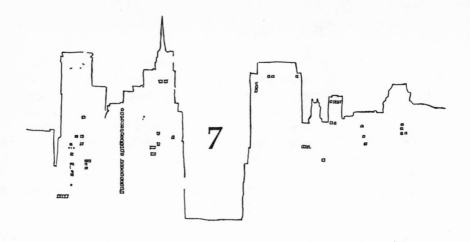

7

The Rainbow Man was willing to pay two or three hundred dollars for an orgasm. Probably more.

Joseph Warburton didn't want to spend a nickel for his.

Lou Ann's sodomist paid André—what? Ten or fifteen bucks.

With tongs, Kate lifted a piece of crisp bacon from the pan onto a paper towel laid over a folded section of *The Times*.

She had slept from ten Monday night to seven fifteen Tuesday morning. She had slept a heavy, dreamless sleep.

She stood before her stove, face washed, hair brushed, bed made, preparing her breakfast.

The world was not as complicated and confusing as she had felt it to be. When? Only fifteen or sixteen hours earlier.

She now possessed certain elements: orgasm, price. But there was more, and the additional factors had not yet become clear.

Thoughtfully, Kate chewed bacon and scrambled eggs and rye toast. She alternately sipped orange juice and black coffee.

At the moment when she killed Joseph Warburton she had not been afraid; she had felt rage. What she did and the way she felt were right and proper.

If the police had been called, though, what had been a clear-cut sequence of events would have become jumbled and ambiguous.

For starters, the police would have wanted to know what she was doing with an unregistered gun. Then they would have asked her how she was so certain Joseph Warburton intended to rape her. He had no weapon. There wasn't a mark on her. The police would look for a record on Joseph Warburton. The chances were he didn't have a record. The same policemen who had herded the massage parlor women into the escape-proof bus would say, "Miss Delling, why don't you tell us what really happened?"

Frowning now, Kate washed her dishes.

She tried to remember something, music and words, that she had never thought through.

Judgment, a certainty. Yes, along those lines. Retribution. Brisk, firm, final.

The rhythm of the word "final" brought to mind the musical passage she had been trying to recall. The beat was that of the bass drum in the *Dies irae* of Verdi's Requiem.

Kate placed the first record of the set on her record player and followed the Latin text with the English translation in the program notes.

Dies irae, day of wrath. Boom, boom, boom, boom.
How great the trembling when the Judge shall come by whose sentence all shall be bound.

And further along:

Nothing shall be hidden any longer, no wrong shall remain unpunished.

Kate listened to all four sides of the recording, then played the last side again.

On the last record, the mezzo-soprano expresses, lyrically, the hopeful view that God's light will fall on the saints forever.

Just who the saints are wasn't made clear, Kate realized.

Finally, the soprano sings, Free me, *Libera me.*

And she isn't kidding. She's singing, Deliver me from eternal death on that terrible day, as if she means it. Then the music is interrupted by the ominous Boom, boom, boom, boom of the *Dies irae.* The Requiem ends with a whispered, pleading *Libera me.*

The *Dies irae,* on the other hand, is not tentative.

Kate slipped the records back in their cases.

Verdi, and the medieval monks who came up with those words, believed someone was in charge.

At this very moment, there were people on the island of Manhattan who still believed a trumpet would sound, the earth would tremble and God's perfect judgment would be executed. The junkie who mugged the old lady, the owner who hired an arsonist to torch an occupied apartment building for the insurance, would not escape. Those believers were certain the books would be balanced.

Kate poured herself another cup of coffee. It was now almost eleven on Tuesday morning. She set the mug on the coffee table and sat on the edge of the sofa. She stared at the little mound of ashes on the sooty floor of the fireplace. The summation of Joseph Warburton.

Back to the equation: orgasm = price.

If she had not killed him, Joseph Warburton would not have paid one cent in the satisfying of his lust. He would have left her in the culvert and strolled past the people on the benches in Riverside Park. No one would have noticed the paunchy man with his now-limp penis tucked back in his pants. If she were still alive, Kate would have been shown dog-eared books of mug shots of sexual offenders. If his photograph were in a book, it would mean he had raped or been accused of rape before. And that he had been freed to rape again.

Kate went to the fireplace, stooped and stirred the ashes into powder. Joseph Warburton, knowing he was dying, admitted his mistake.

She returned to the sofa and her coffee.

Joseph Warburton had paid in full.

Kate sat back now and stretched out her legs, crossing them at the ankles. She studied the bricks above the fireplace.

Alexander Harding, on the other hand, had died in pure frozen water with a Miss Beverly Danforth. That meant he had not yet fallen out of love with Miss Danforth, had not yet needed to tell her, "What can I say? I'm sorry, but that's the way I am."

Alex had never paid.

Nor had Gordon Van der Kemp. Uncle Gordon had been stricken by a massive coronary while seated on the dais at a Foreign Affairs Council luncheon. He was dead before the paramedics arrived.

People who still believed in the *Dies irae* believed men like Uncle Gordon and Alex Harding would eventually cower before a fearsome God.

Kate was certain Alex and Uncle Gordon died impenitent. They would remain forever dead. There was no ultimate Judge. Death was final. They had escaped.

So had Lloyd, although he was still alive. Aunt Sarah wrote, in her last formal, semiannual letter: "Your father shows no improvement. Dr. Dornan is not at all optimistic, I am sorry to report. The latest specialist he called in for consultation was unable to suggest a different treatment. Your father's retreat from reality is so advanced that Dr. Dornan thinks the present institutional custodial attention is all that can be done for him. Your mother's disturbing obsession with those miniature landscapes she is carving in seashells is a source of concern for both Aunt Catherine and me. We will, I assure you, continue to do what we can for your parents, Kate."

Lloyd lay curled on his side in a criblike bed, wearing one of those soft cotton gowns that fasten at the back, and large-size paper diapers. At the private Foothills Doctors' Hospital, a nurse, by grasping his knees and shoulders, turned him from one side to the other every hour around the clock.

"He looks exactly the same on either side. His hands are crossed over his chest in the manner of knights' sarcophagi of the thirteenth century," Anne had written. "I am fascinated by the perfect symmetry his psychosis dictated. Meanwhile, I remain even more fascinated by the challenge of the lovely inner skins of abalone and Pismo clamshells. One day you must see what I'm doing. Not yet."

Lloyd was catatonic, and had been for three and a half years. Aunt Sarah and Aunt Catherine were paying for his care. Anne was scratching the insides of shells with jewelers' tools. Aunt Catherine wrote that Anne worked with a magnifying contraption strapped to her head.

Anne was still squinting at whatever it was she saw.

The last sight Lloyd was known to have seen was his color television set exploding after he threw a full half-gallon bottle of Pepsi at a paid political message that had interrupted an Abbott and Costello movie.

So much for Lloyd.

Kate slowly began to pace her apartment. She established a

course that took her from the living room, through the tiny entry hall, between the sofa and coffee table to the barred street windows, back past the record player, past the fireplace to the hall, to the bedroom.

The equation had become clearer and more complete: orgasm = price = payment. The price for an orgasm must be paid.

There remained serious questions. For the equation to be valid, it must apply to the living. One should not be able to walk away with impunity from what one did to another, or saw being done to another.

Kate sat at the small table she used as a desk. She pulled a pad of yellow quadrille paper from the single drawer and placed it on the polished walnut top. With a fine felt-tipped pen she slowly blocked in a square in the center of the sheet. Then, leaving three empty spaces, she filled in a square to the right and left of the first. She drew a line from the square to the right and left of the first. She drew a line from the square on the left to the center square, and from it to the one on the right. Where the line touched the square on the left, she made a neat arrow mark.

She deftly tore off the sheet and set it to the side.

On the fresh sheet she lettered: Gordon Van der Kemp, Alexander Harding and Lloyd Delling. This, in a column on the left. Then she drew a line through each name.

In the next column were the names: Scotty Rogers, Peter Hamilton, Dr. Waldo Crawford, Massage Parlor Men.

In the third column she printed: André, Lou Ann's Sodomist, Joseph Warburton, Rainbow Man. She drew a line through Joseph Warburton.

Above the first column she printed, Uncollectible; above the second, Liable; and above the third, Overdue.

Kate placed the two sheets side by side, leaned her elbows on the desk and rested her chin on her fists.

It came down to André, Lou Ann's nameless hulk and Margaret's Rainbow Man.

André would be cut off at the knees by another pimp or an irate father from West Virginia. No one would notice or mourn his departure. The man André sold Lou Ann to was probably a salesman passing through the city on his way to Hartford and Boston. The two of them were unable to pay what they owed.

The Rainbow Man.

Kate slowly drew a circle around the Rainbow Man.

The Rainbow Man was paying Waldo's bills, and that would keep Waldo in brunches for a while. He would pay for Margaret's dentist. He would pay Margaret's rent if she asked him to. Her food, her laundry bills. Her telephone bill. Her magazine subscriptions.

But that wasn't the point.

The money he gave her was not sufficient payment for the orgasm he experienced by battering her with a piece of driftwood.

Money was not important to the Rainbow Man. He was rich and famous. He was going to hire more women and smash them until he ejaculated. Eventually the Rainbow Man would kill one of them and a very expensive lawyer would take care of his problems. He would say he couldn't help himself and he was sorry, that was the way he was. His family and friends would find explanations of one sort or another, and they would forgive him.

Kate looked from one yellow page to the other.

She slammed her fists on the sheets of graph paper.

"No, you shit!" she whispered.

She lifted her fists and slowly brought them down again on the paper.

"You evil, stupid animal!" Her mouth was so dry the words came in a hushed, brittle staccato. "I don't forgive you!"

There was the humid, stuffy room beneath the shuffling feet and the cocktail party voices. There was the thump and rush of the ocean waves, the man with powerful shoulders and hands and thighs, the man with hurried explanations, the man with an enormous hard-on, the man with fear on his face, the man who did what he did because that was the way he was.

And there was nothing she could do about any of it.

But there was.

Kate lined up the sheets of paper on her desk. She looked from one to the other. Orgasm square, price square, payment square. The three columns of names.

She had, in fact, done something.

Joseph Warburton's name was crossed out. Kate turned to her left. A smear of ashes lay on the otherwise clear floor of the fireplace. Proof of payment. That still left the Rainbow Man. Whoever he was.

Margaret Elias knew his name.

Kate's phone rang.

Startled, she grabbed the two sheets of graph paper, crumpled them into a ball and tossed them into the fireplace.

She picked up the phone on the third ring.

"Kate?"

"Yes?" She looked at the yellow paper in the brick cave across the room.

"Hi. It's Miriam."

"Hello, Miriam."

"What in hell is Scotty trying to pull? Yesterday he said you were on vacation. This came out of the blue, needless to say. Today he tells us you're on sick leave for two or three weeks, for what he called nervous exhaustion. Except he made it sound as if you were a candidate for the funny farm. Ralph was in here a few minutes ago. He'd just heard that Scotty's gloating because he undercut you on the Welles-Keeler project. So what's going on, Kate?"

"Scotty undercut me on Welles-Keeler."

"You must be furious." Kate could hear the click of Miriam's cigarette lighter.

"Yes, I am furious."

"Does Hamilton know about this?"

"Scotty set me up in Peter Hamilton's office yesterday morning."

"That sonofabitch."

"Which one, Miriam?"

"Yeah, which one. Listen, do you want to have dinner? This is Jake's group night so I'm free."

Kate watched the yellow ball slowly unfold. "Not tonight. Sorry."

"But I want to know what's going on. I want to know what Scotty and Hamilton are pulling on you."

"Could we have lunch?" A triangular piece of yellow paper, a corner, had become free and was stark and bright against the blackened rear wall of the fireplace. "I mean, in a few days?"

"Okay. Kate, you must really be pissed."

"Yes, I am."

"But what are you doing?"

"Well, I have things to do." The two sheets appeared to form a yellow flower blooming, as in a slow-motion film.

"Are you going out of town? Kate, you sound odd."

"I'm tired."

"So what are you doing tonight that you can't have dinner? I'll take us both."

"A concert."

"Oh, okay. You already had tickets?"

"Yes." Kate jerked her face away from the fireplace. "I'll phone you later in the week. I'd like to tell you what happened."

"We'll have lunch."

"Right."

Kate replaced the receiver. She went to the kitchen for wooden matches, struck one and set the yellow papers on fire.

She had not been paying attention to Miriam Graun. She had been considering Margaret and Angie and Doris and whoever was caring for Margaret today.

Kate walked to the new gourmet deli on Columbus Avenue and bought one container of salmon mousse and another of apricot custard.

Angie answered Margaret's door.

"She's asleep," Angie said.

"I brought something easy to eat." Kate held out the white paper bag.

Angie peered into the bag. "That's very nice of you. I've got some coffee on." She looked tired. "We should be quiet. You know? Maggie's pill's working and she doesn't sleep much. Only for a while after the pill takes hold."

"Thanks." Kate moved in past the tentative Angie. "Just half a cup. I'll be quiet."

Angie went to the kitchen. Kate followed her.

Margaret's apartment was a mess. The ashtrays were full. Newspapers and magazines were tossed on the couch and the oak table. Dirty dishes were piled on the counter and in the sink. Empty Tab and Fresca cans were stacked on the floor beside an overflowing wastebasket.

Kate and Angie carried their coffee to the living room.

Angie fiddled with her mug, then with her cigarettes and matches. "I thought Maggie said you worked for a computer company. And this is a Tuesday."

"My boss is on my case."

"You mean you were fired?" Angie's small tawny eyes rounded. "That's why you're home today?"

Kate bent over her mug. "Yes. But I'm appealing."

"You can appeal?"

"I'm trying. But I have to wait."

"What if your boss wins?"

"Then I'm going to have trouble paying my rent." She faced Angie. "I can't go back to my office for a couple of weeks. They're supposed to mail me my checks, but I'm certain my boss is going to sabotage me there, too. I'm really broke. I had to pay first and last month's rent, plus the agent's commission. I have a very serious money problem."

Angie finally lit her cigarette. "Okay. Now I get the picture. You want to use Maggie's book." She puffed angrily on her Marlboro. "Do you know what those names are worth? Maggie didn't get her tricks from a pimp, friend. She has a very select book, friend, and she got those johns on her own. Referrals, friend." She jammed out her cigarette so hard she flipped two butts out of the ashtray. "You want clients, buy an ad in *Frig* and take your chances like other new girls." She crossed her arms hard over her breasts.

Kate felt heat on her cheeks and ears. Her eyes stung. She had been incredibly stupid and unsophisticated. She set her empty mug on a stained copy of *People*.

"Angie," she said, "you misunderstood. I can just quit and get another job if I want to. But I'm mad at the way my boss has been jerking me around. I'm trying to fight back. That's all. He knows I'm in a money bind now. I'm sorry I dumped on you." She gave Angie what she hoped was a sincerely embarrassed and confused smile. "I like Margaret and I'm terribly sorry about what happened to her. That's all. I don't know anything at all about her book, or anyone else's."

Angie relaxed her arms, but kept them where they were. "It's funny. I heard someone say once, the most paranoid people are hookers and cops. Isn't that weird? That's because they feel the only people who can sympathize, you know, understand how they see life, are other prosses or other fuzzes. No one else. Take you. You're broke now. So I act paranoid and instantly figure you're after Maggie's book."

Kate took one of Angie's Marlboros and lit it. She had smoked heavily in college, but she had given up cigarettes after she met Alex. He said her tongue tasted better when she didn't smoke.

"This is one of the most ridiculous positions I've ever been in."
Kate felt comfortable with the cigarette in her hand. She had not
been an automatic smoker for a long time, so she found she could
use the cigarette as a bit of stage business while she considered
her next approach. "I didn't bring Margaret something to eat so I
could wheedle away her book, as you call it. I didn't even know a
list of clients was called a book." She inhaled and exhaled Marlboro smoke. "I was here alone with her for a long time, Angie. I
found your name in what she called her book. The one by her
phone. I was in trouble at work then."

"Look, I'm sorry. Maggie's said you were great that night and
the next day. You didn't have to do all you did. Okay?"

Kate waved her cigarette in half-moon swoops to dismiss the
apology. "But say, though, I really am flat broke and backed
against the wall. How could I make contact with those horny
men with money? You see how dumb I am?"

"For one thing, a straight rich guy doesn't hire. He doesn't
have to. Especially if he's famous enough to make the *Post*'s
"Page Six" once or twice a year. He has to fight off groupies from
outer Queens who'll go down on him under the table while he's
eating his lunch. And thank him. See, that's why Maggie's book
is so valuable. Her clients are mostly kinks. But they're rich and
reliable kinks. The supersickies have been eliminated."

Kate leaned forward to stub out her cigarette. She spoke as she
picked up the two butts beside the ashtray. "Was the client who
beat her up new?"

"No. He's been one of Maggie's regulars for a couple of years.
I'll tell you this about that pig, the word is out on him. He'll be
getting whatever he'll get from a *Frig* ad from now on. Or from
the street."

"Margaret said he was well-known. Is he a politician?"

Angie pursed her lips and shook her head. "No names. Not
from me. Why should you care who the fucker is?" She stood.
"Have you met Connie?"

"No. Would I recognize his face? I'm just curious."

"Sure, you'd recognize his face and his voice, even. You've met
Doris. I didn't know if you'd met Connie, too. She's coming in a
little while. I want to shovel this place out before she gets here.
Oh, and thanks for whatever's in the bag. I'll tell Maggie you
brought it for her."

* * *

After she had closed and locked her door, Kate slowly walked to her desk. Her saliva tasted like paste and her palms were wet. She was going to have to find the Rainbow Man on her own. So be it.

Kate printed Rainbow Man at the top center of a fresh sheet of yellow paper. Under the letters she filled in three squares, as she had before, and connected them with arrows. She would thoroughly explain the equation to the Rainbow Man.

Two inches from the left side of the paper Kate made a list:

> Silencer
> *Frig*-ad
> Phone?
> Answering Machine?
> Where?

The odds against the Rainbow Man being the first man who would respond to her ad were enormous. A possibility, but remote. Kate tapped the top of her pen on the pad of graph paper.

She would, she decided, simply have to use her best judgment about those who answered her ad before the Rainbow Man did.

She added another note to her list.

> Appearance/Disguise.

Kate tilted back in her chair.

She tried to think of someone she knew, had ever known, who would understand why she was going to do what she was going to do.

She brought the front legs of her chair back to the floor.

Not one of those other little girls Uncle Gordon had used instead of a double Scotch before one of his recitals would understand.

And that was probably just as well. The little girls were all grown up now.

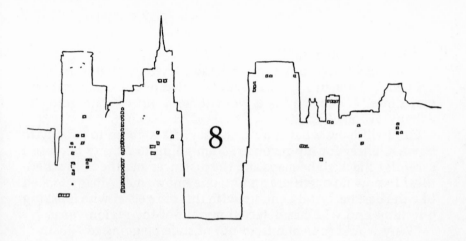

8

How marvelously green the grass, weeds and trees were. The lushest of Southern California springs, in the very best of the coastal canyons or in the higher, inland mountains, couldn't come close to the intensity and variety of greens in the succession of overgrown and neglected farms in the Hudson River Valley.

Kate sipped coffee from the threaded plastic cup of her thermos and gazed through the window of the Amtrak heading toward Albany. She was riding to Albany to gather information about, and if possible, purchase a silencer for her .32.

"I prefer fall," the elderly man seated beside Kate stated firmly, his first words since the train had left Grand Central Station two and a half hours before. "Not this early summer. Not spring or winter. Fall. And the color. Don't you find this mile after mile of green boring?"

"No. This is beautiful," Kate said.

"All this green?" The old man planted his speckled, heavily veined hands on the armrests, elbowing Kate in the process. "I suppose you're running up to the capital to hand an envelope to some state senator's assistant. Because your boss forgot to."

Kate finished her coffee, wiped out the cup with a tissue and screwed it back on the thermos.

113

"Well?" the man said.

"I am not going to Albany to hand someone an envelope."

"Hm." The man's spotted fingers rolled over the armrest several times. "Then why is a woman from out of state going to Albany, if I may ask?"

Oh, hell! Now what should she say? I am going to Albany to buy a silencer for my revolver? I am going to Albany because I carefully checked the maps and the distances and the train schedules? I know no one there and no one knows me? Albany looked like the best bet? And I end up with this old geezer who is asking questions and who has detected my out-of-the-region voice.

"Why would someone from out of state be going to Albany?" Kate asked pleasantly.

"You have your reasons. Not to see the sights. There are no sights in Albany. Probably a maiden aunt's estate. A will." He folded his hands over his belly and glared at the aisle.

Kate turned back to the window.

In the train station Kate went to a row of phone booths and leafed through the Yellow Pages. She settled on the listing:

"Barclay Bros. Buy—Sell—Trade Full Police Equipment Top of Line Models Repairs—Ammunition—Accessories—Drilling—Refinishing—Customizing."

If Barclay Bros. didn't have what she needed, no one would.

Kate gave the taxi driver an address on Kenilworth Street that she estimated to be three blocks east or west of the Barclay Bros. store.

"You mean you want Save-More Fabrics? On the corner of Kenilworth and Adams?"

"Yes. Thanks, I must have written the wrong number."

"My wife gets all her sewing stuff there. Place is a real jumble, she says. But if you know what you want, you can get a good price."

"So I've heard."

"Came up to Albany for a bargain, did you?"

"Mmm."

Kate paid the driver and went into Save-More Fabrics. The large, old, high-ceilinged discount fabric store was indeed in chaos. She wandered the crowded aisles for five minutes. No one asked if she needed help.

The Barclay Bros. store was five blocks east of Save-More

Fabrics, between a dental supply wholesaler and an upholstery shop.

The Barclay Bros. had not washed their front window for many years. Maybe that was because the heavy crisscrossed grille over the window made washing it too difficult.

The inside of the store smelled like cigar smoke, lubricating oil, hot metal and old sweat.

Rifles and shotguns were lined against both side walls, close together in racks that held them barrel up, trigger guards facing the customer.

Two men stood behind a long counter at the rear talking with a patron. The evident subject of the discussion was a heavy black holster on the glass counter top. The three men glanced at Kate and resumed their conversation.

Kate walked to the far right of the glass display counter and looked down at rows of handguns. There was one very small ornate gun, the kind a woman in a late late TV movie pulled from a beaded purse to aim at a sneering man wearing a ruffled shirt. There were several large squarish guns, also from late late movies. They were to be seen worn by Nazi officers. Lugers?

Each handgun bore a gray ticket attached to its trigger guard by a loop of white string. A few guns were embellished antiques. A few were very businesslike antiques. Three-quarters of the guns appeared to be modern and in mint condition. Kate counted fifty-one of those guns, each different. They lay in rows upon golden oak under heavy glass. A duplicate of her own .32 was among the short-barreled revolvers.

The customer left without his black leather holster. The older of the salesmen carefully wrapped the holster in tissue while the younger man began to rub the carved walnut stock of a rifle with a soft orange cloth. Neither asked if he could help her.

Kate turned from the counter and began a slow circuit of the store. She felt light-headed and disoriented, as if she were an invisible visitor to an utterly alien civilization. She was surrounded by magnificently aged, formed and polished hardwood; by meticulously tooled, machined and finished metal.

No two shotguns or rifles were the same. Each stock, each forestock, each barrel, sight, chamber and receiver was slightly different.

She read the handwritten tags.

Hunting shotguns, skeet shotguns, rimfire rifles, center-fire rifles, target rifles. Bolt action, pump action, autoloading and over-and-under. Deer guns, tournament, duck/geese, big game, boys, left-handed.

The inked words and numbers on the tags attached to every trigger guard were, Kate came to realize, not for the illumination of someone like herself. Nor were they for the edification of someone in the market for a Model 378 Fieldking Pump Action Center Fire .22 Br. 9" R-H Twist. The tags meant nothing to her, and for persons in the market for a rifle, the tag was probably unnecessary. They could tell from a glance what sort of gun they were looking at. A state or federal regulation, no doubt.

Kate counted two hundred and forty-one shotguns and rifles.

Not one of those long guns was without grace.

Two hundred and forty-one different manufactured objects, each painstakingly designed and, presumably, mass-produced. A stupefying display of form and function. Kate assumed the guns operated.

"Something I can do for you?" the younger of the salesmen said softly from about a yard behind Kate.

She did not look away from a large rifle equipped with what the tag described as a 4X Cosco Scope. "That looks efficient."

Kate heard the man's sigh. "Lady, are you with one of those gun control organizations?"

"No." She walked around him back to the glass counter-display case. The older salesman carried the wrapped holster into a back room. "But I would like some information about guns."

The tall, slightly stooped man took his place behind the counter. He was about Kate's age. He wore beige-tinted spectacles. "I've been watching you. You don't know very much about guns, do you?"

"Nothing. Nothing at all."

He nodded. "I can always tell. Never seen a real one up close before?"

Kate looked over her shoulder at the rifles and shotguns. "That is rather overwhelming."

He nodded harder. "Yeah. Beautiful, aren't they? You're seeing top-of-the-line firearms in this shop. No plastic. Some of the best makers have begun to use high-grade-synthetic stocks. We won't carry them. My name is Jack Barclay. My grandfather was one of the original Barclay brothers. My father's father. We're all named Jack. The other original brother was named Chester. He never had kids. I have three kids," Jack Barclay beamed. "A son and two daughters. The wife finally gave me a son. Jack. He's four and a half months old. One girl's two and the other's three. So what can I do for you?"

Kate stared down through the glass top of the counter at a display of antique police badges. Three children three years old and younger? And now he has one he can call Jack?

She lifted her face and smiled. It was not at all hard to do, she found.

"I think I need your help," Kate said.

"Well now, what do you want to know?" Jack Barclay's brow lowered, his head tilted a bit to the left. He was giving Kate his full attention.

"Mr. Barclay, I am up here for a few days taking care of a few legal matters for my grandmother." If an old man on the train and a taxi driver had picked up her non–New York accent there was no point trying to fool the man who had inherited a store full of guns. "I own a boutique. There have been robberies in the neighborhood . . ." Kate let her voice trail off.

"Call me Jack, Miss . . ."

"Snyder."

"Well, Miss Snyder, I figure you are in the market for a firearm."

"I have been told that a thirty-two-caliber revolver is the gun I should consider."

"Well, Miss Snyder, I figure whoever told you that may not be the best man to listen to. Say you're in your little store and an armed robber comes in. I'd say you should throw up your hands in a hurry and do whatever he says. See, he'll have his gun out and aimed at you. Now, you open a drawer and pull out a thirty-two." He shook his head. "He sees that and you're dead or seriously injured."

"I would keep the gun in a back room. Either I or one of my employees is almost always there."

"Oh, I see. Well now, then you'd try to shoot the man from—how far?"

"Ah, six feet."

"And you think a thirty-two's the gun?"

"That's what I was told."

"You were given the wrong information. I'll tell you why. Even if you and your other ladies were good shots, you'd have to get off two or three shots to do the job. By that, I mean knock the man down before he blasts you with a forty-five or a three fifty-seven mag. Now, he could be carrying a toy gun or one of those South American–made guns that can blow up in your face. You or your ladies won't know that." Jack Barclay removed his glasses and wiped them on a clean, ironed white handkerchief. "A thirty-two is not the firearm for you, Miss Snyder."

"Then what is the firearm for me?"

"A thirty-eight at the very least."

"Ah, a pharmacist in my neighborhood killed a robber with two shots from a thirty-two."

"Well, Miss Snyder, you can kill a man with one shot from a thirty-two or from a twenty-two. You can kill a man with a BB gun or a slingshot. I'm trying to tell you that, for your purposes, you do not want a thirty-two-caliber revolver or automatic. A firearm of that caliber would give you what's called a false sense of security. Do you follow me? That pharmacist was more lucky than he was a good shot. I've heard stories, and I know them to be true, where all six cartridges from a thirty-two were emptied into men's chests and they just kept coming."

"Hmm." Kate looked down through the glass at the gun identical to the one with which she had shot Joseph Warburton. "Then what do I need to be certain?"

"Certain? Well, you'd need a twelve-gauge shotgun with a triple aught load. That would blow the robber all over your dress shop, Miss Snyder. But it would ruin your merchandise, I suppose. And you might maim what's called an innocent bystander. The kick would probably dislocate your shoulder, in addition."

"You're being very helpful." Kate felt sweat forming on her forehead and her upper lip. Her cotton blouse was stuck to her back. "I think a shotgun is out of the question. Isn't there an effective handgun of some sort?"

Jack Barclay considered that. "Well now, you could protect yourself and your property with a handgun." He unlocked the sliding door at the rear of the showcase and lifted out a larger version of the gun presently hidden on the top shelf of her closet in Manhattan. "This is a thirty-eight-caliber revolver, Miss Snyder. It's even got a short barrel. Short barrels aren't as effective . . . Well, I won't go into trajectories." He held the gun so she could examine it. "You load this thirty-eight with Schiller Safety Slugs and you aim straight, you'll stop your man."

"What happens if I put those . . . safety slugs in a thirty-two?"

He firmly shook his head. "Won't really be the same. You should have a thirty-eight or a forty-five and the Schillers. Your problem is, Schillers are illegal to sell." She watched his mouth, his lips, slide toward his ears. He was smiling, evidently, but the expression of his eyes did not change. "Maybe you can buy them, along with such items as plastic explosives and silencers, in Canada or Mexico or on the black market."

They stared at each other for a good ten seconds. Jack Barclay's mouth was fixed in its inexplicable grin. Kate's palms were cold and wet.

"Mr. Barclay, I am not in the market for a bomb." She moved slowly to her left along the counter, away from him. The man was playing a drawn-out game with her. He had been from the first, she realized.

"Jack," he said again. "The thing is, I think the same way my father and grandfather did, Miss Snyder."

"How is that?" Kate felt herself to be in control of the situation for the first time. She made a second slow circuit of the room. One gun, her .32, was ominous and lethal. The forest of polished and oiled metal and wood in the Barclay Bros. store appeared almost innocuous now. "How did they think?"

"What I told you in the first place. A robber comes into your little dress shop and he tells you to give him your money, lay down on the floor, take off all your clothes—then that's what you should do if you want to stay alive. You see, your majority of women don't have what they call the proper temperament that is needed to own a gun."

"Why is that, Jack?" She folded her hands on a large square of padded flannel on the counter.

"Well, the majority of women are weaker than the majority of men. That is a fact of nature, so there must be a reason for it. Now, you put a firearm in the hands of, say, a woman who's just had an argument with her husband. I am not saying here, Miss Snyder, whether or not the wife has a reason to be angry. The point is, Miss Snyder, if the husband is angry, he may slap the lady around a little. The lady, being weaker, won't be taking a poke at her man. If she did, why, he'd just poke her back much harder. Women know this. But, say, the lady's pretty upset and she can lay her hands on a firearm, knows how to load and fire a gun. She could kill her man. ·Now you have a real tragedy. Fatherless children. Mother in jail. Do you see what I'm saying?"

"Yes, I do. And I want to thank you for all the time you've given me. You've certainly talked me out of buying a thirty-two." She stepped back. "I'm glad I decided to discuss this with an expert like you."

He pulled back his shoulders. "I feel a real responsibility for the firearms I sell."

"That is admirable, Jack. Again, thank you." She was halfway across the room when she hesitated and then turned. "Oh, by the way, you mentioned that silencers were illegal. Why is that? They show them so often on TV."

Jack Barclay had sagged back into his slump. "Sure silencers are illegal in the·U.S. Can you think of a lawful use for a silencer, Miss Snyder?"

She ran her index finger under her chin. "No. No, I can't. I hadn't thought of them until you mentioned them. Thanks again."

Kate closed the door of Barclay Bros. She walked back to Save-More Fabrics. She waited half an hour for a taxi to the station, and then had a forty-five-minute wait for the next train to Manhattan.

Her seatmate this time was an elderly Asian woman who had immediately addressed herself to a thick sheaf of bound documents. The printing on the papers was in characters. Kate could see no English words. That, however, did not mean the old woman was unable to read English.

She slipped a three-by-five lined pad from her bag. She held her Cross pen over the top line and considered how best to organize her thoughts.

She printed *T* three-quarters of an inch inside the narrow double red lines marking off the left-hand margin. *T* for Trace.

She had touched the door handles of two taxis and the gun store. They were the only smooth surfaces she had touched in the city of Albany. Nothing in Save-More Fabrics, only the flannel pad at Barclay Bros.

Jack Barclay, and the salesman who had disappeared with the black leather holster, knew she was from out of town and what she looked like. Only one of the taxi drivers heard her speak more than the words "Train station." The old man with speckled hands who had sat beside her had worn thick, rather dirty spectacles. She was a woman after her aunt's money, a fabric bargain-hunter and Miss Snyder who owned a boutique.

She circled the *T*.

Next, she printed an *S* beneath the *T*. *S* for silencer and safety slugs.

She could easily verify the availability and legality of silencers and Schiller Safety Slugs by calling other gun stores from public phones. The black market was as complicated and dangerous as were trips to Canada and Mexico.

The imperatives were simplicity, foresight and self-control.

Perhaps a silencer was a far greater complication than she had assumed. And unnecessary. Yes. No one in Riverside Park had heard the two shots that killed Joseph Warburton. Different types of cartridges should be investigated, though.

Kate circled the *S*.

Under the *S* she printed *B*. Just how reliable were the assertions of a man who was heir to the Jack Barclay world view regarding the dependability of a .32 in the hand of a female?

That man in Riverside Park was dead. He had not faked the blood gently pulsing through his shirt. Nor had he faked the dry and immobile eyeballs.

Kate looked up from the lined pad and gazed at a deep cigarette burn on the back of the seat in front of hers.

Perhaps she had been lucky with Joseph Warburton. Alex had cautioned her to wait until the attacker was only three feet away, so there must be an efficiency factor. She did not know what sort of cartridges she had shot Warburton with. She did not know how a Schiller Safety Slug differed from the cartridges in the Hush Puppies box. She did not even know what a triple aught load was.

Many little boys who grew up in rural areas, nine- and ten-year-olds, could walk into Barclay Bros. and instantly identify and cite the characteristics of those rifles and shotguns and handguns. The same way little girls could stroll the aisles of Save-More Fabrics and tell the difference between challis and chambray. They learned what they learned from a mother's or father's knee. She had learned about neither guns nor fabrics from Lloyd and Anne.

There was, Kate decided, always the library.

She placed a question mark beside the *B*.

That still left the Where, the *Frig* ad, the Answering Machine, the Phone and the Appearance/Disguise.

Kate bought a *Post* in Grand Central Station and caught the Forty-second Street crosstown, and transferred to the M10. The uptown bus was less than half-full. She found a seat near the rear and then the short article on page 19.

A man, tentatively identified as J. Wardontor, was found shot to death in a Riverside Park culvert late Tuesday evening by Patrick X. Morgan as he was walking his two dogs. J. Wardontor had been the victim of a robbery, police said.

Tuesday night? And then only after two dogs had sniffed out the corpse? Twenty-four hours later?

That could very well have been her own body.

Kate closed and folded the paper.

She looked up and into the eyes of a man seated directly across from her. The bright greens and the old black stone of Central Park slid along behind the window upon which the back of his head rested. The lower half of his face was covered by a full, yet trimmed beard and mustache. His upper cheeks and forehead were disfigured by old acne scars.

The man was probably in his late thirties, Kate assumed before she looked to her left, toward the front of the bus. She saw the man as lazily ominous, seated as he was with his arms crossed over his chest, his head tilted back and his gaze aimed straight down his nose right toward her eyes. He wore wrinkled khaki trousers, hiking boots and a faded black sweat shirt.

All right, Kate, carefully go over every move from the time you sat down. Do not act the way you feel—afraid. You did skip through the *Post* until you found the little article titled, "Robbery Victim Dead in Park." You read that article and only that article, and then you folded the paper. You did not notice where the bearded man in the black sweat shirt, or anyone else, was seated when you got on at Forty-second.

The man could, if he was observant, know exactly what she had not read, and what she had read.

She planned her next movements. She would extract a tissue from the packet in her bag and glance across at the man while she pretended to blow her nose.

Kate pulled forth the tissue and blew her nose. The man was

openly and insolently staring at her. But now his right eyebrow was arched. His arms remained crossed over his chest.

The bus passed the Tavern-On-The-Green sign.

Kate looked to the rear of the bus.

"You dropped this."

Kate whipped her head around.

The bearded, scarred, sweat-shirt-clad man was leaning forward, holding out the Albany train schedule. "It fell out of your bag just now." He was broadly grinning. "When you were blowing your nose."

Kate said, "Thank you." She grabbed the thin paper, shoved it back in her bag, went to the rear door and pulled the cord.

She waited for the signal to change.

"Lady." The man had followed her from the bus and was now standing close beside her. "I have been watching you since you got on at Forty-second. You have a great big problem."

Looking straight ahead, Kate felt her mouth go dry. She said nothing.

"Lady, don't you want to hear what I know about you?"

Kate stepped from the curb and hurried across the broad street.

"Then I'll tell you anyway." The man's voice was low and angry. "You are paranoid. That's what you are. You've been acting like I wanted to pick you up. You must be kidding yourself. You're a pig. A pig like you shouldn't be paranoid. Shit, I've kicked better-looking women than you out of bed."

The man stayed close to her as he spoke.

Kate saw a patrol car slowly cruising down Central Park West in the next block. She gambled.

"If you don't leave me alone, I will scream for the police." She pointed toward the patrol car.

"Fuck you, paranoid pig." The man spat on the sidewalk and turned.

Kate continued to the next corner before she looked back. The man in the black sweat shirt was hurrying across Seventy-second Street. He joined a small group of people who were boarding a bus. Kate waited until she saw him step into the bus, until the doors of the bus closed. Only then did she blow out her breath and walk slowly to her brownstone.

First, Jack Barclay and his gun games, then the ugly bearded sadist in the black sweat shirt.

But she had learned something very important today. She had been able to bluff both men. She would not have signaled the patrol car. Swell—her name on a police report! No way. But Black Sweat Shirt hadn't known that. Then, Barclay was convinced he had discouraged her from purchasing a gun of any kind. And he was quite smug about it.

Art was backing through the outer door bearing a two-foot-high stack of old newspapers and magazines as Kate reached the top of the brownstone's stoop.

"Kate. Good. Hello. Wait a sec." He felt his way down the stairs, tapped the row of metal trash cans with the toe of his dirty blue Adidas until he got an echo, kicked off the lid, dumped in the papers and replaced the lid. "You should see what's still left in my apartment to haul out." He climbed the stairs, wiping his hands on his faded Levi's. He sat down in the center of the top step. "Do you have a couple of minutes?"

"Sure." Kate sat down and leaned her shoulder against a carved stone post. "Do you clean house when you're between jobs?" She discovered, now that she was seated, that her knees were quivering. A delayed reaction to Black Sweat Shirt.

"I'm not between jobs."

He offered her a cigarette. Kate felt comfortable accepting a cigarette from Art.

"Aren't you finished with filmmaking-on-the-streets-of-New York, or are you working on a new article?"

"You, Kate, are responsible for the piece I'm doing. Christ, I don't know whether I should thank you or not. I have a moderately good offer from *New York*, in any case."

When the smoke slipped over her tongue and hit the back of her throat she felt herself begin to relax. "Is this the article on white slavery in the nineteenth century?"

"You should have heard me impressing the editor with my research."

Suddenly he pointed across the street to an intent girl of about fourteen who had rapidly placed three squares from a roll of paper towels under the rears of three squatting standard poodles. All three of the dogs obliged, the girl gathered up the papers and their contents and dropped them into a large brown bag. The girl looked up at Art. He gave her several exaggerated nods and vigorously clapped his hands. Holding all three leashes in her left hand, the girl made a sweeping and graceful gesture of acknowledgment before she continued on.

Art laughed. "Have you seen Vanessa's routine before?"

"No. And I still don't believe it."

"Vanessa's been a dog walker around here since she was about eleven. After the pooper-scooper law went into effect, some old lady on Seventy-fifth hounded the police until Vanessa was socked with a fine. Did Vanessa give up and turn in her leashes? Do you know, that kid now has a lengthy waiting list?"

They watched the girl stride toward Columbus Avenue with her charges.

"Amazing," Kate said. "Why does she need money that badly?"

"She doesn't need money badly. Vanessa lives in a town house in the East Sixties. The whole town house. With her parents, of course. Or so she's told me."

"Then why is she over here on the West Side walking dogs?"

"I asked her. She said West Side dogs didn't have as many hang-ups as East Side dogs." He tapped her wrist. "Back to this *New York* piece you got me into. I was very impressive in my presentation to the editor. When I was finished, he said, 'Art, this is for next August, not the last century. I'd like a piece on now with a very little then thrown in.' As of Monday, I've been hanging around with selected personnel from two midtown vice squads. When I asked for such information as numbers and statistics on the kids, the response was horselaughs. One detective said, 'You think pimps fill out 1040s? You think johns use American Express?' "

"The police weren't even aware that girl I saw was brutalized, to say nothing of her very existence." Kate hugged her knees, which had begun to tremble again.

"Yes. I've asked for ball-park figures. No one could give me any." He stood and offered his hand. "What I need for this piece are specifics, because I'm sure as hell not coming up with any generalities."

"Lou Ann was not a generality."

Kate opened the outer door, Art unlocked the lobby door.

"Was that the girl's name? Lou Ann?"

"The older hookers and her pimp called her Lou Ann."

"You're still shook up about that girl, aren't you?" He leaned his elbow against the wall by her door.

"Yes."

"Those men in Vice see four or five Lou Ann's per watch, they tell me. Week after week and . . ."

"Month after month and year after year?"

He nodded. "Maybe they need to separate themselves from their work for big hunks of time, the way oncologists do. Doctors who specialize in cancer."

Kate unlocked the locks on her door. "Whom do the selected personnel in Vice perceive as the cancer, Art? The hookers or the johns?"

"You left out pimps. This morning, a detective working out of Midtown North let me, and I use the words 'let me' advisedly, let me take a call with him. Seems there was a guy left in the trunk of his car under the West Side Highway near the Circle Line pier. Everyone recognized the victim's face. It hadn't been touched. He'd been . . ." He carefully swallowed. "Someone had gone at him, ah, professionally, with an acetylene torch. The man in the trunk of the red Olds was a small-time pimp."

"Did anyone know his name?"

"Everyone knew his name. And it was confirmed by his driver's license. Andrew Felix Jordon."

"Andrew Felix Jordon?"

"Yes. According to word on the street, Mr. Jordon, at age twenty-two, with a current string of six or seven little girls from the Midwest, decided to branch out more heavily into the drug biz. My detective friend figures Mr. Jordon was used as an object lesson by a local dealer one notch higher. I threw up."

"What about your detective friend?"

"He ate dry roasted peanuts."

"What shade of red was Andrew Felix Jordon's car?"

"I wasn't paying attention to the guy's paint job, Kate. I've never seen a human being's body, not to mention the expression on his face, in that condition before." He jerked himself away from the wall. "I may not have the stomach to finish this piece. And I was Press for ten months in Vietnam in Sixty-eight. The people on the ground there never had names."

Kate said, "May I bum a couple of cigarettes?" He gave her his half-full pack. "Thanks." She felt old and tired and peaceful. "Art, I once read that in even the most primitive of societies, infants are given a name. You know about Margaret! She has a name!"

He grimaced and gave his head a vigorous shake. "You've got it. And that's why I have had, and have, extremely serious reservations about the subject matter of this piece. I tend to not want to know what I don't know, in some instances. I was totally stoned the entire time I was in Vietnam, for what that's worth. But once I have a firm offer, I always deliver. Take care, Kate."

"Oh, I will."

She closed her door and locked the locks and attached the chain.

That was André in the trunk of the red car. She was certain.

So his true name was Andrew Felix Jordon. He had been given that name.

Kate poured a glass of chilled Chablis, turned on her record player, lit one of Art's cigarettes and sat back on the sofa to listen to the last record of the Verdi Requiem. As the *Dies irae* played she wondered what name the Rainbow Man's parents had given him.

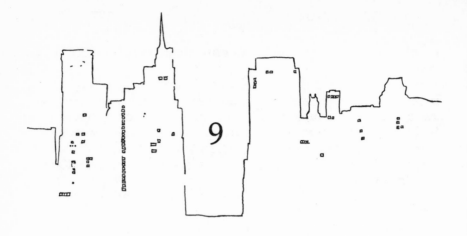

9

Thursday morning after she turned off her alarm Kate did not immediately get out of bed. She pulled her second pillow onto the already warm one and lay back on them both. She slid her legs over to a cool place on the taut bottom sheet and, with her eyes closed, thought about Tucson, Arizona.

Specifically, she thought about the hours and days after she had stood in front of Alex's cluttered desk, when she had asked him, "When did you fall out of love?" and he had replied, "Late October," and she had said, "That was over seven months ago, Alex," and he had said, "Kate, honey, what can I say? I'm sorry, but that's the way I am."

She could never remember how she had gotten back to her duplex. She must have driven herself home. Who else would have? Her car was parked exactly as she always parked it, she later discovered.

She went over and over the words he had spoken over the stacks of printouts on his desk. They boiled down to—that's the way I am.

Seated behind his desk that day in late May he had appeared and sounded like a sixteen-year-old who was relieved to have over with an inevitable and unpleasant confrontation. Now that everyone finally understood the way he was, honey, he could relax a little and continue to be the way he was.

128

Windows closed, drapes drawn against the Tucson sun and nights, Kate sat in the imitation Eames lounge chair she had bought for Alex and computed the hours she had spent alone waiting for her phone to ring. From late October to June. Seven months during which she was so obsessed by Alex she could not finish a short magazine article or watch a TV program to its completion. While she was out at a movie she was wondering if that was the time when Alex was able to call. Sometimes he called at 2:00 or 3:00 A.M., when he said Sharon and the boys were asleep. His voice was so low she needed to strain to catch every third word. Fifteen minutes at 3:00 A.M., a half hour on a Sunday afternoon ten days later. Daily, impersonal conversations about A.C.S. programs. A greasy lunch or breakfast at the Red Dot Café and an hour and a half on the mover's pad in the back of Alex's station wagon, an average of once every five weeks. Of those ninety minutes, twenty were spent undressing and dressing in the short, shallow space.

There was a reason why she believed him, continued to believe that he loved and needed her over those seven terrible months. After she clumsily bared herself to him he began their lovemaking, always, as if her mouth and face and body were marvelous mysteries. She was for him uniquely desirable. How could he or anyone else simulate such ardor? His search for her orgasms? Not his, hers.

Kate sat in the fake Eames lounge chair with the drapes drawn and recalled every minute within the steamed windows of the Chrysler station wagon.

During seven months, or thirty-two weeks, or two hundred and twenty-four days and nights, Alex had telephoned her forty-four times. She remembered each call. She remembered each time they had made love. Seven times. The only time he had been to her duplex he had nervously drunk a cup of coffee. He had not sat down. He had looked around and said, "Very nice. Very comfortable, Kate. I can't stay now. You understand."

She sat in the darkness and gradually understood something. Alex's mouth on her body was minimum wages for the naive woman who was holding his business together. The hushed and hurried phone calls—the same. Better give Kate a quick call. Touch a base or two.

She had touched one human being, and only one human being, for a total of three hundred and fifty minutes over a period of seven months.

Lying now on her bed on a warm Thursday morning in New York City, Kate wondered why it had never occurred to her to take the shiny gun Alex had given her and shoot him with it. She knew where he lived. She could have followed him. Something. But it had simply never occurred to her to kill him. She had blamed herself for being imperceptive and unrealistic and stupid. How else could she feel?

Kate showered, shampooed her hair and shaved her legs.

She hummed along with Judy Collins' version of "Clouds" as she sat down at her desk. On the pad of yellow graph paper she printed:

Frig
Where
Phone
Answering Machine
Deposits for Con Ed and Phone
Compose ad

All right now. Approach this logically. You can buy a copy of *Frig*, but you can't place an ad until you have a phone number, and you can't get a phone until you have an office or a room in which to have the phone connected. The answering machine is last.

She had seen copies of *Frig* and other porno tabloids and slick magazines on racks inside newsstands all over Manhattan. They were inside the kiosks, Kate assumed, to prevent theft and free perusal, rather than to keep them from eleven-year-old boys. Kate had been embarrassed by what she had seen of the covers, never more than quick glances: large bare breasts, well-built young men wearing tight briefs that emphasized their genitals, the faces of young women with blank eyes who appeared to be licking their lips.

Kate walked up Central Park West to Eighty-sixth Street and rode the crosstown bus to Lexington Avenue. She wore faded jeans, an old gingham shirt, clogs, sunglasses, a small scarf she had tied at the back of her neck and no makeup. At the busy newsstand she picked up a *News* and pointed to the stack of *Frig*s on a ledge behind the vendor.

"Yeah? This what you want?" The stocky man gave her a quick side glance as he pulled a *Frig* from the pile.

Kate nodded.

The vendor shrugged and held out his hand.

Kate bent over the tabloid to read the price.

"Dollar seventy-five, honey," the man said. "Plus the *News* you got there."

She handed him two singles.

"Enjoy, sweetheart," she heard him say as she hurried away.

Kate folded the *News* over the *Frig* and shoved them in her canvas tote.

Back in her apartment she made instant iced coffee and sat down to look through the pornographic tabloid.

The first third of *Frig* contained photographs of nude men and women together, several nude women together, a great many women alone and a few men. Most of the women's bodies were contorted in one way or another. The men's bodies were not contorted, but their faces were, presumably from ecstasy.

The remainder of the tabloid was given over to classifieds. Under Classified Information the publisher declared *Frig* would print no phone numbers or addresses or prices for services, and the first ad must be placed in person, payment to be made in cash, cashier's check or money order. Renewals could be made by mail, payment in cashier's check or money order. No credit cards accepted.

Every ad was accompanied by one or more phone numbers, many also with addresses. As for prices, in the ads where fees were stated, they ranged from twenty-five dollars for "a trip around the world, the Swedish way," to "all fantasies accommodated, $125 complete—one hour."

Although the services offered in the ads did not seem to be arranged in any discernible order, Kate broke them down into categories.

The "Hi, my name is Jennifer, and that really is my picture." Jennifer or Tina or Marni then informed the readers of *Frig* that they were only available to discriminating gentlemen whom they would entertain in their luxurious penthouses in the East Fifties or Sixties.

The College Students or Stewardesses or Housewives Looking For a Good Time and Trying to Make Ends Meet.

The Two or Three Lovelies for the Price of One.

The Mistresses Natasha, Kali, Sheila and so forth. Those women were shown wearing long black gloves, high leather boots, black garter belts and Lone Ranger masks. They all stated they had bodies made to be worshiped, despised men and possessed a large inventory of metal and leather goods and contraptions.

The I'm a Little Girl at Heart Who Wants a Daddy. Men Over Forty Only.

The closeup photographs of female genitals or breasts with only a few crude words and Call Lila or Penny or Monique. And a phone number.

Three-quarters of the ads contained photographs and a woman's first name. But Kate noticed that in the last six pages of the section, in very small letters, the words, "girls wanted" or "models needed" were printed at the bottom of ads. Kate had an excellent memory for numbers; she flipped back to the "Hi, . . . that really is my picture," and College Students and Mistress Kali and Little Girl and found that many of the numbers were the same as those in the back section. Presumably by calling one number, a man could arrange for the services of either a Stewardess or Ella the Submissive or Yolanda the Dominatrix or a penthouse in the East Sixties.

In all probability the women in the photographs could no longer be reached at the given number. No doubt when the man called he would be told Shirley or Millie or Brandy was unavailable, but he was in luck. Kitty was exactly the Girl or Mistress or large-breasted woman he wanted.

Kate determined that almost two-thirds of the ads' phone numbers were repeated twice or more. The remaining third, the independents, covered the same specialized services and combinations. These were abbreviated for the most part. Kate could guess what only half of them were: B/D, English, French, Greek, Roman, S/M, L/L, Water Sports, Rough Stuff, Photo/Phone, Golden Shower, F/F, Rim, H/H, G/T, D/T, C/B, F/S and Scat.

A photograph of herself was out of the question.

She studied ads without photographs; approximately a fifth of the ads contained no photographs or drawings. Kate broke them down into three general categories: salons or escort services, explicit and direct strings of obscenities, and the smallest number, a box containing a few words and a name and a phone number.

Kate made herself another glass of instant iced coffee and lit the last of Art's cigarettes. It was now almost two in the afternoon, and her apartment had become hot and stuffy. She closed the living-room windows and turned on her air conditioner for the first time. It screeched and groaned into its High and

Medium Cold phase, and once there settled into a high-pitched, grinding noise. She turned on WNCN and turned up the volume on the second movement of Sibelius' First Symphony to cover the sounds of the air conditioner.

As she settled at her desk she considered the irony of Sibelius' stark Finnish music being played on a hot and humid day in a claustrophobic city. He had written of birches and snow and space.

Oh, well.

Kate began on a fresh sheet of yellow graph paper.

She printed The Rainbow at the top of the sheet. Under that and to the left, she printed Discreet. In the center of the line she printed Accomplished, and to the right, Fastidious.

Beneath the space between Accomplished and Fastidious she printed Only by Appointment.

Beneath Discreet she printed "Minimum Fee $175."

That was fifty dollars more than any other figure in *Frig*. And that was important. The value. That should also eliminate ninety-five percent of the men who bought the tabloid.

All that remained was a name and a phone number.

God, she needed to be so careful from here on.

The connections so far were covered: Albany and the Barclay Bros., Joseph Warburton, the purchase of *Frig*.

She set fire to the sheets of yellow paper and changed into a dress and beige Jacques Cohen espadrilles.

Ohrbach's, she thought, would be the best of the large stores in which to shop for a wig. Macy's and Gimbels provided salespeople to see a sale through. At Ohrbach's she could try on a number of wigs and take the one she finally selected to a cashier who rang up sales for long lines of customers.

Kate walked to the Citibank at Broadway and Seventy-second Street and stood in line for the one functioning stainless-steel machine with its computer screen and push buttons. She inserted her card in the slot, punched in her number code and then, after being queried, asked for two hundred dollars. The heavy roller rolled one way, then the other, and laid out ten crisp twenties. Kate pushed the Record yes button and, screening the bills from the people behind her, shoved the money and record in the inside zipper compartment of her shoulder bag.

Within the next day or so she decided, as she hurried across Broadway to catch a downtown 104, she should begin to keep a record of expenses.

Ohrbach's, at three forty-five, was crowded. Good. She joined
the milling black, tan, Asian and white women examining and
trying on an almost overwhelming number and variety of wigs.
The majority of the wigs were black—shiny strands of black that
had been formed into short, medium and extravagant Afros, or
long pageboys with bangs, or thick, short-cropped straight hair
with bangs. Then there were black wigs with waves, curls, tight
ringlets.

Kate's skin, eyebrows and eyelashes precluded black or the
vivid reds and pale blonds. That narrowed the possibilities con-
siderably. She could get away with a dark blond, light or medium
brown or, perhaps, auburn. The auburn wigs, though, were of
distinctly abnormal shades.

Kate lifted a curly brown wig from one of the many light-
bulb-shaped stands. She pulled it on and tucked her hair away.
She looked like Rhoda from TV. She tried on a light brown
Farrah Fawcett wig and felt ludicrous. A dark blond, swept-
to-one-side pseudoforties wig. That did not suit at all. She found
it hard to visualize herself in any of the hairstyles listing on the
stands. A glance in a mirror showed her that her own hair had
become quite disheveled. No one noticed. The other women
were absorbed only by their own wig quests.

The purpose of a wig, she reminded herself, was to cause her to
appear unlike herself, not to enhance her features.

She watched a black woman with straightened hair, a woman
in her late forties, tug on a crisp medium Afro. The expression on
the woman's face changed; her posture altered; she moved her
hands differently. Kate did not understand how that wig transformed the woman, although it did. Quite a few strands of
straightened hair straggled free, and the woman did not poke
them back. She gazed at herself, full face, in a mirror with
adjustable side wings. She did not look at her profile or the back
of her head. She stood there for about three minutes looking
steadily at what could be seen from the central mirror. Then,
while continuing to look at herself, the woman peeled off the
wig. Her eyebrows raised and lowered, she patted her own hair
in place, dropped the wig on a stand and walked away into a
main aisle. The woman was carrying an unraveling straw purse
in one hand and an almost-mint Saks midsize shopping bag in
the other.

Two Hispanic girls were experimenting with Bette Midler
wigs. They giggled and nudged each other.

Kate eyed a brown wig with a moderate curl, almost shouldei length, she guessed, darker and curlier than her own hair. She settled it over her head, pushing her lighter hair under the elastic band. She fluffed the wig out and swept the long, curled bangs a little to the left. She did not look like herself. She looked like a harder, older woman. She inspected herself in a three-way mirror. Yeah. Just a little tough from every angle. She accepted the image: a no-bullshit secretary or bookkeeper for a no-questions-asked kind of business. The way she saw herself was the way she expected others to see her.

The wig cost thirty-four dollars and eighty-two cents. She carried it home in a round plastic box, along with a carton of Kent Lights she had bought from a combination discount cigarette and head shop on Thirty-fourth Street.

When she turned the dial of the air conditioner to On, the machine grated, rasped and then fell silent. Kate twisted all four knobs. Nothing happened. She pulled the three-pronged plug from the wall socket and called Mario's number. No one answered the super's phone.

She called air-conditioner repair services until she found one that could send out a repairman in less than two weeks. Fuller's on West Twenty-third Street could have a man out on Saturday, at time and a half.

"Fine," Kate said. She intended to deduct the bill from ner next month's rent.

After a tuna salad and cottage cheese dinner, Kate looked through her closet for clothes to match the wig. She would use the same appearance while looking for a room or office and when making arrangements for the phone and the answering machine.

She was sweating heavily as she tried on pants and tops and skirts and tops and dresses. First she eliminated pants—too casual or too tailored. None of her dresses worked. That left skirts and blouses. She finally decided on a madras wraparound and a light, loose V-neck bouclé chenille top.

In the bathroom Kate was studying as much of herself as she could see in the wall mirror over the sink with the aid of a hand mirror when she heard a thump from the bedroom. She jerked off the wig, grabbed her toenail scissors and faced the little hall that connected the bedroom, bathroom and living room.

Roberto padded into the hall, sat down just outside the bathroom doorway and blinked at Kate.

She sat down on the edge of the bathtub and blew out her breath. The scissors slipped out of her hand onto the tile floor. The fingers of her other hand were tangled in the hair of the wig. She carefully pulled the wig free and set it on her knee. Roberto wandered off toward the living room or kitchen.

"Good," she said. "Very good cat."

She had not thought out *leaving* the brownstone wearing her wig and the clothes that went with it.

Kate put away the wig, changed clothes and brushed her hair.

The woman who answered Margaret's door had been awakened by Kate's knock. "Oh, thank you," she said huskily when she saw Roberto. The left side of her face was creased by sleep marks and her hair was damp and pressed against her head. "Maggie's been worried about him. Are you the woman on the first floor?"

"Yes. My name is Kate Delling."

Roberto began to tense.

"Bring him in and I'll close the door. He must have gone through the kitchen window last night before I closed it."

The cat jumped onto the back of the couch and then to the floor.

"How is Margaret today?"

"Her doctor was here when I arrived around one thirty this afternoon." The woman sank onto the couch and leaned forward, elbows on knees, hands dangling from the wrists. "Her doctor, in whom I have no confidence, has given her an injection of antibiotics. She now has a fever which may or may not be related to her injuries. I'm Barbara Cipriano, and no, I'm not a pross. Maggie and I have been friends since Hunter."

The apartment was in even greater disarray than it had been two days before. The ashtrays had been emptied, but fine ash clung to the sides and lumps of black tar stuck to the bottoms. Four spiral bound notebooks lay atop a scatter of magazines and newspapers on the coffee table. A quilted bathrobe was bunched at one end of the couch—Barbara's improvised pillow.

Kate sat in the wing-backed chair. "You don't look very well yourself."

The brown-eyed woman on the couch, who wore her black hair straight and parted in the center, looked like an American Indian who was suffering from malnutrition.

"Just tired. I have a two-and-a-half-year-old daughter and I'm hoping to finish my master's by the end of July. You work with computers?" She leaned back against the cushions and closed her eyes.

"Indirectly. Why don't you go back to sleep or go home? I can take care of Margaret if you'll tell me what her doctor . . ."

"Someone named Connie is supposed to be here at nine."

"It's past ten."

"She said she might be late." Barbara yawned. "Before I conked out I was thinking, maybe what happened to Maggie may be for the best. She's far more intelligent than I am. She has money in savings accounts and mutual funds. She's only twenty-six, for God's sake. She can go back to school, not college necessarily. Seriously study photography. She's a marvelous instinctive photographer. Has she shown you any of her pictures?"

"No. I hardly know her."

"Well, she's damn good. I think the guy who did that to her did her a favor, in the long run."

Kate laid her hands flat on the arms of the chair. Her palms were wet and her mouth was dry. "A man pounded her into that condition with a piece of wood."

"He didn't kill her. I've been afraid one of her customers would kill her. Maggie's always claimed she could sort out the crazies from the kinkies." Barbara tipped her head toward the bedroom. "The guy who did that has been a regular customer for several years. So much for her instincts."

"What about the next prostitute he hires?"

"If the guy kills her, then he'll go to jail, or to a funny farm." Barbara yawned again. "Would you like some coffee? There's instant."

"Shouldn't Margaret be taking a lot of liquids for her fever?"

"She drank some ginger ale awhile ago. I hate to wake her up to force her to drink. When she's asleep she doesn't feel the pain as much."

Kate went into the bedroom. She removed a half-full glass of flat, lukewarm soda, dumped it in the kitchen sink, dropped in four ice cubes and poured in fresh ginger ale. She set the glass on the bedstand and pulled up a chair. After a few minutes a thin slit appeared in the swollen flesh around Margaret's eyes.

"It's Kate from downstairs. I brought Roberto back. Can you drink a little of this?" She held the glass to the puffed lips and

Margaret sipped, stopped and sipped again. "Good. Try again in a while, okay?"

"Been dreaming," Margaret said. She was able to speak a little better. "My grandmother. Thinking."

Kate held the glass to her lips again and Margaret drank thirstily. Some of the ginger ale dribbled from the corners of her mouth. Kate dabbed at it with a tissue. Margaret wanted more. She emptied the glass. Kate hurried to the kitchen for a refill. Barbara was asleep on the couch, her head nestled in the crumpled bathrobe. Roberto was lying on his side on the window ledge in the kitchen.

Margaret drank half the contents of the second glass.

"Gramma Rose. Seventy-three. Broke her hip. In bed in rest home. Hates it. Very expensive. Own room. Special food. Hates food there. I bring pizza, Big Macs, French fries. Nurses furious. Bad for her. Crap. More soda?"

Kate held the glass to her mouth and Margaret drank.

She lay still for about ten minutes.

"Boiled meat. No salt. No garlic. No onions. No wine. Nurses say live longer. Gramma Rose—rather die. Gobbles pizza before nurses smell oregano. Barbara gone?"

"No. She's asleep on the couch."

Margaret grunted.

"We're waiting for Connie."

"Barbara's husband like nurses. Panicked about chemicals. Paranoid. Poor little girl. Never pizza, bacon. Bean sprouts and bran. Got to pee."

Kate helped Margaret to the bathroom. Some of the bruises were turning slightly yellowish, but the swellings did not appear diminished.

Back in bed Margaret began to moan. Kate had seen a bottle of pills on the coffee table. Barbara was softly snoring. A sheet of paper beside the pill bottle was headed, ONE EVERY FOUR HOURS. Days and hours when pills had been administered had been noted in different inks and scripts. Under Thursday, Kate read, three AM, seven AM, eleven forty-five AM, two ten PM, six fifteen PM.

Kate washed the glass, filled it with ice and 7-Up because she could find no more ginger ale. She gave Margaret a pill, after noting down the time.

Margaret groaned and tossed about for fifteen or twenty minutes. At last she lay still and sighed.

Kate leaned close to Margaret and said softly, "Tell me about the man who hurt you."

"Worried about his hand," she said dreamily.

"Why was he worried about his hand?"

"Artist."

"He's an artist?"

"Fucking artist," she muttered.

"Is he a painter? A sculptor?" Kate leaned closer.

"Actor. Phony."

"He's an actor?"

"Phony. Always acting."

"What is his name?"

"John. Fucking john." She turned her face away.

Kate sighed and sat back. Margaret was breathing deeply and heavily.

Barbara answered the knock on the hall door.

Connie had arrived bearing two plastic shopping bags. "I got ginger ale, Tab, Diet Pepsi and cranberry juice. My arms are coming out of their sockets."

"Don't let the cat out," Barbara said.

"I also got cat food and litter for his box. Christ, I'm pooped. This stuff is heavy. Oh, hi. I'm Connie," the new woman said when Kate came into the living room. "How come two of you are here? Is Maggie worse?"

"Kate here came to return Roberto," Barbara said. "I'm Barbara."

"She drank the last of the ginger ale and a glass of Seven-Up," Kate said. "And I gave her a pill at ten thirty. I'll be going now."

As Kate stood under a cool shower she wondered if the man's name really was John or if Margaret now thought of all men as johns.

He was an artist? An actor? Or an artist who was always acting?

And he was worried about his hand. That was significant. Margaret had mentioned his hand before. He had first struck her with his hand, then he had used the driftwood. And Angie had said she would recognize his face. He was, presumably, famous for something.

Kate poured a glass of sherry, lit a Kent and looked across the room to the bricks around and above the black rectangle of the fireplace.

I think, Barbara said, the guy who did that to her did her a favor.

He didn't kill her, Barbara said.

He didn't kill her, did he? He didn't bite off her nipples, did he? the street whore said about Lou Ann.

No one will believe you, Kate. I know. You could prove nothing, Uncle Gordon said.

That's the way I am, Alex said.

Then he'll go to jail, Barbara said, or to a funny farm.

Lloyd Delling went to a funny farm. At this very moment he was in a funny farm. He heard, saw and thought nothing. According to Aunt Sarah he did not feel anything: neither pleasure nor pain; he experienced neither recollection nor anticipation nor the taste of salt on his tongue.

Kate poured more sherry. She did not understand what Margaret had been saying about her grandmother who craved salt and pizzas and garlic. Something about what Margaret said made her uneasy. She visualized a perky little old lady with darting and clear brown eyes, a wizened woman in a hospital bed who was attached to pulleys and electronic monitors, stealthily taking a great big bite from a slice of cold pizza with pepperoni and anchovies and green peppers and mushrooms and rings of onions. Stealthily and triumphantly.

Margaret's Gramma Rose, Kate thought, should not have to gobble her pizza-with-everything as if she were guilty of an offense against geriatric medicine, while Lloyd Delling swallowed Cream of Wheat with the same instinct and simplicity as a seven-week-old infant.

Kate played the last side of the Verdi Requiem twice. That helped.

The second time that she listened to the *Dies irae* she pictured Joseph Warburton lying on the little sharp stones in the culvert, not yet dead.

Now, he was certainly dead. Even the *Post* said he was dead. And his death had been an accident. She had not set out to kill anyone on Monday.

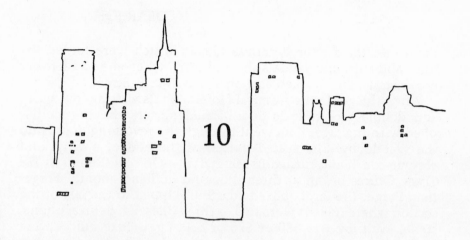

**10**

$K$ate locked herself into the end stall in the women's rest room at Macy's and fitted the brown wig over her head. She stooped to looked at herself in the mirror she had hung over the coat hook on the door. She applied the darker lipstick she had bought at a busy discount drugstore on Thirty-fourth Street, the sort of store where every aisle is monitored by a closed-circuit TV camera and a private security guard with a holstered gun eyes everyone entering and leaving.

She touched her fingertip to the lipstick and rubbed the color into her cheeks. That would have to do. There had been no attendant in the rest room. Kate checked her watch. Twenty minutes. All the women who had been in the outer room would be gone by now.

At the long mirror she carefully inspected herself. She had become simultaneously an efficient and indifferent woman who had been hired to get a job done. She was now a hardened woman in her early thirties who had stopped taking or giving bullshit to the boys when she was seventeen. The woman in the mirror, the woman in the madras wraparound skirt and peach-colored top and dark curly hair and vivid makeup, was one tough cookie.

Kate bought a *Times* and a *News* from a newsstand, stuffed them into the zippered canvas tote in which were folded the jeans and shirt and sandals she had worn when she had left her brownstone, and walked east on Thirty-fourth Street.

When she got to the Admiral Hotel with its waiting tour buses and double-parked taxis and harried porters shoving dollies piled with luggage, Kate went through the revolving doors into the vast lobby. She seated herself at the end of a vinyl and chrome couch and turned to Manhattan—Offices—Rental in *The Times*. Offices began at three thousand dollars a month. Forget that. Forget the large, boxed ads. She skipped to the last of the section where the ads were two or three lines. Lg. deluxe, phone, steno, avail. by wk. $80 or $70 or $60. Lg. deluxe offices were avail. from one end of Manhattan to the other. There were quite a few in Lower Manhattan, five in Greenwich Village, some on the Lower East Side, some above 110th on the East Side, many in the West Thirties and Forties. Lower Manhattan was too inconvenient, and anything above 110th was out of the question. She began to jot phone numbers and addresses on a pad of lined paper.

"I'll bet you're a businesswoman who's in business for herself," Kate heard a man saying.

The man had seated himself on the hard vinyl cushion next to hers. He was speaking to her in an out-of-town voice. She looked at his shoes, brand-new Spaulding white-on-white saddle shoes with red soles. From cuffs to knees she saw crisp, creased seersucker trousers.

She turned a few degrees away and rested *The Times* on the arm of the couch.

The man laid his arm over the back of the couch. Kate smelled a wave of scented deodorant. A finger grazed her shoulder.

Kate faced the man. "Please leave me alone," she said firmly.

"I've been hearing about a nice little Italian restaurant down in the Italian section," he said. "Some gangsters were machine-gunned in the place while they were eating spaghetti. How'd you like me to take you to lunch there?"

The man was broad-shouldered and double-chinned. He was at least forty-five, but his voice was the tight tenor of a nineteen-year-old. His eyes were clear and bright blue.

"Go away," Kate said.

"Come on now," he said. "I'm only here in New York City one more day."

"Then go and eat Italian food." She hunched farther away from him. She was resting her weight on her elbow and was almost doubled over toward the armrest.

"Miss," a new and deeper voice said, "are you registered here?"

Kate looked up. This man was wearing black trousers and a red uniform coat with silver buttons. "I am waiting for a friend and this man here"—she jerked her head toward the man whose seersucker-clad thigh was pressing against her—"is bothering me."

"Sir, are you registered here?"

"Yes, I am. I'm with the R.S.A. convention."

"Miss," the man with silver buttons said, "I'm afraid you'll have to wait for your friend somewhere else."

Kate crossed her arms over her peach-colored top. "I said this man who has shoved me up against the arm of your couch is bothering me. He is being obnoxious and I would like you to pry him away from me." She glared at the man beside her. She could see that the remainder of the sofa was empty; so presumably could the hotel's employee.

"Miss," the hotel's employee sighed, "come on. Nobody wants trouble. Come on."

"Look, I was sitting here looking at the paper when this registered guest of yours . . ."

The man in the red coat bent from the waist. "You look, honey. Get your ass out of here before I count to ten or I'll call Vice." He straightened.

"Are you implying that I am trying to proposition this yokel?"

"One, two, three . . ."

Kate jammed her *Times* and notebook in her tote, stood and hurried across the lobby toward the revolving door. On the sidewalk she groped in her purse for her sunglasses. Her hand was shaking as she strode to the corner.

Do not look back. Goddamn that horny saddle-shoed lummox.

She had been so incensed and then astonished by first Seersucker and then Red Coat, she had acted very, very stupidly. She should have said absolutely nothing. Not one word. She should have immediately left the lobby. But nothing like that had ever happened to her before.

Could a wig cause such a transformation? Could Red Coat tell she was wearing a cheap wig? Why didn't he ask the jerk to lay off? Why did he first ask her if she was registered?

She found a coffee shop farther on.

"Just coffee," she told the fat man behind the counter.

Kate removed the crumpled newspaper, smoothed and folded it lengthwise so that she could lay it on her portion of counter space. She wrote addresses and phone numbers and weekly rents on the lined paper. The counterman refilled her cup. She said, "Thank you." He grunted and turned away without adding a second cup to her tab.

She tucked away *The Times* and opened the *News*. The *News* carried only four potential ads that had not been in the *Times*.

The coffee was sixty cents. She left a dollar.

From a pay phone in the lobby of the Empire State Building she called the first number on her pad.

The woman who answered said, after Kate asked, "No, no, what're you crazy, sugar? They rent out those little boxes and make their money from the phone and whatever else you need. They won't let you put in your own phone. What'd be the point for them?"

The next eight women and men who took her calls were less patient than the first woman.

A man answered Kate's tenth number. "Come on over and I'll see what we have."

The address was on Forty-first between Fifth Avenue and Madison Avenue. One self-service elevator bore an Out of Order sign, a preprinted sign made of slick cardboard that was affixed to the chipped black door with masking tape. There were layers of Scotch tape and masking tape and even adhesive tape under the fresh masking tape. Terrific.

The other elevator carried her to the fourth floor. The hall was narrow and smelled of something stronger than Lysol. Her eyes stung. Under number 401 was a black plastic sign, Service Manager. Kate tried the door. It was locked. She rang the bell.

"Yeah? Yeah? Who's there?" the same raspy voice she had heard over the phone called from the other side of the door.

"Gwen Lester. I just called you about renting an office."

"Yeah. Yeah." He unlocked three locks and opened the door to a very heavy chain and peered at her. "Yeah." He shoved the door closed and opened it for her. "Come on in."

Kate was struck by a wall of old and new cheap cigar smoke. She walked through it into the room and seated herself on a straight chair in front of a heavy, old oak desk.

"The name is McGiveny. You're after an office?"

"Yes. I'm in town to take care of publicity for two groups from San Francisco. They'll finish their tours here in September and October. I don't need anything fancy. But I will need twenty-four-hour access."

"You came to the right place. You work by yourself?" He lit a chewed cigar stump.

"For now. By August we'll need, oh, a suite of four or five rooms. We can discuss that later."

"Okay. Yeah." He nodded. "Maybe I can help you there too."

Kate shrugged and looked around impatiently. Mr. McGiveny's square room contained the desk, two four-drawer file cabinets, an overstuffed chair by the window and an old-fashioned oak swivel chair with arms and a thick, foam rubber pad on the seat.

"I will have to have a private phone installed."

"We have phones in already. They come with the offices. You go through the switchboard."

"I've already told you I don't mind paying for the switchboard service. But I also want my own phone and my own number, and I want to be certain no one messes with it. I got stuck with a six-hundred-dollar call to London last month and I don't want that to happen again."

"Yeah, yeah. What about when you're not in? Ringing telephones at all hours drive people crazy."

"Mr. McGiveny, I will have an answering machine. I have more to do than sit in an office all day."

"Yeah. A machine. Okay. Then I'll show you what I've got. We lease the fourth and fifth floor and provide all the services for our tenants."

They rode the working elevator to the fifth floor. All the doors were closed. Kate heard a typewriter behind one, and a man arguing over the phone about a delivery of what sounded like "scissors" behind another. There were no sounds behind seven other doors.

McGiveny unlocked number 517.

The stifling room was a dark mustard color and faced several dirty windows in a building about fifteen feet away. Her office was just large enough for a metal desk painted army green and three chairs. Two phones lay on the desk.

"Tenant before you wanted the same arrangement with phones." He turned on the room air conditioner. "You get charged for electricity. You'll have to pay that in advance too. Rates are more in the summer because tenants use more electricity in the summer. Heat's free. Ha-ha."

"Why don't you let me sit here for a few minutes to see if I can stand it?"

"Yeah. Okay. I'll go back down. Slam the door shut when you leave."

Kate counted to three hundred, then closed the Medeco lock. She lowered and pulled closed the venetian blinds and turned on the overhead light.

The standard black phone with 517 in the center of the dial ring was dead and so was the Touch-Tone with a VE number. She followed their cords to the wall. The 517 phone was attached to a small box on the wall behind the desk. The box and an inch of the cord were covered by several layers of green and mustard-colored paint. The Touch-Tone was plugged into a jack in a new beige plastic plate just above the floor, two feet from the old, painted-over box.

Seated again in McGiveny's office, Kate said, "I've decided to take it."

"Where'd you say you were from? California? You people have to meditate in a room before you know whether you want it?"

"That is a very small room, Mr. McGiveny. What is it? Seven by ten?"

"Seven and a half by ten and a half. Okay. You want five seventeen. I'll have to have two weeks' rent; that's one twenty. I'll have to have thirty for mail and phone service. I'll have to have twenty for your electricity. And I'll have to have seventy-five for security. Okay." He slowly placed a very worn sheet of carbon paper between two pages of a receipt book and wrote numbers and words. "That comes to two fifty."

"Jesus!" Kate said.

McGiveny shrugged. "You're in midtown Manhattan. I'll tell you what, though. When you want that suite later on, I'll try to get you a very good deal."

"I hope the rooms are larger than five seventeen."

"What'd you say your name was again?" His ball-point pen was poised over the top section of the receipt.

"Gwen Lester. But make it out to D and M Services, 306 Chestnut Street, San Francisco 94115." She counted out two hundred and fifty dollars in twenties and tens.

"That's a lot of cash to carry around," he said as he flipped through the bills.

"The company I work for has found that time is saved by paying cash. I'll need a copy of that receipt. With paid in full on it."

"Yeah." He wrote paid in full and signed the receipt. "About your other phone. You'll have to see about that yourself. Locks have been changed already." He opened his desk drawer and removed a thick square of red plastic upon which was stamped 517. Two shiny new keys and one old key were attached to it. "Your switchboard service will be on in an hour or two. That other key is for the ladies' room."

"Thank you, Mr. McGiveny."

"Yeah. Okay. Stop by if you want anything."

Kate went back to office number 517 and tried the keys. They both worked. The "ladies' room" was around a corner and at the end of a hall. She unlocked that door and hurriedly closed it. She could hear and smell someone vomiting while someone else was saying, "Never, ever buy shit from Ben. Didn't I tell you never buy shit from Ben?"

The nearest office of New York Telephone was over seven blocks away. Fortunately there was a Citibank branch with a machine on the way.

Kate explained to the clerk at New York Telephone that she had just returned from four years in England and Sweden and therefore could not provide a current credit rating or credit cards or a previous phone number as references. Yes, she certainly did understand that New York Telephone would require a deposit in addition to the installation fee and the monthly base rate. She counted out more twenties and asked for a receipt.

The phone would be installed between 8:00 A.M. and 5:00 P.M. on Monday. He could not give her a more exact time.

Kate signed the form, using her own pen. She wrote Gwen Lester on the applicant's line by resting only the flesh above her wrist on the counter. That served the purpose of distorting her handwriting and leaving no fingerprints on New York Telephone's papers.

She walked over to the library on Fifth Avenue and bought a hot dog with sauerkraut, onions and mustard and a can of root beer from a vendor. She sat on a bench with three old men and a shopping bag lady. The men, who sat in the center, spoke with each other in a language Kate did not recognize. The shopping bag lady, who sat on the opposite end from Kate, spoke words Kate did not understand either. She addressed them to objects she removed and then shoved back into her two crammed, quadruple-layered shopping bags. Her voice held no inflection; it sounded like an electronic voice synthesizer that had been misprogrammed. The woman's ankles and feet were filthy and distended. She wore large, unzipped and battered rubber galoshes. Kate glanced at her face; she could not tell the woman's age. Her hair, though, was only lightly streaked with gray.

The men who talked in what was probably a Slavic language were in their late seventies or early eighties. Their clean white shirts were buttoned to the neck, although they did not wear ties. Their plain black shoes were polished. They acted as if the shopping bag lady did not exist. Yet, when Kate had sat down, the man beside her had glanced at her, nodded and smiled and moved an inch closer to his companion to give her room. Crazy was crazy, in Czechoslovakia or on Fifth Avenue.

When Kate finished her hot dog and root beer and smoked a cigarette, she dropped her rubbish in a can and walked seven or eight steps toward the sidewalk before she stopped, turned and went back to the bench. She did not know why she did what she did. She stood before the shopping bag lady and said quietly, "What is your name?"

The woman did not look up. She lifted an empty yellow Kodak film carton from a bag and spoke to it.

"What is your name?" Kate asked a little louder.

All three old men stopped talking and were staring up at her. The center man vigorously shook his head at Kate. The one she had been sitting beside made the universal gesture with his finger circling the air around his ear.

"She no have a name," the center man whispered.

The woman continued to talk to the little yellow box in her grimy, leathery hands.

"Everyone has a name," Kate said hoarsely, because her throat had become very tight.

She hurried away. She was frightened. She did not know why she had spoken to the shopping bag lady or why tears were sliding onto the lower rims of her sunglasses. She was not sad, not at all. She was angry and confused. Not because of the three old men; because of the mystery of that woman. No one would ever know who she was or where she came from or why she had gone mad. No one would ever know how or why she managed to remain alive. At some time she had been someone with a name and a history. Then at some moment she had stopped being that person and had become a genus. Lost, without coherence or volition.

Her peach-colored top was now wet with sweat. Kate slowed. She was only a block and a half from her savings bank. The woman with longish brown hair she saw reflected in the oblique plate-glass window was visibly agitated. She had forgotten all about the wig and the extra makeup.

Christ, she had gotten so upset about a babbling old lunatic she'd almost gone into a place where at least three people knew her by name.

The lines in the McDonald's were long, but only three teen-aged girls were in the rest room anteroom. Kate closed herself in one of the four stalls and rapidly removed the wig. She had trouble with the sodden top, but none with the skirt. She pulled on her jeans and buttoned her cotton blouse. Seated on the toilet looking at her face in the mirror on her lap, Kate rubbed as much color as she could from her cheeks and lips.

"Hello, Miss Delling. How are you today?"

She smiled at the tall blond man whose nameplate proclaimed that he was Vardell Trockij. She had never known how to pronounce his last name and could not bring herself to call him Vardell. So she said what she always did, "Hello," and shoved her savings book and a withdrawl slip across the marble counter. Today it was a withdrawal slip; usually she handed over her book and a check and a deposit slip.

"And how would you like the thousand, Miss Delling?"

"A cashier's check made out to me."

Vardell Trockij rapidly tapped numbers in his computer terminal and watched greenish figures array themselves on his screen. "This will only take a few minutes, Miss Delling."

Ten minutes later Kate had her cashier's check and her savings book in her purse and was headed for the Citibank branch where she kept her checking account. She was only four blocks from Federated Computer Systems.

The lines were long at her Citibank branch and the tellers there did not know her by name. This was a Friday and busy.

"Will you please see that this money is credited to my account as a cashier's check?" Kate asked the teller.

"Um-hum." The woman did not look up. This woman, whose little plastic nameplate stated she was Stella Arlita, never looked up.

Kate did not know about the young man at New York Telephone; she had never dealt with him before. She had dealt with this teller, though, and she had never once seen her eyes.

Stella Arlita was in her late thirties, Kate guessed; older than the other tellers. Her curly black hair was beginning to gray and she was a stout woman who wore a loose, unbelted dress and flat, laced shoes. Always before, Kate had ground her teeth when the next available teller was this hunched-over, olive-skinned woman. She was so damn plodding and leaden.

"Will you please have this cashier's check verified by someone who can confirm it?" Kate said. "It's the same as a cash deposit."

"Um. Just a minute," Stella Arlita said and slowly, very slowly, wended her way through metal desks.

Kate watched her stand about two feet from the desk of one of the assistant managers, Jane Conklin, with Kate's deposit slip and cashier's check in her hand.

Jane Conklin was a slim, brisk woman with whom Kate had occasionally needed to do business. Jane Conklin was at least ten years younger than Stella Arlita. While Stella Arlita stood beside her desk, Jane Conklin spoke on the phone and smoked a cigarette wrapped in brown paper. As she was hanging up, the nervous man who was in charge of the safe-deposit boxes walked up and placed some papers in front of Jane Conklin. She bent over them, scanned and scribbled something on the lower-right-hand corner of all eleven pages. Stella Arlita stood. Jane Conklin's phone rang. She signed the last page as she picked up her ringing phone with her left hand. She lit another brown cigarette. Stella Arlita did not move. The assistant manager named Al Torres pushed a form in front of Jane Conklin who read it as she listened and spoke on the phone. She signed Al Torres' form and he walked off with it to his own desk where an elderly man and woman were seated. Stella Arlita stood.

Customers at the windows of other tellers came and went as the next available teller became available.

Kate glared at the indurate form of Stella Arlita. Her fellow employees acted as if she had, in fact, petrified. Kate drummed her fingers on the counter. Jane Conklin laughed at something she heard over her phone and hung up. Stella Arlita did not move. Finally, Jane Conklin looked up and spoke to Stella Arlita who took one step forward, extended Kate's check and deposit slip. Jane Conklin scanned them and raised her eyebrows questioningly. Stella Arlita turned and pointed toward Kate. Jane Conklin rolled her eyes and led Stella Arlita back to her teller's window.

"What is the problem, Miss Delling?" Jane Conklin asked crisply.

Kate took a deep breath. She was about to tell the assistant manager that she had been standing at that goddamn window for exactly seventeen minutes on a busy Friday afternoon and what in the hell kind of incompetents did this bank employ, when she saw Stella Arlita's face for the first time. Stella Arlita's eyes were visible for no more than two seconds.

"No problem, really," Kate said. "I simply wanted to be certain this deposit will be immediately credited to my account as cash."

"Mrs. Arlita can see to that for you. We treat a valid cashier's check, which I'm certain this is, as a cash deposit."

"Thank you."

Kate dodged through the shuffling patrons in the bank's lobby.

*Mrs.* Mrs. Stella Arlita.

Mrs. Stella Arlita's eyes and mouth had held two quite patent feelings—rage and defeat. Nothing else. No wonder she never looked at a patron.

Kate squeezed aboard a crowded M1 heading down Park Avenue South.

Clutching her zippered tote, hanging onto an overhead strap and staring at the heavy black graffiti on the tinted upper bus

window, she wondered if she had imagined or misinterpreted
the expression on Mrs. Arlita's face. She had never paid close
attention to the woman before. Maybe she was still trying to
understand the enigma of the shopping bag lady: had she been
looking for a shopping bag lady candidate who still possessed a
name? Someone who was being crushed by a fury that could be
neither borne nor expressed, until—poof. A curtain descends and
there are no more people, no more pain, no more feeling. Only
old newspapers and little yellow boxes. No more impatient customers and arrogant supervisors and God alone knew what Mr.
Arlita was like. Perhaps there were even little Arlitas. Perhaps
one of the little Arlitas would become a Lou Ann. Perhaps Lou
Ann would become a shopping bag lady.

The slashes of graffiti began to undulate.

Kate shut her eyes and whipped her head hard to her right.
She was terrified that those lines and curves would modulate
into a figure and a face, something intolerable having to do with
Stella Arlita and the shopping bag lady and Lou Ann and Margaret and Anne.

"Out," she called. "Getting off."

Kate muscled her way to the front door, paying no attention to
the mutters and exclamations.

She found herself on Broome Street and Broadway. That was
okay. Canal Street was not much farther downtown. Three or
four blocks.

Kate set the tote down on the sidewalk so that she could flex
her hand. As she opened and closed her left hand to ease the
cramp, she bit down on her lip.

For a while there she had forgotten and had fallen back into
that old strangling feeling where her hands became shrunken
and useless and pale.

She picked up her tote and walked around the two men who
were lying next to each other, flat on their backs, out cold,
mouths wide open.

Cousin Larry's Discount Office Machines on Canal Street was a
long narrow store containing a confusion of typewriters, calcula-
tors, copiers, cash registers, dictating machines, answering
machines and very loud voices. Kate found a section two-thirds
of the way back where telephone answering machines were
stored on shallow shelves against the wall. An aisle and a glass-
topped counter separated her from the machines and their little
red price tags.

A salesman was demonstrating professionally produced messages to a man who wore dirty Levis, a faded work shirt and new Frye boots. As Kate squinted and tried to read the red price tags, the salesman played twenty-second samples on a machine.

Boris Karloff's voice, with an echo, saying, "Unfortunately you have reached the correct number. . . ."

A giggling woman backed by wild party sounds.

A twangy Down Easter uttering a lot of "yups."

"You need help?" A short, burly man with pale green eyes planted himself in front of her.

"Yes. I want an inexpensive telephone answering machine."

"Business or personal?"

"Hello there, sweetie," a husky female voice purred from the demonstration recording a foot from Kate's elbow.

"Personal," she snapped. "I'm missing many calls because I work irregular hours and must be out of town frequently." Goddamn, she shouldn't be acting defensive.

"How much do you want to pay?" He was not interested in her attitude.

"Do you have anything under a hundred?"

He pulled a machine from the shelf behind him. "Here's a very good used Message-Mate on sale for sixty-seven seventy-seven. What kind of wall connection do you have?"

"A, ah, one of those plug-in jacks."

"We'll throw in a converter. No charge. You'll have to notify the phone company, of course."

"I will?"

"Sure, you have to tell the phone company." He gave her a quick wink. "City, state, federal and intergalactic regulations."

He explained how the machine operated. It was quite simple. You pushed the Record lever and spoke your five- to twenty-second message into a microphone built into the front of the machine. You pressed a lever to receive your messages, and another lever to replay them. A dial indicated the number of calls you had received. There was a thirty-second duration on the tape for every call. If the caller hung up without leaving a message, you could either listen to thirty-plus seconds of previous messages or press the Fast Forward lever to the next call. You could replay a message as often as you wanted. You could rerecord your own message as often as you wanted by pressing the Record lever. A new message obliterated the old one.

When the salesman asked Kate to try out the machine, she said,

"I've heard your normal voice. I'd rather hear how you sound on the tape. That would be a better illustration."

The salesman pressed the Record lever and said, "This is Cousin Larry's speaking for a nice lady who's about to buy a bargain Message-Mate for sixty-seven seventy-seven. Plus tax." He pressed Playback and pursed his lips as he listened. "Not bad. I should be on the radio. On one of those dramatic programs they're bringing back."

"But how do you, or how does that, sound over the phone?"

"Depends on New York Telephone and your connection. You know, like a regular voice on the phone. You can back yourself up with a barking dog. Some people are doing that now. All you have to do is find a cooperative Great Dane. You can have music. You can have children fighting. Little kids. A burglar giving your number a test figures—little kids—a baby-sitter. Forget that apartment. I'll put in a new tape for you."

"How does the converter work?"

He opened a drawer and drew forth a three-inch cube. "You plug this"—he pointed to a plastic-sheathed projection—"into your wall jack. Then you plug your phone cord into this opening here, the one marked Phone. You plug your machine into the one on the right. Where it says Machine."

"And that's all?" She had assumed all of this would be much more complicated, especially the installation.

"That's all. I'll give you a three-month warranty. Parts and labor. If you buy a new machine we give a two-year warranty."

"Three months. Fine. I'll take this one."

The salesman produced a large, square, triplicate receipt form. "I need your name for the warranty."

She was not prepared for this. How stupid. "Rose," she said. No disguise for this as she had planned. And now he wanted her name!

"Is that first or last?"

"Pardon?"

"Is Rose your first or last name?" He was eyeing a beautiful and imposing black woman in tight suede pants who was trying out a calculator with motions so fast her hand was a blur.

"Last. Helena Rose. Three eight one East Eighty-eighth Street. N.Y.C."

"Phone?"

"It's unlisted."

"Okay. I'll go ring this up, then."

Kate paid cash.

The machine weighed over five pounds. Three blocks from the store it felt like a hunk of solid cement.

She took a cab home. Seven fifty.

Her apartment was very hot and stuffy and she was very tired. After Kate opened every window, she thought, if both Roberto and Phyllis have the energy to make it through the bars they can just spend the night. And, if the repairman couldn't fix the air conditioner, she would damn well have him put in a new one and send the bill to AVCO, Inc., the company that had knocked out walls and converted the brownstone from what had probably been a flophouse twenty years ago. Before Lincoln Center.

The answering machine in its heavy-duty plastic shopping bag could go on the floor of the little hall closet. She took the madras skirt and peach-colored top from her tote bag, shook out and hung up the skirt and dropped the top in her laundry basket. The wig went back in its box. Kate placed the receipts from McGiveny and Cousin Larry's in an unmarked envelope. She slipped her savings account book in Denis de Rougemont's *The Idea of Europe*.

As of nine twenty Friday night, the only real hazard lay in the Hush Puppies box. It was at the back of the top shelf. Everything else could be explained any way she liked.

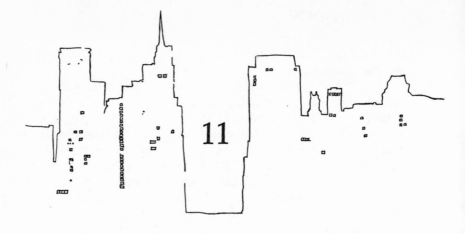

# 11

The repairman from Fuller's rang Kate's lobby buzzer at 7:12 A.M. When she looked at the clock beside her bed she assumed, Oh, hell, one of Margaret Elias's friends.

"Isn't this a little early?" she asked the man whose name was Joe, according to the oval patch over his shirt pocket.

"You want me to look at your air conditioner or not? You're first on my schedule."

"Yes. All right." She let him in.

He paid no attention to her robe and bare feet. "You better believe—all right." Joe clomped directly to the air conditioner. "You tell me it's not all right, I go to the next party on my list." He unsnapped the plastic grid, exposing the machine itself. "You want to sweat, sweat. No shit to me, you know?" He plugged in the heavy cord, then twisted all of the knobs. "Mother's dead." He knelt and unscrewed a panel. "It's Saturday, you know? You should hear my wife. How come I have to work on Saturdays? I tell her, I don't work on Saturday, you don't go to that fairy that fools with your hair on Tuesdays. Know what I mean?" Joe pushed needle-nosed pliers through an opening.

Kate yawned. "Do you think you can fix it?"

Joe continued to probe with the pliers. "Christ, lady, I don't know what's wrong with it. Jesus Christ. Three minutes, I'm

156

supposed to know?" He unplugged the cord and unscrewed another small plate. "This fairy my wife goes to on Tuesdays? Fruit's name is Leo. How's that for a fag name? Leo. Like in Leo the Lion." He reached into his toolbox for a Phillips screwdriver.

"Will you excuse me? I'm going to get dressed." She felt disoriented.

"So get dressed." He pulled the heavy machine from its wall sleeve.

Kate closed her bedroom door and hurriedly put on the jeans and shirt she had tossed over a chair the night before.

Joe was bent over the top of her air conditioner, absorbed.

"Would you like a cup of coffee?"

"Why not? I take it black and no sugar."

Kate filled her teakettle and set it on the stove. She was not yet fully awake.

"This Leo, the fairy?" Joe said as he worked. "That's all my wife talks about. Leo says to see a movie, we have to see the movie. Leo says, read some book, my wife goes out and buys a book. She never read a book before Leo. Damn thing's frozen." He grimaced as he tried to turn something with his pliers.

Kate spooned instant coffee into two mugs and poured boiling water into them. She set Joe's mug beside his toolbox on the floor.

"Thanks. This Leo is my wife's best friend, the way she talks about him all the time. Know what I mean? Her girlfriends, with them she does the kids and what's on sale at Alexander's. With Leo, she does world affairs and Channel Thirteen and psychology. How about that? Psychology with a fruit?" Joe hunched over the air conditioner, turning his pliers back and forth. "She's really gotten confused because of Leo. You a women's libber?"

Kate was hungry, her stomach gurgled. "I think women are not and have not been treated fairly."

"You employed?" He sat back on his thick haunches and glared at the machine.

"Yes."

"What do you think about being a Ms.?"

"I haven't thought about it much."

"My wife wants to be called Ms. all of a sudden. At thirty-two, with three kids and a husband. You know where she got this? Not from her old girlfriends. Not them. She's getting this from

Leo the pansy, that's where she's getting it. What I can't figure is what Leo's getting out of all this, unless it's a conspiracy. You know, to tear down the whole society." He plugged in the machine and turned a knob. The air conditioner came to life. "I've seen this guy. He wears tight, I mean tight, pants with no pockets. He's got a rear end like a girl." He replaced the plates, screwed in the screws and pushed the air conditioner back into the wall sleeve. "So I don't know what she wants anymore. Your fan bolt was locked with corrosion. Machine has an automatic shutoff so it can't burn out." He snapped on the plastic grid, put away his tools and stood. "Okay if I use your desk here?" He sat at her desk and rapidly scribbled on his service form. "Comes to fifty-two twenty. Time and a half for a Saturday job. I only charged you the minimum." He tore off Kate's copy.

As she wrote a check he said, "My wife was better off before that beauty shop hired Leo. Before, she wasn't always asking questions about everything all the time. Know what I mean?"

"Thank you for repairing my air conditioner." Kate handed him the check.

"Should work okay the rest of the summer. Machine's almost new. I mean, I lay her every single day. I mean, every day. Some men won't do that. Now she wants to talk instead. I don't know what she needs to talk so much for, I'm not interested in what she's saying."

Kate locked the door after Joe and made herself another cup of coffee. It was five after eight. She couldn't go back to sleep. She had assumed she would have to wait all day for the repairman. She hoped the man from New York Telephone would arrive at eight on Monday morning.

So Joe's wife had found a friend? She wondered if Joe told everyone with malfunctioning air conditioners about his wife and Leo. She was relieved that he was able to repair her machine as rapidly as he did. God only knew what would follow after telling a stranger he screwed his wife even when she was having her period, and wasn't he a swell fellow?

She decided to go to the restaurant at Seventy-second and Columbus for breakfast. Bacon and eggs, home fries and a large glass of fresh orange juice. She did not eat both pieces of toast; she wondered how many people ate both pieces of toast in that neighborhood of weight-conscious youngish men and women.

Back in her apartment she washed underwear in the bathroom

basin, made her bed and vacuumed all the floors. It was only ten forty-five.

She went over her ad again, in her head: The Rainbow, Discreet, Accomplished, Fastidious, Minimum Fee $175, Only by Appointment.

There was still the phone number. There was still the name.

Grace? No, too passive.

Judith? Too imperious.

Victoria? Too obvious.

Alice? An ambiguous name.

Jean? No, Jeanne. That felt right. Just, Jeanne.

Now it was eleven fifteen.

In the middle of the day on a sunny Saturday, Central Park would be as safe as it could be. What she wanted to do was walk, not run or jog, walk for miles on curving paths under trees. If she walked for several hours she would be tired in a good way, as she had been when she was a child. Worn out from hiking on trails covered by pine needles in the San Bernardino Mountains. She had seen chipmunks and crested jays and western tanagers and squirrels and, sometimes, deer. She had gone so far from the lake that the sound of powerboats could no longer be heard. Then she had eaten dinner and taken a bath and fallen asleep without hearing Lloyd's voice explaining why some sculptor was excellent or incompetent, or Anne stumbling along the hall or knocking over her glass.

Kate got down the Hush Puppies box and unwrapped the gun.

She carried only her canvas bag with the shoulder strap. She wore sunglasses and a straw hat.

Men and women were running along all the paths, mainly young men were zipping along on bicycles, many teenagers and children were roller skating in shoe skates with large yellow and red wheels. Couples lay on the grass talking or reading or making love. People sat on benches reading, staring, smoking dope, drinking beer and wine.

Kate saw squirrels and pigeons. The trees were green, the shrubs and grass were green. The noise of traffic on Central Park West and Fifth Avenue was muffled. She walked for an hour and a half before she began to slow.

"Hey, you look tired out, lady."

Kate looked up. A boy of about fourteen or fifteen was pushing a ten-speed bike along the path with her. Two half-full shopping bags hung from the handlebars. "Not really." She continued walking.

"If you had a bicycle like this you'd get very good exercise."

"I like to walk." The kid was too encumbered with his bike and shopping bags to pose a serious threat.

"How about a watch that is accurate to the millisecond?"

"I have a watch."

"What about an AM-FM radio?"

"No thanks."

"A genuine fourteen-carat-gold Dunhill lighter for thirty bucks?"

"You're kidding." Kate stopped and smiled at this freckled boy whose brown hair fell over his forehead like one of Mark Twain's characters. He even had a cowlick.

"No bull." He reached into one of his bags, drew out a Dunhill case and opened it. Nestled in the velvet was either a new gold Dunhill lighter or an incredibly good imitation.

"Very impressive."

"You don't want it?"

"Afraid not."

"Shit." He looked first in one bag and then in the other. "Guess I'll have to replenish. You want to give me an order for anything?"

"Such as?"

"You just tell me, and it'll fall off a truck. Camera, jewelry, a programmable pocket calculator. Anything I can carry. All you have to do is name it."

Kate hesitated. The boy in the light blue cords and striped blue-and-green rugby shirt and beige suede Adidas looked as if he could qualify for a TV hot breakfast cereal commercial.

"I need some protection," she said.

"Yeah," he nodded seriously. "I see. My best friend's in jail for dealing coke to a friend of his who turned out to be a cop."

"Just thought I'd ask. Thanks, anyway." She certainly understood his caution. He didn't know who she was, and she didn't know who he was. The entire exercise was dumb. "Good luck with that lighter." She walked toward a broader path thirty feet ahead.

"Hold it, lady. Don't be too cool. Are you serious?"

"Yes."

"That'll cost you."

"How much?"

"What did you have in mind, protection-wise?"

"A thirty-eight. Not one with a long barrel."

"Shit, lady, you don't want much!"

"Forget it, then."

"No, no. I've got to go to my warehouse and see what's there. I'll be back in, oh, forty-five minutes." He consulted what appeared to be an authentic Rolex. "Make it an hour. I'll meet you over there by that big rock." He pointed to a large, rounded black outcropping. "This'll cost you a hundred. Can you get a hundred in an hour?"

Kate said, "Yes."

The boy rode off on his bike, shopping bags swinging.

She was on a path between West Drive and Central Park West near the Museum of Natural History. Kate left the park at Seventy-seventh, crossed the avenue and hurried to her apartment.

There was one hundred and forty-two dollars in the wallet in her purse.

She had to think this through. She turned on the air conditioner and sat at her desk.

If the kid had a .38 in what he called his warehouse, how could she tell whether or not it worked? An American-made .38 in good condition sold for at least double one hundred dollars cash. Then there was the question of .38 cartridges. She had not asked about them.

Kate lit a second cigarette from her first.

That was the first problem.

Second, there was the kid himself. The fact that he looked like a transplanted Penrod meant little; he was offering hot items to strangers in the park. Or perhaps he wasn't. Perhaps he was connected in some way with the New York Police Department. Maybe they hired kids to entrap people. Maybe he was working for the police in a kind of work-release program for juvenile offenders.

Third, there was the question of one hundred dollars cash. It was now two thirty-five. He hadn't asked her to meet him after dark, although the rock he told her to meet him beside was surrounded by trees and shrubs on three sides. Cute. A woman alone in Central Park carrying one hundred dollars cash. The kid did not know she was carrying a .32 in her canvas bag.

Kate thought about the .32, one hundred dollars and more for cartridges, if he had any, and her own safety.

She would have to leave the .32 at home.

The kid could mug her and steal the cash. The kid could be connected with the police, in which case she would be arrested for buying stolen property or for illegal possession of a firearm. That was the worst. A good lawyer could get her off. "Your Honor, this is obviously either entrapment or gross stupidity. Why would a woman like Miss Delling want or need a stolen gun?" If the .32 were zipped in its compartment, the police would be very interested. Very.

Fourth, was the acquisition of a .38 worth the risk? If Jack Barclay of Barclay Bros. was to be believed, yes, it most definitely was. Joseph Warburton had died quickly from two bullets. Barclay said she was lucky. Warburton may very well have been luck. The more she controlled the odds, the better. Simple logic dictated that the fewer bullets and the more effective the bullets, the better.

Kate wrapped the .32 Alex had given her among the raw white boulders in a gully outside Tucson, Arizona, put the gun away in the Hush Puppies box, and walked back to the far older and smoother black rock in Central Park.

She sat down on a bench about fifteen yards from the foot of the black outcropping. Men, women and children ran, bicycled and roller-skated along the path beside which she sat alone under a tall tree with lacy leaves.

The time for the boy's appointment came and went. Kate had not considered the possibility that he would fail to show up at all. She was no longer apprehensive, she was growing angry.

After her trip to Albany, she had persuaded herself that she had no choice but to use the .32, even with its disadvantages.

When the boy did not show up after almost an hour, Kate stood and walked south on the path.

"Hey, lady." The boy pedaled up beside Kate, grinning, a new Gristede's bag hung from his handlebar. "Sorry, I had to check around to see whether you were by yourself. Walk over to that path there." He tipped his head to the left.

Kate saw a path in deep shadow, almost a cave of overhanging branches. "No. I'm not going in there." She looked around. Across a stretch of grass was a stand of trees, enough protection for both of them if they were both being aboveboard. If one could consider a hot-goods dealer and a prospective hot-goods buyer virtuous. "I'll only talk with you in those trees. Or nowhere."

He glanced over at the trees. "No."

"All right. How about right over there on the grass?"

"Okay. But over near the bushes."

The grass grew up into a V that was edged by dense and entangled shrubs. They settled on the grass, about twenty feet from the nearest shrub.

"Shit. I've been all over town for you." He made a sort of triangle for them—the shrubs on two sides and his bike on the third. Without exposing it, he showed her a large, squarish gun. "This one's a Smith and Wesson automatic. It's a nine millimeter with an eight-shot magazine and hammer-release safety. Also, it's a nice short-coil double action with a slide lock on the last shot." He sounded as if he'd grown up in Jack Barclay's store.

"I'm sorry, I didn't tell you that I don't want an automatic. I've been told that unless you're experienced with their care they can present problems."

"True."

They sat beside each other on the grass, Indian fashion.

"That was all you were able to locate?"

"Oh, no," he said. "I have a twenty-two, a thirty-eight and a forty-five. All revolvers. The forty-five is a real cannon." He held open the mouth of his Gristede's bag.

Kate saw three more cloth-wrapped bundles. The automatic had looked to be in as good condition as the new guns under glass at Barclay Bros.

"Let me see the thirty-eight."

He reached inside the plastic, fumbled for a moment and brought a gun almost to the mouth of the bag so she could see it. "This is a thirty-eight S and W with a two-inch barrel. A model fifteen. Double action."

She leaned over so she could better see the gun. "How do I know this isn't junk from Guatemala?"

"I told you it was a Smith and Wesson. Says right on the gun—Smith and Wesson and the serial number."

"All right. I'll take it." She said it as if she had been debating between several pork loins at the butchers. "Do you have ammunition for the thirty-eight?"

"All I have for the thirty-eight revolver is a box of fifty specials. That will cost you twenty bucks more if you want them."

"What are specials?"

"They're express load hollow points."

"Are they like Schiller Safety Slugs?"

"I've never heard of them."

"Then why are your cartridges called specials?"

"Because they aren't conventional round-nosed bullets. They travel faster and expand when they hit someone. They're tough fuckers."

"Are they American-made?"

"You better believe."

"I suppose I'd better."

"The thirty-eight is new. Factory fresh." He rewrapped it, but held the bundle inside the shopping bag. "That will be one twenty."

"How are we going to do this?" Kate looked to the boy for an acceptable order of exchange.

"Will you show me your bills? Just hold them in your bag so I can see them. I'll kind of bend over and slide the gun and cartridges into your bag. Then you make a roll of your bills and lay your hand on the grass. I'll lean back and pick them up. Okay?"

"Okay."

Kate did as he suggested. In half a minute, she had the gun and box of cartridges and he had her one hundred and twenty dollars.

The boy stretched out his legs. "Be careful with that."

"Oh, I will." Kate was on her knees now.

"You know how to use a revolver?"

"Yes."

"Women are getting really paranoid in the city these days," the boy said. "I've sold seven guns to women in the last two months."

"What do you do when you aren't selling guns and Dunhill lighters?"

He screwed up his face. "Go to school."

"Must be a terrible school." Kate offered him a cigarette.

He shook his head. "My father smelled smoke on me he'd puke purple."

Kate lit hers. "Really?"

"Yeah. He's an M.D. and dedicated." The boy stood, wriggled his shoulders and threw his leg over his bike. "Well, be careful with that." He slowly, gracefully, glided down the gentle slope and disappeared around the shrubs.

Kate watched him from behind her sunglasses.

She waited five minutes before she got up and walked back toward her apartment.

On Central Park West, between Seventy-sixth and Seventy-fifth, she saw Art's friend Vanessa with a dachshund and a schnauzer.

Kate was on the building side of the street, Vanessa on the park side. Vanessa was immediately successful with the dachshund. The schnauzer required petting and four tries before he was able to lower his rear over the paper towel the girl laid on the cobblestones for him.

The hot-gun kid said his father was a doctor. According to Art, Vanessa lived in an East Side town house of her own. Were these attractive, enterprising children bored? Were they trying to prove something? To whom?

Not much made sense to children. Not while they were children.

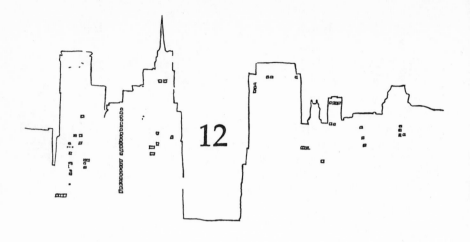

12

Only one customer was ahead of Kate when she arrived at the Avis agency at 7:00 A.M. Sunday. Only one clerk was on duty. The customer, a six-five black man, was demanding the Opel he had evidently ordered several weeks before. The clerk was telling him the Opel had been rented to someone else by mistake.

Kate suspected the argument had been going on for some time. About ten cork-tipped cigarette butts lay on the floor by the man's huge right shoe. He was smoking a cork-tipped cigarette. His matched leather luggage rested beside his left foot.

The black clerk, wearing a name tag that read Cleon, said, "I'll try Queens again." He used a phone at the rear of the employees' enclosure. He returned to the counter and the thick, robbery-proof Plexiglas. "Theirs just came in. They can have it ready in half an hour, forty-five minutes."

"How long before they can have it here?"

"You won't like this. You have to go out to Bayside and pick it up. Office there can't spare a driver."

The tall man rose on the balls of his feet. Kate could see his flexed muscles through his tight body shirt. He slowly lowered himself. "Am I supposed to pay the taxi fare to Bayside?"

"I'll request an adjustment on your bill."

166

"Do that. Just where in Bayside is number two?"

The clerk wrote the address on a card and slid it under the Plexiglas. "Your car will be clean and filled up and checked over, sir."

The customer picked up his luggage. "Um-hum."

"Look, man. The night manager made the mistake, not me."

"Um-hum." He carried the two large bags out to the street as if they were empty wicker baskets.

"Help you?" Cleon asked Kate. "Name, please."

"I don't have a car reserved."

"Miss, this is a Sunday."

"I'll take whatever you have. I will only be using it today."

He shook his head. "I'll see if they have anything." He went back to the rear phone and pushed two buttons. "We have a Chevette and that's all. You're lucky there's anything on a Sunday morning in the summer. Next time be sure you make a reservation."

Kate handed over her driver's license and American Express card. Cleon rattled off the various charges so fast Kate could not follow him. Yes, she wanted insurance.

He rolled a form into a big typewriter, punched keys, then stepped back and blew his nose while the machine speedily filled in the spaces.

Kate initialed the insurance coverage line and signed her name next to the red X.

Her brown Chevette descended to street level on a heavy-duty elevator.

She drove north on the Henry Hudson Parkway to the George Washington Bridge and crossed the river to New Jersey. She was not at all clear about where she was going. Somewhere north and west.

Twice she had been invited by Miriam to spend weekends at what Miriam called Graun's Snuggery in the Poconos. Jake and Miriam owned, together with Jake's two brothers and their wives, a cottage on the shore of a small lake with an unpronounceable Indian name.

By a complicated and agreed-upon arrangement, the three families took turns using the cottage. Duration of stay had to do with seasons and holidays, according to Miriam. One week during August equaled two weeks in November, for example. Or Labor Day weekend was equivalent to two weeks in April.

Kate had been a weekend guest in a July and in an April, when
Miriam and Jake had possession for two-week stretches. She had
needed to rent a car, as the nearest bus stop to Lake Mitchanina-
bai was thirty miles away. For that she had gotten a New York
driver's license. She had been fine as long as she had stayed on
Interstate 80. Once off 80, she had become lost—both coming and
going, both times.

Kate remembered the long stretches of narrow roads in northwestern New Jersey and northeastern Pennsylvania. Miles
between dwellings, only an occasional muddy pickup or heavy
sedan, pastures, dense forests. Vast dense stands of woods, and
old abandonded barns.

She turned off 80 at the Stanhope-Netcong sign. There had
been light traffic on the highway and there were few cars on the
two-lane road bearing north. She drove slowly now, looking for
an acceptable site.

This trip to the country, she had finally decided late Saturday
night, was the only choice she had.

The one-hundred-dollar .38 revolver either was a new Smith
and Wesson or else someone had gone to incredible trouble to
produce a counterfeit. The twenty-dollar cartridges in the green-
and-yellow box were made in Bridgeport, Connecticut.

Just about the only honest information Alex had given her was
that she would hate living in Tucson, Arizona, and how to shoot
a pistol. Therefore, she knew a .32 with conventional bullets was
going to feel and sound and recoil differently from a .38 with
cartridges of a higher velocity. She could spare from ten to
fifteen cartridges for practice.

What she was searching for was an abandoned barn that was a
mile or more from any habitation.

She passed plenty of barns—new, old and still in use, and old
and collapsing. But in every instance they were close by a house
that showed signs of life or a closed-for-Sunday farm machinery
repair yard or a short walk from a mini-shopping center with an
A & P and drug, hardware and sporting goods stores.

The odometer indicated she had driven eighty-two miles. Her
watch read ten twenty-five. Time to try the one-lane roads. She
turned onto Crane Creek Road and passed through woods that
came to within three or four feet of the paving. A mile and a half
farther the woods abruptly ended. The land was relatively level,
but slanting toward hills about ten miles straight ahead. Rows of

young corn grew right up to the woods she had just left. Nothing but corn to the right, the left and ahead. No fences, no mailboxes, not even utility poles bearing electricity and telephone service.

About two hundred yards ahead she saw something squarish and pinkish on the right. She slowed before she reached the very faded and buckling billboard.

Future Site of Sussex Village—Garden Apartments—Luxury Condominiums—Year Around Country Living—Enjoy Boating—Fishing—Winter Sports.

Kate brought the Chevette to a stop with two wheels on the grassy shoulder between the road and the corn. She got out and stood on the front bumper. She did not find the body of water where the boating and fishing were to be enjoyed, but she did see a weatherworn red barn several hundred yards to the left. Corn appeared to grow right up to its bowed walls on four sides. She crossed the road and walked forward until she was almost opposite the barn.

Had she been in the car she would have missed the two-rut dirt track that slanted toward the barn. The grass between the track and the pavement bore only faint tire marks.

Kate trotted back to her car.

Corn had been planted to within three yards of the sides and rear of the barn. An area in front of the doorless front of the barn was untilled. Kate turned off the ignition and sat smoking a cigarette for a few minutes.

The only sounds were produced by birds, insects and the ticking of the Chevette's cooling engine.

Inside the barn she found a few badly rusted and ancient-looking parts of machines, and apple crates. Midway back was a seven- or eight-foot-high pyramid of baled hay. The wire was corroded and the hay was moldy.

Perfect.

She brought her attaché case into the barn and unlocked it. She tore a piece of 8½-by-11 yellow graph paper from the pad, removed four poultry skewers from an envelope and fastened the paper to a bale of hay. Next, she placed six of the new cartridges in the chamber of the new revolver.

Standing five feet from the hay, Kate aimed the gun at the yellow rectangle and pulled the trigger. The explosion, in the silence, sounded like a bomb, and the kick jarred her hand and arm and shoulder.

"Holy shit!" she whispered, as she gaped at what had been the lower-left-hand corner of the yellow paper.

The hole was almost an inch across.

She affixed a fresh piece of paper over the first with the skewers, and from the same place she had stood before, Kate fired two shots, one after the other. The first hit the right lower corner, the second, the left upper corner.

"Hmm." She was pulling, but the sound and recoil didn't seem as intimidating as before.

On the third sheet, one bullet was near the center and the other was an inch beyond the paper, to the right.

Overcompensation. She ejected the spent shells and put five more in the chamber.

Both bullets were near the center of the fourth sheet.

She stood back two feet for the fifth target.

Both shots were near the center, although the second was to the left again by two inches.

Nine cartridges. Enough. Her arm and hand ached.

Kate ejected the shells and the two cartridges. All nine casings went into a fresh envelope, and the unused cartridges went back in their box. She wiped and wrapped the gun and put it in the attaché case.

With a long-shafted screwdriver she poked through the hay for the bullet that had not gone through a target. The other eight would be easier to locate and extract.

She struck metal between five and six inches into the hay.

Jesus, and that was tightly baled hay!

Sweat was running down the sides of her face, her bra was wet and her blouse stuck to her back as she worked the bullet free. She stared at the lead. It looked like a jacket button, round and flat.

She found and gouged out one slug after another, carefully and intently. Three were together in the same pit, bent and misshapen. Before she went after the last one, she stuck the screwdriver in the hole, wadded up the tattered sheets of yellow paper and tossed them into the attaché case.

That was when she heard the wheezing.

She was midway between the hay and the warped apple crate upon which the attaché case lay. Very slowly, Kate turned toward the bright blue-and-green light beyond the doorway. The .38 was empty and wrapped in flannel, the cartridges were lined up in their box. Someone was standing just outside the entrance to the barn; she could not see who it was, but she could see the figure's shadow, and she could hear the heavy wheezing.

How long since she had fired the last bullet?

At least a half hour ago. During that half hour or more she had not been so intent on retrieving the slugs that she would have missed that wheezing. Whoever was out there was suffering from a serious allergy or asthma. One of her cousin's boyfriends from the East had been allergic to something at Lake Arrowhead during the spring vacation when Kate was seven. Kate had been terrified by the transformation in the arrogant, broad-shouldered young man, who within hours had been transformed into a helpless, gasping, wild-eyed cripple.

Whoever was out there, standing almost immobile, she could see from the shadow, could not present a great physical threat.

"Who's there?" she called firmly, lowering the timbre of her voice as far as she could.

"Who is there?" Kate said, this time more softly.

The shadow moved closer to the doorframe and paused.

"You better come out from there," a woman said. "This's private property."

Kate pulled the screwdriver from the baled hay and slowly walked toward the bright light.

Just beyond the doorway, to the side, stood a woman who wore jeans, a long-sleeved shirt and dime-store sneakers. Her face was pale, with gray-black circles around her eyes. Her mouth was open and her chest was heaving.

Kate lowered the screwdriver. "Can I help you?" she said to the woman.

"Take your gun and your car off the property." The woman managed a rapid nod. "Or I'll tell the police."

"I'm not . . . hunting. I was . . ."

"You're to get off the property."

"Of course."

"I don't want trouble. I didn't know it was a lady over here." The woman stood very straight. She was frowning fiercely, concentrating.

"Sorry, I didn't see No Trespassing signs."

"Cornfield's private property."

"Do you live nearby?" Kate wondered how far the woman had walked. The Chevette was the only vehicle in the yard before the barn.

The woman jerked her head in the direction of the way Kate

had been headed on the road before she had come upon the old billboard. "Near enough."

Kate went back into the barn, dropped the screwdriver in the attaché case, closed it and went to her car. "Look, I'm sorry if I caused you trouble. Can I drive you, ah, home? You aren't well."

"I'm allergic."

"Walking can't help."

"That's not your business. You just get off the property."

The woman bobbed her head and stood back.

"Okay." Kate turned the car around and drove as fast as she dared over the bumpy dirt tracks.

At the road she turned left, in the direction the woman had indicated she lived. Two hundred yards from the track to the barn the road dropped into a very shallow hollow, at the bottom of which flowed a stream at right angles to the straight road. Kate slowly drove over the narrow bridge. The mobile home was an early model and rested on cinder blocks in a bare patch of dirt just off the road and on the far side of the stream. Laundry lines sagged under the weight of extra-large men's overalls, T-shirts, boxer shorts and blue work shirts, as well as an almost negligible amount of a woman's clothes. She saw no car or truck or bicycle or motorcycle—only the trailer and the clotheslines in the cleared space in the cornfield near the stream. The road gradually ascended a few hundred yards farther and leveled out. Kate stopped and looked back. Even knowing that little hollow existed, she could not see the break in the cornfield.

So, she had not been completely witless. But she had been dangerously careless.

The sound of the gun was audible to people several hundred yards away. Of course it was, in that silence.

All that woman had to do was walk to the top of the little hollow and look for a car. If she could not see a car on the road, why the person shooting the gun had to be in the neighborhood of the old barn.

Jake Graun had once said, with great disgust, "Never go into the woods to take a leak in northwestern Jersey. Those farmers and their kids shoot at anything that moves. Twelve months of the year."

Which was why Kate had assumed no one would pay attention to her nine shots in that endless cornfield, if she could be heard. Groundhogs, gophers, target practice, just fooling around.

Crane Creek Road met a three-lane highway four miles beyond the stream and the trailer on its cinder blocks. She turned left, southeast.

That woman had seen a strange woman emerge from a barn. The man who wore the huge clothes was evidently elsewhere. But the countrywoman had heard the nine gunshots, and she had seen the woman with the reddish-brown hair and her car with the New York plates.

Kate had had to use her own driver's license and her own American Express card to rent that car. She had touched only the hay in the barn. She had retrieved eight slugs from the hay.

The ninth was still five to six inches in the bale of hay.

"You have a problem," Kate said as she was driving back to New York City on Interstate 80.

One of those button-shaped slugs was still in the hay.

"A possible problem."

No, she decided as she approached Fort Lee.

The odds against the wheezing woman effecting a connection between a past event on Crane Creek Road and future events in Manhattan were enormous.

The risk needed to be taken, given the demonstrated efficiency of the hundred-dollar gun and the twenty-dollar bullets.

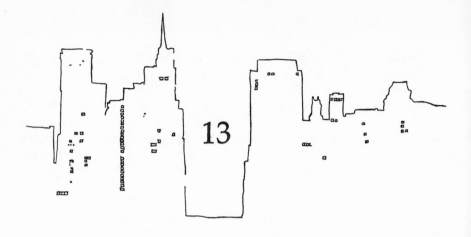

# 13

By eleven thirty Monday morning Kate had read *The Times* and the *News* and was having trouble with her nonvented cigarette smoke.

She turned off the air conditioner in office 517 and struggled to open the windows. One opened as far as it was built to open, the other only raised an inch. She estimated the temperature to be around eighty-five and the humidity to be around eighty percent. There was no air movement in the well between the mustard-colored office and the building across from it.

The thermos in which she had brought coffee was empty.

She dialed 9 on the phone connected to the switchboard.

"Yeah?" the operator said.

"This is five seventeen," Kate said.

"I know you're five seventeen. I can see your light on the board."

"Where are you located in the building?"

"Why?"

"I'm waiting for a telephone installation, and I wondered if I could go out for coffee and leave a message with you in case he came while I was . . ."

"No way, honey. You're on five. I'm on eight. I don't open this door for anybody. Never. No way. Leave a note. That it?"

"Yes. Thank you."

The line went dead.

Kate folded her hands on the ugly green desk.

She would need to carry a small, clean mirror. She could not very well lay her ear against the chest to listen for heartbeats. A mirror held an inch or so from the mouth would fog if a person was still breathing. The mirror in her compact was always dusted with powder. If she wiped it off, she might leave bits of powder.

So much to plan for and foresee.

Here, half of Monday was now gone, wasted waiting. If the telephone installer was not in the office by four, at the latest, she would be unable to get to the *Frig* office and place the ad. If she could not place the ad by five today, her ad would not appear until a week from Thursday.

That would be too late.

The Rainbow Man had mauled Margaret a week ago Saturday, ten days before. He needed a prostitute for two or three weeks, then not again for six or eight months, Margaret had said. She had 517 for only two weeks. But, of that time, only eleven days now remained. And, of the eleven days, she would have only eight if the *Frig* ad came out this Thursday.

The .38 was the gun she was going to use. Based on those nine firings, it was, along with the cartridges, manifestly one of the few remaining evidences of American technological superiority and craftsmanship—that could be purchased by someone who was unable to afford a space satellite or a big computer, anyway.

Kate thought about the slug she had needed to leave in the hay. That one disc of lead was the only mistake she had made so far. The marks on it were unique to her .38, like fingerprints. There the damn thing lay in hay in a barn in the middle of a cornfield eighty-five miles from Manhattan. The asthmatic woman had seen the Chevette; she couldn't miss the New York license plates. The license number could easily be traced to Avis and from Avis's records to Kate Delling.

The one time she had used her own name and a credit card! Goddamn!

She squeezed her hands together and raised them and slammed them on the desk.

The wig felt heavy and hot and too tight.

Kate wiped her sweating hands on the madras wraparound skirt. "Think this through," she said.

Okay, the mildewed bale of hay was a gouged-up mess. What would the woman make of that? Or the man who wore the large overalls? The woman had not seen the .38 revolver. She had seen the attaché case, but there was no reason for her to assume Kate had not been using a rifle and had already put it in the car. Would a woman with a bad allergy poke through rotting hay in an abandoned barn in her cornfield? Would her man? That probably depended on how curious and possessive they felt about their property and how suspicious they were of strangers from New York.

Kate visualized the mobile home and the clotheslines in the cleared space beside the stream. The falling-down billboard. No utility poles. Those people could not have much excitement and stimulation on a one-lane road approximately six miles long, on which theirs was the only visible habitation.

"Wait," she said, relieved.

The people who lived in the trailer did not own those cornfields. Whoever owned all that land and all that corn would not be living in that old trailer without electricity. Kate had seen no storage sheds or farm machinery on Crane Creek Road. The people in the trailer were only caretakers.

The woman had said . . . What had she said? Private property. And the property. Never, my or our property. And she did not want trouble.

Why would a man whose clothes indicated he labored on a farm want to amuse himself in his spare time by looking for a slug he did not even know was there?

You see, you are being paranoid, she told herself.

When her phone rang she jumped. It rang twice.

"Yes?"

"McGiveny here," the raspy voice said. "You all settled in, Gwen?"

"Almost." Gwen? Not Miss Lester?

"No problems?"

"I am waiting for the telephone installer."

"Okay, yeah. He'll come. You set him up for today?"

"Yes."

"Yeah. Listen. I'm onto your suite for August. I'm going to get you a very, very good deal."

"Thank you, Mr. McGiveny. I appreciate your help. Now I must get back to work."

"Anything you want, you let me know. Just tell the switchboard girl you want McGiveny. Gwen, I mean, anything you want, you give me a call. I'm very well-connected."

"Thanks. Bye." She forced herself to replace the receiver slowly and gently.

I'll bet you're well-connected, you obscene old creep.

McGiveny was no better than the late André. Accepting cash and no identification. Did he really believe her story about publicity for two groups from San Francisco? He no doubt assumed she was doing something illegal, or at the least, disreputable. He also, no doubt, possessed duplicates of her two shiny new keys.

And what would he find when he came sneaking into office 517 when she was not there? One answering machine illegally connected to an outside phone. He could easily play her message and those of her callers. Her telephone number would be on the phone, he could look through current porno tabloids and find The Rainbow, if he was sufficiently interested. But, so what?

She would simply need to be certain she knew when he had been in 517 and whether or not he had listened to her tape. If he had, why, she would just erase the messages without responding.

Tomorrow, after the phone was connected and her ad was placed, she would work on the message itself.

As Kate was examining the door for a simple and effective means to keep track of McGiveny's comings and goings, she heard a man talking in the hall. She heard him say, "Five seventeen?" A different male voice said, "That way . . . Left . . ."

The knock came a few seconds later. "Telephone man," the voice boomed.

The man from New York Telephone did not take long.

"I've already been in your basement, Miss Lester."

"You have?"

"Yes. Your connections down there are new. Some switches in buildings around here are in pretty bad shape."

"I'm glad my switches are working."

He exchanged the Touch-Tone on her desk with an identical one, plugged it into the wall, punched numbers and said into the mouthpiece, "I need a confirmation. This is 555-0204, new inst."

He waited, standing straight, looking at the wall, his heavy leather belt creaking under the weight of his tools. "Okay. Thanks."

"That's it?"

"Yes, ma'am. Your phone is in service. Will you sign here?"

Kate wrote Gwen Lester in the same contorted way she had before.

She locked the door after him.

I am Jeanne. My number is 555-0204.

I offer the rainbow, Rainbow Man.

Her watch read two twenty. The *Frig* office was on West Twentieth. Kate took a taxi.

*Frig* occupied the entire third floor of a well-maintained building. The elevator was operated by a polite, smiling man in worn gray uniform trousers and a frayed, short-sleeved white shirt.

The doors opened onto a reception area that looked more like the waiting room of an emergency hospital than the lobby of a pornographic tabloid. But a small, hand-lettered sign painted on the heavy glass partition that separated the reception area from men and women working at desks and tables read *Frig* just like the tabloid's logo.

"What can I do for you?" A man walked up to the wicket in the wall of glass.

"Is this where I place an ad?"

"Is it camera-ready?" He was as matter-of-fact as a clerk in an auto parts store.

"No."

"Then do you want us to typeset the ad for you?"

"Yes."

"Do you have artwork or photos you want used?"

"No."

He produced a large pad of white paper. "Okay. Show me what you have."

"I want to dictate my material. Can I do that with your operation?" This was Jeanne/Gwen Lester, tough lady.

"Sure, dictate."

"I want this in a box with a plain black border. In the center, top, I want two words, The Rainbow. Under that, leaving adequate space, on the same line, reading from left to right, the word, Discreet. Then the word, Accomplished, and finally, on that line, Fastidious."

"Those are long words." The man looked at his printing. "Give me the rest and we can juggle."

"On the third line, again leaving plenty of space, on the right, Only by Appointment. And on the left, Minimum Fee One Hundred and Seventy-five Dollars."

"Are you serious about the one seventy-five?"

"Yes." She hissed the word.

"It's your ad." He shrugged.

"On the bottom line, the phone number 555-0204 and Jeanne. That is spelled J-E-A-N-N-E. Number on the left, name on the right."

"You should state the area code: 212?"

"Yes."

"I can have the area code in a smaller type. Is that okay?"

"Yes. I want the top line in capitals."

"You want The Rainbow in caps?"

"Yes. The rest, only caps on the first letter of each word."

"Sure. What kind of type? Frilly? Block?"

"Neither frilly nor block."

"You want dignity?"

"Yes." Another hiss.

"Okay. And a plain black border?"

"Yes."

"Our deadline for the next issue is"—he looked at his wrist-watch—"less than two hours."

"I know."

"When do you want this in the publication?" He called *Frig* a publication.

"I want it in your next issue." Hard and firm.

"I'll take care of setting it up for you, but you won't have approval for the first issue. Too late."

"I've told you what I want and how I want it. I can't afford to wait a week."

"Sure. We'll take care of your ad. The girls trust us to play square." He studied his tidy printing. "I can't guarantee how this will pull; you may be charging too much. If it doesn't, come back, and we'll leave everything as is but the price. No problem to change the numbers in the corner." He jotted numbers on scratch paper. "If you want to pay for six issues there's a twenty percent discount."

"I'll pay for two issues now."

"I can't give you a discount on only two issues."

"That's okay. I want to see how this does."

"Figures." He was fast with letters and spaces. "Fifty-one dollars a column inch. You want it laid out this way, it'll go two columns, two inches. All that space you want. Comes to two oh four, plus our charge to make the ad camera-ready. That's thirty-one. Comes to two thirty-five for the first issue. Four thirty-nine for two issues. Jeanne." He smiled. "We don't accept Master Charge or Diners Club."

Kate had the cash ready. She had already calculated the cost.

He gathered up the bills. "Your phone will be ringing by nine A.M. Thursday, Jeanne."

"I'm sure it will."

She walked to the elevator and pressed the down button. The same smiling, polite operator delivered her to the street floor.

How very cooperative all these men were: McGiveny, the elevator operator, the *Frig* ad taker.

Tomorrow she would dispose of the .32 revolver Alex Harding had given her for protection. The .38 was not for protection.

Tomorrow she would dispose of the .38 casings and the .38 slugs she had fired into the baled hay on Crane Creek Road.

Wednesday she would go down to Orchard Street for clothes, and she would market, and compute her expenses, so far, and give herself a manicure.

All she had touched in the *Frig* office had been money.

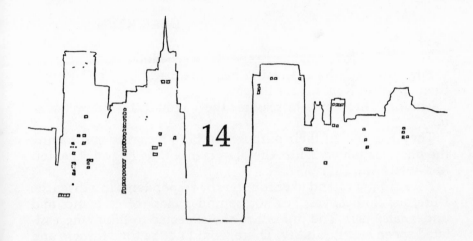

# 14

"Kate, if you won't have lunch with me today at Konrads I will assume everything Scotty is saying about you is an understatement."

Miriam Graun called as Kate was finishing her breakfast.

"Today's fine. When?" Kate asked.

"How about twelve thirty?"

"Twelve thirty it is."

"I'll make the reservations, then." Clunk.

Kate drank her second cup of coffee and flipped through *The Times*. She was not paying much attention to the articles, because she had much to do and much to think about. Lunch with Miriam would last from twelve thirty to two, at the latest. She could drop off the answering machine at 517 on the way to Konrads. After lunch she would tape her message. Maybe she should keep the .32 for insurance in case the .38 malfunctioned. No, she did not want two guns. And all of the slugs and casings and so forth needed to be gotten rid of. Between five and six thirty in midtown when the sidewalks were most crowded.

"Ah." A small ad caught her eye.

The Gallardon concert had been rescheduled for August third. Ticket holders could come to the box office at Carnegie Hall for replacements.

181

That called for a change in the day's schedule.

First, drop off the answering machine, backtrack to Carnegie, then down to Konrads for lunch.

The time had come to reassess the wig and the heavy make-up.

They had served their purposes in both ordering and having the phone installed. Ditto, the placement of the *Frig* ad. That left McGiveny and 517.

Kate did not intend to encounter the respondents in a disguise. Different clothes, yes, but not behind a mask of cosmetics and under false hair. The procedure she expected to follow necessitated speed and flexibility. There would not be time for wig and makeup taking off and putting on.

How then to avoid McGiveny? If he came to the door of 517 she would tell him she was busy and to go away. She could control her own office. The elevator? She would tell him, if he appeared to notice, that she had dyed and restyled her hair. Certainly if McGiveny saw her she would know he had and she could decide her next move. She would simply have to risk McGiveny.

The madras skirt and the peach top and the wig would have to go. They had been pretty much of a uniform. Slugs and casings had to go. What else should she be remembering?

The people.

The old man on the train, the man on the bus who had seen the Albany train schedule, Jack Barclay, the clerk at New York Telephone, the telephone installer, the man at Cousin Larry's, the kid in Central Park, the woman on Crane Creek Road. Who else? The clerk who took her money at Ohrbach's? The man in the *Frig* office?

"Calm down," she snapped.

She inhaled deeply and slowly exhaled—in and out six times.

McGiveny was not in the lobby, the elevator or the hall. Kate set her answering machine on the green desk.

The line at Carnegie Hall moved very slowly. It was ten after twelve before Kate was able to complete the exchange of her ticket.

She arrived at Konrads fifteen minutes late.

Miriam was nursing a vodka and tonic. "You don't look unstable, Kate. You look very well."

Kate seated herself across the white tablecloth from Miriam. "Unstable?"

"You should hear Scotty. Kate Delling, mumble, unstable, mumble, pushing herself, mumble, over her head, mumble. So what have you been doing for a week and why is Scotty gloating and why are you late?"

The waiter set a glass of white wine before Kate.

"Thanks for ordering for me." She sipped the Chablis.

Miriam gazed through her enormous round designer glasses, both elbows on the table, a platinum watch on her left wrist, fifteen thin gold bracelets on her right wrist and forearm, a wide gold wedding band on her ring finger and fingernails bitten to the quick. As always, whatever the season, she wore blue. Today a sapphire cotton blouse with a darker blue skirt.

"Let's work backward. Why are you late? You are always, always early."

"I am sorry. I stopped by Carnegie to exchange a ticket and it took much longer than I expected."

"Ticket for what?"

"A Gallardon concert."

"Isn't he always sold out?"

"Yes. His last concert was canceled and rescheduled. I was picking up a ticket for . . ."

"That's number three. Now to number two. Why is Scotty Rogers telling everyone at F.C.S. that you're crackers, but talented, or sharp as a tack, but batty, and other peppy smears?" She signaled their waiter, who hurried over. "Another of these for me and menus."

"Very simple. He doesn't like me and he needs me. He's been using me and he's using you. I went over his head to Mr. Hamilton, or tried to, about Welles-Keeler. When I walked into Hamilton's office, unannounced and without an appointment, Hamilton had my personnel records on his desk and Scotty was sitting there looking sanctimonious."

Miriam's big brown eyes closed to slits. "Those two shits. Kate, quit. If you come back next week or the week after, Scotty will have gotten to everyone you work with. People will be kind and look at you funny. I'm not finished, but we'd better order."

They both chose Konrads' Caesar salad and an order of garlic cheese toast to share. As the waiter was writing on his pad, Kate glanced at Miriam who was busily squeezing her wedge of lime into her drink. She had suggested Konrads because she knew Kate loved the Caesar salad.

"He must be afraid."

"Scotty?" Miriam said. "Or Hamilton?"

"Scotty. Is he really telling people I'm crazy?"

"He hasn't come right out with crazy. The implication he's trying to convey is that of a brilliant and unfortunately unbalanced female who, modest shake of the styled locks, needs to be under the firm supervision of a sensitive and supportive man like himself."

Kate fell back in her chair and guffawed. "Are you making this up?"

"Actually I'm doing my level best to edit the insights and observations of Scotty Rogers for rational consumption."

They watched their waiter, with flourishes, create their salads.

"In essence, and you should know this, Kate, Scotty figures you'll cave in. He figures you're an insecure patsy from out West somewhere. And let's face it, you don't come on as a street fighter."

"Just how do I come on?"

Miriam chewed pensively for a few moments. "Very efficient. Very smart. But not, oh, I don't know the right way to say this. Kate, you're just too damn ladylike."

"Really? Too ladylike?"

"Yes. I don't mean Eastern preppie and Vassar." She bit into the garlic toast. "Mmm, I love this stuff. What you are is ladylike without an edge. That schmuck knows you're doing his work and he likes it. Gives him a sense of power. You should quit. I don't know why you've stayed at F.C.S. this long."

"Why do you stay?"

"One of the reasons I called you last week and this morning was to tell you I am considering an offer from Allied Systems. A very good offer."

"But they're in Westport."

"That's why I didn't instantly accept the job. Jake and the kids don't want to leave the city and I haven't decided whether the job is worth the commute to Connecticut. But, Kate, your options are open-ended. Wouldn't you enjoy walking into Scotty's office and telling him to stick it? I have written down the name and phone number of the division head at Allied I've been talking with." Miriam reached into her purse and pulled out a sheet of F.C.S. memo paper. "I have told Don Garza about you and he's very interested. Call him, okay? He doesn't have a problem with intelligent women."

Kate took the paper. "I'll think about it. Thanks. I promise I'll think about it."

"You cannot come back to F.C.S. after what Scotty's done and is still doing."

"No, I can't."

"So? Now tell me what you've been doing. Have I told you you're looking great?"

"I feel good. I've just been reading and fixing up my apartment and catching up on films and exhibits. Nothing exciting. How are Jake and Charlotte and Mark?"

Later they split the check, and Kate went back to 517.

No sign of McGiveny. Kate had laid a two-inch-long length of brown thread on the floor where anyone entering the office would have to step on it. It was exactly where she had left it that morning.

She set up the answering machine and pushed the Record button and said, "Hello, this is Jeanne. I'm sorry I missed your call. Wait until you hear the tone and let me know who you are."

She played back her message. Her voice was high and tight and mechanical. She tried again, speaking more slowly.

"Hello, this is Jeanne. I'm . . ."

No.

She began again.

"Hello, you have reached 555-0204. I'm sorry I missed your call. Wait until you hear the tone and then leave a number where I can reach you."

That was better. No name. No implications of hustle. But her voice was still too tense. She needed to convey more confidence.

Satisfied after the fifth take, Kate connected the phone and answering machine to the converter and set up the machine to receive calls.

From a public phone three blocks away, Kate dialed 555-0204.

To her, the voice was that of a stranger. The effect, though, was almost exactly what she was after.

She said, in her normal manner of speaking, "Sorry, I've dialed the wrong number," after the beep sounded. Then she took a bus back to her apartment.

The disposal of a gun and slugs and casings would have been far simpler in the winter when one could wear gloves. Kate solved the problem by extracting, with tweezers, envelopes from the center of the stationery store package. She dropped scrubbed slugs into the first envelope, wiped casings into a second, skewers into the third. The .32 went into a large manila envelope, folded over. The wig was stuffed into a larger brown envelope. The madras skirt and the peach top were cut in four-inch-by-four-inch squares.

Every envelope was placed within an envelope.

They were distributed, this time, on Third Avenue and Lexington Avenue between Fiftieth and Fifty-eighth in trash cans near hot dog and pretzel and Italian ice vendors.

Art and a woman were coming down the stairs from the second floor when Kate entered the inner vestibule of the brownstone.

"Kate, hello."

"Hello, Art." Her folded shopping bag containing the now empty envelopes was under her arm.

He led a tall, attractive, broad-shouldered woman to her.

"Kate, this is Laurel Flexner. Laurel, Kate Delling."

There was no doubt at all that this was the woman Art loved.

They said "Hello" at the same time.

"How is your dissertation coming along, Laurel?"

"You're kind to ask. The dissertation is evidently in good shape. I'm cross-eyed. My veins are pumping caffeine and my dreams are filled with footnotes in French."

"When do you expect to be finished?"

"By the end of July. I hope."

"Good luck."

"This nice man here," she poked Art, "said he had tickets for the new Foster Goldman play and he would pop for dinner."

"And she promised to stay awake during the entire performance."

"How's the article?"

"Plugging along. Not much new. Things are quiet."

"Well, have a nice evening."

Kate showered and ate a bacon and tomato sandwich.

She put an English suite on the record player and sat at her desk to itemize her expenses.

Rent for 517, New York Telephone, Cousin Larry's, the wig, Avis, train fare to Albany, the .38 and the cartridges, taxi and bus fare.

Seven hundred and four dollars so far.

Tomorrow, Orchard Street for dresses to be worn exactly once.

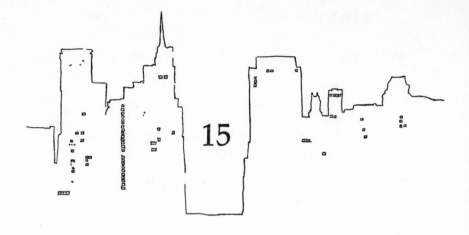

**15**

Ordinarily Kate could not spare the time that shopping on Orchard Street required. Wednesday she had the entire day and was determined to find what she needed—designer clothes marked down by from thirty to fifty percent.

She wended her way through crowds of shoppers, past tables on the sidewalk that were piled high with underwear or men's sneakers or bedspreads and blankets or children's clothes or sweaters made in South Korea.

At Elegance Styles, a shop between a hat and glove store and one that carried only nurses' uniforms, Kate found that most of the clothes crammed into the racks against the walls were for autumn.

A young Puerto Rican employee pointed toward a six-foot-long freestanding rack. "Summer sale," she said. "Supercheap."

The sundresses, street dresses, evening dresses and two-piece sets were hung together in no order whatsoever. Kate began at one end and searched for size elevens. There were eights and tens and fourteens and sixteens and eighteens. A twelve might do if she could find one. Halfway through she came upon an eleven, a backless white dress. No. The only twelve was a gaudy red-and-black-and-green full-skirted dress that would have attracted attention at a disco.

188

The next store she tried was of the same dimensions as Elegance Styles. They were all the same size: narrow and deep. This one was called Ladies Vogue.

Ladies Vogue also featured fall clothes. It also had a rack of greatly reduced summer dresses. Kate found five size elevens. In a four-by-three cubicle behind a curtain that could only be pulled three-quarters of the way across the pole, she tried on the dresses and went out into the store where she waited her turn for the mirror.

Two dresses met the requirements: simple, good lines, stylish. The effect she was after was casual, elegant and decorous. One dress was café au lait with a small, unobtrusive brown figure; the other was a solid avocado green. The green was a Henry Devon. Goody. The label on the other had been removed, but it was a designer dress. Perhaps it was flawed. That was no problem, given the price and the knowledge that it would be worn only once.

By four twenty, she had found nine dresses that met her criteria, and she had spent three hundred and twelve dollars and sixteen cents.

If she was very fortunate, she would need to destroy only one or two of them.

Two purchases at Ladies Vogue and one each at the other stores. On Orchard Street, dresses were not folded within tissue paper and laid in boxes with carrying handles. All nine dresses fit in one oversized bag she bought for twenty-five cents from a vendor. The shopping bag was decorated with an ad for a chain stationery store in Pennsylvania. She did not care what it said; it was heavy plastic and had a strong handle.

Kate felt quite pleased with her merchandise. At Bloomies or Saks or Bergdorf's she would have paid over twelve hundred dollars, at least.

She stood at Delancey and the Bowery waiting for a bus.

Good, she had gotten what she had hoped to find.

Bad, she had now spent over a thousand dollars in less than a week.

No matter. Money was only the subject of intellectual curiosity now.

Men from sixteen to eighty lay, sat, shuffled or else stood in one place wavering. Forever blitzed, crocked, owled and plowed.

They looked like stiff-kneed puppets who all wore combinations of soiled brown and black and dark blue.

There was no green, and each man was rigid within his small space in the doorways or on the sidewalk.

Kate looked for a bus. Six or seven blocks downtown she saw one.

Some of these men knew each other. How could they avoid knowing each other?

She thought of the tenor-baritone duet in the *Pearl Fishers*. So uniquely beautiful. She could not recall another beautiful duet between two men. Duets, yes, but not beautiful; antagonistic or at cross-purposes. Yet composers had written so many lovely duets for sopranos and mezzos. Male composers. She was puzzling over that and shifting her heavy bag from left to right hand when she saw the headline on the two high and neat piles of *Posts* in the center of the newsstand.

THREE MUTILATED BODIES IN EIGHTH AVE. HOTEL

She bought a paper.

On the bus she read the article about the bodies.

They were female. Police discovered the grisly scene while investigating a complaint of a thick, red fluid dripping through a ceiling fixture in the room below. Identification may prove difficult. Faces had been maimed and the hands and feet were missing. Police speculate a prostitution-ring conflict. An intensive investigation has begun.

With great care Kate closed and folded the paper.

Three women whose hands and feet had been hacked off? Blood soaking through the floor? One woman taken by surprise? Okay. But a second and a third? Had the second sat and watched? Then the third? Or did each wait outside the door until she was told, "Next." The article did not mention screams.

But then, Lou Ann must have screamed.

And what, precisely, did "prostitution-ring conflict" mean?

Kate drank two great swallows of Calvados from the bottle.

When the resulting hiccoughs subsided, she carefully hung each of the new dresses in her closet, and went up to Margaret's.

Waldo Crawford, M.D., answered the door.

"Is she worse?" Kate asked.

"No, she is much better. But you, my dear, smell as if you are burning on a low blue flame. Come in, won't you?" He held open the door.

Kate walked into Margaret's apartment. It was clean and tidy, but not the way it had been the night Kate had eaten cassoulet on Dansk stoneware at the Shaker table. The furniture and objets d'art were too squared, the way an impersonal cleaning service would have placed them.

"Who's there?" Margaret called from the bedroom.

"Your obliging lady friend from downstairs."

"Kate?"

"The very lady." Waldo placed his fat hand on Kate's arm. "What have you been drinking? My eyes are watering."

"I had some Calvados awhile ago. I am not drunk."

"Oh, I can see that. But Calvados so early in the evening?" He escorted her into the bedroom. "Here is your angel of mercy, Maggie. And I must say you are both looking quite fit. All things being relative."

Margaret was propped up on pillows, a paperback facedown over her knees. Her hair was brushed and shining. "Hi, Kate. Waldo just dropped over because his favorite color is yellowish-purple and there are so few opportunities to hear it talking."

"You are better." Kate stood at the foot of the bed.

"It was bound to happen." The swelling of her face was reduced, although the flesh around her eyes and mouth was still puffed. Her arms and shoulders were discolored. She now wore a splint on two fingers of her right hand. She held up the hand. "Waldo didn't pick up a few broken bones the first couple of times he came by, but then no one's perfect. How's the computer systems business?"

"You make a living by understanding those evil machines?" Waldo said. "Cybernetics is at the root of all current paranoia."

"Margaret, the *Post*'s front-page story tonight is about three women who were murdered and mutilated. The police think they were prostitutes."

"Why?"

"They were all found together. Is there any possibility that the man who beat you . . .?"

"Where were they found?" Waldo asked.

"In a hotel room on Eighth Avenue."

"Then they were probably working girls. Maggie, have you led this nice lady to believe you ply your trade on Eighth Avenue?"

"Shut up, Waldo. Kate, I doubt if my ex-client has ever been southwest of Fifty-seventh and Broadway for anything other than the theater, accompanied by his wife."

"Three women in a hotel room, mutilated, you say? I guarantee you that when the pathology reports are in they will show evidence of heavy drugs. Further, I guarantee that the cops will know who their pimp was within thirty-six hours. That is a pimp snuff if I've ever heard one."

"But how will they find the pimp if they can't identify the women?" Kate asked.

"Darling, even if those girls were imported into the city yesterday, people on the street will know who their pimp was."

"Their faces were smashed in and their hands and feet were hacked off!"

"Oh, my God!" Margaret whispered.

"That is disgusting!" Waldo sputtered. He abruptly seated himself in the chair by the window. "Well, Maggie, now aren't you glad you've always been independent?"

"Kate, my ex-client couldn't possibly . . . I know him. I thought I knew him. Okay, he flipped and beat me up. But he isn't a butcher. A bastard," she shook her head, "but not a butcher. Jesus!"

"I stand by my explanation," Waldo said. "A pimp of unsound mind."

"Can I get you anything from the market?"

"Thanks, no. Doris took care of that this morning, and I'll be able to go out in a few days. Waldo, why don't you hoist your fat body and give Kate a drink?"

"I can't stay. Don't get up," she said to the man who made no move to do so.

"Come back when you can stay. And don't worry so much."

"Computers and paranoia. They go hand in hand." He waved good-bye.

Kate let herself out.

So the Rainbow Man was a bastard, but not a butcher?

Three dead women and one or more crazy pimps?

The police would find the pimp or the pimps.

Then there were the customers. No one ever mentioned the customers.

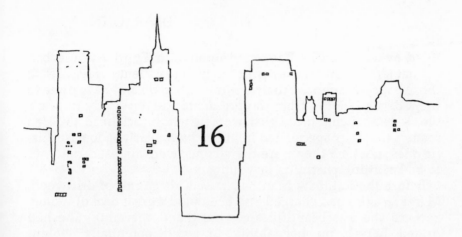

16

Not many men who expected to pay a hundred and seventy-five dollars would be standing at a newsstand at 8:00 A.M. waiting for the latest copy of *Frig* hot off the truck. Certainly not the Rainbow Man. Kate was certain that men who were regular perusers of the tabloid were familiar with a very high percentage of the ads. Most ads were repeats, whatever the name, photo and come-on.

Her ad was simple, and there was a great deal of space between the words that, of themselves, implied that Jeanne could be anything from a top-notch executive secretary to a lawn-party consultant. However, her black-bordered ad was in neither *The Wall Street Journal* nor *Town and Country*. Jeanne's services were announced along with those of Hot Wild Co-eds and Nicole—Guys, Gals, Couples.

Kate soaked in her bath and tried to relax.

She would know the Rainbow Man's voice, she had no doubt at all about that. Not recognize it—know it.

Margaret's friends seemed convinced that they had effectively spread the word about him to their associates in the network of high-priced professionals. Margaret considered the idea of him making a casual pickup on the West Side, at any rate, unthinkable. Also, his needs were such that he could not expect them to be filled by a woman he happened upon in a Third Avenue bar.

That left *Frig* and the other porno tabloids. Plenty of females in those pages announced their willingness to do and have done to them deeds ranging from the prosaic to the physically impossible. Kate was convinced that women who proclaimed to *Frig*'s readers that they specialized in kinks, particularly sadomasochistic ones in which they were the victims, were almost certain not to be beautiful, charming or young.

Before the Rainbow Man had raised his chunk of driftwood, Margaret Elias had charged and been paid a great deal of money because she was beautiful and young and charming. She had prided herself on her ability to avoid potentially violent clients.

Kate sensed that the Rainbow Man would not find the satisfaction he desired from mauling a woman whose body and face were already damaged, no matter how acquiescent she was. He could hire a woman from one of the expensive escort services that advertised in *Frig*, one who could be expected to be physically attractive and young. But whoever ran the service would not be willing to provide him with a second "date."

That meant he would need to find an independent who was not connected with Margaret's and her friends' circle, one who could be paid off, as he was paying off Margaret.

Kate stepped from the tub and dried herself.

The Rainbow Man had exactly seven days in which to buy and read his copy of *Frig*. Those seven days were within his pattern. He would be attracted rather than put off by her ad and the price. And he would call.

And so would other men.

She took pains with her makeup and her hair. Her ad promised discretion and fastidiousness. That she would produce.

Thursday's dress was a moderately full-skirted tea rose cotton.

She carried her Gucci-copy shoulder bag. The .38 fit nicely in an inner side compartment over which she tucked a cotton scarf.

McGiveny was not in the lobby or the elevator at three in the afternoon.

Kate pressed the Rewind lever until she heard a click. She pressed Playback.

Beep. "Sorry, I've dialed the wrong number." That was her normal voice, with traffic sounds in the background.

She looked at the back of the machine for the switch that would play the message her callers heard.

"Hello, you have reached 555 . . ."

She listened intently.

Excellent, the two voices were quite different.

She reset the "Hello, you have reached . . ." cassette and pressed Playback.

Scratchy sounds and a low, resonant buzz, then:

Beep. "Jeanne. Oh, baby give this stud some head. Yes. You hear me, baby? I want for you to see what I'm . . ." Click.

Beep. "This is Ted Carmichael. I'm staying at the Aldine on Forty-ninth. Please call 555-4098 before noon." Click.

Beep. "Hi, Jeanne. You sound good. I'll call back tomorrow." Click.

Beep. "What's this one seven five shit? Poon's poon, so what makes you think there's something so special . . .?" Click.

Beep. "Jeanne, Ken here. Gloria and I are after a third to swing. Call 555-7522. We pay very well." Click.

Beep. "Baby, show me your beaver shot first, and we'll talk about one seventy-five. I mean, why should I pop for . . .?" Click.

Beep. A woman's voice. "If you have seen George Duncan, please, for God's sake, please call his mother. He is retarded. 555-4490." Click.

Beep. Several people giggling. "We're having a circle jerk. . . ." More giggles. "We're . . . We want you, Jane. Hey, Jane . . ." Click. Kids.

Beep. "Hello, Jeanne. That's a very nice ad. Call Uncle Thad at Select Escorts. Number's in *Frig*. We can do business. Safe and big bucks." Click.

Beep. "If your rainbow includes English, call . . ." She could not hear the number.

A phone rang.

Kate looked from the 517 phone to the Touch-Tone.

She pressed the Stop lever on her machine and let the Touch-Tone ring twice more. She could not think what to say.

"Hello?" Her voice was barely audible.

"That you, Jeanne?" A booming baritone.

"Yes?"

"Good. I'm Ben. I have an hour beginning at four thirty. You're kidding about the one seventy-five, right?"

"Wrong."

"Come on, honey. Tell you what. I don't need much. I'll give you eighty. That's ten more than my shrink gets."

"I don't give discounts, Ben."

"Ninety? I only paid ninety once in my life. In London."

"Sorry."

"No shit? Inflation's hit the trade this bad? Or maybe you got something nobody else's heard about?"

"Maybe."

"Shit. Okay. Sorry we couldn't do business."

Kate laid the receiver back on the Touch-Tone.

Not you, Ben.

Ben was not the Rainbow Man. He evoked only annoyance, not the rage she would require. Perhaps no one but the Rainbow Man would provide that. And if that were so, she would need to destroy only one of the nine Orchard Street dresses.

The second time she answered her Touch-Tone she tried to sound like Jeanne.

"Hello." Lower and slower. Very steady.

"Jeanne?"

"Yes."

"Hold on a minute," the man said. Another man was talking or laughing in the background. "Jesus, shut up a sec, Cal. I can't hear her. Jeanne, my friend and me want some action. We've got the one seventy-five. Now you can talk, Cal. Speak up and tell the lady."

"We got it ALL, baby," a second voice hollered into the phone. "Twice as much as . . ."

"I'm booked for the rest of the day. Thanks for calling."

"But . . ."

She hung up and listened to the twenty-one remaining recorded messages. There were more drunks and crazies and masturbators and one earnest young female who, in thirty seconds, managed to condemn Jeanne and her kind and solicit a tax-free donation to the Ashram of Perfect Purity in East Orange, New Jersey. But a third of the remaining callers sounded as if they were seriously interested in a meeting with Jeanne. Some left numbers and others said they would call back.

None of them was the Rainbow Man.

"Hello, Jeanne," a man said at four twenty. "I'm intrigued by your ad." He sounded like a younger, more assertive version of Peter Hamilton.

"My ad was meant to be intriguing."

"Are you free early this evening?"

"What time did you have in mind?"

"Six thirty. I'd like to make it sooner. Unfortunately, I have a meeting and one of my colleagues has the suite until six. I think we'd better play it safe and give him and his lady friend a half-hour leeway. I'm not in the mood for swinging. The suite is number 95C at the Wallingford. You'll find anything you need there. I mean, anything, Jeanne."

"I have a small problem, friend."

"Call me Al. What's your problem?"

"You have the voice of a very interesting man, Al. I would like to see you."

"So?" He sounded suddenly cold.

"Sometimes the police set up dummy apartments. I wouldn't want us to be in the midst . . ."

"Oh, honey." He gave a deep, relieved chuckle. "I forgot. Of course you high-class solos need to be careful. I've been using one of the company's dating services for so long I'd forgotten. I promise I won't have a partner hiding in a closet. The suite is leased and listed under the name Harvan. That's H-A-R-V-A-N. I'm with the Fort Davis, New Jersey, office."

"Well . . ."

"Honey, you aren't worried about money? Jesus, I'm the chief sales engineer."

"No, I never worry about money, Al. I just want to be certain we have a memorable time."

"Memorable time! I love it!"

"See you at six thirty."

When Kate hung up the Touch-Tone she became aware of the tic in the muscle above her jaw. It hadn't acted up for weeks.

Al's company leases a suite in the Wallingford that is equipped with anything you need, Jeanne? And Al is intrigued by Jeanne's ad, so much so that he isn't availing himself of one of the company's services. Really? A suite complete with prostitutes is a Harvan perk for the fellows? Gee whiz, maybe F.C.S. leased a suite for the boys. That's where Scotty spends his three-hour lunches?

Kate's watch indicated four forty-five.

What if the Rainbow Man called and she was not there?

He would not leave a message. He might, though. No. Yes.
No.

The Touch-Tone rang regularly. A few earnest potential customers sprinkled among a much larger number of creeps. She
told them all she was unavailable.

At five fifteen she erased the previous messages and set up the
machine. She walked around to the bathroom on the fifth floor. It
was empty and not at all clean. She applied fresh makeup and
urinated.

In a phone booth on Madison Avenue she asked Information
for the number of the Harvan Company in Fort Davis, New
Jersey.

The operator did not have a Harvan Company, but there was a
Harvan Division of the Jonathan Richmond Corporation.

"Harvan Division," a well-modulated female voice answered.

"The sales engineer's office, please."

"Do you want Sales Engineering or Mr. Babkus' office?"

"Mr. Babkus' office."

"Just a moment."

Two buzzes. "Mr. Babkus' office."

"Hello. May I speak with Al?"

"I'm sorry, Mr. Babkus is in New York today. May I tell him
who called?"

"Yes. This is Fran Johnson from the Hudson River Committee."

"Shall I ask him to call you?"

"No. I'll call him at home tomorrow evening. Thanks." She
hung up.

So he is Al Babkus, with his own secretary and a key to a suite
in the Wallingford?

Who would pay for Jeanne? Would she be asked to make out a
receipt? One hundred and seventy-five, free-lance, paid in full?

Kate walked slowly up Madison, stopping to look in store
windows. As she stood before the plate glass she watched the
reflections of men: quite a few well-dressed men striding purposefully along.

She had not been prepared for the Harvan suite at the Wallingford—equipped with anything a Jeanne could need.

Mirrors on the ceiling? A TV with porno videocassettes? A
giant aerosol can of mint-flavored whipped cream? The enema
paraphernalia some of the *Frig* ads offered? Nurses' uniforms,
nuns' habits, gestapo outfits?

Good God, did Harvan pay for the Anything? How was this presented in their annual report? Operating Expenses? Or did the fellows in middle and top management chip in for the new heavy-duty Tunisian vibrator with attachments?

She stood at the plate glass of a radio and camera store and in the glass she saw the reflections of men's trousers. The flies. Faded Levi's, tailored Italian silk, baggy drill, shiny gabardine, pleated corduroy, tight chinos.

Behind those flies hung flesh from which pleasure had been and could be experienced. There was no evil in that flesh. Not in the flesh. A penis was not a weapon unless the man to which it was attached considered it such. Lou Ann knew about that.

Very interesting. What did Al Babkus envision the rainbow to be? Evidently something more or different from the services provided by one of "the company's dating services." What, that he had not already felt, did he expect was possible in an hour or so for a price of one hundred and seventy-five dollars?

Not love, certainly. Not even affection.

Sensation. A pleasurable sensation or a series of sensations that would intensify until, for a few minutes, he would be in a voluptuous frenzy.

For the happy spasms of Al Babkus and his colleagues, an executive at Harvan authorized a large amount of money for the suite and a running tab at several out-call operations. Harvan, not Al Babkus.

What would Al Babkus do when Jeanne did not appear at 95C? He would call her number and he would hear, "Hello, you have reached 555 . . ." By seven he would know Jeanne was not going to show. For how many hours did he have the suite reserved for himself? Two hours? Could one of Harvan's services provide a woman on such short notice?

Tough shit, Al. But then, maybe your suite 95C was equipped with one of the mechanized/body temp./real-feel latex/three openings/4 speed/remote-control female "forms" advertised in *Frig*. Reusable.

Kate was six and a half blocks from the Wallingford's canopy on Lexington Avenue, and she was now filled by a terrible curiosity to see what an Al Babkus, a chief sales engineer with a key and a corporate suite, looked like. This stranger who had flipped through *Frig* and been "intrigued" by words and numbers arranged in a certain way in a certain context. She took a deep breath as fury tightened her chest.

So that makes you number two, Al.

Kate walked toward Lexington through after-work crowds.

The Wallingford was a busy midtown hotel, three notches higher than the Admiral. Busy, less touristy. More expensive: the wives of the conventioneers wore less polyester.

She went matter-of-factly to the elevators beyond the desk.

If the desk or any of the bellmen saw her as other than a guest there was no indication. Above each elevator was a clocklike face, the hands of which moved in the direction of the elevator, stopping at floors, passing floors, up or down.

Two gregarious middle-aged women entered the elevator with Kate. She waited until they pressed 6, then she pressed 12, smiled and stepped back.

At the twelfth floor Kate walked from the elevator in the direction of the illuminated exit sign. She opened the fire door and went down the cement steps. At 9 she tried the hall door. A minor gamble. If it opened, it opened. If not, she would have sore feet by the time she got to the ground floor.

The door to the hall was not locked.

A stocky, well-muscled man with a receding hairline and a trimmed salt-and-pepper beard answered her ring. "Jeanne?"

"Hello."

"You are Jeanne?" He seemed hesitant. "Come in."

"You're Al?"

"The very one." He closed and triple-locked the door after her. He had unbuttoned the top button of his oxford cloth white shirt. His tie was well loosened. "Welcome. Make yourself comfortable." His voice was uncertain as he waved Kate into a very large sitting room that had been furnished in Lucite, brushed chrome and suede with large hard-edge and pop art canvases on the walls.

"Very nice."

"So you're Jeanne."

"Yes."

He had obviously been expecting a Jeanne to look and act differently from a Kate Delling, which was what he had gotten.

"Sit down anywhere. Can I get you a drink?" He turned a knob and a portion of the wall swung around, presenting a well-stocked bar.

"No, thank you."

"I only got here myself." He poured four ounces of vodka over ice cubes and squeezed lemon juice into the glass.

Kate lowered herself onto a large four-cushion couch covered by lime green suede. She gave him the kind of smile she would give a stranger at an F.C.S. business meeting. Al drank deeply and sat beside her.

"You certainly don't come on like . . . God, you've put me off balance, Jeanne. And that ain't easy."

"Oh?"

"You see? You don't use any of the moves. You say, 'Oh?' "

"What are the moves, Al?"

He leaned back. "I am going to like this. Your initial ploy is—the truly inexperienced date. Plus, you don't remotely look like a hooker. I like that, too."

"How long do we have, Al?"

"Sweetheart, we have until nine thirty. That is a very big three hours."

"I need to know about you." She faced him.

"Jesus, I like this. You don't dive on me. Subtlety. You're going to be good, creating suspense, easing into it. Now, what is the rainbow?"

"That depends on you, Al. I need to know about you."

He leaned toward her and lightly ran his hand over her breasts, then sat back. "I've fucked most of my wife's friends and most of my friend's wives. Christ, what hypocrites! 'Al, darling, you're the first man since I've been married!' "

"Maybe you were, Al."

"I cannot tell you how much time and energy I spent on those nice ladies." He adjusted himself. He was getting an erection. "I like the way you listen, Jeanne. Turns me on."

"Go ahead and tell me."

He laid his hand on her thigh. "By then I was moving up at Harvan and qualified for a key to this place." He indicated the suite with his free hand.

"Al, why did you decide to call me?"

"I've been getting very bored with the girls from the services. Cute, well-built, clean kids. It's gotten so they're all interchangeable. They must all go to a Fundamentals of Hookerdom school. No imagination. Very mechanical. Total predictability. I was intrigued by your ad."

"So you said over the phone."

He had begun to move his hand up her thigh. "When do I find out what the rainbow is, Jeanne?"

Kate lifted his hand from her leg by the wrist, dropped it on the lime green suede, picked up the imitation Gucci bag at her feet and stood. "Now is a good time." She pulled out the .38 and aimed it at his chest.

Al Babkus sat back, crossed his legs at the ankles and laid both arms on the back of the couch. "Say, you do have a very unusual shtick. I've done a little B and D, although none of those tough cookies came close to a toy gun in their routines."

"Al, this is not a toy gun. It is a thirty-eight revolver loaded with real hollow point cartridges, and I am going to kill you with it."

"Okay. Now am I supposed to tell you I need to be punished by some sort of surrogate nanny? The truth is, I don't get off on S and M. So, let's cut this part short."

"There is no next part, Al."

He brought his arms down and sat up straight. "I hate to tell you this, honey, but you're turning me off."

"Good." The gun was beginning to feel heavy. She had lowered the muzzle an inch or so. She raised it.

He bent forward and reached into his back pocket.

"Do not move."

"I am getting out my wallet to pay you. I don't want to play anymore. Got that? Shit, I'll never call another Minnie Mouse *Frig* ad again." He slapped his wallet on the suede cushion.

"That is correct, Mr. Babkus."

His eyes blinked, then widened. "Hey, just what the fuck is this? Is this some nasty little joke my wife thinks . . ." He licked his upper lip. "How did she know I'd call you? I mean, nobody knows I called you. I only decided . . ." He stared at the gun. "Is that really real?"

"Yes. Now, Al, before you die, I want you to think of the women whose bodies you've used. From what you've told me, there are quite a few."

"Ah, what do you want me to think about them?"

"That you are sorry, Al. Deeply and sincerely sorry."

"Ah, okay. Yes. I . . . Yeah. I see what you mean. I've been a shit-stick and I'm truly sorry."

The bullet smacked into Al Babkus' clavicle a bit to the left of center. He jerked up, arching his back.

Kate hurriedly stepped backward as blood audibly burbled from a jagged red cavity. Before he slid over onto his side she saw a shaft of bone. Blood was soaking into the lime green suede sofa cushion.

The smell of gunpowder was now mingled with the stench of excrement. Al Babkus' sphincters had relaxed.

The smell. A smell. She had not considered smell before. She had never fired a gun within a closed space before.

She went to the hall door, pressed her ear against the light gray paint and listened. She heard the voices of a man and a woman. They were speaking in flirting, bantering voices. Then she heard a third and a fourth voice. An annoyed man and woman talking about the criminal costs of something.

As the couples crisscrossed past the door of 95C, no one remarked about the smell of gunpowder or the sound of a gun. The flirters flirted and the complainers continued to complain.

Al Babkus was now almost the same color as the walls. There was no need for the clean little mirror. Blood was barely trickling now from the hole at the base of his neck.

She lifted the credit cards from his wallet by their edges. His driver's license, in a plastic slip, stated that Allan Blanton Babkus had been born on August 7, 1945, and he resided in Upper Montclair, New Jersey. Four one-hundred-dollar bills and five twenties were neatly tucked in their pocket. She removed the four hundreds, returned the cards and rubbed the wallet against the suede-covered arm of the sofa.

Kate walked through the suite, pushing open doors with her knee. On the drainboards in the kitchen were almost two dozen dirty glasses. In the bathroom, used towels were tossed in every corner, as well as in the bathtub and shower. The beds in both bedrooms were unmade, and the bottom sheet on one bed was covered with long, reddish-brown smears.

She went back to the bathroom. Using a clean face towel, she turned on the basin's faucets and washed her hands and forearms with a tiny cake of hotel soap. She flushed the soap down the toilet and dried herself.

What else?

The handles on the outer door of the ninth floor and the inner one of the twelfth floor. God, she had almost forgotten the fire doors.

Kate put the .38 back in its compartment in her purse. She put the four hundred dollars in her own wallet. She heard no voices from the hallway. Using her cotton scarf, Kate opened the door. No one. She went to the fire stairs door, opened it and wiped off both handles with the scarf. She walked up to the twelfth floor and, as she waited for her breathing to slow, listened. Nothing. She wiped the outer and inner handles and went to the elevator where she pressed the button with her scarf.

She was unable to determine whether the elevator had ascended or descended to the twelfth floor. At the fifth floor, three couples, preceded by the fumes from gin and bourbon, crowded into the elevator. She left the Wallingford in the train of the folks who were headed for Luchow's.

Nothing was in focus as Kate walked up Lexington to Fifty-seventh. She was worried about whether or not anyone else could smell what she still smelled. If she crowded into a bus, would someone look around and say, "I smell the smell of a gun," and look at her face and know? If she took a taxi would the driver note the smell of a fired gun and remember her address?

Kate walked the twenty-three blocks to her brownstone.

Until she pulled the trigger she had not known she would do so. But on and on he had talked, a man too arrogant and insensitive to lie. A whore like Jeanne was not worth concerning himself about. All a Jeanne could care about was avoiding trouble with Vice and receiving her payment. And when Jeanne asked him to tell her about himself, he just naturally assumed her curiosity was limited to his sexual history—the better to please him.

She knelt on her bathroom floor and vomited into the toilet. Again and again, until there was nothing more to vomit. Shakily, she rose, rinsed out her mouth and scooped water on her face, soaking her hair and the front of the tea rose dress.

She did not change. She put the final side of the Verdi Requiem on her record player and turned up the volume and sat forward on her couch, listening intently.

Boom. Boom. Boom. Boom. *Dies irae.* Day of wrath. That dreadful day came for Allan Blanton Babkus and he was truly judged by fire. He knew he was being judged. He admitted his culpability.

Al Babkus wanted the rainbow because he was bored. Well, he would never be bored again. There was that.

And Jeanne had come through with the "Accomplished."
As the final *Libera me* was whispered, Kate began to relax.
She tore off the tea rose dress and shoved it into a grocery bag.
The only smell left was her own sweat.

Kate read *The Times*'s account of Al Babkus' death as she rode
the bus up to 116th Street. Two paragraphs on page 17.
Allan Babkus, an executive with the Jonathan Richmond Cor-
poration, was shot to death during a robbery at the Wallingford
Hotel. A police spokesman stated that several leads were being
followed. Mr. Babkus, of Upper Montclair, was survived by his
wife, Arlen.
No children? What if there had been three or four children?
Alex Harding had children and he died in an avalanche with
Miss Beverly Danforth.
Gordon Van der Kemp had children. And his children had
little friends.
She dropped the bag containing the tea rose dress in a trash
can on Broadway across the street from Columbia. She dropped
the spent cartridge into a grating on Riverside Drive and 110th
Street.

Art Gilman was talking with Vanessa at the corner of Colum-
bus and Seventy-fourth.
"Hello," Kate said to them both. "They're beautiful," she told
Vanessa about the two half-grown golden Labs she held on
chains.
"Yes, they are. And they love to be petted."
"Do you two know each other now?" Art asked.
"No, I'm an admirer, though. I'm Kate Delling."
"Hi, I'm Vanessa. I saw you last Saturday on CPW when I was
walking the dachsie and the schnauzer."
Kate stooped to pet the dogs. They both wanted to be petted at
once. They climbed over each other and Kate and tangled their
leashes. Vanessa held the chains and maneuvered them like a
puppet mistress.
"Okay, that's enough, children." Vanessa lined up her charges.
"Off we go. Nice to have met you," she said to Kate, and off she
went with her paper towels and brown bag.
Kate and Art walked toward their building.
"Are you on vacation or just taking the day off?"

"Vacation of sorts. Art, what do the police know about those three women who were killed in that hotel room?"

"They were full of heroin, for starters. The police don't know who they are yet. Their names, that is. They're certain the women were prostitutes. My contacts at Midtown West say the killing was not done by a maniac. It's a pimp-drugs tangle they haven't figured out yet. Someone on the street will drop a word in the next day or so, if they haven't already done so. Evidently all of the whores are scared to death."

"Of whom?"

"Their pimps, other girls' pimps, the dealers. Oh, I have a tidbit from the East Side that won't make the papers." They were at the foot of their stoop. "Some guy who did have a name was killed at the Wallingford last night."

"Oh?" Kate leaned against the stone banister.

Art nodded. "The cops are telling the press the guy was shot by a robber. What they aren't telling the press is that he had a hundred bucks in his wallet, all his credit cards and a gold Swiss watch on his wrist."

She could feel the tic pulsing. "Then he wasn't shot by a robber?"

"They're certain he wasn't. Seems the company the guy worked for kept this very expensive suite at the Wallingford for their brass to entertain their girlfriends in. By girlfriends, read prosties. Three or four out-call services are known to have been regular providers."

"Who do the police think killed the man?" Kate remembered all of those glasses in the kitchen. Some of them certainly held the fingerprints of prostitutes.

"They don't know, and the company the man worked for is trying to keep a lid on the entire story. The man, by the way, was a very steady customer of the services. The East Side has fun and games, too, Kate."

"But can a private business prevent a police investigation?"

"I doubt it. Anyway, why would a hooker kill him and leave a hundred bucks cash in his wallet? The services are falling all over themselves to appear cooperative. Appear. No way are those operations opening their ledgers to Homicide. Homicide slides the pages to Vice. Vice can decode the initials and addresses. As opposed to Forty-second Street pimps, the high-class, East Side

services try to take good care of their girls. And more important-
ly, the services are out of business if they don't protect their
customers."

The tic in her jaw stopped as suddenly as it had begun. "Always the customers." She looked up at him with a bemused
half-smile. "Art, in your researches into the white slave trade in
the last century, did you ever come across names of the customers?"

He sat down on the bottom step and rested his chin on both
fists. Kate sat opposite him. She concentrated on the lighting of
her cigarette.

"Yeah, there were some names on those old yellow papers. But
not on purpose." He held out his hand for a cigarette. "The kids
were designated by first names only and age and a brief description. Some Unitarian minister's wife developed a kind of decod-
ing method in 1932. No one gave her a nod, of course. She
figured out who many of the buyers were from the initials and
the designations and the prices and the dates. For example, you
see the buyer was an H.R.M. in a town in southern Indiana and
the price for the kid is eight hundred bucks. By the minister's
wife's detecting, that could only be Henry Robertson Manticle, of
Manticle Farm Machinery."

"You mean, the Manticle Foundation?"

"And the Manticle Fellowships, and so forth. Yes. No one else
in that part of Indiana had eight hundred or five hundred dollars
over the period of time in question to pay for a child from a
certified white slavery operation. No one else within five
hundred miles had fifty dollars to his name."

"Did she publish the information?"

Art slumped forward even farther. "Are you kidding? By 1932
the descendants of some of the steadiest customers—from Pennsylvania to Oregon and Maine to Mexico—were U.S. senators
and Cabinet secretaries. Their family names were logos on everything from baking flour to hand lotion."

"I see. How stupid to ask if she'd published her names." A
great surge of confidence rose from Kate's gut right up through
her throat.

"The lady's husband, the minister? Their names, by the way,
were Amy and Roger Barton. The husband had a heart attack
right here in New York outside the offices of a magazine publish-

er that had thrown out his wife and her material. After he died, she turned over all her papers to Lawler College and was last heard from in 1938 in what was then called Spanish Guinea."

"Have you seen her papers?"

"Um-hum. At Lawler College. Anyone can go through them. What happened was, the so-called Victorian psyche underwent a reevaluation. A man like Henry Robertson Manticle did what he did because he was repressed, you see. And his wife was repressed. H.R.M. was a victim of his society. *Plus ça change, plus c'est . . .* et cetera."

"Will you include the expensive prostitution services in your articles?"

"Only briefly, and only for purposes of comparison. My focus is the very young West Side street hookers."

"What about those murdered women?"

"I'll use that. Do you know what a vice cop told me? The only reason that case made the front page was there were three, count 'em, three mutilated whores. Pimps kill and/or mutilate their women with great regularity. But, one at a time. It's a way of life. Jesus."

She pulled herself away from the wide stones of the banister and started up the steps. The music of the *Libera me* had begun to slide around in her mind.

"You get up and walk away? I'm losing my objectivity on this. Maybe that's good. Maybe I'll win a Pulitzer." Art lay back on the stairs. "You haven't heard the end of this one, Kate."

The piece of string lay where she had left it on the floor of 517.

She had not bothered with pads of paper and envelopes and pencils on the desk. If McGiveny sneaked into her office he would play the machine and know she was a call girl. That was not a felony. The only call she intended to return from her tape was the Rainbow Man. The others were erased. Al Babkus' call was not on tape.

At four thirty Friday afternoon Kate sat at her desk in the avocado-green Henry Devon dress and pressed Rewind.

Today two different callers had left messages in Spanish and one in Chinese or Japanese. Otherwise the messages varied little from Thursday's. She recognized the voices of five men who had said they would call back and who had.

A little after five the Touch-Tone rang.

"Is this Jeanne?" a woman asked.

"Yes." A female john? That had not occurred to her. But then *Frig* carried ads for women who were for hire to women.

"I am calling for Mr. Berwald. Hold on, please. I will connect you."

"Tell Mr. Berwald I'm booked up for today."

"Oh, that's too bad. Well, he'll get back to you next week."

Kate replaced the receiver.

Mr. Berwald had his secretary place a call to a prostitute? Maybe Mr. Berwald was so busy he had his secretary run through the *Frig* ads for him.

More men dialed her number. Men who obviously wanted to use her as they masturbated. Men who wanted to hire her, but from the way they spoke and the hotels they named or the addresses they gave, did not intend to pay one hundred and seventy-five dollars, not even fifty. One man, elderly, with a cultured voice, wanted her to come to his East Seventy-eighth Street apartment and sit on his lap for an hour or two. Nothing more was required. Kate told him she was not available.

She continued to be unavailable until seven thirty-five.

"Jeanne?" An almost musical bass.

"Yes."

"Your ad is very clever. Who advised you?"

"No one."

"In that case, I'm doubly impressed."

"Thank you."

"*Frig* is not a publication in which one expects to find evidence of subtlety and imagination."

"So I gather. Are you a regular reader?"

"No. Oh, I've looked through it occasionally. Very little changes from month to month and year to year." He spoke like a man who was accustomed to speaking before an audience. "You did not grow up in this area?"

"No, I didn't."

"And you have attended college?"

She sensed that he wanted Jeanne to have gone to college. "Yes, I have attended college."

"May I ask where?"

"Yes. And may I tell you that is none of your business under the circumstances?"

"Excellent, you have succeeded where others have failed. Are you available this evening?"

"As you have probably gathered, I am as selective as I hope my clients are."

He laughed. "You aren't asking for character references, are you?"

"Hardly. However . . ."

"I can understand your position. Let's see. How can I alleviate the apprehensions of a woman in your circumstances?"

Kate waited. This pompous bird wanted to play big word games? Okay.

"May I assume that if I can allay your concerns you are free for several hours this evening?"

"I am available. I am by no means free."

"Your fee is no problem. All right, I can't very well avoid giving you my address, can I?"

"Not very well."

"And when you see my card in the vestibule you will know my name. This has become rather silly. My name is George Scoresby. I'm a member of the faculty at NYU."

"I'll be able to see you from ten thirty to twelve thirty, Dr. Scoresby."

"Excellent." He gave her a deep, rich chuckle. "We won't be meeting at my home, of course. I don't live in Manhattan. I do have a quite comfortable little place in Chelsea where I'm able to catch up with my writing and see certain students. Ah, privately."

"Your address?"

He described his building on West Twenty-third Street as being "Mixed, but quite safe."

Now it was seven forty-five. Over two and a half hours before Scoresby expected her. A college professor who maintained a pied-à-terre where he saw certain students, ah, privately? No mistaking what he meant by ah, privately.

He was not the Rainbow Man, though. And this was the second day.

The phone continued to ring and she continued to answer it. She could sit there until one or two in the morning and wait for the Rainbow Man or she could go to Scoresby's. If the professor checked out she would go to Chelsea. If he didn't, she would come back to 517.

At nine-fifteen Kate erased Friday's messages and set up the machine.

There was a grimy, underlit used book and record store on West Forty-eighth. The place was open late and was such a disorganized mess, Kate was certain the husband and wife who ran it were fronting for something illegal. Several times she had spent hours poking through thousands of LPs and no one had paid her the slightest attention.

Near the bins of used records was a collection of out-of-date college and university catalogs. In 1978 a George F. Scoresby, Ph.D., was a full professor in the Political Science Department at New York University.

On the counter behind which the old man sat in a greasy overstuffed chair, Kate found a two-year-old copy of *Books in Print*.

Scoresby, George F., was the author of three books that, judging from their titles, analyzed employment patterns and urban growth patterns and urban voting patterns. And each had been published by a different university press.

A plumbing fixtures store occupied the street level of Professor Scoresby's building. A polished brass panel in the small, well-maintained and brightly-lit lobby held the names and numbers of the tenants. Floors two, three and four were given over to the offices of lawyers, dentists and a podiatrist. Five, six and seven appeared to be residences. There were two tenants per floor.

George F. Scoresby was listed as 7-B.

With her knuckle Kate pressed the button beside his number.

"Yes?" came a tinny voice from the speaker.

"Jeanne," Kate said.

He buzzed her through the heavy door into the inner hall where a self-service elevator waited. Beyond were stairs. She again used her knuckle to press 7.

The hall flooring was parquetry under a clear layer of polyurethane. A small Navaho rug lay before 7-B. The door was dark, fine-grained wood.

George Scoresby extended his hand. "Welcome. You are more than prompt. You are early by six minutes."

Kate shook the man's hand and walked past him into 7-B. The main room looked as if it were a reading room in a library:

floor-to-ceiling bookshelves, a large, carved refectory table that was covered with stacks of folders and papers, and in the corner a small couch and two easy chairs were arranged around a round coffee table.

"You must be comfortable here, Dr. Scoresby."

"Oh, I am. Very. Would you like to see the rest before we sit down for a minute or two?" He led Kate through an arch into a square hall.

The kitchen and bathroom were immaculate and had been expensively remodeled. The bedroom held one large armoire and a king-sized bed. Nothing else, not even a carpet on the polished hardwood floor.

"You must indeed be comfortable." That was the first time Kate had ever used "indeed."

"Indeed," George Scoresby said. "I'm drinking cognac. What can I give you?"

"Nothing, thanks."

"Oh, I must insist you join me."

"Cognac, then."

He went to the kitchen and returned with two snifters. She seated herself on the small couch. Scoresby, after handing her a glass, took one of the easy chairs.

"Jeanne is not your name," he said and then sipped his cognac.

"Really?" She drank from her glass and immediately regretted it. Her face became flushed. She was suddenly very apprehensive.

"No one who advertises in something like *Frig* uses her own name." He crossed his legs and leaned his head back.

She watched him watching her.

George Scoresby had once been a tall, slender man with strong features. Now, he was slightly stooped and his flesh sagged. He combed his brown hair flat and straight back from a sharp widow's peak. He was, Kate realized, a man who had been steadily drinking for a long time, rationing the booze, juggling, never completely sober, yet never out of control.

She waited for him to speak. He was smart and he was observant. She needed to know if he had researched her as she had him.

"You are a cynical young woman, Jeanne, or whoever you are. And you are playing no games with me. Correct?"

"Correct." She did not know what he meant.

"Ah. I do not need to go through the motions with you."

"No."

"What a relief. You don't ask, 'What motions?' Do you know who I am?"

"I know your name. You gave it to me."

"Then you don't follow the . . . Never mind. Have you been told you are an unorthodox prostitute?" He finished his cognac.

"Yes."

"May I . . .?" He glanced at her glass. "No. I'll be back in a moment." He was. And his glass was more than half-full. "I have never before needed to hire a woman," he said as he resettled himself in his chair. "I have more volunteers than I can handle."

"Oh?"

"This isn't the sort of thing one shares with one's family and colleagues." His full, drooping mouth rose at the corners. "An average student, a rather homely senior who needed an A from me for her G.P.A., came up here for a consultation. Thirty-two hours later I was like one of those empty insect casings. That ugly girl had fucked me dry. For a grade, and I was fully aware of her intentions the entire time. I could not help myself. Do you know what I did?"

"No."

"I could not bear the smug glances she gave me afterward. I flunked her."

"Did you?"

"Yes. I gave her an F in my course. Now, wouldn't you think, Jeanne, or whoever you are, that the word would have gotten around?"

Kate set down her glass. "Yes, I would."

"Well, it hasn't. They continue to troop up here."

"And what do you do, George?"

"Ah! George! I only need to give money to you. What do I do? I must try to explain demography and statistics while some twenty-year-old is exposing her pantieless cunt to me."

"Why must you do that?"

"Because I am expected to do that." He was drinking faster as he became angry.

"Explain demography and statistics or peer up your students' skirts?"

He stood, bumping his shin against the coffee table. "Come to the bedroom. Your money is in the envelope there." He flapped his hand at the refectory table. "I didn't think I would need to justify myself to a whore! This way!" He held his arm rigidly, his index finger aimed toward the hall.

Kate set her purse on her lap. "Tell me something, George."

"What?" he shouted. "I am not pleased with you, Jeanne!"

"I can't think why you would be."

He leaned against the doorframe. "On the other hand, you don't expect anything from me except money."

Kate reached into her purse and found the gun's handle. George Scoresby was almost seven feet from where she sat. Much too far. She rose, holding her purse with her left hand; the gun was in her right hand within the purse. She walked toward him.

As she approached, he turned and strode to the bedroom. "You have yet to show me what this rainbow of yours is." He sat on the foot of the bed.

Kate followed him. When she was four feet away she lowered her purse and raised the .38.

"Is that a gun?" He squinted at it.

"Yes. I came here to kill you, Dr. Scoresby."

"Oh, this is silly. I should have realized from the first this was some kind of attempt to embarrass me politically. You aren't a whore at all, are you?"

"No."

"Well, you see? All right, now you have your stupid little tape recording of my indiscretions. Get out!"

"Dr. Scoresby, you called me, remember?"

"Yes. Well?"

"You found my ad and my number in *Frig*. You called me. I didn't call you."

"Oh, my God!" His hands were bunching up the thin batik bedspread. "Is this a robbery?"

"No, Dr. Scoresby, this is about the students you've taken advantage of. On that bed you're sitting on."

"Well? Are you a representative of some campus feminist group?"

"No. Remember, you called me? From a *Frig* ad."

This could go on and on, she realized. George Scoresby had been taunted and threatened before. But never, she thought, by a woman in his bedroom, holding a loaded gun.

"I want you to know you are going to die."

"We're all going to die, Jeanne."

"I want you to acknowledge the . . ."

He twirled away and down, onto his right knee. Kate fired and the bullet caught him in the small of his back.

"Oomph," he said, with surprise, as blood and a chunk of fat splattered over the bedspread. But he scrabbled, crablike, back to the main room. Kate's hand was trembling. She shot him again as he ducked under the huge carved table. This time, below his shoulder. He did not stop. He crawled toward the entry door, trailing blood. Very slowly now and gasping.

He curled against the door.

Kate stood over him, aiming the gun at his face.

His eyes rolled toward her and stopped. She was the last sight he saw, if at that moment he was still seeing.

"Oh, hell," she said, looking at the large drops and smears of blood in a trail across the floor.

And he was still bleeding.

Kate hurried to the bathroom and brought back two large bath towels. She tugged George Scoresby away from the door and pushed the towels around him. She was remembering the blood that dripped through the ceiling in the Eighth Avenue hotel room.

Then she listened.

The walls were thick, but the blam of the gun in that bare bedroom must have been audible two blocks away.

Hurry!

Her hands were shaking as she washed and dried her snifter and put it away, using a clean tea towel to open and close cupboard doors.

The envelope. She should take that; the one hundred and seventy-five dollars might provide a clue. She shoved it in her purse and, stepping over George Scoresby, opened the door. No one in the hall. The elevator was elsewhere, she saw.

Kate took off her shoes and ran down the stairs. Midway between the second story and the lobby she slipped them on and walked across the small lobby to the vestibule door. As she turned the polished doorknob with her scarf, a deliveryman carrying a carton of liquor bottles opened the street door. He swept his eyes over her as she passed him in the little space. He smelled of garlic and wine.

She climbed onto an uptown bus at Twenty-third Street. A young black man with long muscular legs sat on the rear seat listening to very loud rock from a large transistor radio. Kate sat in the middle of the bus, staring at the opposite window. She needed to think, to recall all that had happened in Scoresby's building, but she could not concentrate because of the pounding beat and bawling voice. She looked at the other passengers on the half-empty bus; none of them seemed to notice the noise, or care. She glanced at the man, frowning. He smiled and turned the volume higher.

Kate got off at Columbus Circle and walked up Central Park West.

Nothing had gone right with George Scoresby. He had not even known why she had killed him. And the deliveryman had gotten a good look at her face.

From the park came the distant tat-tat-tat of firecrackers and the thuds of cherry bombs.

On the other hand, the deliveryman had been drinking. But he would presumably remember the time he had seen her and the store he worked for would have a record of the delivery. When Scoresby's body was found, the police would question everyone who had been in the building at approximately eleven fifteen Friday night.

In her apartment, Kate removed the avocado-green dress, balled it up and shoved it in a brown bag. She examined her shoes. A nickel-sized splotch of George Scoresby's blood had soaked into the sole of her left shoe. She dropped the shoes into a second bag. The two spent casings went into an envelope.

The gun probably needed cleaning, but she was too tired. She wrapped it and laid it on the top shelf of her closet.

And now for your envelope, Dr. Scoresby.

Kate slit it open with a letter opener and counted the bills. She counted two tens and five fives.

She laughed until she choked.

Forty-five dollars!

He had had no intention of paying for the rainbow.

"Either way, Jeanne flunked you," Kate murmured and put the record from the Requiem on her machine.

That night Kate did not sleep well. She dreamed and could not remember the images when she half-wakened. Then she fell back into a restless doze and dreamed again.

After a late breakfast Kate lifted the avocado-green dress from the bag and carefully examined it. No bloodstains. She rode the Eighty-sixth Street crosstown to Fifth Avenue. The shoes went in a basket near a vendor selling pretzels and soda in front of the Metropolitan, and the dress in a trash can in front of the Guggenheim. She emptied the casings from the envelope into a storm drain at Eighty-sixth and Madison.

She bought a *Times* and a *Post* from a newsstand but did not open them until she was back in her apartment. In neither paper was the killing of Dr. George Scoresby mentioned.

Then no one had heard the two gunshots, or if someone had, no one had reported them. He said he lived elsewhere. His family probably did not expect him home until today, or even tomorrow. If anyone rang the 7-B button no one would answer. Eventually he would be found, though, and the police experts could fix his approximate time of death. The deliveryman would be questioned.

So, two potentially serious problems. The deliveryman at Scoresby's and the one slug left in the hay on Crane Creek Road. The slug was by far the more dangerous mistake.

She began to pace. Her hands were sweating and her face felt hot.

One slug in Allan Babkus. The police already possessed it. Two in George Scoresby: the police would have them in a day or so. The police knew Babkus had voluntarily admitted his killer. Scoresby had also opened his door to the person who shot him.

If the police checked Scoresby carefully, they would surely find students he had invited up to his Chelsea apartment, and why. Then they would know that both Babkus and Scoresby had sex with a great many women while they were in Manhattan and away from their homes.

Back to the slugs.

She paused long enough to light a cigarette.

The police would know all three slugs had been fired from the same Smith and Wesson .38 revolver, almost certainly by a female.

Kate sat for a moment on the arm of her sofa.

That woman in northwestern New Jersey could not have much to do. No TV. No phone. Asthma or a terrible allergy, yes. But she did live in the middle of a cornfield. She had managed to walk from her trailer to the barn. She had heard the nine gunshots. That was seven days ago.

She stubbed out the cigarette and resumed her pacing.

Unless the woman on Crane Creek Road was mentally retarded, she would have given an occasional thought to a stranger from New York who had driven to a deserted barn and shot a gun at baled hay. No matter that she was only the caretaker. What else did she have to think about out there?

And when she went back to the barn to satisfy her curiosity, she would see that the woman had taken the trouble to dig her slugs from the rotting hay. She would wonder why. Of course she would.

The one neat and ungouged hole in the hay. That was the question. Would the cornfield woman realize it was also a bullet hole? What else could it be?

Kate leaned her head against the cool bricks above the fireplace.

Think!

Okay. The woman on Crane Creek Road extracts the last slug. Then? She looks at it. She has it, that fat lead button, lying in the palm of her hand. Now what does she do with it? She shows it to the man who wears the huge overalls. What does he do? Does he say, "We should take this to the police"? Does he clomp into the office of whoever the police are out there and say, "My wife found this slug in a bale of hay in that old barn on Crane Creek Road and we think this is very suspicious. My wife even has the license number of the car the woman from New York was driving." No, he doesn't do that. Jake Graun said almost everyone in that region owned and fired guns.

The woman puts the slug away in a drawer. She writes down the license number of the Chevette, if she can remember it, and forgets about them. Why would she connect her trophy with the murder of Allan Babkus, who received only two paragraphs on page 17 of *The New York Times*? And even after George Scoresby's body is found? And the Manhattan police detectives announce both men were killed by the same revolver?

All the woman had was a disc of lead. She had not seen Kate's gun. For all she knew, Kate could have been firing a rifle.

With the exception of the kid in Central Park, the only people who had ever seen Kate with a gun were dead—Alex, Joseph Warburton, Allan Babkus and George Scoresby.

"Oh, God!"

She pushed herself away from the brick wall.

The hot-goods kid!

He could tell the police that he'd sold her a .38 and the hollow point bullets, where in the park they had met and, she was certain, a very good description of her. He had to be a very observant boy.

And, unless the boy became scared and stopped selling stolen items, he was bound to be caught.

But would the police ask him to describe every person he'd sold a hot gun to? He'd told her he'd sold seven guns to women in the past two months. He had not told her how many guns he'd sold to men during the past two months. How many .38 revolvers? Surely he did not test-fire his stolen guns and keep spent slugs. He wouldn't, would he?

Her phone rang.

"So tell me what you've been doing," Miriam said. "You haven't been home for two nights."

"I've been out." Kate sat at her desk.

"Doing what?"

"What do you mean, doing what!"

"God, Kate, you just popped my eardrum. So don't tell me what you've been doing." Kate heard the click of Miriam's cigarette lighter. "Don Garza, the man at Allied Systems? He called me at home, naturally, and asked if I'd talked with you about going up to Westport to see him."

"Oh, yes. About a job." Kate felt her shoulders relaxing. "No, I've been so busy I haven't had a chance yet."

"You're so busy trying to be the first human to look at every single article on display at the Met that you don't care what's going on at your current place of employment?"

"What's going on?" She had begun to doodle on her pad of yellow quadrille paper. She had printed CCR for Crane Creek Road and HGK for hot-gun kid. "Has Scotty been made a vice-president and taken over Hamilton's potted plants?"

"The org. chart for Welles-Keeler came out Thursday."

"Oh, yes. Welles-Keeler. And what has Scotty done?" She crossed out CCR and HGK and printed OK FOR NOW beside them.

"You are listed as Staff under Scotty Rogers' name. Off to the side. All by yourself. Just, Staff, as in you're at the same level you've been, except you're no longer head of your group. Ralph and I have your people. As in, Scotty's really shafted you."

"Miriam, are you saying that because I raised my voice in the presence of Peter Hamilton I've been . . .?"

"You've got it, friend. As Scotty tells everyone, you are a talented girl who can't handle pressure. Which is why you're to call Don Garza today. I hope you noticed that Don's office and his home numbers are on the paper I gave you on Tuesday."

"A talented girl?"

"Verbatim. A talented girl. He's also said, 'talented gal.' As in, he can put this talented gal to very good use as his right-hand assistant where she can work directly under just one man, thereby relieving you of distractions."

"Relieve me of distractions! That sonofabitch has been distracting me and you and Ralph with his own goddamn work for three years!"

"There went the other eardrum. Now what am I supposed to do for hearing? Kate, Ralph and I have shoved his quote assignments end quote right back at Scotty and told him we can't or we're too busy. He's gotten go fuck yourself from my body language as well as my language language. What you and Ralph and I know is that you've been shoveling it for Scotty. Ralph even wants you to call Don Garza. I hope you don't mind I told him about that."

"I don't mind your telling Ralph. I like him."

"He likes you. He said if he didn't have an ex-wife and those three kids, plus his present wife and those two kids, he'd have quit a week after Scotty was made department head. But he's fifty-three and scared. He didn't tell me that—about being fifty-three and scared. You know how it is."

"I can afford to go elsewhere and he can't."

"You've always been quick and crisp with words."

"I won't be coming in on Monday, Miriam."

"Thank God! Great! So while Scotty's wondering why you're uncharacteristically late, you'll be on your way to Westport. Oh, I almost forgot. Jake and I want you to come out to the Snuggery for the Fourth weekend."

"Thanks, Miriam. I wonder, though, who will Scotty use to do his work for him?"

"He will begin an immediate search for another Kate Delling."

"Will he find one?"

"Sure he will. You'll be able to come out for the Fourth, I hope?"

"Hmm." Kate printed SR for Scotty Rogers on the graph paper and drew a square around the letters.

"Kate, are you paying attention?"

"Yes. Westport."

"No. Snuggery on the Fourth."

"May I call you about that in a few days?"

"Jake and I do not lightly invite, you know."

"I know. But I'm rather involved . . ."

"You can bring him, too. Call me. But call Don Garza first."

After she hung up, Kate looked at the boxed SR.

No.

Even if he were to call Jeanne's number he was untouchable.

"Miss Delling," the homicide officer would say, "I understand you may have had a few grievances against the late Mr. Rogers. Will you tell me where you were on the night of . . ."

She drew an X over the box that contained SR.

As Kate sat at her desk in 517 listening to the beeps and clicks with the words between, she felt weary and unfocused. The entreaties and demands and insults and strings of filth became a blur. Drunks, panters, bellowers. A few unimaginative and evidently genuine offers were recorded. None was the Rainbow Man. And only six days left.

For almost two hours Kate told sincere and insincere men that she was not available. A man who said he was an oilman from Midland, Texas, offered Jeanne five hundred dollars plus a big tip if she would care to join him and a friend for a few hours at the Americana Hotel. He may well have been happy to pay five hundred dollars to whoever he imagined Jeanne to be. Kate Delling did not know how she could shoot two men from Texas when she'd had trouble with one caved-in professor in Chelsea. She told the Texan she was booked up.

This was Saturday night, approaching ten thirty. And here she was in the mustard-colored office wearing a brand-new, soft-apricot chenille dress.

"Hello, Jeanne," the man spoke rapidly. "I hope you're free tonight." He was calling from a public phone.

"Hmm," she said. His voice reminded her of someone.

"I'm at the convention center here and I am a man who is tired and I have earned a good time."

"What's on at the convention center this week?"

"RVs. Recreational vehicles."

"Aren't you people having trouble because of the gasoline shortage and prices?" She could not bring to mind who this man sounded like.

"Yeah. But I saw that coming, Jeanne. In 1976 I sold my West Wind franchise for a bundle. I walked across the street and bought the Honda franchise. So you must know I am not hurting for money right now."

"Where are you from?"

"St. Louis. Say, Jeanne, I'm only going to be in New York City until tomorrow afternoon, and I am in great need of the rainbow."

Now she remembered. Saddle Shoes in the Admiral Hotel lobby. That's who he sounded like. "What shall I call you and where are you staying?"

"Oh, great! Buck Turner is ready for more than one rainbow tonight. With the right girl I've been known to hit the pot of gold as many as six times. Great. I'm at the Big Apple Inn on Seventh Avenue. Room 2347."

"What time did you have in mind, Buck?"

"How about eleven thirty? I have to close down a few matters here before I can leave."

"Eleven thirty."

Kate smoked two cigarettes, then erased her machine, set it to Record and laid the thread on the floor.

She called the Big Apple Inn from a pay phone.

"Do you have a Mr. Turner registered?"

"One moment." She was put on Hold. "We have two Turners. Which one do you want?"

"He, ah, prefers to be on an upper floor."

"Oh, you want Donald Turner in 2347. The other Turner's on six."

"Thank you."

The convention center number produced a recorded message informing callers it was closed and another number for emergencies.

Terrific. No way to check him out, and the Big Apple Inn would be just the place she herself would set up a trap for a call girl if she were the police.

However, Buck Turner sounded very Midwestern.

Kate followed her judgment.

The Big Apple Inn's lobby was busy.

The announcement board with changeable letters listed the events being held in three of its dining rooms and five of its conference rooms. She glanced at it and walked purposefully to the row of elevators and waited for one of the expresses to the top fifteen floors.

The elevator was empty. She pushed 23 with her knuckle. The wood-paneled box shot up. At 20 it came to a stop. A housekeeper pulled in her cart, punched 21 and pushed out her cart when the doors opened again. Her back had been toward Kate the entire time, except for a downward and backward glance as she entered. So she saw a pair of simple tan pumps.

A sign opposite the elevator indicated that the odd-numbered rooms were to the right. Four or five men were partying in number 2321. She heard their muffled voices. The sound insulating was much better than she had expected.

Room 2347 was halfway along the second hallway. When she knocked on the door she heard no sounds from within the room. Almost a minute after she had knocked she heard the chain lock being undone.

A man who was well over six feet tall opened the door and held his fingers to his mouth for silence at the same time that he gave her a broad wink. "Jeanne?" he whispered.

She nodded and went into the room.

The phone was lying on the bed. Four or five pillows were piled against the headboard. He gestured for Kate to sit in one of the two armchairs as he lay back on the bed and picked up the receiver.

"Sorry, sugar. That was just a maid bringing fresh . . ." He listened and winked again at Kate.

"Aw, now, sugar, don't . . ."

"But, sugar . . ."

He listened.

"Yes. Monday at ten forty-five. I'm getting a hard-on just thinking . . ."

He listened and lit a cigarillo.

"What's this—do I love you?"

He listened.

"More important than . . ."

He listened.

"Sugar, I am as tired as I've ever . . ."

He poured Scotch into a water glass.

"I'll see you Monday, sugar. Bye." He hung up and drank deeply. "Oh, man! You want a drink first, Jeanne?"

"No, thanks. Is your wife checking up on you, Buck?"

"She called awhile ago. That was my girlfriend."

"You are a busy man." Kate walked to the bathroom. No one there. She opened the closet door. Nothing but Buck Turner's clothes and two suitcases. "Have you enjoyed your stay here?"

"Lots of work. Some fun." His hands were clasped behind his head as he watched her. "The girl I had up here last night was cute enough, but dullsville. A guy at the RV show gave me a couple of numbers." He shook his head. "Cute, but no talent at all."

"So you want the rainbow?"

"That's a great ad, Jeanne. I like it. Gets the old mind going. The cock follows."

"Did you discover me yourself, or do I come recommended?"

"Sugar, I bought that magazine after dinner tonight. I didn't ask for recommendations. You know why?"

"Why?"

"Because if you're as good as I hope you are, I didn't want someone else to get to you before I had a chance."

"Then you didn't tell any of your friends about Jeanne?"

"I'll do that after I find out about the rainbow, sugar." He finished his neat Scotch and refilled his glass. "I'll bet part of the turn-on you give is you look so wholesome. Like fucking a really hot schoolteacher."

Buck Turner was fiftyish. His long, full sideburns were curly gray, while his hair was black and straight and had been combed sideways over what was obviously a bald spot. His stomach bulged over his beltless waistband.

"Buck, will you hand me a pillow?"

"Sure, sugar. Why?" He tugged a pillow from the pile behind his back and held it out to her.

"The pillow is important." She laid it over her purse.

"No kidding? Okay."

Kate pulled the gun from its compartment and held it under the pillow while she set her purse on the floor beside her chair. Holding the pillow before her with her left hand, she went to the side of the bed and looked down at the man.

"I like a girl to undress me," he said. "Very slowly. To begin

with. Don't worry if I come while you're doing it. I get it right up
again in just a few minutes."

"Buck"—she lowered the pillow so he could see the .38—"I am
going to kill you."

He gaped at the gun. "Shit! A rip-off. Goddamn!" He brought
his arms down from behind his head and hunched up straighter.
"All I wanted was a good time. Those other girls were dullsville."

"So you've said. How much did you pay them?"

"One got fifty and the other sixty-five. Look. I still have over
three hundred dollars cash in my wallet."

"How much do you pay your girlfriend back in St. Louis?"

"My girlfriend?"

"The one you were talking with on the phone."

"Nancy? She's the bookkeeper at my franchise!"

"How much do you pay her?"

"What the fuck is this?" He straightened farther. "Are you
robbing me or running a Dun and Bradstreet?"

"So. Nancy is paid, what?"

"That's none of your damn business!"

"You have a strange sense of circumspection, Donald."

His head snapped forward. "Just who in hell are you?"

"Donald, did Nancy become your girlfriend before or after you
hired her to become your bookkeeper?"

He formed a little O with his mouth and relaxed just a little.
Kate knew what he was thinking—this is a crazy woman and I'll
just humor her along for a few more minutes. Why else would
she be pointing a gun at me and asking about my bookkeeper at a
motorcycle franchise in St. Louis?

"Well, now, the truth is, I needed a bookkeeper. Nancy," he
shrugged, "came by. I interviewed her. She sounded good. She
needed the job. The chemistry was there right from the first."

"Are you paying her more or less than you paid your first
former bookkeeper?"

"Oh. The other bookkeeper was a man, so Nancy's getting . . ."

"Less."

"Not much less."

"Donald, in the past week or so I've killed three men."

"You have?" At that moment Buck Turner realized the woman

holding a pillow and a gun was going to shoot him. "You have."

"Yes, Donald." She arranged the gun behind the pillow. "How long has Nancy been your bookkeeper?"

"Not quite, oh, three years."

"Not quite three years! Oh, you bastard!"

"Yes, well, maybe I should give her a raise. If you don't shoot me with that thing, I will give her a raise. Okay?"

"Tell Nancy you're a bastard, Donald."

"Okay. I'm a bastard, Nancy."

Kate fired four shots through the pillow. They went thwoo, thwoo, thwaa, thwee, the pillow flew apart and Buck Turner's stomach and chest burst open. Feathers swirled and then floated down over the bed, the floor and Buck Turner. His left hand rapidly slapped up and down on the bed, then stopped and quivered. She watched the hand until it lay still, then she turned away and slumped onto a chair. The feathers settled.

She dropped the gun on the rug and waited.

This great clod, Donald Turner, was the one who caused her to lose her concentration. Because he was so oblivious in the first place.

But no one banged on the door, hollering, "Police! Open up! Hands over your head! Lean against the wall!"

Almost half an hour passed.

Her right hand and forearm ached. She had probably strained a few tendons pulling that tight trigger so often and so fast.

Wearily, she bent over and picked up the .38. She placed it in its compartment and closed her purse. Anything else? She looked around the room. Only what was left of the pillow. She had touched the doors to the bathroom and closet.

Kate wiped those handles with tissues from the bathroom, then dropped them on the floor. She pulled two more tissues from the bathroom dispenser and with them pulled the door closed in the hallway. Those tissues she squeezed into a ball and left in the elevator. No fingerprints on those.

At Fifty-sixth Street and Sixth Avenue, Kate signaled a taxi.

She sat back on the torn plastic seat in a cab that reeked of perfume and booze and marijuana and the driver's BO.

Smell had become increasingly important. Why was that? The sense of smell is the most primitive of a mammal's senses. Then hearing, then sight, in an ascending order.

The colors and lights blurred through the dirty taxi windows.

That probably meant she was sinking back into some atavistic state, before the mind learned to control instinct.

She closed her eyes and, bouncing as the taxi went over potholes, tried to remember the evening. The office, yes, and the brown thread. The call to the Big Apple Inn. The housekeeper and her cart. The tall, heavy man with bushy gray sideburns. The feathers sticking to the bloody flesh and the bloody bed. Had she wiped off all of her fingerprints? Yes.

She absently paid the driver, trying to remember something, an expression. Something important. She let herself into her apartment, showered, poured a glass of wine. After the second glass of wine she put on the Verdi.

Boom. Boom. Boom. Boom.

You, Donald Turner . . .

Ah, that was it! The certain fear when she had called him Donald.

She had known the name he had been given.

Sunday morning rain fell steadily and the temperature was in the low eighties. Kate took the Seventy-second Street crosstown to Fifth Avenue, rode down to Washington Square and dumped the pale apricot chenille dress in a trash can. She dropped the four empty shells into four different storm drains.

Despite the umbrella her terry tunic top was soaked as she sat in the M5 heading back uptown to Seventy-second and Broadway.

She saw Vanessa ahead of her between Amsterdam and Columbus. The girl was wearing a yellow slicker and a pith helmet. She had what appeared to be two lambs on her leashes. As Kate closed the distance she could see that they were woolly light gray dogs.

"Hi," Vanessa said. "These are my newest charges. Aren't they lovely?"

"I thought you'd gone into sheep walking for a moment." Kate stood under her umbrella looking down at the dripping dogs.

"They're Bedlington terriers. The first ones I've ever gotten to know. They're very intelligent and very sweet. You should see them off their leashes. They actually gambol! I've never seen anything actually gambol before."

"Do you mean they skip?"

"Kind of. They run along, then just go straight up, the way lambs do in cartoons. Except, they're dogs."

The dogs' tongues were lolling, and as they watched Vanessa's face, their skinny little tails wagged vigorously.

"I suppose you know that Art and I are fans of yours."

Under her pith helmet, Vanessa blushed. "I guess I've liked every dog I've ever met."

"Do you have dogs of your own."

"No. My father is disturbed by barking, and noise in general."

"Then how did you learn so much about dogs?"

Vanessa bent and scratched the dogs' heads. "Some kids don't figure out escape routes soon enough. I'm lucky, really."

"I don't understand."

"Oh, things are seldom what they seem. You know, from Gilbert and Sullivan?"

"I still don't understand."

"Dogs are what they are." She looked up at Kate. "They don't know how to pretend. The way people do. You know what I mean. I can tell from your face."

Kate did not know how her face appeared to Vanessa, although she did know how she felt. Angry and frightened and desolate. "Are you safe?" She peered at the girl.

Vanessa nodded once. "Take care." She loped to Columbus and disappeared around the corner.

The dogs bounded before her. One of them did give a kind of straight-up bounce.

Vanessa's family was very wealthy, according to Art. What if her father was an Uncle Gordon?

Kate continued to stand on the sidewalk under her umbrella. What if one or more of her cousins' friends had told what Gordon Van der Kemp had done to them? What could they have done? Nothing.

But that did not mean that every father was perverted and every adolescent was in jeopardy.

She splashed home. She was spinning within a narrowing spiral in which her perceptions were contracting. That was dangerous. She needed to be more aware, not less.

She bought a heavy Sunday *Times* from the old man at Seventy-second and Columbus.

She had even put Buck Turner of St. Louis from her mind. He received a half column.

Donald Turner, an executive from Missouri, in Manhattan on business, had been brutally assaulted and robbed in his room at the Big Apple Inn. Mr. Turner's body had been identified by a business associate. Lieutenant Hernandez of Midtown Homicide stated that the police were pursuing substantial leads, including possible eyewitness descriptions of the assailant. The Big Apple Inn had imposed stringent new security measures to ensure its guests' protection. The victim was survived by his widow and two children.

And Nancy, the bookkeeper.

But why, Kate wondered, did the police think Buck Turner had been robbed? His wallet was presumably in his trouser pocket. Under the blood and the feathers. And what robber would shoot a man lying on a bed? Four times?

She had pulled his hall door closed, but she had not locked it; she assumed it locked automatically. A burglar could have been prowling the halls trying doorknobs. But what would a burglar have made of the blood-and-feather-covered corpse of Buck Turner? He would have run like hell.

There was something askew in the article.

The bullets, of course.

The bullets from Buck Turner were the same as those from Allan Babkus. Then, what would the police know? That both men had hired prostitutes? Then what?

An announcement from Lieutenant Hernandez of Midtown Homicide cautioning all men in the Manhattan area to forgo the use of hookers? The hooker you hire may be homicidal? How about that for a catchy subway poster? And then, eventually, Dr. George Scoresby would be discovered.

She went to the barred street window. The steady rain continued. She thought of going to 517. A rainy Sunday. A claustrophobic day. She tried to remember the weather on the night Margaret had been battered by the Rainbow Man.

Margaret had been wearing a raincoat.

She had come back around three in the morning following that night, though. Yet she said he was not a middle-of-the-night john. Maybe now he had changed his pattern, cut off from his usual sources by Angie and the network. But the latest Kate had stayed at 517 was the night before. Eleven.

Tonight she would not go to the office until eleven.

That was eight hours away.

Vanessa was out there in the rain and the air with her dogs. She was safe. Vanessa had looked and she had seen and she had walked away via the escape route she had found.

Eight hours.

Kate found the television section of *The Times*.

At four, the choices were the middle of a baseball game and two movie reruns, the beginning of a *National Geographic Special* on polar bears, a panel news show and *Christopher Webberton at Home*.

She turned to Christopher Webberton. The paper did not list his guests for today's program.

The handheld camera approached the door of Webberton's Gramercy Park town house, the door opened, the camera proceeded through a black-and-white-tile entry hall, swung left through high double doors into a drawing room, moved slowly over furniture, statues, paintings and came to rest on Christopher Webberton himself seated on his Mies van der Rohe chair, looking like the middle-aged Thomas Jefferson.

He dipped his head and smiled in welcome before he turned in his chair to introduce his guests urbanely, an Academy Award–winning actress presently starring in a Broadway play and her husband, a best-selling science fiction writer.

Now a stationary camera took over.

Webberton crossed his legs and leaned toward his guests, his wiry hair backlit, his aristocratic profile in sharp focus.

"What a phony he is," Kate muttered.

But he always managed to obtain celebrated and interesting people for his program. Never interesting and unsung people, though. He had had as his guests men and women whose only other television appearances were on network news programs.

He laced his fingers and laid his hands, palms down, over his knee. He listened as the actress told him she wanted him to take her sailing

Christopher Webberton was a world-class yachtsman. He was also known as a gourmet cook, a writer of witty essays and a watercolorist. This, in addition to his being one of the heirs of Boston's Webberton Paper.

Phony. Always acting.

Who else had said that about Christopher Webberton? Or had it been said about him? Or someone else?

Kate held her hands over her eyes and tried to remember.

No, Margaret had said the Rainbow Man was a phony who was always acting. And that he was an artist. And he was rich and famous. And he was strong.

She stared with horror at Christopher Webberton chatting amiably with the movie star and the science fiction writer.

Kate watched until the program was over.

Margaret answered her own door.

"God, Kate, and I thought I was looking so much better."

"Yes, yes, you do. Margaret, I have to talk with you."

"Come in." She stood aside. "What's the matter?"

Margaret was greatly improved, although she moved slowly and with evident pain. Her face was still deeply bruised and swollen.

Kate sat on the front edge of an armchair. "Is Christopher Webberton your client?"

Margaret tried to purse her lips as her eyebrows rose. "I don't discuss my johns, Kate. Not by name, anyway."

"You could deny that he's one if he isn't."

"Did you watch him just now?"

"Yes." She could not interpret the expression on Margaret's face because the flesh was so puffy and discolored.

"The way he comes on like Gramercy Park's Renaissance man?"

"I know."

"Would you like to know what his peculiarity is?"

Margaret clicked her tongue and shook her head. With that, Kate knew Christopher Webberton was not the man who had beaten her.

"What?"

"It's pretty peculiar. He has his old Japanese cook sit near his bed in a rocking chair. Rocking. She must be eighty years old. Once was enough for me, I'll tell you. Very, very weird."

"Yes. Weird."

"You were able to pick Chris up as a kink from his program?"

"Yes, I suppose I did."

"God. I hadn't realized he was that obvious to a nonpro."

* * *

Kate was three steps from the second-floor landing when Art stomped up the stairs from the first-floor entry.

"Have I had a frustrating day," he said. "Come in and I'll fill you in on what's breaking with Midtown Vice and Homicide."

He unlocked his door. Kate followed him into his apartment. "About the prostitutes whose hands and feet were cut off?"

"Them, too." He waved her to a chair. "Want some coffee?"

"All right. Yes. Thanks." She sat on a scratched and nicked maple captain's chair.

"I had a loose appointment with a detective in Vice for nine this morning," he called from his kitchen alcove. "Guy named Bennett. Sunday mornings are usually quiet for Vice. Other than paperwork from the night before."

"Have they found out who butchered those women?"

"Not yet. Milk or sugar? This is instant, by the way."

"Neither."

He came out of the kitchen and handed her a mug. "Have you ever heard the name George Scoresby?"

Kate looked away from Art, whose glasses had slid three-quarters of the way down his nose. "No. Who is he?" She rested the mug on her knee. Her hands were trembling visibly.

Art lowered himself into his big, dumplinglike chair. "He was a professor at NYU who made a lot of money on the side as a consultant to politicians. He specialized in urban demographics."

"That isn't my field."

"Just wondered. He must have needed to avail himself of computer expertise in one way or another to come up with his statistical patterns. Anyway, he was killed."

Be careful! "Oh?" A slight questioning tone.

"The reason Bennett had to postpone our meeting this morning was because George Scoresby's body was discovered around two A.M. last night. Remember the man I told you about who was shot at the Wallingford? Man named Babkus who was using his company's suite to entertain out-call girls?"

"Yes. What does your detective in Vice have to do with . . .?"

"There is a very smart, very ambitious lieutenant in Midtown Homicide named Hugo Hernandez who has every available cop assigned to him at the moment."

"I'm not following you, Art."

"Okay. Babkus was killed at the Wallingford Thursday night. Last night, a man named Donald Turner was blasted in a room at the Big Apple Inn. Scoresby's body was found last night, but the ME says he died Friday night."

"But, what does Bennett . . .?"

"Wait until I finish. Babkus was known to use women from expensive out-call operations. Turner, a motorcycle franchise owner from St. Louis, was reported to have had a different hooker up in his hotel room each day of the three nights before he was killed. Scoresby, on the other hand, Hugo Hernandez rapidly learned, had been entertaining undergraduate females, and an occasional male, at his home away from home in Chelsea for years. For free. In fact, the co-ed who found his body and is presently under heavy sedation had been given a key to Scoresby's pad. She's been, ah, accommodating him every night he was in the city for the past five weeks. She told the officers Dr. Scoresby suffered from insomnia. She was evidently his current sleeping pill. Friday night she had been unable to visit him. She'd told him that." He stopped for breath and drank from his mug. "You haven't tried my great gourmet instant coffee."

"I was waiting for it to cool a little." With both hands she brought the mug to her mouth.

"The most interesting part is—all three men were killed by bullets from the same gun." He waited.

Think! What should she say? "I'm still confused. What can be the connection between a motorcycle franchise owner from— Where did you say?"

"St. Louis."

"Between him and an NYU professor and the other man?"

"That's where my friend Bennett came in. One angle Lieutenant Hugo Hernandez was pursuing was a possible tie-in between the three shootings I've been telling you about and the killing of those three prostitutes in the hotel room. That is, did a hooker wig out because those mutilated women were friends of hers and become a one-woman avenger? What do you think?"

Be Kate the Logical. "Didn't you say the three women were probably killed by a pimp?"

"Almost certainly."

"Then if a friend of theirs was after revenge wouldn't she go after pimps rather than customers?"

"Excellent! That was where the thinking was when I left Midtown Vice and Homicide. The women were killed by one or more men and the men were killed by one or more women. Bennett told me the ME's report on the three women has convinced him that at the time of their deaths none of them could have qualified for much more than Eighth Avenue street hooking. They were pretty shopworn, so to speak. Any good friend of theirs would have been rather conspicuous at the Wallingford or the Big Apple Inn."

"What about the professor?"

"Hernandez has some of his team working on what Bennett called the Scoresby Conspiracy Angle." Art shook his head. "That one's really out in left field. I told you Scoresby advised politicians?"

"Yes." Kate set her mug on the floor.

"What if a woman who is or was affiliated with a politician defeated by one of the politicians Scoresby advised blamed Scoresby for that defeat? She's become mental, as they say in England. She plots and plans. The man she's after is Scoresby, but if she shoots only him, the police will limit their investigation. But if two other men, completely unrelated to Scoresby, are shot and killed, the police won't know which way to go."

"Is that what Bennett thinks?"

"No. He doesn't think Hernandez believes in a conspiracy either. He still has to put some people on it though, because the idea was suggested by a biggie downtown."

"Who does Bennett think killed the men?"

"He has no idea. He's a vice cop, not homicide, and he's been a vice cop for almost twenty years. The man is a fantastic source for my piece. Total recall. But he views the men and women who live and have their being in the general vicinity of Forty-second and Eighth Avenue with complete impassivity."

"How can that be?"

"What?"

"Impassivity about what's happening on Eighth Avenue!" Kate grasped the arms of the captain's chair and leaned toward Art. "Are you telling me your friend Bennett would have looked impassively at Lou Ann bleeding on that filthy VW, with the drunks laughing at her and her pimp scooping her up to sell her again just as soon as she can walk?"

"Kate, look. Bennett's seen thousands of Lou Anns in twenty

years. If he lost his objectivity he'd maybe flip his lid and start kneecapping pimps with his Police Special. Helpful as he's been to me, he doesn't think my article will make one bit of difference. He says, 'You think the pimps and hookers read that stuff? You think the johns after kids'll throw up their hands and repent?' Kate, that place is like the Augean stables. Bennett does what he can do."

She slumped back. "Augean stables. What chance does Lou Ann have if someone like Margaret can't protect herself?"

"I didn't know about Margaret until late yesterday."

"Not until yesterday? I thought you knew that day when we were on the stoop watching Vanessa and the dog."

"Well, I didn't realize. Her mail was in my box by mistake. I took it up. She says she's much better now. I'm glad I didn't see her right after it happened. Jesus! But, then, she's been living a very dangerous life. She said you've been very helpful, by the way."

"I did see her right after it happened." Kate picked up her mug and stood. "Thanks for the coffee. I have things to do."

"So do I. Bennett said he might be able to spare some time tonight. If not tonight, tomorrow."

Kate sat at her desk looking at a blank sheet of yellow graph paper. After a while, she printed, Sunday, Monday, Tuesday, Wednesday = Four Days Left.

The odds against the Rainbow Man calling Jeanne were increasing enormously. This, at the same time the odds in favor of Lieutenant Hugo Hernandez with all his police officers finding Jeanne were also increasing enormously.

According to Art, Hernandez was smart. How smart was he? When would he figure out that the killer was a woman all three dead men had assumed to be a prostitute? He would send an officer with a search warrant to every hooker with an ad in *Frig* and the other porno tabloids. There she would be sitting in 517 with the .38 tucked in her purse.

Ah! But what if the police came to 517 and searched Jeanne and her purse and the desk, and the gun was not there? The most they could do would be what? Arrest her for soliciting? But how could they prove, from her *Frig* ad, that she was soliciting?

She would need to leave the gun at home.

Damn! She should have considered that before today!

Her phone rang.

"My darling Kate. Today is Sunday and the rates are so much cheaper on Sundays, aren't they?"

"Hello, Mother." She had not spoken with Anne for months. "How are you?"

"How am I? I'm very, very busy with my work, of course. My work is absorbing. Sarah was saying recently that she doesn't understand why you choose to live in that place with all the muggers and strikes and filth. As for me, the papers are so full of violence and ugliness, I stopped reading them long ago."

"Did you have a special reason for calling?" She always did.

"Yes, I do. Kate, darling, I've agreed to let a small gallery show some of my work next month."

"The seashells?"

"Abalone. Only abalone now. Only abalone with the most subtle gradations of color. Only the softest tones of grayish-pink into a slightly deeper pink, and then into a faint rose. And, you know, within that range is an almost miraculous variety of colors. One must learn to see them, of course."

As Kate listened to her mother describe the pinks and grays and roses and the almost microscopic engraving she did on the shells' hard, lustrous skins, she gazed down at her yellow graph paper. Four Days Left. Is Anne insane, with her absolute absorption? Am I insane? Mother, I have shot and killed four men. Killing men isn't pinkish-gray. Red. Bloody feathers. Blood smeared and puddling on a hardwood floor. Blood soaking into lime green suede. And none of them really matter at all because I still haven't found the Rainbow Man and I only have four days left and the police are after me. The police are after me!

"My god!" She looked toward the bedroom doorway. The gun the police were after was on the top shelf of her closet, only a few feet from the floorboards of Art's apartment.

"What, Kate? So, I'm quite satisfied with the way my work will be displayed. How long it's been since I've been to Catherine's beach house. I can't remember the last time. I don't know why she keeps the place. Probably for the children because . . ."

"Why are you going to Laguna, Mother?"

"Because that's where the gallery is. Did I forget to tell you? The lighting is so important. Mr. Fogarty of the Fogarty Galleries is a genius with lighting. He understands the exact effect I want. Catherine is giving a little reception after the opening. She said she had considered having a chamber group play. But she still hasn't recovered from Gordon's death after all this time. You're well and busy, darling?"

"Yes. Well and busy." She pressed her hand over her eyes.

"Poor Lloyd. He always loved our visits to Laguna. The wonderful breakers, one after another, crashing on the beach. The sound of them at night after everyone was asleep and the house was quiet. Kate?"

"I'm here."

"I've just remembered something. I suppose you're old enough now, for heaven's sake. Your father told me not to confront you with it at the time."

"Confront me with what?" Her forehead was now resting on the pad of yellow graph paper. The receiver was against her ear, but the mouthpiece was dangling downward.

"Lloyd could never bring himself to tell me what you'd done to so upset Gordon. You were so young and all. I gathered, though, you had defaced something at their beach house. But what could it have been? Of course I was drinking heavily then, so I could have missed the whole thing. What was disfigured?"

"He did it, Mother!"

"I can't hear you, Kate dear. We'll talk about what you did at Laguna another time. This is not a good connection. Even though it's a Sunday."

Kate heard the disconnect buzz. All the way from California.

What I did at Laguna?

Anne supposed she was old enough now.

The brown thread was in place when Kate let herself into 517 at eleven thirty-five that night. And still no evidence of McGiveny or Lieutenant Hernandez and his people, or anyone else on the fifth floor of the building.

The tape held thirty minutes of everyone but the Rainbow Man. She listened to the message between calls from men who wanted to pay a woman one hundred and seventy-five dollars, or less, or more, or who wanted to be paid themselves. Those who wanted to be paid were drunk or on drugs.

Lawrence Pendelton called at 1:15 A.M.

She did not learn his full name until later.

He badly needed her, he said. He would not even touch her. He would give her her money first, he said.

"Why did you call me?" Kate asked.

"I have found that many women affiliated with out-call services, or who sell themselves cheaply, are addicted to drugs. I demand a woman's complete attention. Do you understand, Jeanne?"

His words were spoken in a flat, taut line. He sounded like a crazy meld of George Scoresby and Scotty Rogers.

"You demand complete attention?"

"Yes. But intercourse is not required. Are you able to visit me tonight?"

"Where are you?"

"On Seventy-ninth between Columbus and Amsterdam. Please try to make the most presentable appearance you can. Remove most of your makeup. I am Pendelton in number one oh eight. The Yarmouth."

She considered Hernandez. Pendelton was like none of the others. Not in any way.

She rode a taxi home, picked up the .38 and walked to the big, sturdy, no doubt rent-controlled fifteen-story building.

From the street she could see a guard wearing a gun in a holster sitting behind a metal desk in the inner lobby. A transistor radio lay beside the crossword puzzle magazine he was looking at.

She was buzzed through the inner door after she had counted to only three.

The guard glanced at her as she walked past him to the elevators. He had no panel showing the locations of the two elevators, and there was none above the elevator doors. The tenant had buzzed her through, she was the tenant's problem. She removed the scarf as the elevator ascended.

Pendelton immediately answered her knock. "Come in," he said urgently.

Kate walked into a larger, high-ceilinged entry hall. A small console table against the left wall held a bouquet of fresh flowers.

He closed and locked the door. "Follow me."

He led her through a spacious, conservatively furnished living room. She saw a dining room off to the right. They walked down a hall past a bedroom. Then a bathroom. At a closed door, Pendelton removed a key ring and unlocked two locks.

Oh, shit! A torture chamber!

Kate reached into her bag for the .38, wrapped her hand around it. If necessary she could shoot through the purse.

Pendelton flung open the door and walked before her into the room.

At first, Kate did not understand what she was seeing.

Arranged around three sides of the twelve-by-twelve room were fifteen or sixteen artfully lighted dioramas in cases sided and topped by glass. A minimuseum.

"I made them all," Pendelton said. "Scratchbuilt. The models. The scenics. The weapons. The horse furnishings. Every detail."

Kate slowly walked to the closest display.

A polished brass plaque was affixed to the outer wooden base of the case. The words VIONVILLE—DEATH CHARGE were engraved on the plaque.

Under the glass was an amazingly lifelike miniature scene of soldiers and horses suspended in the midst of an appallingly brutal battle. Men were falling from horses which were trampling men writhing on the ground while other men aimed rifles and shoved swords into torsos.

The case next to Vionville was SEDAN, SEPTEMBER 1, 1870. It contained more soldiers, horses and carnage, exquisitely rendered.

Kate looked at Pendelton. He was a small, slender, immaculate man of about forty years. His neatly trimmed light brown hair, his creased gray trousers, his light blue shirt, his tightly knotted tie, his polished black shoes conveyed the message: circumspection. His features were even, his cheeks pink, his eyes clear blue, his teeth white. Yet his face was vapid.

"What is all this?" Kate asked.

"You're impressed, aren't you? Some people call what I do militaria. I have specialized in the Franco-Prussian War. I must insist that you examine each of the groupings before we can get on with the other matter."

Kate made a circuit of the room. Every case held soldiers in scrupulously detailed uniforms of what she assumed was the period of the Franco-Prussian War. All were in the act of killing or dying.

"I chose to specialize in the Franco-Prussian War because in a number of respects it represents the beginning of the present time. Our era."

"It does?"

"Any one of my scenes would take a prize in the British Model Soldier Society competitions. Unfortunately, I can't openly compete."

"Why is that, Mr. Pendelton?"

"My work prevents it."

"What sort of work are you in?"

"I am the executive director of the Manticle Foundation. I also serve as a director for several corporations."

"Manticle, as in Manticle Farm Machinery?"

"Yes."

"That originated in southern Indiana? The medical research and fellowships?"

"We're finished in here." He walked to the door, waving Kate to go into the hall.

She watched as he turned off the master light switch that extinguished all of the little lights in the cases as well as the room lights, then he double-locked the door.

"Now, we're going to my bedroom. Oh." He pulled an envelope from his back pocket and handed it to Kate. "Please count it now."

"What do you expect for your one hundred and seventy-five dollars, Mr. Pendelton?"

Kate counted eight twenties, one ten and a five.

"You'll see." He went into the bedroom.

In the center of the room was a single bed and several chests. From the bottom drawer in one of the chests he removed a large contraption made of powder blue leather, studded with rhinestones.

"This is a harness, Jeanne. You are to remove all of your clothes, including your shoes. You are to slip into the harness. I'll help you. It's based on a dog's halter and can be adjusted." His words were speeding up and beginning to run together. "Then I will lie down on my bed and you will circle the bed on your hands and knees until I tell you to stop. I will hold a crop." He lifted an ornate white riding crop from the same drawer. "From time to time I'll threaten you with the crop. When I do, you must look like you're afraid I'll hit you with it. I won't, though. Even so, you must act like you're frightened. You're perfect for me. I can tell. Natural-looking. Only a little makeup."

"Do you do this often, Mr. Pendelton?"

"No. Only five or six times a year. And after we're finished, we'll have a drink and you can call me Lawrence."

He turned to the bed to prepare the harness and Kate drew the .38 from her purse.

"How do you think those women felt, Mr. Pendelton?"

"How they feel isn't part of it. I pay them. I really don't care."

"You know, the fact that you're crazy is not beside the point."

He turned around, and when he saw the gun, dropped the powder blue leather and raised his hands over his head. "Oh, God, you're a robber!"

"Your name is Lawrence Pendelton."

"Yes. Lawrence K. Pendelton."

"I'm going to kill you, Lawrence."

"Because of my miniatures?"

"Because of everything. Including the Manticle Foundation. Do you show those soldiers to the women you hire?"

"Yes. I only ask them to look at my battles, that's all."

"Why?"

"Some girls become truly fascinated and horrified by my scenes."

"You can see this is a genuine gun?"

"A thirty-eight Smith and Wesson. My arms are getting tired."

"Tough. Do you know what hollow point slugs are?"

"Yes. But they're illegal. Do you . . .?"

"Lawrence, tell all the women who crawled around your bedroom that you're sorry. Wherever they are."

"I'm sorry. I'll never do it again. I . . ."

She shot him through his right eye.

Lawrence K. Pendelton fell like a sack of cement dropped from a great height.

Kate tied the scarf over her hair before she stooped by Lawrence Pendelton, who lay more contorted than any of the dead soldiers in his collection. For the first time, she was not certain.

She withdrew the clean mirror from a side pocket in her bag. First she held it an inch from her own mouth. In a few seconds vapor collected on the glass. She held the mirror before Pendelton's mouth and counted slowly to fifty. Nothing.

Using tissues from the man's bathroom, Kate unlocked the hall door. No one.

Now for the guard in the lobby.

The elevator ascended to ten from four or five floors below.

The guard did not look up from his crossword puzzle as she walked across the lobby.

All the guard would be able to tell Lieutenant Hernandez was, "The woman wore a raincoat over a green-and-white print dress. I couldn't tell her hair color because she had a gold-and-brown scarf over it."

She saw no one on the sidewalk. She walked rapidly, keeping close to the curb. It was now close to 3:00 A.M.

There were no taxis and no buses. She was not far from home. If necessary, she could walk down the center of the street.

At Columbus she turned right and took three steps.

A car squealed to a stop ten feet in front of her and two men leaped from it shouting, "Freeze! Police!"

Then she saw three figures struggling in the entry of a padlocked bakery.

The police sprinted to the dark, grunting forms.

Kate wheeled and ran back to Seventy-ninth. She heard the thudding footsteps behind her.

"You! Police! Stop!" A man was yelling.

Kate stopped in a panic.

A panting policeman shone his flashlight in her face.

"You should look scared shitless, lady," he said furiously.

Kate said nothing. The .38 was still warm. She should never have gone into a guarded building at that hour. Of course she had looked suspicious.

"I'll need your name," he said more gently. He took a notebook from his shirt pocket. "Jesus, lady, what in the hell are you doing walking around here at this time of night?"

"Ah . . ."

"You saw the two guys mugging our guy?"

"What . . .?"

"Our decoy."

"I don't know what you're talking about." Although she had begun to understand.

"Our decoy. You had to see the mugging."

Kate's legs trembled from ankles to crotch.

"All I saw was a tangle of dark figures in the doorway before I ran away." They were neither Homicide nor Vice.

"Hell. Come with me. Please." He plodded around to where a uniformed policeman and an officer in crumpled slacks and sports shirt held the arms of two handcuffed teenaged boys.

"She see it?" the uniformed officer asked.

"Only the end of it." He aimed his flashlight at the muggers' faces. "You think you can remember them?"

Kate nodded. "But I really didn't see any of this."

"But you can remember their faces?"

The boys stared in her direction. They could not see her face in the darkness beyond the powerful flashlight.

"I suppose."

"Okay." The officer who had run her down walked her back around the corner. "Give me your name and address and a phone number where you can be reached."

"Fran Johnson. I live in Fort Davis." She gave an address on Birch Street and the phone number of the Harvan Division of Jonathan Richmond. It was the only number she could think of and she was surprised she remembered it. Plus, Fran Johnson of the Hudson River Committee.

"What are you doing out at this time of night?"

"That is none of your business!"

"Okay." He gave a half-shrug. "You'll be getting a call in a day or so."

Kate strode away. She did not look through the doors of Lawrence Pendelton's lobby as she passed it.

She had to walk the long way home.

When Kate awoke on Monday her hair was wet and sticking to her eyelids. Hot, hot, and the clock read two seventeen.

More than anything, she was hungry. She had no food. And cockroaches of all sizes scampered over her drainboard.

For the first time since she was a very little girl, Kate did not make her bed.

She showered and walked to the restaurant on Seventy-second. The newsstand had sold out its allocation of *The Times*. She bought a *Post*.

While she waited in a small booth for the cheeseburger special, she read that the eminent teacher and consultant, George Scoresby, had been shot by an intruder in his Chelsea apartment.

He made the third page and was given a double column.

Lieutenant Hugo Hernandez, of Midtown Homicide, told reporters that the police were following several solid leads and he could say nothing further at this time, except that the police did not think the killing was politically motivated.

She skimmed the lengthy list of George Scoresby's accomplishments and honors. He had advised many local and national politicians of both parties.

His wife was in seclusion at the family home in Manhasset. He was also survived by two married daughters and a son, presently living in Japan.

"Hello, Kate." Art slid into the seat across from her. "I saw you through the window."

"Hello."

The shirt-sleeved waiter placed a heavy platter before her. "You want something?" he said to Art.

"Coffee, thanks." Art folded his hands on the scratched vinyl tabletop. "Kate, I have to talk with you. I've been looking for you."

She bit into her cheeseburger and nodded.

"I didn't think you'd gone to work today. I could hear you listening to music at four A.M."

"Oh, I'm sorry." She swallowed. "You can hear my record player from your apartment?"

"Sometimes." He shoved his glasses back up where they belonged. "You know how it is in these renovated brownstones. All that remains from the nineteenth century are the thick outer walls."

She took another bite and chewed. "Did you have your meeting with your friend Bennett the Impassive?"

"Around eleven this morning the man who directs the Manticle Foundation—remember our conversation about the Manticle Foundation? He was found by his housekeeper. He had been shot through the eye."

Kate laid her cheeseburger on the platter. She carefully wiped her hands on the large paper napkin. The waiter set Art's coffee on the table. Art waited until he had moved to another booth.

"You aren't saying much, Kate."

"I'm eating and listening."

"But you've stopped eating."

"Go ahead." She sipped her coffee.

"All right. You haven't gone to work for over two weeks."

"I'm considering a new job in Westport."

"But you haven't worked for the past two weeks?"

"No."

"Hernandez has new evidence."

"Does he?" Kate shoved aside her coffee and lit a cigarette.

"Yes. In each killing, he's found, now, that two factors have been the same."

"This man from the Manticle Foundation is part of the conspiracy with the professor from NYU?"

"In each killing the bullets have come from the same gun and there was a copy of the last issue of *Frig* on the premises." He drank his coffee in two swallows.

"That's very interesting, Art."

"I think so."

"What does Lieutenant Hernandez make of it?"

"The closest I can get to the inner circle at Homicide is my friend Bennett. Bennett says the killer is one woman and so, he says, does Hernandez."

"What do you think?"

"I think the men have been shot by a woman who is not a hooker, but who is posing as a hooker. And that she is a very smart woman who has gone to great lengths to cover her tracks."

"Do you?"

"Yeah. The whole thing smacked me in the gut around five A.M. this morning. I hoped I was wrong. I didn't want to see Bennett, but I went down there anyway. Lawrence K. Pendelton of the Manticle Foundation was shot through the eye around three A.M. last night." He looked away from her and toward pedestrians walking along Seventy-second Street. "I remembered our conversation of yesterday, when I said that if Bennett were to lose his objectivity, he'd cork off and start shooting pimps in their kneecaps. Do you remember that?"

"Yes."

"The dead men weren't pimps."

"No, I gather they weren't."

"They were all johns. And from what Bennett's told me they weren't your run-of-the-mill johns. He said the contents of Mr. Pendelton's apartment will not bring peace and pleasure to the trustees of the Manticle Foundation. The woman who's been killing the johns is very selective."

"How would a woman go about being selective about johns?"

Art turned away from the window. He did not look at her. He fiddled with his spoon. "First, she'd have to dream up an ad for *Frig* that would capture the attention of . . ." He smacked his spoon on the table. He leaned toward her, his weight on his forearms. "I bought a copy of *Frig* this morning."

"Then what is your thought on this?"

"My thought on this is that I hope to God I'm smarter than Lieutenant Hugo Hernandez. But then, I can hear you at all hours, and he can't. And he doesn't know about Lou Ann and Margaret, Jeanne." He reached across the table and took her hand and held it. "*Dies irae*, Kate. *Dies illa. Quando Judex est venturus. Day of wrath. Day of mourning. When the Judge shall come. Dies Irae. Dies illa.*"

"Are the walls and floors so thin, then?"

"Yeah. Hugo's close, Kate. You can still close it down." He released her hand. "The Requiem ends, you know, with the *Libera me.*"

"I wish I believed that."

She laid money on the table.

From the restaurant, Kate took a taxi to 517.

The brown thread was not in place. She found it, twisted, under the desk's kneehole.

McGiveny.

She sat down and tried to think.

Of course the police had questioned McGiveny about the people who rented his offices. The women. By now Hernandez had had his people call every phone number in that edition of *Frig*. That would present no problem for them. They could also easily trace the address for every phone number from New York Telephone.

Be logical!

She could not be arrested for a *Frig* ad, nor for her phone message. She had gone over that.

If the police burst in at this moment, what could they do? She did not have the .38 with her.

She stared at the Touch-Tone when it rang.

Not to answer it, if it was the police, would, perhaps, create suspicion, since she had disconnected the machine. Then she needed only five minutes to clear all evidence from the office. They had called before; they knew what Jeanne sounded like. Give them Jeanne.

"Hello," the Jeanne-voice the police had already heard said.

"Is this Jeanne?" The man spoke with an accent.

"Yes."

"Wonderful. I require you today. Please cancel your other appointments, my dear. Naturally, I will compensate you for losses. Well?"

"Yes," she whispered.

"I am unable to hear you!"

"Yes," she tried again. She knew that voice. She had heard it on ABC, NBC, CBS and *Christopher Webberton at Home.*

"You will come to me at precisely seven this evening. If a limousine is still before my home, you are to wait. Do not approach the door until the car is gone. Do you understand?"

"Yes."

"I require you for two hours, perhaps three. You are to be modestly and beautifully dressed, my dear. Otherwise you will not be admitted."

"All right."

"My home is 205 East Sixty-fifth Street. Jeanne, I await the rainbow."

"The rainbow."

"Yes." He hung up.

Kate laid the receiver back in its cradle.

Immediately, the phone rang again.

She let it ring.

Tears dripped on the desk top. From ineffable rage and betrayal.

Rich and famous. With an image.

Sure you'd recognize his face. And his voice even.

He'll pay. Fucky. Shitty. Everyone will take care of everyone.

Artist. Fucking artist. Actor. Phony. Always acting.

Crazy. Strong man. Very strong.

Hand. Once. First. Then driftwood.

Worried about his hand.

The pianist is indisposed.

Kate extracted both tapes from the machine. She went to the women's bathroom and brought back five damp paper towels which she used to wipe the answering machine, both phones, the desk, the chair, the air conditioner, the door, the windows. When she let herself out she wiped off the hall doorknob. In the women's bathroom, she unwound the spools and flushed the tapes down the toilet, along with the towels. She dropped the clear plastic spools in a trash can on Madison Avenue before she climbed aboard an uptown bus.

Upstairs she could hear the faint sound of Art typing. She had not noticed that before. So, of course, he had heard her records. Especially when she turned up the volume.

She took care with her hair and makeup. She decided upon her navy cotton-twill blazer from Bergdorf's, the Perry Ellis straight skirt and the Saks blouse with the tiny round collar.

This time Kate rode across town in a taxi. She told the driver, "Sixty-seventh and Fifth." She walked down two blocks and turned the corner at Sixty-fifth. The limousine was pulling away from the curb. She was unable to see who the passenger was.

A strikingly handsome black man wearing trim, dark brown trousers and a short-sleeved white shirt and a brown bow tie answered her ring.

"I'm Jeanne," Kate said. "To see Mr. Gallardon."

"He is expecting you. Please come in. This way, miss."

He led her up a wide, curved, blue-carpeted stairway to the second story. They were now at the foot of a narrower staircase, carpeted in ruby red. The man stepped back.

"At the top of these stairs, continue to the rear of the house, miss. The studio door is the only one you will see."

"Thank you," Kate said.

Her heels sunk into the red pile. She climbed slowly and with great deliberation.

A life flows up to and through moments and there are always more and next moments. No one expects finality, not in midmoment. *Dies Irae, Dies illa.* That day will never arrive because days are impossible, only moments are conceivable.

He opened the door before she knocked.

"Ah, Jeanne." He gave it the French pronunciation. "Welcome."

She looked up into his face, searching his eyes. They were deep blue; smile crinkles fanned at the corners of his eyes, his intelligent, sensitive eyes.

"I see you know who I am. Well. That can't be helped." He closed and bolted the door. "Come, sit down with me."

The room was enormous; even the Steinway concert grand near the center appeared small. At the far end, at the front of the building, was a large bed covered by fur throws. A grouping of chairs and a couch upholstered with soft leather made a wide half circle before the fireplace. There were no windows and the walls and ceiling were faced with cork panels. On the floor lay a purple wall-to-wall carpet.

"This is my sanctuary, as you can see. I am quite insulated from the world and the sounds of traffic here. I have a small kitchen and bar. A toilet. Whatever clothes I need in that closet. Now, you must say a few words or I will think you are without a tongue. That would be most unfortunate for me, wouldn't it?" He helped her from her blazer and laid it over a chair. "Now, you're more comfortable!"

Kate sat on a chair that had been upholstered with pale pink velvet. "I have listened to your recordings of Beethoven's Fourth and Fifth many times. Also the Rachmaninoff Second and Third, and the Brahms First and Second. But, most of all Chopin. The Ballad in G Minor."

"An aesthetic whore! I cannot believe my good fortune! I will play a little Chopin mazurka for you as an aperitif."

He seated himself on the padded adjustable bench, bent his head over the keys for a moment and began to play.

Jean-Paul Gallardon, playing a piano in a cork-sealed room in his own home, looked just like Jean-Paul Gallardon playing the piano on the stage at Carnegie or Avery Fisher. His great aristocratic head was angled toward a point near the bottom of the music rack and, while he was wearing linen slacks and a fishnet shirt and leather sandals, rather than tails and a white tie, he carried himself with the same power and grace.

"You play more beautifully than anyone I have ever heard," she said when he sprawled on the leather couch.

"We are finished with music now. For the money I pay, I expect your devotion to my body until I am finished. You will devote your attention and efforts to nothing but a single purpose."

"Your orgasm."

"Exactly." He sighed. "And now you may begin. I will make known to you . . ."

"You know, you sound like an absolutely crazy blend of Buck Turner and the man who ran the Manticle Foundation and my Uncle Gordon. Isn't that strange?"

"What is this?" He raised his head an inch or so and languidly peered at her. "An edge of hostility to begin? Well, then, let us observe the effect." He lowered his head to the leather.

"Have you given much thought to Margaret Elias?"

He straightened a little and looked down at the purple rug between the leather couch and the pale pink velvet chair. "I am very sorry about what happened to Maggie. Of course, I have given thought to her." He massaged his right hand with the long, strong fingers of his left hand. "I disappointed a great many people when I needed to cancel that performance."

The .38 was in her hand now, still inside her bag. "You beat her with a piece of driftwood."

He nodded and glanced toward the fireplace. He knew exactly where the chunk of dun-colored driftwood was. Ready. "I am not an evil man." His head slowly moved left and then right in denial. "No." Then he shrugged. "What else can I say?" He let his head fall back against the couch.

"Now you sound like Alex Harding and Joseph Warburton."

"More names? Come now, I am a busy man. I do not enjoy conversation with whores. Their tongues, yes. Their words, no."

"Margaret Elias is my friend."

He regarded her through half-opened eyes. "Yes. A lovely body." He sighed. "Let me see yours now. Do not remove your shoes first, if you please, Jeanne."

"My name is Kate." She stood and aimed the gun at his gut. "And I came here to kill you, Jean-Paul."

"This is absurd!" He crossed his arms over his chest. "I hired you to give me pleasure, relaxation. I am becoming tense."

"Margaret no longer has a lovely body or a lovely face."

"Leave me!" He jerked his head toward the door.

"Jean-Paul, look at me. I'm so goddamn tired."

The first bullet struck him to the left of and below his belt buckle. He gave a roar and lunged for her. The second bullet blew off the joint connecting his left arm to his shoulder. On he came.

Her heel caught in the thick rug as she backed away, and she fell against the pink velvet chair.

The gun. She dropped the gun.

Gallardon threw himself on it, screaming.

Kate tried to turn away as he fired.

The bullet entered the fleshy part of her upper arm, missing the bone, and tore a chunk of flesh from her shoulder as it exited. She slammed back onto the pink velvet.

He had stopped screaming. He was, she saw, prone on the rug and he was concentrating utterly on aiming the .38 at her chest.

She fainted as the bullet went into the cork ceiling.

Hell was great pain.

Jean-Paul Gallardon was far away, surrounded by a vast expanse of purple and red. His face was pressed into the purple and one knee was drawn up as if he were in a terrible spasm.

He was no longer bleeding, but Kate was. Her blouse and bra were soaked. Her waistband was, for the moment, catching the flow of blood.

She found she could stand, with the backs of her legs braced against the pink velvet chair.

Okay. Get to the closet.

She tugged a dark blue knit shirt from a hanger.

Her Saks blouse was soggy with blood. She used it to wipe the closet pull, then dropped it on the purple rug.

She bloused Gallardon's loose shirt so that it covered her waistband and would not hang below her blazer. She laid one of his soft wool scarves over her shoulder and eased into her blazer.

The next problem was the retrieval of the gun. She kicked it from his hand.

Don't bend over. Stoop. Slowly. Slowly. Breathe evenly and deeply. Ah. Slowly, slowly; now up. Gun in purse. What have you touched? Blood all over. What about door, Kate? Unzip purse and take out scarf. Close door with scarf. Stand and listen. Walk down stairs. Man in white shirt is coming to meet you on the blue stairs. "Miss, you'll be all right. Miss, here." He shoved paper in her hand. "The car will take you home. Good night, miss. He can't help himself."

A new man in a dark car. "Where?"

"Port Authority."

"Port Authority Bus Terminal?"

"Yes."

"Okay."

He opened the door for her.

He didn't look at her face. He was afraid of what he would see. God knew what he'd seen come through that door.

"He can't help himself," the butler had said.

On the sidewalk under the noise and exhaust fumes. Oh, God. Am I dripping blood on Eighth Avenue?

A cab.

"You all right, lady?"

"No. Lincoln Center."

On the sidewalk again.

Another taxi.

"Seventy-second and CPW."

She had touched nothing in either the car or the cabs. She was so very tired of trying to remember to touch nothing.

Kate leaned against the bricks in the vestibule of her brownstone and pushed 3-R.

"It is Kate. Help me." She enunciated very carefully.

Margaret and the woman who had been studying for her master's helped her inside. Barbara Something.

"Call Waldo," Kate pleaded.

"Are you sure you want Waldo?"

She was being helped inside by the two women.

"Yes. Keys in purse."

"Kate, he isn't a very good doctor," Margaret said.

Barbara fumbled to find the right keys for the three locks on Kate's door. "She's bleeding, right? And she's got more than keys and some bloody tissues in her purse. Get her in here fast, and call Waldo, Maggie."